RULES OF REVENGE

Visit us at www.boldstrokesbooks.com

By the Author

Hostage Moon

Show of Force

Rules of Revenge

RULES OF REVENGE

by

AJ Quinn

2014

RULES OF REVENGE

ISBN 13: 978-1-62639-221-2

This Trade Paperback Original Is Published By
Bold Strokes Books, Inc.
P.O. Box 249
Valley Falls, NY 12185

First Edition: December 2014

CREDITS
Editor: Ruth Sternglantz
Production Design: Susan Ramundo
Cover Design By Sheri (graphicartist2020@hotmail.com)

Acknowledgments

For as long as I can remember, my dream has been to write. So I will always be profoundly grateful to Radclyffe and Bold Strokes Books for taking a chance on me and making my dream a reality. I want to extend my heartfelt appreciation to Ruth, Cindy, Sandy, Connie, Sheri, Lori, Toni, and all the others who work so tirelessly to make everything possible. And I especially want to thank you, the readers, who allow me to enter your lives through my stories. Thank you for your e-mails, your encouragement, and your support. It's an honor and a pleasure to share this time with you.

Dedication

To my first and only chosen daughter.
Thank you for coming into my life.

Before you embark on a journey of revenge, dig two graves.

—Confucius

CHAPTER ONE

Imam Sahib District
Kunduz Province, Afghanistan

In the shadows cast by the first light of day, death waited patiently. Still. Silent. Focused.

That she found herself in the remote tribal lands of northern Afghanistan near the Tajikistan border was of little importance. What mattered were the conditions, and they were as close to perfect as they could get for the job at hand. No wind, the temperature was mild, there was unlimited visibility, and the region's rocky hills and thick brush afforded plenty of natural cover.

A perfect kill zone.

Lying on her belly, legs spread out and feet arched down, partly embedded in the ground, she stared through the scope on her rifle. By her calculations, it was 630 meters from her current position to the road. But even after she compensated for bullet drop, wind drift, and ambient temperature, she knew her target would be well within the range of both her skill and the weapon she held with the gentle touch of a lover.

For just an instant, she paused. Reassessed. But one final glance confirmed what she already knew. The benefits of the location she'd selected outweighed any risk. It afforded the best vantage point—an unobstructed view of the road—and the suppressor would reduce the sound of the muzzle blast.

She knew a ballistic crack would still be heard, but it wasn't a concern. In the unlikely event anyone other than her target happened to be in the vicinity, they would find it almost impossible to determine where the shot had come from. And with the bullet traveling at three times the speed of sound, her target wouldn't hear anything before it was too late.

Satisfied, she settled in to wait. Remaining alert for anything unexpected, her thoughts turned back to her target. A man named Ivan Fyodor Sakharov.

According to the intel she'd obtained—information she routinely augmented regardless of who sanctioned the job—the former Russian military officer was a major player in the business of trading military-grade weapons for heroin. And he had found the perfect place to ply his trade.

Afghanistan. A country known to produce roughly 3600 tons of opium annually, almost 90 percent of the global total.

The opium was harvested from farms across the country and taken to factories in the remote Pamir Mountains, where it was turned into heroin. Large quantities were then transported—by truck, motorcycle, even on foot—into Tajikistan, where a kilo of good quality heroin could net a wide array of weapons, including assault and sniper rifles, rocket-propelled grenades, handguns, and cases of ammunition. Even American-made Stinger missiles could be had for the right price.

The weapons inevitably found their way into the hands of the numerous terrorist groups which proliferated around the globe, while the heroin made its way into Russia, across Europe, into the UK, and into North America.

It was a dirty business. But it was Sakharov's rapid rise through the ranks in the Russian mob—the *Bratva*—that had raised flags in international circles. And someone in the chain of command at one of the alphabet soup of intelligence agencies—MI6, CIA, DGSE, NSA—wanted him neutralized.

She shrugged mentally at the clinical euphemism and allowed herself, if only for a moment, to wonder at the pointlessness of the contract she'd accepted. Because she knew one inescapable truth. For every weapons or drug dealer who disappeared in the lawless borderlands, there were a dozen others ready to take his place. Monsters were like that. Each seemed to come with a ready-built succession plan. And life simply went on without skipping a beat.

But in spite of what she viewed as self-evident futility, she had made herself available. Her choice. It was always her choice when it came to which jobs she accepted, which ones she turned down. And her feelings about death were seldom wrong.

By accepting the contract, her clients were assured whatever she did would be done quietly and efficiently. She was very good at what she did. She had never failed to deliver. And she ensured there was no blowback—no unintended consequences—from any covert operation she took on.

As for her targets? They were terrorists. Extremists. People who trafficked in drugs and weapons and humans and put innocent lives at risk. They had made their own choices.

As seconds and minutes passed, she continued to stare at the dust-covered road. But in the heat and silence, with nothing to do but wait, her thoughts turned in a familiar direction and she was conscious once again of the questionable moral compass that guided her existence.

Trust no one.

Kill or be killed.

They were the tenets that guided her life. Truths she never questioned. She knew a lot of people would suggest it wasn't a comfortable way to live. And perhaps they'd be right. But it was the only existence she'd known for a very long time. More importantly, through constant vigilance and by remembering each and every lesson she'd been taught, she'd managed to stay alive.

Flashes from the last fifteen years filtered through her mind. The lessons begun by her mother, then continued by others—the ones who had taken an interest in her over the years. The things she'd done. The mistakes she'd made along the way, as well as the successes.

The violent fury that once drove her had long since flamed out. She'd learned to channel it and had even managed to make some sort of peace with the fates that had set her on this path. She focused on keeping things simple and normally didn't let emotions dictate her actions.

She was no longer the same person. But in any case, that would have been impossible because death changed everything. And Cairo and Damascus, Tikrit, Gaza, Tel Aviv, and all the places and years in between had left their mark.

She was often uncertain what time zone she was in—or even what country. And she traveled under so many different passports, some days her own name sounded foreign to her ears. What she had was her work. Her reputation. A violent past, a volatile present, and financial security, whether she cared about that or not.

At one time, she had thought it would be enough.

Until recently, it had been enough.

But it was not a lot to show for twenty-eight years of living. She had no personal life. No ties, no family, no lovers waiting anywhere in her shadowy life. There were fewer than a handful of people she trusted. Only one or two she might even call friends. And it probably explained why she found herself revisiting her choices so frequently of late, making her think perhaps she had stayed in the game too long.

Her former handler labeled it *spook burnout*.

He worried she was accepting too many jobs, taking too many chances. Maybe crossing too many lines that shouldn't get crossed. When he had finally broached the subject before she'd left for Afghanistan, she knew he'd expected her to argue. But she couldn't see the point.

She'd already figured out that, over time, the job could either steal your soul and turn you into an emotionless killer or come close to breaking you. And sometime in the last year, when she hadn't been looking, her ability to distance herself emotionally from her work had begun to shred.

Retirement, she supposed, was always an option. She was an expert at being a ghost. She could disappear and settle anonymously on a small island somewhere. A place filled with life and color—lush greens, endless blues, and vibrant reds. A place as different as you could get from the places work frequently took her and still be on the same planet. A place where she could reinvent herself and begin to rebuild her life.

It wasn't as if it was the first time the idea had occurred to her.

The thought of going native and living in a tropical paradise inspired a smile. But only for an instant, because the bigger question was whether the people who had helped create her and routinely utilized her skills would ever let her retire. People in her profession seldom did.

There was also the added worry that even if she managed to walk away, her own need for adrenaline might have her crawling back to this life, like an addict in search of a fix. *What if this is the only place where life makes sense? The only place you belong?*

It was that particular fear that was plaguing her now, reverberating in her head. With no answers in sight, she forced herself to shut out all extraneous thoughts and return her focus to her current assignment. Ivan Sakharov.

She took several breaths, began going through a routine she had gone through many times before. She'd learned long ago how to compartmentalize, how to tune out everything but her target, and she began the process of clearing her mind.

Just as slowly, she released all the tension from her body and began lowering her heart rate until it was forty-five beats per minute. Seeking the still point until only the whisper of air over sand and rocks existed. And then even that ceased to exist.

With her body and mind quiet, she could wait like this for as long as she had to. No other reality existed. Everything now came down to timing. The eternal wait until the moment came, followed by the instant when instinct and reflexes and training told her to act.

Minutes or possibly hours later, her patience was rewarded, the silence disturbed by the sound of an approaching vehicle. As expected, Sakharov was driving an open Jeep, throwing a cloud of dust as he approached, his long blond hair shining like a beacon. His posture was relaxed and unconcerned. Unaware his fate was sealed and he had but a few moments left to live.

A second passed, then another as she took a couple of deep, controlled breaths. She focused on the lone occupant in the vehicle.

One last breath. And as she exhaled, she gently squeezed the trigger.

❖

In the last light of day, Darien Troy slid her bag into the overhead compartment and sank into the comfortably oversized seat in first class.

For the next few minutes, she scanned her e-mail while half listening to the muted sounds of her fellow passengers as they boarded the Boeing wide-body and settled in. One particular e-mail caught her attention. Marked urgent, it came from Ben. It was short and to the point, but then Ben seldom needed to say more.

Need you in Paris. ASAP.

Had it been anyone else...

But this was Ben Takahashi. Her first case officer. Her handler, mentor, surrogate mother and father, and the older brother she sometimes wished she had, all rolled into one. He'd seen to her education, her training, and had saved her young and foolhardy life on more than a couple of occasions.

And somehow, when she wasn't looking, he'd become so much more. He'd slipped past her defenses, and somewhere along the way, they'd forged a friendship—the unlikely pairing of a well-connected son-of-a-diplomat-turned-spy and his too-young, barely-in-control protégé.

She hadn't cared about surviving when he took her in. And yet somehow, by the end of their first year together, Darien had found herself doing more than just surviving. She'd blossomed, thrived under his tutelage. Developed a healthy appreciation for life. And over time, her connection with Ben enabled her to cultivate a patina of sophistication she might otherwise have never achieved.

If nothing else, she owed him.

Without further thought or question, she began swiftly entering the keystrokes that would change her current flight plans from Afghanistan. Minutes later, it was done. Tomorrow would still find her in Dubai. But Frankfurt, then London, and ultimately Paris were now scheduled in the days that followed.

There was still room to fine-tune her connections. And she'd need to stop long enough to pick up a few things before catching up with Ben. Like her motorcycle...and some weapons. But when it was all done, she'd make her way toward the Latin Quarter.

There, in a sixteenth-century house she never seemed to find the time to finish renovating, Ben would explain what was so urgent he was willing to break the one rule he knew she insisted on. A commandment engraved in stone that said she never worked back-to-back jobs.

Of course, she knew without asking what job she'd find Ben working on. She'd seen the newspaper headlines while waiting for her flight. Had seen the horrific photos, the aftermath of the three passenger airliners simultaneously brought down on their final approach to Washington, Paris, and London.

Five hundred ninety-three lives gone in the blink of an eye.

MI6 probably pulled Ben in before the dust had settled. And even if they hadn't, CIA would have asked for him. Because even before NTSB had boots on the ground, she knew they would find US-made surface-to-air Stinger missiles had been used to bring down the three jets.

Light to carry and easy to operate, Stingers were a fire-and-forget weapon, employing a passive homing seeker that needed no direction from the operator after firing. The operator wouldn't need to maintain a lock on the target and could disappear immediately after firing. That made them perfect for hit-and-run acts of terrorism. And utterly lethal against civilian airliners, which weren't equipped with the countermeasures found on military aircraft.

It was also commonly known that hundreds of Stingers were still missing from the arsenal supplied by the CIA to the mujahideen in the Soviet-Afghan war, in spite of attempts to buy the weapons back.

Darien wasn't keen on being in bed with the CIA. But she knew what Grace Lawson wanted, Grace Lawson got.

What didn't make sense was why Ben and Grace would feel they needed her particular expertise, especially this early in what would undoubtedly prove to be a long investigation. That thought was troubling and left her feeling unsettled as too many images from the past suddenly bombarded her.

Shutting down her smartphone, she closed her eyes. There were limits to the number of personal rules she would break—even for Ben—and the answers to her questions would have to wait until she got to Paris.

After the flight crew had completed last-minute preparations, after the pilot had welcomed the passengers aboard, and after canned instructions and warnings had been issued, the jet began to roll along the runway before gaining momentum and surging into the late-evening sky. Shifting in her seat, she turned her head and stared out the window.

Below her, Kabul and the Hindu Kush mountains receded in the darkness. Only then did she allow herself to relax.

"Is everything all right? Is there anything I can get for you?"

She turned toward the voice and gazed into the lovely smiling face of a flight attendant. Returning the smile reflexively, she shook her head. "Nothing, thanks."

Watching the gentle sway of the flight attendant's hips as she walked away, she slipped her iPod out of her jacket pocket. What she needed was music, something aching and bluesy, and a moment later a sax softly wailed as she closed her eyes.

She was tired and welcomed fatigue as it crept upon her. Allowed it to carry her toward sleep, where she hoped there was no room for worrying thoughts or regrets.

Chapter Two

Charles de Gaulle Airport
Paris, France

What now? The question ricocheted in Jesslyn Coltrane's head on the heels of a sudden premonition. A tingle at the back of her neck—her version of a spider-sense—had sent out an unexpected warning. Moments later, she spotted a colleague walking into the departures lounge she was in.

It could have been a coincidence. But it wasn't. She knew that even before Garth Smith approached and pulled her from the line of passengers preparing to board Air France flight 324 to JFK.

That her first instinct had been to tell him to go to hell and continue boarding her flight was a clear indication of just how tired she was. But then she'd just spent ten months with her team in Pakistan. Developing and working assets. Gathering intelligence. Endlessly reviewing data, video, and audio recordings. Considering possibilities, interpreting and discarding them.

She must have eaten and slept at some point. Right now she was far too tired to recall when. But too many days fueled by coffee and adrenaline would do that to anyone.

Closing her eyes, she could still hear them…angry voices shouting anti-US slogans in multiple languages. She could still see them…crowds comprised mostly of youths who took to the streets in violent protest. Clashing with embassy security forces, throwing rocks and bottles, smashing windows, and burning American flags.

Jessie repressed a shudder as her composure threatened to abandon her. Swallowing, she took an extra moment. Concentrated on her breathing and tried to let the tension drain from her body. It helped that even with her eyes closed, she could feel her team—Elle, Rob, and Adam—form a protective circle around her, although she knew they had to be as tired as she was.

Maybe if she counted to ten, by the time she opened her eyes again Smith would be gone.

Right. Or she could click her heels together three times, find herself in Oz, and marry the scarecrow—or better yet, Dorothy.

She opened her eyes, pushed back a flash of anger, ran a hand through hair at least three weeks past needing a cut, and sighed. She knew the score.

Smith didn't deserve her anger. He had no way of knowing he was the fifth thing gone wrong today. Or was it the sixth? No matter. He was simply doing his job. It wasn't his fault he'd caught her on the slippery downward slope of an adrenaline crash. Just as it wasn't his place to provide her with any kind of explanation.

He did what he was supposed to do. What he'd been instructed to do, no doubt. He informed her that the Deputy Director of Operations was in Paris and had requested a face-to-face meeting with her. Preferably within the hour.

Jessie was certain she'd misunderstood. "I'm sorry. What did you say?"

Smith shrugged, indicated it wasn't a battle worth fighting, and repeated the message. But hearing it a second time didn't make it any easier because the words remained the same.

Terrific. She was tired, hungry, and not in the mood for a confrontation. She had also grown up in the shadows of the business, the daughter of two legendary agents, and knew better than most that any request to meet with the deputy director was a polite way of saying she had no choice in the matter and she'd better get moving.

Because what Grace Lawson wanted, Grace Lawson got.

It took Jessie several seconds to gather her thoughts and regain her equilibrium. Several more seconds to pull on the mask of professional detachment. Several final seconds to think things through.

Given the lateness in the day and the rain which had been falling
on and off since early morning, she could well imagine the traffic
waiting to ensnare her beyond the self-contained chaos that was
Europe's second-busiest airport.

"Just me or the whole team?"

"She asked for you and Jackson." Smith indicated Elle with his
index finger. "The others are expected to go on to New York."

The team immediately separated. Rob and Adam took a step
back, their expressions clearly indicating they were grateful for the
reprieve they'd just been given. Elle, on the other hand, young and
coming off her first field assignment as a tech analyst, moved closer
to her and mumbled, "Boy howdy," through her teeth.

Unable to reassure Elle for the moment, she looked at Smith.
"And where are we supposed to meet the DD?"

Smith shrugged. "She said you'd know where."

Jessie swore under her breath and slowly rubbed the bridge of
her nose, knowing that while no headache yet existed, one would
likely start in short order. Doing a quick calculation, she realized it
could take the better part of half the time she'd been given just to get
through the concourse. But she'd already accepted this wasn't going
to be one of her better days and was equally determined not to let it
show.

Beside her, Elle picked up her small carry-on while Rob and
Adam shifted uncertainly. A few feet away, she could also sense
the gate attendants, hovering impatiently just beyond her peripheral
vision, waiting for them to board their flight so the Jetway could be
closed.

Without uttering another word, she grabbed the leather satchel
at her feet. Shrugged and muttered a brief farewell to Rob and Adam,
then silently indicated for Elle to follow her. Leaving Smith to deal
with the airline people, she slung the satchel diagonally across her
body, walked out of the departures lounge, and waded into the fast-
moving stream of people intent on making their connections.

Excuse me. Pardon me.

She winced as an elbow connected and wearily acknowledged
she'd have bruises before she got out of the airport. But she was on
the clock now. Cursing softly in three different languages, she kept her

head down and persevered through the noise and bedlam. Aware Elle was silently keeping up, she didn't bother to check her momentum until she felt the first faint breeze ruffle her hair.

It was immediately obvious the weather hadn't improved. But it matched her mood, so that was all right. As she pushed the rest of the way through the doors, Jessie glanced toward the brooding sky, blinking a couple of times to clear the rain from her eyes. Shivering, she pulled her leather jacket closer and inhaled cool, damp air laced with aviation fuel and vehicle exhaust fumes.

Elle spoke for the first time. "Do you know where we're going?"

"Yes."

Over the next few minutes, providence intervened. The line for a taxi proved blessedly short and moved swiftly. And in less time than Jessie could have possibly hoped, she and Elle were tucked comfortably in the back of a Mercedes, only slightly damp. She gave the driver the address she wanted on Boulevard Saint-Germain—a café once known to be the haunt of Hemingway, Picasso, and John-Paul Sartre.

"I don't know if it will make a difference to you," the driver responded, "but you should know it will take a miracle to get a table there at this time of day."

"I'm afraid we don't have much choice. We're supposed to meet my boss there." Jessie paused and tried to imagine the deputy director being told no table was available. The image was almost enough to make her smile. "I'm not worried, though. My boss is as formidable as they come, so I'm confident she'll have managed to find us a table by the time we get there."

The driver glanced in the rear view mirror and for an instant Jessie met his eyes. "And does mademoiselle wish to be late or on time for this meeting with her boss?"

Jessie choked back a laugh. "All I can tell you is we have a little over thirty-five minutes to get to our meeting, and unfortunately, being on time is the only option we have. So if there's anything you can do…"

She got a quick grin back from the driver as he nodded and merged aggressively into traffic. "Then I shall see what I can do to get you there on time."

As the car accelerated, Jessie realized the driver meant business. Almost immediately, he began to weave in and out of the rain-clogged lanes of traffic in the seemingly random fashion perfected by Parisian drivers. Ignoring horns and curses and the occasional red light, he dodged motorbikes, trucks, and other cars with finesse.

Releasing a sigh, she leaned back and watched Paris life blur by.

She'd learned over the years that attempting to guess what was on the deputy director's mind would be a colossal waste of time, so she didn't bother. She simply listened to the discordant notes playing in her head—the flats and sharps that made up the overture—and wondered what it all meant.

❖

Forty-three minutes after leaving the airport, Jessie paid their fare, tipping the driver generously. Pushing her hair back from her face and pulling up the collar of her jacket, she joined Elle on a crowded sidewalk where music, voices, and the tantalizing aroma of food drifted on the evening air.

The café was just ahead, and with the rain having stopped, the street corner was filled to overflowing with artists, students, and business people. But in spite of the crowd, she had no trouble spotting Deputy Director Grace Lawson—an attractive woman in her late-fifties, dressed in a business suit that fit in with the chic Parisian crowd.

As expected, she was sitting alone at a corner table, having chosen a vantage point screened by the crowds that also afforded a perfect view of the café and the surrounding area. She might not have been in the field for a number of years, but her instincts were clearly still sharp from more than twenty years of fieldcraft. The deputy director didn't like surprises, and no one would be able to approach her position without her knowledge.

Jessie led the way as she and Elle reached the table. "Sorry if we kept you waiting," she said as a greeting. She pulled off the satchel and let it drop to the ground before taking an empty seat across from Grace while Elle slid silently into the third chair. "As you can imagine, traffic coming back into the city at this time of day was a bitch."

She could feel sharp hazel eyes appraising her. No doubt taking in the rain-damp hair, the pale face, and shadowed eyes. But whatever Grace noticed, she refrained from making any comment.

She simply offered a faint smile and said, "You made better time than I had any right to expect. I hope you don't mind, but I anticipated your arrival and ordered drinks for you." With that, she raised her hand.

Almost immediately, a waiter approached, poured a German beer into a glass and put it in front of Elle, then placed a wine glass on the table in front of Jessie. "Kir," he said. "With crème de cassis."

"Thank you." Jessie looked at the glass and allowed a small smile to show. "You know, I'm not sure what astonishes me more. The fact you always remember what to order, no matter who you're with, or that you manage to get this level of service in Paris."

"Don't sound so surprised. I know fifty is rapidly becoming a distant image in my rearview mirror, but should I not remember Elle likes German beer? Or that you always preferred Kir with black-currant liqueur rather than blackberry?" Grace paused and a first, rare smile appeared. "Or that we were sitting here the first time you tried it? And as for the service—"

"The waiter's one of yours, isn't he?" Jessie tried unsuccessfully to hold back a quick laugh.

Grace nodded and seemed almost pleased.

Aware Elle was nervously watching, Jessie flashed a tight smile. "Well, as lovely as this is, I'm sure you have more pressing matters to deal with than to sit in a café in Paris reminiscing while having a drink with Elle and me. So why don't we take care of business. What can we do for you? What do you need that has you in Paris and warranted pulling us from our flight back to New York?"

Grace's smile faded and her features suddenly tightened. "Believe it or not, I came to ask for your help on a matter of some urgency." Grace paused, studied Jessie, then gave a faint shrug. "Now I'm not so sure it's the right decision. You look tired, Jesslyn."

More fatigued than Jessie cared to admit, the faintly maternal-sounding concern produced nearly the same physiological effect as hearing Grace Lawson admit she needed help from anyone. Jessie stiffened. It was an instantaneous reaction, even if it was unintentional. She simply couldn't help it.

Just as across the table, Grace clearly couldn't help but notice. She reached out with one hand and brushed Jessie's fingers. "I'm sorry, Jessie. But old habits are the hardest to break."

Half a dozen sarcastic replies immediately sprang to mind, but Jessie cut herself off, kept her comments to herself. "It's all right." She sipped her drink, using the time to regroup. "How about we put family history aside for the time being while you explain what kind of help you need? Can we do that, Mother?"

Her comment caused an eyebrow to rise. "So you do remember from time to time?"

"Remember that you're my mother?" Jessie blinked, shook her head. Elle momentarily forgotten, she knew the frustration in her voice was unmistakable but couldn't help it. "The last time I checked, I still work for the CIA. And even if I wanted to deny my DNA, there's no escaping the reality both my parents are legends in the Agency, so no one's likely to let me forget."

"Did we make things so difficult for you?"

Jessie smiled thinly. "I joined the CIA for a lot of reasons. Maybe not all of them were good ones. Mostly, I think I wanted a chance to prove myself." She pushed aside the messy motives and emotions attached to the past and moved her shoulders in a faint, restless shrug that was a match for her mother's. "But the truth is I could have just as easily gone to work somewhere else. It's not as if I didn't have other options. Both the NSA and NRO were interested in recruiting me before I finished school."

"Well, of course they were. They'd have been fools not to be."

She didn't bother trying to suppress her laughter this time. "Spoken like a mother."

"I'm not sure I would go that far," Grace responded dryly.

The humor might have been unintended, but it broke the tension. "I've got an idea. Why don't we get whatever business we need to discuss on the table. After that, perhaps we can take a few minutes to sit back and enjoy an evening in Paris before you have to leave." She watched and waited for Grace to nod. "I assume we're here about the three jets that were brought down. Tell me how you think Elle and I can help."

"All right. Those three planes—all those lives lost. They didn't just fall out of the sky. And there was no warning. What happened was instantaneous, catastrophic, synchronized, and highly sophisticated. Someone went to a lot of trouble to plan and carry out what can only be described as an act of terrorism. And my every instinct tells me this is only the beginning," Grace said.

"Of what?"

"There's chatter, as always, but there's certainly more than the usual. In particular, a listening station monitoring mobile communications in Eastern Europe intercepted a cellular transmission between Prague and Paris."

"What was the gist of the conversation?"

"The transfer of funds. All our analysis indicates they're arranging for something bigger. Something truly large scale. Everything points to a planned terrorist attack on US soil. That's why I'd like you working on this here."

Jessie took a sip of her drink, gazed at the people and the street scene surrounding her—such a beautiful spot and totally incongruent with the conversation they were having.

There was no question, of course. She would do whatever was being asked of her. As she'd already made clear, it was in her DNA. And it was her duty. Swallowing, she found her throat dry and reached for her drink once again while Grace continued to speak.

"We're running this on two separate fronts. We've already got a team in place on the ground ready to follow the money. As soon as the transfer takes place, their sole focus will be to follow the money to whoever is orchestrating the purchase. But we also want to identify the salesman. Replace him with one of our own and filter the shipment. That's where you come in. After your time in Islamabad, you're already familiar with a lot of the players. That's why I need you and Elle working on this end with MI6."

Grace watched her for a moment with a level of scrutiny that unnerved most people. But Jessie didn't blink. "All right. Who's running the team here? Who are Elle and I going to be working with?"

"Actually, it's someone I worked with quite closely when I was still a field operative. An old friend by the name of Ben Takahashi. That's the best possible scenario since Ben's been out there for a very long time, and you'll be operating in a world he's quite familiar with. Smartest thing you can do is follow his lead. Your survival may well depend on it. And if luck holds—and I'm hoping it does—he'll have already arranged another old contact to work as the fourth member of the team." Grace paused. "No comment?"

Jessie's breath caught in her throat and the murmur of voices around her faded. "I'm sorry. Is one required?" she asked mildly.

A dark chuckle said it all. "Smart girl. Just keep your eyes open and your head down and you'll be fine."

"Thanks."

"Don't thank me yet," Grace cautioned. "This isn't going to be easy."

"It seldom is."

Chapter Three

Paris welcomed Darien back like an old friend. The Eiffel Tower, Notre-Dame Cathedral, even the tourists and college kids crowding the sidewalks and cafés seemed to welcome her as she circled and backtracked through a labyrinth of narrow streets and ensured no one was following her.

Traffic was heavy, but no more than usual for a cool and damp evening, and she made good time. She moved past the Saint-Michel Metro station into the Latin Quarter and haphazardly wound her way through a warren of centuries-old narrow streets. Twenty minutes later, she silenced the engine, turned off the headlight, and coasted through the shadows before coming to a stop.

She took a quick glance at her surroundings, checking for surveillance. One final scan of the street and sidewalks for possible threats. Around her, the world continued to move. But nothing pulled at her. She saw no one paying particular attention to her, heard only the distant sounds of music and laughter and the ticking of the cooling motorcycle engine.

Satisfied, she parked a short distance from the house. Grabbing the saddlebags, she left the motorcycle gleaming dully in the half-light the French called *l'heure bleue.*

The blue hour. Twilight. Between dawn and sunrise—or dusk and sunset, in this case. When the world and everything in it lay suspended between light and dark, painted in a blue-shadowed hue. Her favorite time of day.

Timing was everything and dressed as she was, in dark jeans and black leather, she blended easily with the shadows. Making her way through the gloom along a damp footpath, she took the stone steps two at a time, unlocked the front door, and stepped over the threshold. The house silently greeted her as the door closed behind her and darkness closed in around her.

The alarm sensor glowed a steady green, indicating someone had already turned it off. But she wasn't concerned as, almost immediately, her already primed senses picked up the light citrus scent of Ben's aftershave. The familiar fragrance brought a measure of reassurance in spite of the absence of sounds or any aroma from the evening meal.

Ben was probably somewhere upstairs with his head buried in computer files and had, no doubt, forgotten to eat. Much like someone else, she thought wryly, as the pangs she felt reminded her she hadn't eaten in some time. Had it been lunch yesterday? Or was it the day before? She knew better, but she'd been too tired to pay attention.

Driven as much by hunger as by the need to delay finding out what Ben wanted from her, Darien wandered toward the kitchen, dark except for light spilling in from the hallway. Dropping the saddlebags onto the floor and laying the keys on the counter, she opened the fridge.

Clearly Ben had not spent any time shopping, as only a couple of apples, a piece of cheese, two bottles of Bière de Garde, and a half-empty bottle of wine sat forlornly on the top shelf. She selected one of the apples and hoped it would at least tide her over, already knowing it wouldn't satisfy her hunger.

She sighed tiredly, felt the early stages of a headache. Tomorrow would be soon enough to go to the market. For now, she wanted nothing more than to grab a quick shower, then find Ben and see if perhaps he could be persuaded to order pizza. And then she wanted to curl up in her own bed for the first time in more than a month and sleep.

In the process of undoing the chin strap on her helmet, her senses suddenly picked up something her tired brain hadn't fully processed yet. Her heart began to race, but even as adrenaline flooded through her, her mind became focused and clear.

"Looking for something?" a voice asked from a few feet behind her.

Darien straightened slowly. But even without turning around, she already knew three things. The person behind her was a woman. Young. And she had no doubt she would find a gun leveled at her chest when she finally turned to face her.

"How did you get in here?" the woman asked, nerves evident in the voice. That was interesting and potentially troubling. Guns and nerves seldom combined to yield happy outcomes.

Her blood quickened, but Darien kept her movements slow and steady. She put the apple down and reached for the keys she had left on the counter, holding them up for the woman to see while she turned to face her.

The keys were a perfectly timed distraction—a magician's sleight of hand. The woman's eyes automatically followed the motion of her arm as she held it above her head and away from her body. As the woman focused on the glint of the dangling keys, it bought Darien the time she needed to slip her other hand unnoticed inside her jacket pocket. Enough time for her fingers to curl around the cool metal of her SIG Sauer.

Keeping her hand where it was, she tilted her head and silently contemplated her next move. Shoot first, ask questions later?

An instant later, the decision was made for her, even before someone turned on the lights and a familiar voice shouted from the doorway, "Darien—Dare, no. Don't kill them. They're with me."

Darien stilled. She hadn't needed Ben's warning to hold back because another woman had just stepped into the kitchen and captured her attention. She experienced a strange sense of déjà vu.

Five eight. Slender physique. Delicate features framed by collar-length blond hair. Eyes the color of warm honey. A sexy mouth.

Grace. Only younger.

"If I'd wanted to kill them, they'd already be dead."

The wry intonation in the faintly accented voice was unmistakable, even behind the motorcycle helmet's face shield. Jessie heard Elle sputter angrily in response, but there was nothing she could do for her. All she could do was work to control her own reaction, gather her composure, as the tall, leather-clad woman Ben had called Darien tossed the keys she was holding on to the counter. In the next instant, she stripped off the helmet.

The act shook loose a waterfall of hair as dark as night and revealed a face that immediately caught and held Jessie's attention. She was trained to notice faces, but even if she hadn't been, she would have noticed this one. Late twenties with ice-edged cheekbones, dark eyes fringed with thick lashes. She'd been blessed with a flawless golden skin that was faintly sunburned and spoke at mixed heritage. Possibly European and Middle Eastern.

Stunning, yes. Without a doubt. But the simple statement rang true. She could hear the truth of it in the woman's—Darien's—voice. See it in eyes that had seen a lot and weren't at all trusting. And in her predatory stance. Disciplined. Intense. Deadly.

This woman could kill them. Of that she was equally certain.

"And to be clear, it's not that I had some wild epiphany," she continued softly, her voice low and smoky as she briefly slanted cool eyes toward Jessie, "but that one looks too much like Grace to be anything but a relative. Her daughter, I would guess."

"I'm thinking right now that's a good thing," Ben muttered.

Jessie's suspicion was piqued. "You know my mother?"

Dark hair swirled as Darien turned to look at her once again. Her lips parted, allowing the tip of her tongue to momentarily appear, as if tasting the drawn out silence. "It was a long time ago. Almost Jurassic. But, yes, I know your mother. You've got Grace's face, your father's eyes. Makes me wonder if you resemble them in any other ways."

"I'd like to think so, but at a minimum, my attitude's my own," Jessie responded dryly. Observing Darien, she sensed an air of danger about her that took her aback even as her voice seemed to hold a trace of humor.

She quickly told herself it was her imagination. Before she could think to say anything else, Elle interrupted. "Maybe you believe recognition stopped you, but I was the one holding a gun on you. So just how were you planning on killing anyone?"

Darien's stare was dark and sharp as she turned to face Elle, and Jessie had no doubt most people backed down from that stare. Without saying a word, Darien's right hand disappeared into her jacket pocket. When it came back into view, she was holding a SIG Sauer P229, her index finger resting lightly by the trigger.

"Well, damn," Elle whispered.

Jessie stared at the weapon a moment longer, then smiled faintly. "That would have certainly done the trick," she said. "But it would have made a hell of a mess of your jacket, don't you think?"

"Wouldn't have been the first time." Darien's voice was soft and amused. "But it would have been a shame. The jacket's a favorite of mine."

The stunning face was suddenly lit by a surge of silent laughter before it ghosted away, leaving only a memory of it in her eyes.

Unprepared for the effect the smile had on her, Jessie stared for just an instant longer. It was the kind of smile that made a woman think of doing whatever she could to see that smile again. Her pulse leaped and nerves danced skittishly across her skin.

As thoughts began to jumble in her mind, she realized she'd have to steel herself the next time she saw that smile and kept her eyes on the gun as it disappeared back into a pocket.

Ben chose that moment to step the rest of the way into the room. "Personally, I still prefer the Heckler & Koch HK45 to the SIG." He kept moving until he was in Darien's space, close enough to touch a leather-clad arm, but not yet touching her. "You've been off the grid for five weeks. And then after I sent you that e-mail, you didn't call and I didn't know if or when to expect you."

Darien lifted one hand and rubbed her neck where tension had undoubtedly gathered. But her voice remained measured and controlled as she said, "Hello to you too, Ben."

There was history there, they were obviously connected. Probably not family, Jessie thought, noting there was nothing of Ben visible in Darien's face. But she knew ties when she saw them, just as she knew the ties that bound people together weren't always forged in blood.

Whatever their connection, Darien revealed nothing. "I'm not sure how or why, but for some reason I missed that disapproving tone of yours," she said softly.

Ben laughed aloud. "Dare—"

"Oh, bloody hell, Ben," she sighed. She was clearly fighting a losing battle to keep fatigue at bay, but there was a stubborn set to her chin and defiance in her eyes. "I didn't call because I was in an airplane preparing to leave Kabul when your e-mail reached me, and believe it or not, there are things even I can't control—like flight times and seat availability."

"Really?" Ben raised a brow.

"Yes, really. I wasn't sure how quickly I would be able to make things happen. As luck would have it, at the last minute I managed to catch an earlier flight out of Dubai. But it was plain and simple luck, and I had to move quickly before my window of opportunity closed. I was also still trying to tie up loose ends from my last job, which left no time to call."

Jessie watched the exchange unfold, uncertain what to make of it. Whatever was happening, they'd clearly reached an impasse, and that didn't bode well for the job at hand. Especially if Darien was the colleague her mother had alluded to. She found her gaze drawn back to Darien once again but couldn't see anything beyond the cool eyes and the remote, beautiful face.

Breaking the taut silence, Ben cleared his throat. "I assume you were successful in Afghanistan?"

"I'm here and in one piece, aren't I?"

"Indeed you are"—Ben nodded and indicated the smudges of fatigue under her eyes with a finger—"but you're tired."

"I'll sleep tonight. Too tired not to."

"That's good." He gazed steadily at her, his frown more pronounced. "I know it's not what you want to hear. But after Grace pulled me in, I realized the only person I could think of who might be able to help was you. And since you're here now—"

Darien gave a barely discernible shrug and then released another soft sigh. "I'm here now."

It took Jessie a moment to realize that somewhere in the subtext they'd arrived at some kind of accord. Perhaps even more noteworthy was the unexpected change in Ben Takahashi's expression. Over the course of the days since she'd met him, his visage had always remained the calm, impassive face of a warrior with high, perfect cheekbones, dark eyes, and an unsmiling mouth.

He was smiling now. And there was something else in his face Jessie couldn't quite read, but it looked a lot like affection as he eased into the process of finally introducing Jessie and Elle to Darien Troy.

Darien sent a brief salute across the room, acknowledging Elle who was still bristling and intent on keeping her distance. She then turned to Jessie and offered her hand—long and slender with a cool, firm grip. All business. "Grace only ever spoke of you as Jessie. Is it short for Jessica?"

"It's Jesslyn, actually."

"Nice. It suits you better than Jessica. You're both Company? CIA?"

"Yes." Jessie tried to place the hint of an accent as she accepted the handshake. Definitely some French and Spanish with Arabic and Russian influences thrown into the mix. She waited, one brow rising, but there was nothing forthcoming. Whoever and whatever Darien was, she was volunteering no reciprocal information.

In the span of the next two heartbeats, Darien picked up the apple she'd left on the counter and bit into it, chewing slowly before asking, "So, who's going to bring me up to speed?"

"Jessie, why don't you take the lead," Ben suggested.

She gave a quick nod, but she was still distracted, studying Darien. Still evaluating. Wondering where she'd fit. And how. "Sure, I can do that," she said. "Better yet, if you can give us a few minutes to set things up, Elle and I will show you what we've got and what we've managed so far."

Darien nodded back, agreeing without any apparent reservation. "That works. I've been traveling for three days to get here and I could really use a shower and a change of clothes. Why don't I freshen up, and then come and find you."

Jessie was about to direct her to the nearest bath when it occurred to her that Darien had keys to the house and could probably find her way on her own. "All right. We've set up in one of the rooms on the second floor. The one with the tiny perfect replicas of Michelangelo's *David* all over one wall."

For a moment she thought she heard Darien groan, but she could have been mistaken.

Pushing away from the counter she'd been leaning against, Darien tossed the remains of her apple into a compost container and rinsed her hands before reaching down to pick up the saddlebags.

"You've probably not eaten," Ben said. "Can I interest you in some pizza?"

Darien shrugged. "The apple I just ate must have done the trick because I'm not very hungry anymore. How about I let you know after I've showered?" She moved to go, but as she reached the doorway she paused briefly. "If I can ask one question before I go—of all the rooms available in this house, why would you choose to work in the second floor dining room?"

Jessie looked at her curiously. "I don't think we gave it much thought. Ben said we could use anything on the first two floors and it seemed like a good work space. The room has a long table in it and Wi-Fi, which more than compensated for putting up with the images of *David*. Elle's our resident tech expert, and she was able to set up our computers and hook us up to an agency base station." Unable to see why it mattered, she moved her shoulders restlessly. "Is there a problem?"

Darien cast a glance at Ben before she shook her head. "No. No problem. Go set up. I'll be back down in a bit." Before anyone said another word, she pivoted and left the room.

As soon as Darien left, Elle moved to follow. "I'll go get things ready. Both of us don't need to do it."

Jessie absently agreed and waited to hear Elle's footsteps receding as she climbed the stairs before turning to Ben. "I suppose the good news is that no one's on the kitchen floor bleeding out," she said dryly. "But since we're supposed to be working on this together, the question just begging for an answer is when you were going to tell us about Darien."

She studied Ben's expression, but it remained inscrutable as always and told her nothing.

"I wasn't trying to hold anything back. But there was no point in saying something to you if Darien wasn't coming. And since all I got from her was an acknowledgment she'd received my e-mail asking her to meet us here, I wasn't all that certain she'd agree to help."

"Why not?"

"She's got this…I can't exactly call it a rule, because Darien doesn't do a lot of rules. But she doesn't normally take on back-to-back jobs without some kind of break in between. Not if she can help it, and she just spent the last five weeks in hell-and-gone Afghanistan, deep in the middle of something."

Jessie raised her eyes to his. "My mother described you as an old friend and said she worked closely with you when she was in the field. And you've got a long history with MI6. So I'm guessing you don't need to be told we can't afford to have someone on the team whose head isn't completely in the game. It makes it dangerous for them and everyone around them. If your friend Darien doesn't want to be here…"

"Darien will be fine."

"Because you say so?"

"Actually, yes." Ben's jaw flexed, and for a moment or two, he seemed far away.

Jessie waited in silence until he raised his eyes again. "About Darien?" she prompted.

"Right." He rubbed his hands together and she felt him studying her in much the same way he had when they'd first met, days earlier. "What do you need to know?"

"Maybe start with who she is. Is she MI6?"

"Once upon a time, maybe, but not anymore. She wasn't any fonder of politics than she is of rules. Says she prefers autonomy."

"Who doesn't," Jessie responded neutrally. "But it doesn't mean she won't work whatever side of the street she happens to be on. Does anyone hold her allegiance?"

"Since I'm the only person she's ever trusted enough to be her handler, I suppose I do."

Jessie frowned. "I'm not sure I understand."

"That's all right, because Darien's not easy to explain. But I can tell you I've known her since she was five and quite possibly know her better than she knows herself. I can say that with confidence because I've been the only parental figure she's had in her life for a very long time. Since her early teens."

Jessie listened patiently to what was being said, paying particular attention to anything that wasn't. She watched Ben closely and saw his mouth relax a little before he continued.

"Darien was off the charts in all our tests when she was first brought into MI6, and I played a key role in training her. I was the first, last, and only case officer she ever had, and I helped shape her into what she is today."

"I get that you know her. What you're not telling me is why you want Darien on this."

"Because I've always believed when a job's critical and failure's not an option, you want the best. This job—finding out who brought down those planes and stopping them before they commit another act of terrorism—is critical. We need someone with connections. Someone who knows the territory and can open doors. Someone who can get things done with no blowback. And Darien's the best."

"And I should just believe you?"

"Yes."

She rolled her eyes. "Having that kind of talent running loose without a handler seems inconceivable. And she appears young for such a paragon."

Ben laughed. "Don't let her age fool you. She's really quite lethal and can kill you seven different ways before you even know she's moved." His smile faded as he studied her face. "Trust is rare in our world, Jessie, but your mother trusts me, and I would ask you to do the same. Especially when it comes to Darien."

Jessie weighed what he was saying and wondered if she had any choice. Did it actually matter if she trusted him? Yes, she supposed it did. What the hell. "All right—for now. Can you at least tell me what her role is in all of this? What's Darien going to be doing for us?"

"Whatever we need." Ben gave her one of his quick, rare smiles. "She's one of the best. Bloody brilliant, quick, and cool under pressure. You won't be sorry."

"I hope to God you're right because we really can't afford it if you're wrong."

"I'm not wrong."

❖

Leaving Ben in the kitchen to grind coffee beans and make a fresh pot of coffee, Jessie wandered up the stairs and joined Elle, her head spinning with thoughts and possibilities.

For a couple of minutes, she watched Elle's hands fly over the keyboard on one of the laptops they'd set up as she searched for and located the files she wanted—the ones they'd shortly be sharing with Darien. The task apparently completed, Elle turned and looked at her, unspoken questions in her eyes.

Jessie hesitated for just a fraction of a second. "I need you to do something for me."

"I already tried," Elle responded with a cheeky grin.

"Tried what?"

"Tried to run a deep background check on the scary yet sexy Darien Troy. That's what you were going to ask me to do, wasn't it?"

Jessie stared at Elle. Young and relatively inexperienced, and sometimes a little hotheaded, she more than made up for it by being bright and intuitive—and a technical wizard with a computer. "I should have known you'd get a jump start." She paused, cleared her throat, and released a small strangled laugh. "You think she's sexy?"

"Well, duh. She's smoking hot. And from what I could see of her body in those jeans and that leather jacket—well, let's just say if it wasn't for the fact she scared the hell out of me and she's so far out of my league, I'd jump her. Are you saying you wouldn't?"

Unable to help herself, Jessie grinned. There was no sense in denying Darien Troy brought forth thoughts of hot mouths, entwined bodies, and tangled sheets. "Well, there is that. Why does she scare you?"

Elle's eyes widened. "How about she was ready to kill us? No questions asked. No begging your pardon. And in case you didn't notice, she doesn't make a sound when she walks. If she doesn't scare you, she should."

Jessie thought about that. "Well, she doesn't. But I'll grant you that she's not easy to read. And since I'm shaking with anticipation, please don't leave me in suspense. You know you want to tell me. What did you find out?"

"Nothing. Nada. Zip. She doesn't have one—a background, that is." Elle shrugged and looked uncomfortable. "Whoever she is, she's not in the agency database...which is, of course, impossible. Someone did a really good job of wiping her records, and I'm talking exceptional if I can't find anything. She's a ghost."

"No, no, no. Don't tell me that. What do you mean she's not in the database? That's not possible. She's been brought in by MI6. She's got to be in there."

"Well, she's not. But I'm afraid it gets worse."

Jessie frowned as she rocked back on her heels. "How can it get worse? Do I even want to know?"

Elle looked away, embarrassed or nervous guessing by her body language. It was hard to tell. "I tripped an embedded alarm someone set up when I tried to run Darien's name through classified files. And it wasn't my accessing the system that set off the alarm—it was specifically Darien's name."

Jessie closed her eyes. "Oh, Jesus, that can't be good."

"No shit. Anything that deeply encrypted is never good news. Whoever set it up was good because I didn't spot anything until it was much too late. I couldn't break the encryption, and before I could abort, an alert regarding my extracurricular activities had already been sent."

"Do I want to know where?"

"It went a couple of places. One I couldn't trace, but the other... I'm sorry, Jess, but it went to the Deputy Director of Operations."

"My mother?" Jessie winced.

"Your mother," Elle agreed mournfully.

"That's not good. Not good at all."

CHAPTER FOUR

S he'd kill for some aspirin and a strong cup of coffee.
Darien sighed as she leaned on her palms against the tile wall, closed her eyes, and let the thunder of water beat down on her back. The water was scalding hot, but it felt like heaven. Already, she could feel heat wrap its arms around her, soothing her weary muscles, easing away her tension, and, for the moment, clearing her head of ghosts.

Except there were still too many things on her mind, too many unanswered questions preventing her from lingering in the shower for too long. Starting with the people downstairs. People who clearly expected her to work with them.

Didn't they know she didn't mix well with people? Hadn't Ben explained she was better off—they'd all be better off—with her working on her own? She needed space, but something told her the need for space was not going to be high on anyone else's agenda. Least of all the CIA agents' downstairs.

She rubbed her hands over her face before reaching for the shampoo that smelled appealingly of oranges. As she lathered her hair, she hoped someone would be able to quickly explain why she was here. She knew in time it would all become clear. She just needed it to happen now.

She felt better about things when she stepped out of the shower. After she toweled dry, she grabbed a fresh pair of jeans and a clean T-shirt from the antique armoire in the corner of her bedroom. About to walk away, she caught a glimpse of her reflection in the mirror and hesitated. Stared.

With her face scrubbed clean and tendrils of wet hair hanging loose down to her shoulders, she looked younger than she was. But that didn't matter, because she knew people would only see what they wanted to see, going no deeper than what lay on the surface.

A long, lean body. An angular face. Dark hair. Gray eyes. Symmetry created by nothing more than the chance meeting of chromosomes. A genetic roll of the dice that was part her mother and part who knows.

But still. One of the earliest lessons she remembered being taught was that nothing was ever really as it seemed. It had been a difficult lesson to learn. But it was one which, over time, helped her understand why most people looked at her and never glimpsed the shark swimming silently beneath the calm surface of the water. Not until it was too late.

It was part of what made her good at what she did. But it had been a long time since she'd been forced to work closely with anyone other than Ben, and it made her wonder what the two CIA agents saw when they looked at her. She paused as she thought of them. Elle, the wary tech expert, clearly still green and probably less than a year from the CIA training facility. And Grace's daughter, Jesslyn, whose eyes glowed with the same fierce intelligence as her mother.

It would be interesting to find out.

No time like the present. She shrugged at her reflection, slipped from the room, and headed down the stairs.

Just before she arrived at the second floor room they'd set up—the as yet unfinished dining room with the anatomically correct *David* all over the wallpaper—voices spilled into the hallway. Voices and the scent of freshly brewed coffee. Thank God for that, because she would need her wits about her until everything made sense.

Jessie was pouring coffee as she entered the room. She glanced up, lifted the carafe she was holding, and raised her eyebrows. "Want some? I seem to be incapable of making good coffee, but Ben made this, so it should be slightly more drinkable."

"I wouldn't go that far." Darien sent Ben a baleful look. "But thanks, I'll take some anyway. Black's fine."

Passing her one of the heavy mugs she'd just filled, Jessie added cream and sugar to another and brought it to Elle before going back and filling two more. Ben reached for one while Jessie brought the other to her lips.

Darien took a cautious sip, waited for the jolt of caffeine to race through her system, and instead worked hard not to grimace. Ben still couldn't make a cup of coffee worth a damn. No matter how many times she'd shown him. Releasing a sigh, she put the mug down on the table. "So what have you got?"

Elle responded with a quick tap on the keyboard, and almost immediately, an image was projected on the opposite wall.

It took Darien a moment to process what she was seeing. A photograph and, as she focused, the remains of a burned-out aircraft slowly took shape. The initial photograph was followed by others.

Pieces of charred fuselage. Fragments of luggage. Markers to indicate locations of body parts. As Elle projected new images, the locations changed, but the outcomes were undeniably the same.

"As of earlier today, there's no longer any question," Jessie said. "Explosives residue found at all three sites indicate missiles were used to bring down the three aircraft. But even without it, we've been inundated with reports from people on the ground near all three debris fields and passengers in nearby planes. They've all described seeing missiles rising from the ground. What we've got is a well-planned, highly synchronized assault."

"And what's been the response?"

"Counterterrorism command is reconstructing the movements of known terrorists who could pull off this kind of assault. Local law enforcement agencies in all three countries are working cooperatively on the ground. Following up on tips and checking any available CCTV and security video in the vicinity of the three crashes. So far, no one has claimed responsibility, but we're noting an increase in chatter."

"And where would the intelligence communities be without chatter," Darien murmured.

Jessie took no offense. "True enough. But as you undoubtedly know, chatter is a measure of collective behavior and there's been a noticeable spike in volume from several known and suspected terrorist networks. By itself, that isn't necessarily meaningful. But whenever we notice volume spikes on several networks and compare them with the content of recent communications intercepts and satellite observations, patterns begin to emerge."

Elle looked up from her computer. "And pattern analysis is always more reliable than individual pieces of human intelligence gathered on the ground."

She stiffened noticeably when Darien turned cool eyes in her direction.

"One of the challenges in what we're doing," Jessie continued quickly, "is that the people we're tracking tend to use the same communications circuits that regular citizens use. And between burner phones and Internet cafés, they're also able to use different networks when they communicate. It makes them harder to track."

"Harder but not impossible," Elle added.

Jessie nodded. "For the past few days, we've concentrated our efforts on tracking the movements of known arms dealers. Someone knew who could supply the missiles and had the ability to make it all happen. We just need to find out who that was. And we need to do it fast."

"What makes you say that?"

"One of our listening stations intercepted a message. More funds are about to be transferred, and all indications are there'll be another major buy. And it's going to happen soon. We're not going to be given a lot of time to find out who's behind it and stop them before they strike again."

"Is that all?" Darien asked dryly.

Ben spoke for the first time. "Grace and I have conferred at length with our counterpart in the DGSE, and for once, it appears all the experts are in agreement. Another strike is imminent. I'm hoping that's where you come in."

Darien noted both Jessie and Elle had turned to look at Ben. But for the moment she was only interested in what Ben had to say because hopefully here was the answer to her question. "And why is that?"

"You have the contacts," Ben answered. "Assets you've developed over the years who will only talk to you, give you information. And legends you've spent time building that will let you slip into places the rest of us can't, with remarkable ease. Places where we're most likely to find whoever arranged for delivery of those Stingers. You can hit the ground running. If you can locate and replace the broker, we'll be that much closer to finding the buyer. And that much closer to neutralizing this threat."

❖

"I guess that explains why you're here," Jessie murmured softly. "Ben never actually said, and not knowing any different, I confess I rather hoped we might be able to use you."

She felt as much as saw Darien stiffen and as she turned to meet her gaze, Jessie realized, too late, that she'd managed to insult her.

"Nobody uses me."

Darien's voice was cool and controlled even as something hot and dangerous seemed to flash in her eyes. But then it was gone, and Jessie was forced to wonder if she'd imagined it. *No, probably not.* But she also could see the fatigue etched on Darien's face and, in the interest of détente, thought it was probably best that she make amends.

"I'm sorry. I didn't mean to imply anything negative by my comment."

Darien said nothing.

Jessie tried again.

It took a long moment, but Darien's expression finally began to relax and she gave a halfhearted shrug. "It's all right. No hard feelings."

Her careless shrug seemed to indicate she really didn't care, but Jessie suspected that wasn't entirely true. *Nobody uses me.* She cared, but it didn't appear she was willing to admit it or engage in any further discussion.

For now, the only thing Jessie could do was nod as she thought about how to channel the conversation in a different direction. And vowed to try and avoid words that could be triggers.

"Okay, let's show you what we've got so far." She signaled Elle, who had been staring intently at her computer to the exclusion of everything around her, and heard her tap quickly on the keyboard.

The images of the three crashed airliners on the wall faded to black, replaced by a photograph of a Caucasian man shown exiting a vehicle, a cell phone pressed to his ear. The image was grainy and had been taken from a distance. But it was still discernible and captured a creased weathered face, close-cropped hair, and dark eyes. No visible scars, no tattoos or any other distinguishing features.

"He looks familiar. I know his face from somewhere," Darien muttered, seemingly to herself as she stared at the photograph. An instant later, she raised her head. "Jovan Stankovic."

Jessie studied Darien thoughtfully. "I'm starting to get the feeling you're more than just a pretty face."

Darien scowled. "If you're just figuring that out, you're not as bright as I thought you'd be."

Ignoring the comment, Jessie turned back to the photograph. "But you're right. He was a lieutenant colonel in the Serbian military, cut his teeth under Miloševic. He disappeared after the war. When he resurfaced, he was surrounded by former soldiers and had transformed himself into a top-notch weapons broker."

With a quick tap of several more keys, Elle sent the image to print, and then projected a second, clearer shot—a different man this time—while Jessie collected the photograph from the printer and placed it on the table.

The process continued for a couple of minutes, the silence disturbed only by the sound of Elle's fingers on the keyboard and the humming of the printer as each image was produced. In the end, the rogues' gallery consisted of five faces staring back from the center of the table.

"One of our biggest challenges in trying to identify terrorist groups is that the members know each other, can vouch for each other. That makes it extremely difficult to insert covert agents into a cell," Jessie explained. "Where we've had success is on the fringes of terrorist organizations, tracking groups that support or supply terrorist cells."

Annoyance apparently forgotten, Darien nodded slowly, considering. "And someone had to supply the Stingers used to take down those planes."

"Exactly. Arms dealers have a strong supporting cast—negotiators, financiers, exporters, importers, transport agents—and use them to arrange every aspect of an arms deal. That's where we're hoping to find a trail we can follow. And these five"—Jessie indicated the faces on the table—"are the dealers we've identified as most likely to have been involved in this instance. The Serb we just spoke about, three Russians, and a German-born dealer who's currently living in Florida."

"Why these five?"

Jessie smiled. "Because it's my job to analyze threats and make determinations. And in a who's who of arms dealers, I'd put these five at or near the top."

"Any reason in particular?"

"A few, actually. They're all well connected. Each is capable of moving everything from assault rifles to tanks and rockets to military fighter planes. And they have no known allegiance to any group or cause. They're simply businessmen. Entrepreneurs in a supply-and-demand business."

Her description didn't rate a full smile, just the barest hint, but there was a flicker of amusement in Darien's eyes. It was faint, Jessie mused, but she decided it counted as a smile and still rated it as progress.

"And does anyone stand out?"

"If I go with my gut, I'd have to say the Russians. They've got well-developed networks in both Europe and the US, so for that alone, they bear watching. And they seem to have easy access to an endless stockpile of weapons, both former Red Army and US made."

"Then I guess we'll be paying extra attention to the Russians."

Moving closer to the table, Darien's eyes carefully scanned each photograph before stopping at the second one from the right. Jessie glanced at the image that was holding Darien's attention and got a quick impression of long pale hair and light-colored eyes in a narrow face.

"Ivan Sakharov," Jessie said. "Now, he's a real sweetheart. In the past few years, he's managed a rather rapid ascent in the Russian mob chain of command. It's rumored he's added human trafficking to his repertoire, and he's known for catering to any and all tastes through a pair of brothels he owns. He'll move anything for a price. Drugs. Weapons. Children. With Sakharov, it doesn't seem to matter. Do you know him?"

"Yes. And you can take him off your list."

"Why would we do that?"

"Because he's dead."

Something in Darien's voice, cold and confident, had Jessie turning to look at her more closely. She waited, thought Darien might say more, but she remained silent while Elle's hands flew over the keyboard. Knowing Elle, Jessie surmised she was navigating through CIA data files searching for corroborating information.

After a minute or so passed, Elle waved her hands dismissively at Darien. "She's wrong, Jess. There's nothing here. Nothing whatsoever to substantiate Sakharov's death. Nothing to indicate he's anything but alive and well and living somewhere in Eastern Europe. I've got his last known location in Prague if you're interested."

Darien turned and stared at Elle intently. "Your information needs to be updated," she said in the same tone she might have used to discuss the weather. "Sakharov was killed three days ago. Near the Tajikistan-Afghanistan border."

"How do you know?" Jessie asked quietly, not taking her eyes off Darien's face, watching her expression shift into an unreadable mask.

"Because Ivan Fyodor Sakharov was the last job I completed three days ago before coming to Paris. I know he's dead because I killed him."

❖

"Jesus, she's a mercenary."

Elle's poorly timed remark seemed to echo as a heavy silence fell over the room. Darien saw Ben grimace and Jessie wince. But neither intervened and a wave of conflicting emotions crashed over her.

She knew she couldn't afford to react in anger. So, at least for a moment, she bit off a curse, squared her shoulders, and stood stoically, pretending that what Elle said didn't matter.

It doesn't matter. It shouldn't matter.
But the words cut deep.
To hell with that.

As the last thread of her control snapped, she turned and took a step toward Elle with menacing purpose, causing her to jump to her feet, stumbling as she backed up until she was pressed against the wall. Darien watched the color drain from Elle's face. And then she took another step forward, intent on getting even more up close and personal.

"I get paid for providing my expertise. Just like you do," she said, forcing her voice to remain mild, but ensuring every word was clearly articulated. "None of us would be in this line of work if we didn't believe we were making a difference. The only difference is that you do it only for the CIA, while I do it for a number of intelligence agencies that utilize my skills. Including the CIA."

Elle crossed her arms tightly over her chest. "I just—"

"Right now, you just need to listen. For the time being, Ben has arranged it so we have to work together, which means we're both going to have to learn to live with it. So you need to lose the attitude, the distrust, and all of your agency need-to-know. You may see everything as black and white, but for me, and for most of the world, it's gradations of gray. You're going to want to think about that before you rush to judgment anytime soon."

Elle shot a look of desperation over Darien's shoulder, as if seeking divine intervention. An instant later, Jessie stepped between them before things got more out of hand, and Darien heard Elle release a shuddering sigh of relief.

Jessie stood squarely and met her gaze head on. "Darien, you have every right to be angry, but Elle didn't mean—"

"Actually, yes she did," Darien said quietly. "And I'm not angry. But if Elle has a problem with who I am, what I do, or who I do it for—if either of you has a problem, for that matter—then feel free to leave because in case Ben didn't make it clear, this is *my* home. Find somewhere else to stay and someone else to help you. Just leave me the hell out of it."

"Darien—"

"This isn't up for discussion. You're here because you need help and because Ben seems to think I can provide it. Fine. I'm not sure how, or for how long, but I'll do my best. What I won't do is stand in my own home and be judged or found lacking for decisions I've made in the past or things I've had to do—things you know nothing about. My reasons are my own, and you'd be wise not to venture too close because this is the only warning you'll get."

She paused midstream and closed her eyes. The headache that had been creeping in at the edges of her vision was suddenly pounding, threatening to overwhelm her. She needed to end this quickly and find a quiet place where she could lie down in the dark until it passed. And then she needed a good night's sleep.

Aware that Ben was watching her a little too closely, Darien swallowed the nausea rising in her throat and focused on her breathing. Slow, steady, deep. One, two, three. Feeling slightly better, she forced herself to finish.

"You don't have to decide now. Take tonight to think things through. If I find you're still here in the morning, I'll take it to mean you've decided to stay in spite of my questionable moral character. We'll put this little interlude aside and simply move forward. And if you're not here, well, it really doesn't matter. Am I making myself clear?"

Squaring her shoulders, Jessie stared at her for a long moment before releasing a softly spoken, "Yes. Quite clear."

Behind her, Elle nodded mutely while keeping a safe and deliberate distance between them.

Feeling vaguely mollified, Darien backed away. Avoiding Ben's probing gaze, she tried to keep her temper in check until she could leave the room. She knew she had pushed Jessie and Elle hard enough and it was time to back off. With visions of her bed and the relative darkness of her room enticing her, she headed for the stairs.

She almost made it. But then she heard Elle call out to her.

Stopping shy of the first step, Darien turned. Just beyond Elle, who had come into the hallway, she could see Jessie. Standing in the doorway with uncanny stillness, simply watching her. She forced herself to keep just as still. Tried to read between the lines while she waited to see what Elle wanted.

"I just want to say I'm sorry. I know I don't have a lot of experience to offer and sometimes my mouth moves before my brain engages. But I'm a really good tech and…and I really didn't mean to insult you."

"It's all right, Elle. Life's full of disappointments. I'll live."

Elle swallowed nervously. "So you're saying we're good?"

"We're good. Everyone's entitled to one mistake. The key is to learn and not make the same one twice because when you're in the field, you seldom get a second chance."

"All right"—Elle ran a nervous hand through her hair—"but, you know, just in case. What would happen if I were to mess up again?"

Darien sighed. "Elle, you have no idea what you're playing with. And you really don't want to find out."

CHAPTER FIVE

Jessie didn't remember falling asleep.

By the time she had dragged herself to the bedroom she was using, she'd been at least two hours past running on empty. Stripping as she entered the room, she'd tossed her clothes on a chair, indulged in a bath, then threw herself naked and still damp on the bed with a satisfied sigh.

She had intended to close her eyes for only a minute or two—no more—and then she'd get up, find a clean nightshirt to sleep in, and get ready for bed. But when she opened her eyes, soft morning light was spilling in through the windows, while the heady scent of fresh-brewed coffee wafted in the air.

God, she'd kill for a good cup of coffee. She grimaced half-consciously, knowing the scent of coffee she'd picked up meant she'd be settling for the thick, bitter brew Ben made if he got up before she did.

Was there still time for a quick shower? The clock on the bedside table indicated it was not yet six, and since Ben was already up there was no rush to get downstairs. She made time.

Fifteen minutes later, showered and dressed in jeans and a navy cotton T-shirt, she wandered down to the kitchen, stopping just short of the door. Maybe there was still hope for a decent cup of coffee.

Darien was standing at the center island, harmonizing softly with some classic rock song as it seeped into the room from unseen speakers. She appeared to be completely absorbed, focused on cutting a fresh-from-the-oven baguette, if the aroma was anything to go by, and filling a basket she had placed on a tray beside a carafe of coffee. She then added an assortment of sweet rolls and a bowl of freshly cut fruit.

The sight of food stirred Jessie's appetite. If she was honest, almost as much as the sight of Darien's angular face, lean body, and long jean-clad legs.

Elle was right. She was stunning.

But if she had taken Ivan Sakharov out as she claimed—and there really was no reason to doubt her—then she was also an extremely dangerous woman. Jessie only needed to look into her savagely bright eyes to see that. The one thing she hadn't anticipated was the keen awareness that filled her every time she looked at Darien Troy.

It was almost as if some part of her recognized Darien, had known her for years. Which begged the question, *why?* Or more specifically, *why now?* And *why her?*

She didn't really want to dissect the heat Darien's presence generated, but she couldn't help asking. What was it about timing that made it so hard to get right? Because she knew with certainty she would not be acting on whatever she was feeling anytime soon—if at all. The job at hand was too critical and needed everyone fully engaged, not distracted by thoughts of a much more private nature.

And as a rule, she didn't mix work with personal matters.

So, for the time being, she remained where she was. In the hallway. Content to watch Darien take the song through to the finish.

One moment, Darien's hips were doing a little bump and grind, keeping time with the music as she bent behind the island. In the next instant, she straightened and spun around, aiming a SIG Sauer at Jessie's chest.

"Whoa."

She really needed to remember Darien killed for a living. Jessie automatically raised her hands and froze, not daring to move. Barely daring to breathe, while keeping her eyes fixed on the business end of the gun. "Darien, it's just me, Jessie. We're on the same team, remember?"

It was probably only seconds, but it felt like a lifetime before Darien raised an eyebrow in a perfect arch and lowered the weapon, smoothly sliding it back into an ankle holster. "Sorry. You surprised me. Must still be tired. I'm not used to having anyone around other than Ben and even then—"

"I'm sorry as well." To her chagrin, there were nerves in her voice. She watched Darien break off a hunk of bread and drizzle some honey on it before holding it out like a peace offering.

"Thanks." Jessie accepted the offering, took a small bite, then quickly found herself wolfing down the rest before licking honey off her fingertips. "Damn, that's really good."

"The bread comes from the bakery down the street. The honey's white tupelo and comes from your Florida Panhandle. Ben's hopelessly addicted to it, so I try to keep some on hand."

"I can see why," Jessie said, filing away the small personal revelation for a time when she could consider what it told her. "I really didn't mean to startle you. It's just that I've tried to be the first one up in the morning for the last few days. Mostly it's to make sure I'm the one making the coffee, because Elle is as challenged as Ben in that regard"—she shrugged—"not that I'm much better."

"A lightweight," Darien murmured. "Who would have thought?"

Jessie's eyes widened slightly as she weighed the obvious attempt at humor. "Yeah, maybe, but I consider morning coffee a sacred ritual. It's the only thing that gets me going, and none of the other members of the last team I worked with could make a decent cup either, so I've done without for a long time."

"Where was that?"

"Islamabad. Elle and I were part of a team there for most of the past year. We were finally heading stateside when the two of us got pulled into this."

"Let me guess—by Grace?"

There was the smile again. A simple curving of Darien's lips and an unexpected flash of dimples. But it was as powerful as the first time. Possibly even more potent than Jessie remembered, because she momentarily lost the thread of conversation.

"Jesslyn?" Darien narrowed her eyes and glanced at her quizzically. "Was it Grace that stopped you from going home and sent you and Elle here?"

Jessie swallowed, moistened her dry lips, and found her voice. "Yes—yes, she did. And she left us with no choice in the matter, I might add. No choice at all. She might be my mother, but saying no to the deputy director is considered a career-limiting move."

"In other words, it's still what Grace Lawson wants, Grace Lawson gets. It's nice to know some things don't change."

"You really do know my mother, don't you?" Jessie found herself laughing. "Speaking of getting what you want, what do you suppose it would take to get a cup of that coffee? Because after putting up with what Ben and I have been making for the past few days, I'm desperate enough to beg if what's in that carafe tastes anywhere as good as it smells. And it smells heavenly."

"Begging's not required." Darien offered another smile. "And I promise it'll taste even better than you're hoping."

Jessie's eyes fastened on Darien's mouth, and she was left wondering how often she used that particular expression. Because it was powerful and dangerous and could make someone easily believe they were the center of her universe. "I don't know about that—I've got pretty high hopes."

Without saying another word, Darien reached for the carafe and began to pour coffee into a mug while Jessie waited impatiently, all but grabbing for it when the mug was finally full. She brought the coffee to her lips, inhaling the rich aroma just before she took a tentative sip, and released a sound that was a cross between a sigh and a moan.

"Problem?"

"God, no," she breathed. "This is perfect."

❖

Perfect.

Darien heard the word and had to agree. Although Jessie'd probably only managed a few hours of sleep, the shadows visible on her face the previous evening had lessened and to her ever-watchful eyes, Jessie looked refreshed this morning.

And lovely—especially during that instant when she had found herself staring and swore she could see a fire burning visibly in Jessie's eyes. Swore she could feel the heated flush as it spread across Jessie's cheeks.

Darien tried unsuccessfully to look away as she realized just how edgy Jessie made her feel. She made every sexual urge Darien usually sublimated with work cry out for attention.

Her reaction surprised her, but deciding to ignore it for the moment, she took a breath. Then another. But as her gaze moved over Jessie's face, she saw the tip of her tongue peek out as she licked her lips, and Darien felt an unexpected quickening deep in her blood, lighting something she hadn't felt in quite some time. The air sizzled, making it hard to draw a deep breath. And harder still to resist the urge to reach out and touch.

Not good. Especially considering who her mother is. "I'm glad you like the coffee. But if I can make one suggestion?"

Jessie blinked. "A suggestion? Sure."

"I suggest in future you don't look at me like that."

"Like what?"

Darien's voice dropped to a heated whisper. "Like you want me."

Jessie swallowed visibly. "Is that what you think I'm doing?"

"Lie to yourself if you choose, but don't lie to me," Darien said. "You know it's what you're doing. It makes me question just how strong your sense of self-preservation is. So I think it's only fair to warn you that if you choose to take this any further, you're going to find out I'm not nearly as civilized as anyone you might be used to."

The impulse to touch, to kiss, happened fast. Without taking the time to think through the consequences, she pushed away from the counter and deliberately walked around the island until she was standing in front of Jessie. So close she could see the pulse quicken at her throat, smell her cool and feminine scent, feel the heat radiating off her body. She ran an index finger in a slow, sensual glide across Jessie's full lower lip, along her jaw, and down the side of her neck.

"In fact, I think we should get this out of the way."

With a deft move, she captured Jessie's face between her hands and lowered her mouth. Her lips hovered there for an instant, a whisper away. She nipped Jessie's bottom lip with her teeth. And then she captured her mouth completely. Darien felt an instant of pure electricity, followed by a rush of heat. She responded to it, her hands diving deeper into Jessie's hair as she gave herself up to the exquisite pleasure of her mouth. Drawing Jessie closer, she brought their bodies into contact.

Damn. Jessie tasted of coffee and heat and desire. Her lips were as soft as Darien had imagined they would be and tasted every bit as sweet. They were everything she'd wanted—and she wanted everything.

It was the last coherent thought she had as the kiss deepened and someone—possibly both of them—moaned.

They broke apart almost as quickly as they'd come together. Darien let go of Jessie and moved back until they were a couple of steps apart. For a moment, all she felt was the fire still raging inside her, consuming everything in its path. Fighting to regain composure, she saw Jessie shut her eyes and keep them closed for a second or two, before opening them again and licking her lips.

One look. That was what it took for her to know Jessie wasn't unaffected by her touch. Her kiss. The thought pleased her…maybe a little too much. "That was even better than I thought it would be."

"Was it?" Jessie's voice was huskier than usual, her eyes were shining, her breathing slightly ragged.

Darien swallowed and took another step back, creating more distance between them, and dropped onto a stool. "We both know it was."

Jessie was an intelligent woman, and she clearly interpreted and understood her retreat for what it was. "It was just a kiss," she said lightly. "A damn good kiss, mind you. But it was just a kiss. And now, I guess we won't have to wonder. Just please, whatever else you might do…don't say you're sorry."

"I wasn't going to." Darien hesitated. "I'm not."

For the first time in as far back as she could remember, she felt a need to explain herself. But having never done it, she had no idea what was involved or what she should say. And then it no longer mattered. Anything she might have said, any conversation they might have had was lost as Elle burst into the kitchen in a clatter of footsteps and a blaze of anger.

"What the hell did you do with my computers?" she demanded, shaking off a restraining hand as Ben followed her into the kitchen.

"Elle?" Jessie tried to intervene. "What's going on? What's the problem?"

"I'll tell you what the problem is—she's the problem." Elle pointed a finger at Darien, temper clearly getting the better of her. She reached for Darien and grabbed her arm as she rose to her feet. The height difference caused Elle to pause as she looked up, but only for an instant. "Answer me, damn it. Where are my computers? What have you done with them?"

Darien's body tensed as fury outdistanced common sense and she curled her hands into fists. Then it was gone. Control returned and she stared dispassionately. "This is getting tiresome," she said, the threat implicit in her tone. "You'll want to step back and keep your hands off me."

It took only one long stare to have Elle releasing her hold and inching back. "I'm still waiting for an answer," Elle said with considerably less bravado.

"Dare?" Ben moved closer. "What's going on? Did you do something with Elle's computers?"

Darien directed a look of angry defiance in Ben's direction and lifted her shoulders as if to say *What if I did?* But Ben continued to stand in front of her, waiting for her to respond. Frustrated, she ran a hand through her hair, pushing it out of her face.

"I put them in boxes and stored them in the hall closet." She could feel her temper still spiking, but the initial rage was leveling off and she managed to keep her voice calm.

Jessie gave her a hard stare. "Did you change your mind about helping us?"

"Not at all." Inexplicably, the question and accompanying tone of disappointment stung, and Darien forced herself to take a steadying breath as she met Jessie's eyes. "It was a judgment call. I happen to believe if you're serious about tracking the list of arms dealers you showed me last night, you're going to need better technology than what you've been using."

"Better technology?"

"That's right. And it just so happens what I can provide is the latest from R and D. State of the art."

"State of the art," Elle repeated with a small sneer of disdain. "I'll have you know what I got from the agency is—"

"What you're using isn't bad." Calm once again, detached, Darien looked back at Jessie. "What I'm offering is better. But you don't have to take my word for it. Nor do you have to use it. If you follow me upstairs, I'll show you what I've got and you can decide for yourself. And if you're not happy with it, your old equipment is still here and I'll be glad to set it back up."

When Jessie continued to hesitate and seemed to struggle with a decision, Darien impatiently tapped a hand on her thigh and aimed a long, level look. "It's not that difficult a choice, Jesslyn. What have you got to lose?"

"You're right," Jessie said. "Okay, show us what you've got."

Without another word, Darien led the way back into the hall and up the stairs, not stopping until she reached a room on the fourth floor. After she tapped a lengthy alphanumeric code into the security pad located behind a framed black-and-white photograph on the wall, she flattened her palm against a biometric panel, then stepped aside as the door opened.

Silently cursing Ben one last time for getting her involved in this, she stepped into a room that was high ceilinged, relatively spartan, and painted a soft white. At its center was a sleek espresso-colored console. Horseshoe-shaped, it held several interconnected computers and two large monitors, while on the wall beyond it was a bank of large flat-screen televisions.

Taking a seat at the console, she spoke softly to unlock the keyboard and placed her hand on a second biometric panel. She then drew the keyboard closer and quickly typed the command which initiated jammers and inhibitors, preventing any external signal from penetrating the room. As she worked, she explained some of what she was doing for Jessie's and Elle's benefit.

"I've been in secure rooms"—Jessie gave a sharp laugh—"but this…you seem to have thought of everything."

"I certainly hope so." Flipping one final switch, she turned to Jessie. "I'm going to need you to look at the camera."

"What camera?"

Darien pointed toward a small blinking red light on the console. "It's connected to a three-dimensional facial recognition program that's set to capture all the necessary information. Things like the shape of your face and eyes, the texture of your skin. And I'll need you to say something."

"Anything in particular?"

"So long as it's natural, I don't need much. That'll actually do it. I'll also need to get a retinal scan and your handprint. Same goes for Elle."

Elle's eyes narrowed. "What for?"

"Security clearance. It's the only way you'll be able to get in the room, let alone access any of the equipment. Within reason, of course."

"I'm guessing access doesn't come with administrator privileges," Jessie said lightly.

"You'd be right. But you'll still be able to access all the information you need, and I can guarantee it will be more than you've been getting until now."

It took a few minutes to get it all done. Once Darien was satisfied she had what she needed, her fingers danced across the keyboard as she entered a new series of commands. One by one, the television screens came to life, showing real-time satellite images and endless streams of data.

"Okay, I need you both to listen, because I'm only going to explain this once. Getting into the room is just the beginning. Face, voice, and retina—in that order—will activate the system, but it's the handprint that'll let you input anything on the keyboard. If the keyboard isn't activated within twenty seconds of system activation, the whole thing shuts down and the room goes into lockdown. At that point, there's no way to get out, and the door can only be opened with very specific overrides."

"All right. Good to know." Jessie frowned, still staring at the information dancing across the screens. "What is that? And why does some of it look familiar?"

Darien glanced at the screens. "The one on the left is currently running a search on Langley's database. On the right, we're tapping into DGSE. But you're not limited to only those two. From here, we can access a number of classified systems. MI6, Mossad, SVR, ASIS. You get the idea."

"Wicked cool," Elle whispered. "How the hell are you doing all of this without getting caught?"

Darien shrugged. "That won't happen. Even as we speak, the signal's bouncing around satellites like a pinball, much too fast for anyone to track it."

"Jesus." Her anger and resentment clearly forgotten, Elle looked and sounded as if she'd found the holy grail. "This is so amazing. I think there are only about a dozen hackers that could pull something like this off."

"Probably, but I'm better. I don't leave tracks," Darien responded in all seriousness and fought not to laugh. Elle looked suitably impressed, while Jessie rolled her eyes. "Sorry. Sometimes I can't help myself. The truth is I do work for all the agencies whose systems I routinely access. It's part of the deal. Quid pro quo. But by accessing their systems the way I do, I can also let them know where their areas of vulnerability are and what they need to do to stop others from gaining entry."

"Have you ever been stopped?" Jessie asked before her voice softened. "Or come close to getting caught?"

"No. At least not so far." She shrugged again. "A couple of more things, and then we're done here."

"Okay. What's first?"

"If things start to go south for any reason, if you feel threatened or this location becomes compromised in any way…" She flipped a small switch and a wall opened up, revealing an impressive cache of weapons. Martial arts weapons including nunchakus and a Japanese katana were clearly visible, as well as more traditional weapons. Knives, handguns, several sniper rifles, and boxes of ammunition.

Jessie's eyes widened. "Gotta love a woman with her own private arsenal. Are you sure you don't have a Stinger missile or two in there?"

Darien turned and stared at her for an instant, not unaffected by Jessie's attempt at humor, but not yet willing to give. "No Stingers at the moment, but it can be arranged if you think it's necessary."

"I'll keep that in mind. You said there were a couple of things. What else?"

"This one's simple. For as long as we're obliged to work together, if you want to know something about me, you need to do it the old-fashioned way and ask. Doing end runs and deep searches on the computer won't work, unless you don't mind my finding out. And just so we're clear, that kind of activity tends to irritate me, so you might as well save yourselves the trouble."

Jessie flushed and gave a halfhearted shrug. "Sorry. We didn't mean—" She stopped and muttered something under her breath but quickly pulled herself together and gave Darien a cheeky smile, clearly trying to take any possible sting out of her words. "Actually, I guess we did mean to check you out. And obviously, that was you on the other end of the alarm we tripped—along with my mother. I really am sorry about that."

A reluctant smile tugged at Darien's lips. "It's all right, Jesslyn—this one time. Your instincts were good and given similar circumstances, I might have done the same."

"Maybe, but I doubt you would have tripped that alarm."

"You're right about that."

It was obvious Elle was no longer interested in the conversation as she continued to stare wide-eyed at the console. "Can I—"

Darien entered a new command on the keyboard, then got up and gave Elle her seat. "Help yourself. But Elle?"

She waited until Elle looked up at her and saw the faint smile that was not meant to be reassuring as Darien let a glimmer of the predator show. "I'm not sure how you survived Islamabad, but you've pushed your luck with me twice now. Make sure that's as far as it goes because there will be no more chances. Are we clear?" She paused for just an instant before continuing more gently. "Now, if we're done here, I believe I left breakfast ready downstairs. Shall we go eat?"

CHAPTER SIX

There would always be myriad reasons and countless agendas served when terrorist groups publicly claimed responsibility for acts that horrified most of the global community. A desire for media attention. A way to entice new recruits. A chance to demonstrate resolve and dedication to a cause. Or simply a demonstration of power, intended to instill fear.

Take your pick, Jessie mused. She knew it was only a matter of time before some group finally came forward and claimed responsibility for bringing down the three airliners. Under normal circumstances—if there was such a thing—someone should have already stepped forward. Why not today?

It wasn't as if they couldn't use a break. Nor could she forget they were on borrowed time, sitting on a ticking bomb. One she knew could go off at any time, without warning.

Shutting her eyes for a moment, she rubbed the bridge of her nose. She'd spent the better part of the last week pulling together information on their list of arms dealers. The hours bled one into the next seamlessly until she could no longer tell when one ended and another began. But she needed to assess where the dealers were, who they'd been seen with, then try to anticipate what might occur next.

It was like looking for a needle in a haystack, trying to find possible points of intersection between the dealers and the as yet unidentified terrorists. They had been widening the circles until the amount of information threatened to overwhelm, and she had been staring at the monitor for so long the data had begun to swim in front of her eyes.

Stretching tired and cramped muscles, she tried to run one last set of probabilities but found she couldn't concentrate and released a frustrated sigh.

"Are you okay?"

Jessie glanced up and noted the faint line of concern on Elle's brow. "I'm not sure. I've not been sleeping well." She swallowed and pushed her hair out of her eyes. "And I think I might have done something stupid. Something really, really stupid."

Elle's eyes narrowed fractionally and Jessie felt the weight of her stare. "Well—?"

"Well, what?"

"Well, don't keep a girl in suspense," Elle teased. "Was it a good kiss?"

"I have no idea what you're talking about."

"Don't bullshit me. Now spill it."

Jessie's eyes closed and she tried to shut out the image of Elle's grinning face as she replayed the hot, mind-numbing kiss. It had been a week and she could still taste it. She licked her lips and tried to recall the name of the last woman to kiss her like that. Failing miserably, she couldn't quite contain a soft groan. "Oh, shit."

Elle laughed. "Oh my God, you're blushing. I can't believe it. That good?"

"Ah, Jesus, Elle. Too good. How'd you know?"

"Because I can see something every time the two of you look at each other. Wow, talk about chemistry."

Jessie released another sigh. "Chemistry, maybe. But what the hell have I done?"

"You kissed a gorgeous woman," Elle summarized succinctly. "I'm not sure I see the problem in that."

"The problem?" Springing to her feet, Jessie began to pace, wondering if she was being too defensive. But it couldn't be helped. "The problem is I barely know Darien. And we have to work together."

"You left out the fact that she's a contract assassin. She kills people for a living. But let's not get caught up in the details because what's more important is she's helping us look for the terrorists who blew up those planes. Terrorists who are planning even bigger shit we know nothing about."

"Exactly." Jessie chose to ignore the sarcasm in Elle's voice. "Damn it, Elle, there's too much at stake for me to screw things up with sex. This isn't me. I don't do this. I can't do this."

"Then don't," Elle said with a shrug. "Look, Jess, at the best of times the woman scares me. But it seems to me whatever happened—this kiss—has already happened, and sooner or later, you're going to have to deal with this attraction the two of you seem to have. And nothing says you can't do both…deal with the attraction and do your job."

"What are you suggesting?

"For now, I think you need to stop beating yourself up. You've been going nonstop for quite a while, so why don't you give yourself a break?"

"Give myself a break how?"

"I don't know. Go grab a shower or something, clear your head. Things always look better after a long, steamy shower."

An image flashed in her mind, a bolt out of nowhere. Darien in the shower with her, their bodies entwined. Damn. Blowing out a breath, she ran a hand along the back of her neck, rubbing the tension she found there. "You're right. I think I'll do that."

She walked away, only to hear Elle's voice call out after her. "I'm thinking it must have been one hell of a kiss, though, to get you so worked up."

It was. Damn, it really was.

❖

A quick shower normally cleared her head, but the hot streams of water called up sensations Jessie wasn't prepared for. *Don't think about it,* she told herself—which of course only served to make her think even more. She remembered the feel of Darien's hands in her hair. Remembered the heat of her mouth. Remembered her taste. And realized how much she wanted to do it again.

Damn it all, it was just a kiss, she reminded herself raggedly. She shut off the water and grabbed a towel, then quickly dressed in jeans and a sweatshirt. Leaving her hair to dry on its own, she headed downstairs and wandered toward the kitchen.

She saw Ben was already there. Sitting on a stool at the island, he was watching Darien as she prepared what would be their evening meal. Deftly wielding a knife that looked as sharp as a scalpel, slicing vegetables and adding them to the stir-fry she was making.

All the obvious attractions and she cooks. It seemed like an excess of gifts.

Through the open doorway, she could hear Ben talking. A normal, everyday kind of conversation that seemed to revolve around his father. She noticed his tone was different, more relaxed. Heard him say his father had called to ask when they might be available to have dinner with him.

"I told him we were working on this thing and—"

"And what?"

"Bloody hell, Dare. I'm fifty-three years old. When do you suppose he'll forgive my failure to marry and ensure the family line?"

"It's the only thing he's ever wanted," Darien responded with a laugh. "You know that."

"I do, but now he's gotten it in his head that you can somehow be talked into at least providing him with a grandchild. Marriage optional."

Darien's hands stopped moving and her face became a study of contradictions. Jessie could see amusement and embarrassment jostling one another in Darien's normally guarded expression, as she made a wry grimace. "Your father wants to introduce mongrel and dilute the family bloodlines?"

"My mother's British, so the bloodlines are already diluted. The point you're purposefully missing is he thinks any child you and I produce would be brilliant."

And beautiful, Jessie added to herself while Darien's voice and laughter and scent swirled around her. She let out a long breath and cleared her throat to let the others know they were no longer alone, then walked the rest of the way into the kitchen.

"You know, your father's a really nice man. I always liked him and I hate the thought of depriving him of a potentially brilliant grandchild"—Darien looked up at Jessie as she came into view—

"and I truly don't want to hurt you. But the thought of me with any man, even you—"

Ben grinned. "Is not going to happen?"

"Not ever."

Darien's eyes held a trace of mischief and amusement flitted around her mouth. She added wine to the pot simmering on the stove, then poured some into a glass and took a hasty swallow.

Jessie let her gaze linger on Darien's mouth for a heartbeat, boldly and unapologetically appraising for longer than was probably necessary or wise. But the woman was rapidly becoming a madness in her well-ordered life, the resulting feeling almost primal.

She needed to think about that. About what it meant. But that was for later. For now, even as she told herself she needed to keep her feelings in check, she thought about the kiss again, letting her mind drift in the all-consuming sensuality of Darien's lips pressed against her own.

As if reading her perfectly, Darien's eyes shifted coolly to her. Darien said something, but Jessie was already embarrassed at being caught staring and didn't hear what she said. Her brows drew together with self-directed annoyance and heat flooded her face. It took a moment longer for her to understand wine was being offered when Darien gently shook the bottle she was holding.

"Want some?"

Want some?

Wine. She was offering wine. Nothing else.

She managed to mumble a response. "Sure."

Darien filled a glass and slid it across the island in her direction.

Jessie murmured her thanks. Forcing herself to exhale, she concentrated on bringing the wine to her lips. She wasn't used to having anyone or anything distracting her—especially not when she was working in the field. But twice now, not including the one unforgettable kiss, Darien had done just that. Evidently without even trying. She'd have to remain sharp or it would happen again.

"Can I do anything to help?"

Darien pointed to where the dishes were stacked at one end of the island. "You can help Ben set the table."

❖

As evening faded and slipped into night, Darien found her mood shifting. She recognized she was in what Ben would call one of her quiet moods. Dark and uncertain, emotions churning. But as she looked around, she couldn't isolate a source for her discontent.

Elle had returned upstairs as soon after dinner as she could politely arrange her escape, apparently pulled by some invisible umbilical cord that had formed, attaching her to the computer system.

Jessie, on the other hand, had abandoned any further analysis for the night. During dinner, she expressed her dissatisfaction with the progress they were making. "We just seem to be hitting dead ends in trying to identify the specific weapons dealer involved," she said.

They were being stonewalled, Jessie believed, by the inadequate political will of most governments to implement and enforce measures that would regulate, deter, and punish arms traffickers. "They're allowed to operate virtually unscathed, with no fear of prosecution or retribution. Only a few countries in the world actually have legislation against weapons brokers," she protested heatedly, "leaving them largely free to ply their trade. Despite the fact that they facilitate war and armed conflict, support terrorism, advance crime, and break UN arms embargoes."

As if hearing herself, she stopped abruptly, her face faintly flushed with obvious emotion. "Sorry about that," she said after a moment. "Didn't mean to get on a soapbox. It's just one of those subjects that get me going and it's been one of those days."

After that, Jessie had fallen into a kind of weary silence. But now it looked like she had found a healthy outlet for her frustrations, as she sat contentedly beating Ben at chess for the third straight game, much to Ben's consternation.

Darien watched for a minute or two longer before looking away. No one was actually talking to her at the moment. But she could still hear incessant irritation whisper in her ear, leaving her temper raw edged and her body coiled like a spring.

In an instant of sudden cool clarity, she realized she'd spent too much time surrounded by people over the last few days, something she just wasn't used to. That was it, clear and simple. The problem with the discovery, however, was she could see no immediate solution. Not now and not anytime soon.

When she let out her third shuddering sigh in as many minutes, Ben laid his king on its side, conceding yet another game to Jessie, and stood up. "Dare? What would you say to a workout?"

Darien let out a half laugh. Why hadn't she thought of it, she wondered, knowing physical exertion was the perfect panacea for what ailed her? Considering, she rose, moved with purpose toward the stairs, then stopped. Before allowing herself to continue, she needed to be clear about Ben's intentions.

"You already know I'm in a filthy frame of mind." She said it moodily and bared her teeth, but without heat. "So you're not actually thinking of sparring with me, are you?"

She heard Ben chuckle in response.

It wasn't that they weren't well matched physically. At just under six feet and one seventy-five, Ben was firmly muscled, barely an inch taller, and outweighed her by fifty pounds, while she had the advantage of being more than twenty-five years younger and had greater speed and agility on her side.

But Darien also knew if it came down to it, Ben could never move beyond his heritage and upbringing to actually hurt her, while at heart, like it or not, she was and would always be a street fighter. She wouldn't hesitate to fight dirty if it meant the difference between winning and losing. And she didn't like to lose.

Thankfully, Ben knew her well. "I don't think I'm up to having you toss me all over the floor tonight, so I think this might be a good time to practice kata rather than spar."

Suddenly the rest of the evening seemed to hold promise. Approaching Ben, she did something she seldom did, surprising them both—she touched her lips briefly to his cheek. "Thanks. For some reason, you often seem to know what I need before I do. Let me go change and I'll meet you in the dojo."

She was about to head upstairs when a softly worded question stopped her. "Would it bother you if I came along? I'd love to watch, and just maybe I wouldn't mind getting a bit of a workout myself."

Darien paused and turned to look at Jessie, trying to read her. But she saw nothing troubling. Nothing worrisome. After sending a quick glance in Ben's direction to make sure he didn't object, she nodded. Even smiled a little. "Why not. If you want to go get changed, Ben can show you where we work out."

After quickly changing into loose drawstring pants and a tank top, Darien wandered into the small dojo she'd set up on the fifth floor. Jessie and Ben showed up right behind her, both having changed into sweatpants and T-shirts.

"Ready?"

Jessie nodded and joined Darien and Ben on the floor as they began what was for them a familiar warm-up routine. "God, I needed this." Jessie sighed as they warmed up with basic Pilates, jump rope, and some light calisthenics. "I've been spending way too much time in front of a computer."

"Do you run?" Darien asked. When she saw Jessie's quick nod, she added, "You could come running with me some mornings, if you'd like. Paris is really quite beautiful at five a.m."

"Five?"

"Too early for you?"

"That's brutal."

Darien tried to bury a grin. "Or you might like it. You just need to be prepared to be stared at."

"Why's that?"

"For some reason, a lot of Parisian women don't run as a rule, so when people see you running, you're likely to get stared at…or spoken to by strangers."

"What do you do when that happens?"

"I ignore them and keep running. That's why I prefer running early—before too many people are out and about."

Jessie appeared to hesitate. "I guess I'm willing to give it a try. But am I going to slow you down too much?"

"Don't worry about that," Ben said. "I've trained with Dare quite often over the years, and if you let her set the pace, you'll find she sets a nice steady one. You should have no problem keeping up. It's also a great way to see the city."

"Then I'd say it's a plan," Jessie said and flashed a quick smile.

As they continued through the warm up, Darien kept an eye on Jessie. But she did okay, keeping up without any apparent problem.

Then again, Darien acknowledged, she shouldn't be all that surprised. The sleeveless T-shirt and sweatpants Jessie wore weren't that tight, but they highlighted a slim body with some very nicely defined muscles.

Jessie finally gave way once Darien and Ben prepared to start executing the first in a series of katas. Moving to the back of the room near the door, she sat on the floor while Ben wrapped a bandana around Darien's head, covering her eyes.

Like shadowboxing, Darien used kata to perfect technique and as a form of conditioning. Each kata simulated combat and needed to be practiced as if engaged in a real fight—with the right body dynamics, the right movements, the right sequences, executed at the right moment—and the feeling that the next attack could come from any direction. Each movement bled into the next in a well-choreographed ballet.

She thought that with a bit of imagination, kata could be deadly. She also firmly believed kata enhanced both the body and mind.

The blindfold helped her improve her sense of balance. More importantly, with the aid of the blindfold, she was able to slow down the kata and focus on precise breath control, muscle control, and mind control, which allowed her to move into a form of moving meditation. She relaxed both body and mind and moved into the moment, beyond the chatter and chaos that normally occupied her head.

There was something to be said for that. And for the first time since before she'd left for Afghanistan, Darien felt the external world recede, felt herself begin to unwind.

The Zen moment, unfortunately, proved to be short-lived, shattered as Elle called out their names. Elle's shouts grew closer, accompanied by the rush of her footsteps as she made her way down the hall.

Instinctively, Jessie jumped to her feet and reached out, grabbing Elle's arm and physically stopping her as she slid ungracefully across the hardwood floor in the dojo. She knew that for traditional martial artists, the dojo was considered a special place. Etiquette and protocol dictated how one should enter or leave, and allowing Elle to crash into either Darien or Ben was the last thing the situation—and etiquette— demanded.

She heard Darien bite back a muttered comment as she dropped out of a kick and pulled the bandana down around her neck. Ben took two additional steps before he stopped as well. After exchanging glances, they bowed toward the front wall of the room—a sign of respect—then signaled for Elle and Jessie to follow them out of the dojo. Their meaning was clear. No conversation about terrorists would take place in the dojo.

Elle could barely contain her excitement, unable to wait until they reached the computer room. "We caught a break. A little over an hour ago, a group released a statement claiming responsibility for launching the missiles that brought down the three jets. They've also issued a warning. They say this is only the beginning, and that another demonstration of their power is imminent. The UK has already responded by raising their terror-threat level to severe. No word out of DHS whether the US will follow suit."

"Bloody hell," Ben said. "Do we know who they are?"

"I've already managed to get a bit of research on them, but I've got to tell you, most of it is ancient history. It's going to take time and resources."

"But you've obviously got something." Darien's impatience simmered visibly.

"I do—but I'm trying to warn you what's there is quite old, and it doesn't make a lot of sense."

Jessie placed a calming hand on Darien's shoulder. "Just tell us what you've got."

Taking a deep breath, Elle nodded. "What we're looking at is a group that first showed up on intelligence radar almost twenty years ago. They weren't around long—maybe five years. But what's really interesting is that for the most part, they were never directly involved in any terrorist activities. They just funded other organizations."

"You're saying they were financiers?" Jessie asked. "Bloody bankers?"

"After a fashion, yeah, I guess. Initially, they backed a number of groups dedicated to independence in the Caucasus region and fighting against the Russian government. But then they discovered there was money to be made, and they began establishing ties with other terrorist groups with goals far greater in scope...including jihadists fighting in the Middle East and other parts of the world."

"Where did they get the money?"

"Primarily through money laundering and drug trafficking. But they were also suspected of kidnapping young European and American girls and selling them to wealthy customers in Asia and the Middle East. Or putting them to work in brothels." Elle paused. "They probably would have kept on going, but something happened. It was rumored they were directly involved in the kidnapping and execution of two Israeli citizens suspected of being Mossad. After that, it all fell apart."

"Jesus." Jessie grimaced. "Did these bastards have a name?"

"They called themselves the Guild."

The Guild? Darien stiffened. Denial came hot and hard and fast, and she felt her heartbeat accelerate until it was pounding madly in her chest. "No, that can't be right." She turned to Ben and was surprised to find his expression curiously shuttered.

"I can understand why you'd think that. I mean, other than the execution of the two Mossad agents, the Guild never actively participated in acts of terrorism. They only provided funding. But it would seem they've changed in the years since they went off grid." Elle held out the printout for Darien to see. "Take a look. I printed out the Reuters piece that carried their statement."

"I don't care what it says. It can't be the Guild."

"Why not?" Jessie asked.

"Because the organization known as the Guild was completely destroyed. Almost fifteen years ago." The muscles in her jaw tightened as she forced herself to remain calm, to think. She turned away from the concern in Jessie's eyes and looked at Ben again, only to watch as his brows came together and his eyes shifted away, refusing to make eye contact. She stared at his profile a moment longer and felt an ache deep in her heart.

"I don't know about that," Elle was saying. "My research indicates they went off grid less than five years after they first surfaced—about fifteen years ago—so that seems to match what you're saying. But I spoke with Adam—he's a colleague at Langley—and he said they've been able to confirm this group really is the Guild."

As a sense of dread settled over her, Darien saw that her hands were trembling slightly and fought to get herself back under control. She forced herself to look at Elle, to pay attention to what she was saying. "How was the information confirmed?"

"Deputy Director Lawson. Turns out she had firsthand knowledge and experience with the Guild back in their heyday."

It took a lot to shock Darien. Certainly not violence or the depths of human cruelty, or even death. She'd seen too much and lived with it for too long. But she was shocked now. She could feel the color leeching from her face and her heartbeat reverberating in her bones as she turned and stared at Ben.

He should be as shocked as she was. He should be showing something. *Anything, damn it.* But he simply stood there with a look of regret etched on his face while he continued to avoid her eyes and said nothing.

Darien gulped in a breath and then let her years of training kick in. She forced herself to control the fury that had her entire body vibrating, while she regained control of her scattered emotions. And then she forced herself to accept the unpalatable truth.

"You knew," she whispered. She watched Elle freeze. Saw Jessie's confusion as she glanced from her face to Ben's, then back again. And she felt empty. So very empty. "Damn it, Ben. You and Grace both knew this is what we'd find."

Ben's shoulders appeared to sag under the weight of her accusation. "Dare, it's not what you think. Not exactly. Let me explain."

"No, you don't get to call me *Dare* like we're good friends and think that will somehow make things better." The words tumbled out harshly and disjointed.

Because she wanted to strike out, she shoved her hands in her pockets, closed her eyes, and shuddered out a breath while Jessie and Elle and the world beyond them ceased to exist. "You've been

keeping secrets, Ben. Hiding the truth from me. It's the one thing—
the *only* thing—I ever asked you to promise me. The one thing you
said you'd never do."

Ben reached out for her, taking her arm. "Darien, I'm sorry—"

"No, you don't get to be sorry either because it doesn't change
anything." She pulled herself free from his grasp. "At least have the
decency to admit you and Grace knew what we were dealing with.
Can you do that?"

Ben released a low, frustrated groan. "No one knew for certain.
All we had to go on was chatter. Rumors circulating that someone
might be trying to resuscitate the Guild for reasons we could only
guess at. It was all supposition and guesswork. So we kept it need-
to-know while we watched and waited. Until the rumors could be
verified."

"Bullshit." Darien would be the first to admit she wasn't one for
adhering to rules. But honesty, especially with those she was supposed
to be able to count on, people she was close to, had always been held
as sacrosanct. Knowing Ben and Grace had withheld information
from her shook her. Finding out they'd been less than honest with
her hurt.

Do the ends justify the means, she wondered. "This is why you
and Grace made sure I was here, under your watchful eye, when the
truth came out. Isn't it?"

Ben flinched. "We didn't want you getting hurt. Or doing
anything—"

The unintended but lethal jab was right on target. She wheeled
around as his anger sparked her own. "You wanted to be able to
control my reaction, isn't that what you mean? Well, guess what? I'm
not thirteen anymore. And you can't control me now any better than
either you or Grace could control me fifteen years ago."

"Dare, damn it, listen to me. We can work through this. Grace
will fly in and we can all sit down. If we work together, we can figure
out who's behind the resurrected Guild. We can figure out what
they're after and how to stop them."

Darien shook her head vehemently as something twisted inside
her, but she kept her gaze steady on him. "No, I don't think so. You

had your chance to have us *work this through* together and you blew it. Now it's my turn."

She felt Ben give her a slow, measuring study, but his dark eyes revealed nothing of his thoughts as he asked, "What does that mean? What do you think you're going to do?"

"I'm going to do what I do best," she answered, suddenly feeling tired to her bones. "I'm going to do what you and Grace and my mother trained me to do."

Ben blinked. "You're going to go after the Guild."

"It's what I'm good at, isn't it? And it would no longer surprise me if it's what you and Grace counted on when you brought me in."

"That's not it at all."

Feeling overwhelmingly weary, Darien shrugged him off. "You know what, Ben? It doesn't really matter."

"What does that mean?"

"It means it doesn't matter what you thought or planned or what Grace thought or planned. It doesn't even matter why the Guild is back or what they intend to do. What's important now is getting close enough to shut them down permanently—before any more innocent lives are lost. So I'm going to finish what was started nearly fifteen years ago. Only this time, I won't stop until I know for certain the job is done."

"And how in bloody hell do you think you're going to do that? Can you at least answer me that?"

She might be angry with him, but she was not so far gone that she couldn't hear the frustration, weariness, and yes, even hurt in Ben's voice. Darien stopped, considered, then allowed her thoughts to begin racing as she structured a plan on the fly. And even though she hated herself for it and thought she was showing weakness, she eased back into a long-established pattern of talking her thoughts out...with Ben.

"I'm going to go see Yuri." She turned, sending a whisper of dark hair over her cheek. "If anyone knows anything about the Guild and who's behind it, it'll be Yuri. He'll get me a contact."

"What makes you think so?"

"They said they're just beginning. They want to demonstrate their power and warned another attack is imminent. But if they plan to continue with large-scale acts of terrorism, they're going to need what I can offer. Assault weapons, missiles, weaponized vehicles. Whatever. I don't care. All I need to do is get close enough to look them in the eyes. And then I'm going to take them apart for good." The storm had passed and she was calmer. "There won't be any coming back again after that."

Ben's frown deepened as he appeared to weigh her words. Watching him, Darien couldn't help but wonder if this too was part of some Machiavellian plan he and Grace had concocted. Dangle the Guild in front of her, wind her up, and let her loose to hunt them down. Seek and destroy. Could it be that simple?

Trust no one. Wasn't that what she'd been taught? She didn't want to believe it, but present circumstances were forcing her to consider every possibility.

After a lengthy silence, Ben spoke. "Even if we do it your way for now, you'll need to move slowly. Not do anything rash. Jessie and Elle and I are still here. Grace is a phone call away and will stand ready to provide whatever intel or resources you need. All you need to do is tell me what we can do to help."

Still hurting, still feeling the sting of betrayal, Darien wanted to say there was nothing anyone could do to help. But years of training stopped her, and the truth was if she wanted to do this, and do it right, she would still need help. She would probably need all of them—Jessie, Elle, Ben, and Grace—before this was all over if she wanted to survive. And she intended to survive.

"Before I meet with Yuri, I'll need to see Zoey. I need to set the stage. In the meantime, I'll need one of these ladies ready to go with me. I don't care which—just help whichever one's willing to back me up."

"All right. But it's late. Why don't you leave it until morning?"

"I don't see any point in waiting." She felt his eyes on her face, knew he disagreed but didn't know how to stop her. How to change her mind. "Don't push me on this, Ben. Neither of us will like what happens. I'll be back when I have things in place."

Ben bit off an oath. "Damn it, Dare. Please don't leave like this. Tell me how to make things right."

"You can't. And there's one more thing."

"What?"

"When this is over, I'm no longer your problem. I'm through. I want out and I don't give a damn about the consequences." She sent a slashing, cynical look as she brushed past him and started for the stairs.

"Dare—"

Hurt, unbelievably hurt, and fighting to keep her composure, Darien kept walking. There was nothing left to say, and the sound of retreating footsteps was the only answer she had left in her to give.

CHAPTER SEVEN

Darien did not come back to the house that night. Nor, quite obviously, had she returned by morning. When Jessie walked into the kitchen, there was no delightful aroma of fresh-brewed dark-roast coffee in the air to greet her. There were no bowls of fresh fruit from the market or steaming croissants straight from the bakery down the street.

Admit it, she thought. *You're already spoiled.*

But it was more than that and she knew it. In spite of the physical attraction, Jessie hadn't wanted to like Darien. She had just wanted to get the job done. But Darien had made working together easier than she'd anticipated—and liking her had happened quite naturally.

Staring at the empty coffeemaker, Jessie realized she was worried about Darien. And that was crazy, because if anyone gave the impression they could look after themselves, it was Darien Troy.

Abandoning any thought of trying to make coffee and unable to face the prospect of drinking something Ben might make, Jessie chose the path of least resistance and walked to the patisserie a couple of blocks away. A good decision. The right decision. The early morning sky was an incredible shade of blue, and the air was already warm, filled with scents and sounds, and the promise of a beautiful day.

She took her time, and more than twenty minutes passed before she returned to the house with three coffees and a box containing *pain au chocolat*. Maybe not as healthy as something Darien would have put together, but who could deny the pleasure of chocolate for breakfast?

Ben was up, staring morosely at the empty coffeemaker and wearing the remnants of a bad night. His eyes lit up when he saw what she was holding. "You're a lifesaver," he said. "I was about to murder another pot of coffee."

Jessie smiled at him faintly.

"At least it doesn't look like it's going to rain."

The weather—how original. But if Ben preferred to make small talk about coffee and the weather rather than address the elephant in the room—the argument he'd had with Darien the evening before and whatever had driven her from the house—then Jessie would cut him some slack. She would give him time.

She knew instinctively that whatever had gone down between him and Darien had hurt him deeply on a personal level. She shuddered as she recalled the jagged ice in Darien's tone and felt herself softening.

But her experience and training warned her not to lose too much time. The clock was ticking and they still needed to identify the people behind the organization calling itself the Guild—before they made their next move.

Trust your instincts. She did what she'd been taught to do. She let him make small talk, gave him time as she took a sip of her coffee. It was strong. Very strong. But she figured the jolt of caffeine couldn't hurt.

"She was going to see Zoey. She'll have spent the night with her."

At last. "Who is Zoey?" A lover?

"The best answer I can give you is that Zoey's an artist Darien took under her wing. A very *young* artist."

His emphasis had Jessie trying to read between the lines, along with the expression on Ben's face, with no success. "How young is young?"

"She's maybe seventeen…going on forty." He sent her a wry smile and shrugged. "Dare saved her from an unfortunate incident in an alley in Berlin. Then, for a reason she's never bothered to explain, she kept the kid with her while she completed the job she was there to do instead of saving her and walking away as she should have done. The funny thing is, for a runaway, the kid didn't put up even token resistance. They were like kindred spirits recognizing each other. And then Darien compounded the matter by bringing Zoey back to Paris with her."

"When was this?"

"Maybe four years ago."

Jessie tried to understand, but it felt as if all she could do was try to keep up. "The child would have been around thirteen. Are you telling me with all the technology available upstairs, no one bothered to or was able to find out where Zoey came from? Who she belonged to? No one tried to get her back to her family?"

"Actually, Dare did her usual thorough job. She found out the kid came from Amsterdam, but she said there was nothing there Zoey needed to go back to. So she assumed responsibility for her. She's gone so far as to set her up in what was Dare's pied-à-terre before she bought this place and looks after all her expenses. She also sees to the girl's education."

"I don't get it. Why doesn't Zoey just live here?" She indicated the expansive house surrounding her with a wave of her hands. "It's certainly big enough, so it's not like they'd be tripping over each other."

"That's true, and they tried that route in the beginning. They never said why, but my guess is neither Dare nor Zoey is very good at living in close proximity to other people for too long. And rather than risk Zoey heading back to the streets, they worked out a compromise."

Jessie couldn't miss the light of amusement in Ben's dark eyes or the affection evident in his tone. "But you live here. How does that work?"

"Actually, I don't live here," Ben responded. "I maintain my primary residence in London, but I also have a home in Tokyo. I'm only here because I got pulled into this job."

"Because of your history with the Guild."

Her comment elicited a real laugh from Ben. "You're really more like your mother than your father, aren't you." He made it a statement, not a question. "But to answer your question, yes. I'm involved in this because of history."

"History that includes both Darien and my mother?"

"Yes, again. Darien, Grace, and I were all originally part of bringing the Guild down fifteen years ago. And I expect we will all somehow be involved in stopping them once again. Preferably before they go too much further."

Suspicious by nature, Jessie blew out an impatient breath. "For Christ's sake, Ben. Fifteen years ago, Darien would have been a child."

"She was thirteen."

She tried to picture Darien at thirteen. She'd bet she'd been tall for her age. A slim, long-legged, wild child with haunted eyes the color of smoke. She blinked the image away and turned her attention back to the conversation. "You realize what you're saying makes no sense at all, don't you? How is it even possible?"

"Actually, it makes perfect sense if you stop to think about it. Revenge is a powerful motivator—even for a girl barely into her teens."

"It's still not working for me. What kind of revenge drives a girl to go after terrorists?"

She watched the change as it slid across Ben's face. "The kind that's based on avenging her mother's death."

Because she knew she was responding emotionally, Jessie fought to cover her own reaction. She closed her eyes for just an instant and pictured her own mother. "I can see how that could be quite motivating. But still, for you and my mother to bring a thirteen-year-old girl along as part of some covert operation to take down a terrorist organization? That's just crazy."

"Actually, you've got it backward. It wasn't our takedown. It was Darien's operation all the way. Grace and I considered ourselves lucky that she allowed us to go along with her."

"What are you saying?"

"When we became aware Arianna Troy had been killed—when her body was recovered—Grace and I started searching for Darien. But it wasn't easy. She'd had plenty of training and time to disappear. We found out later that Arianna was set up, but Darien had no way of knowing who was behind it, which meant she wasn't prepared to trust anyone. By the time we caught up to her, she'd been surviving on her own for quite some time, and by then the damage was done. She had compiled a list of targets—people she felt were responsible for her mother's death—and she was operating with one simple premise. She wanted revenge, and if someone got in her way, they bled."

"Then why did she allow you to help?"

"I think because, deep down, she knew both Grace and me. She had known us personally for a number of years through her mother, and in the end her need for help trumped her distrust. Dare had her priorities straight, and she knew it was either accept our help or get killed without being able to exact total retribution."

Reaching into his pocket, Ben pulled out his wallet and extracted a photograph. "This was taken a few months before Arianna died."

As Ben's words faded into silence, Jessie stared at the photograph. Thirteen-year-old Darien had been on the cusp of evolving into something spectacular when she'd posed for it. The painfully beautiful face already sculpted into intriguing angles and hollows. The frightening intelligence clearly visible in the smoky gray eyes, along with the ever-present defiant attitude evidenced by the line of her jaw and set of her chin. But without the damage caused by whatever transpired in the months after her mother was killed.

Jessie got the point. "Shit."

Ben nodded. "I know you have more questions. But unless it interferes with what we need to do to stop the Guild, some of the answers will have to come from Darien. Or from Grace."

"My mother, because you don't believe Darien will answer my questions?"

"Actually, I don't know for certain, but I'll be curious to find out."

She hesitated, wanting to ask more questions before accepting they'd come as far as they were going to. For now. "All right, but I've got to warn you. I grew up surrounded by secrets and I've discovered I have little tolerance for them."

Ben smiled faintly. "Fair enough."

"What happens next?"

"Right now, unless you brought club wear with you from Islamabad, my guess is we need to go shopping."

Jessie couldn't restrain the shudder that ran through her. Shopping? "What do I need with club wear?"

"Have you forgotten already?" Ben raised a brow, an unholy gleam in his eyes. "Darien will need backup for her visit to Yuri's tonight, and Yuri owns a club."

"Are you that certain she'll be back?"

"Without a doubt. Darien's a professional. That means she'll see any job through, but especially one that's personal. And that means she'll be going to Yuri's tonight."

"And what's she hoping to achieve by going there?"

"Hopefully, get a foot in the door and a chance to fill the Guild's shopping cart."

The tightening in her chest was automatic. "Darien's going to offer to broker the weapons deal?"

Ben nodded. "The quickest route to a buyer is to offer them what they want and make it a deal they can't refuse. Dare's got a ready-made legend that's been years in the making. But for this to work, she'll need Yuri to vouch for her, confirm she can deliver the goods, and facilitate the introduction to whoever's running the Guild. To gain access to Yuri, she'll need to be in character, which means she'll be expected to show up with a sexy woman on her arm. If she doesn't, it may raise questions and distract from the purpose of her visit."

"And I'm supposed to pass for arm candy? That hardly seems fair."

"Darien will tell you that life is neither fair nor unfair. Just sometimes surprising." He took a closer look at her face and sighed. "And something tells me you're going to prove as bad about shopping as Dare."

Jessie gave him a wry grin.

"Well, don't worry too much, you're in good hands. I have some friends with shops along the Champs-Élysées. If they can deal with Darien, they should be able to make quick work of what we need for you."

❖

"You look perfect."

At the sound of her voice, Jessie turned, lifting her gaze as if she'd known all along she was there. "Darien."

"You were expecting someone else?"

"I wasn't actually expecting anyone." Jessie frowned as she spoke. "Ben was certain you'd come through. But quite frankly, it had gotten so late I wasn't certain you'd show."

She nearly pulled off the air of indifference she was obviously striving for. But Darien could still hear the edge of uncertainty in her voice. "Well, even if you didn't believe I'd show up, I'm glad you're still dressed and ready to go with me to Yuri's. Ben chose well with that dress."

"How do you know it isn't mine? Lucky guess?"

"I rarely guess."

Jessie shrugged and looked away. "Maybe so, but I'll have you know I feel ridiculous. Like a kid playing dress up. This so isn't me," she said, indicating the barely there black dress designed to accentuate her slim figure and subtle curves.

Darien smiled. "Don't hold back, Jesslyn. Tell me how you really feel."

"I—damn it all, I don't even have a place to hide a gun."

"You won't need one tonight. I've got you covered." Flipping her jacket open, Darien showed a holstered weapon within easy reach, before revealing her backup in its holster at her ankle. "As unappealing as it may sound, your role this evening is—"

"Arm candy, I know." Jessie stiffened and her frown deepened. "Ben made it quite clear." As expected, she didn't like the role she'd been given and it showed.

Darien smothered a laugh she knew Jessie wouldn't like either. "I can appreciate you may not be crazy about the idea, and I wish I had another option to offer. But I don't, since having a sexy woman on her arm is exactly what Yuri and everyone else at the club tonight will expect of Ari."

"Who's Ari?"

"Allow me to introduce myself, Ms. Coltrane." Darien graced her with a slight bow and gave the greeting with a distinctive Eastern European inflection to her voice that was not normally present. "My name is Ari. I'm a freelance photographer and an adjunct lecturer in computer animation and digital photography at the Sorbonne. I'll be your escort this evening."

"Ari…?"

"Simply Ari."

"You're a photographer? So the photography throughout the house—all those amazing black and whites of Masai Mara, Machu Picchu, Nepal, Egypt. They're all yours?"

"Yes."

"Well, Ari no-last-name, you're very talented." Jessie shot her a narrow look. "And that's almost frightening."

"What is?"

"How different you suddenly seem."

Caught off guard by the directness of her comment, Darien tried to consider what Jessie was seeing as she looked at her. She was dressed in unrelenting black, but that wasn't particularly unusual. Other than having her hair slicked back, some artfully placed ink that wasn't showing at the moment, and a small silver hoop threaded through her left eyebrow, she didn't think she looked all that different.

But then Ari was a legend, years in the making. One she'd used on so many occasions she easily slipped into the persona and wore it like a second skin. It was a part of her, like dark hair and gray eyes. "With you, I'm just me."

Jessie shook her head. "Actually, no. You look different, you sound different. You're even moving differently."

"I'm just me," Darien said again, momentarily affecting a lilting French accent before switching back to what Jessie would identify as her natural, faintly accented intonation. "But Ari's Russian. And it's Ari that everyone at Yuri's will be seeing tonight, with the beautiful Ms. Coltrane on her arm."

"That's really good, but you didn't learn that in any school. How the hell do you do that?"

"I don't know." Darien shrugged. "I've always been able to switch languages and accents at will, and I've done it for so long I've never really questioned it. I believe it's part heritage and part having lived in so many different places while I was growing up."

Jessie remained silent, urging her to continue with only a look, and after a moment, Darien complied.

"My mother was Israeli. I was born in Cairo, but my childhood included living for extended periods of time in England, France, Germany, Israel, and Montenegro. Each place meant learning a different language and adopting a different accent so I wouldn't stand out. Now it simply makes it easier when I need to pretend I'm someone else."

"Still, it must have been tough."

"Not really. I loved living like that with my mother. Exploring new places, learning new languages. And pretending to be someone else comes naturally."

Jessie smiled. "I was born and raised in the US, lived there most of my life," she said. "I can't imagine what it must be like to live in so many different countries. What about your father?"

"No idea. Just a lot of rumors I wasn't supposed to hear when I was a child." Darien shrugged. "The most popular ones had him as either an American, British, or Russian spy. But it wasn't important to me. My mother and I were as tight a team as you could get, and there were always father figures around if I really needed one. People like Ben and even your father."

She stopped, suddenly aware she was talking out loud. Talking too fast, confiding things that were personal. But the words had already tumbled out of her mouth and she seemed incapable of stopping them. Briefly, she wondered if she'd regret it later. For now, she had no answer.

"In any case," she continued more slowly, "as far as everyone tonight is concerned, the lovely Ms. Coltrane is American and speaks only English, so she won't be expected to engage in conversations with anyone."

"Actually, I speak seven languages like a native and can sort of hold my own in several others."

"That'll come in handy."

Jessie drew closer, her low voice and subtle perfume surprisingly seductive. "The CIA thinks so."

Darien cleared her throat. "I was thinking specifically of tonight. If the people around you believe you can't understand a word they're saying, there's a greater chance they'll give up something that might prove useful to us."

Jessie nodded her understanding and acceptance of the situation, as well as her role in it. She started to shift away, but Darien gently caught her arm and asked, "Is there anything else you need to do, or are you ready to go?"

"Since I'm not going to find a place for my gun, I'm as ready as I'll ever be." Jessie paused, let a beat of silence pulse between them. "What about you? Are you all right?"

"I'm fine. Why wouldn't I be?"

Frowning, Jessie tilted her head and looked at her. "Because when you left last evening—"

"Ah." The sound was dismissive. "That was nothing that should concern you. I'm fine."

"Are you sure?"

"Quite sure. I'm fine."

Jessie shot her another look. "No matter what I ask, you're going to answer that you're fine, aren't you?"

"Jesslyn, I'm—"

"Fine, yeah, I know. If that's the case, if you're not willing to talk about it, then we might as well go."

We. For some reason, the word caused Darien to pause, to feel something she couldn't name. Possibly because she hadn't thought of herself as being part of a *we* for a very long time. Hearing the word now inexplicably stirred something. The need to share, to not be so alone.

She already knew she couldn't. She knew now was not the time. Too many things stood in the way. But that didn't stop something deep inside from shifting, and she suddenly couldn't remember the last time she was simply herself with a woman. Not pretending to be someone else for the job. Someone like Ari.

Jessie's brow knit for a second, her eyes betraying a momentary concern, as if she'd somehow managed to read Darien's thoughts and caught a glimpse of what was going on inside her head. But then her expression smoothed and became faintly amused as she flicked her gaze over Darien's face. "At least tell me we're not going on a motorcycle. Because this damned dress—"

"The dress is something else." It was a thing of fantasies, Darien thought, and she almost laughed, enjoying the moment—and shoulder-to-waist triangle of delightfully feminine skin left exposed by the dress—more than she should have. "You look beautiful. Ben chose it wisely, and no, we're not going on my motorcycle. I've got a car and driver waiting outside." She held out her arm and waited for Jessie to take it.

CHAPTER EIGHT

Their driver turned out to be a gamine, rail-thin blonde, with a heart-shaped face and a pixie haircut. Leaning slouched against a gleaming Mercedes, she looked terminally young, dressed in skinny black jeans, a black long-sleeved T-shirt, and black high-tops. Her gaze snapped immediately to Darien as they approached, and she straightened long enough to open the door for them.

"Thanks, Zoey," Darien murmured as she slipped in beside Jessie. The young blonde nodded, closed the rear door, and got into the driver's seat.

So this was Zoey, the young artist Darien had rescued. Silently observing her, Jessie wondered what her role might be in this convoluted game they were now playing. She wondered why Darien would choose to involve her at all in their search for terrorists. But she had no answers, simply questions and more questions.

Traffic was slow and they weaved in and out of crowded lanes, headlights and taillights winking, with only Zoey's occasional curses at other drivers breaking the silence. Darien had been quiet since getting into the car, her face impossible to read. Gone was the smiling, faintly vulnerable woman Jessie had glimpsed earlier, leaving what she suspected was Ari in her place.

With a sigh, Jessie crossed her arms over her chest and gazed out the window, watching landmarks and scenery blur by. Slowly the initial shining hues of neon signs that flooded the avenues and boulevards filled with shops, cabarets, and clubs gave way to a grittier part of the city. But she still had no idea where they were going. And she had the unsettling feeling she had fallen through a hole in the fabric of reality and was now in another world.

As a shiver of nervous anticipation danced along her spine, she inhaled and let it out slowly. To hell with this. If Darien wanted her help with whatever she had planned, she could damn well start talking to her.

Aware Zoey was watching her in the rearview, she turned and faced Darien. And though her lips might have trembled slightly, there was nothing uncertain in her voice. "Are you planning to tell me about where we're going or am I playing this evening entirely by ear?"

Darien gave no immediate sign of having heard, and Jessie flushed slightly. Obviously, she had erred. But before she could come up with an alternate plan, Darien half turned toward her, backlit intermittently by the lights of passing cars. But the play of light and shadow did nothing to diminish the intensity of her stare. It was a fixed look, like a cat daring a mouse to move.

Jessie felt her face heat once again. "I'd like to know a bit more about where we're going," she reiterated. "I'm a threat analyst, and I'm not the risk taker you are. So please, if I'm to be at all helpful to you tonight, I need to know what to expect."

"Expect the unexpected."

Jessie frowned. "That's it? That's all you're going to tell me?"

Darien's expression didn't change as she leaned back into the soft leather seat, looking preoccupied with her own thoughts. But then she started talking. "We're going to a club called Oz, owned by a man named Yuri Berezin."

"And he is—let me guess—the wizard?"

The comment earned her a hint of a smile. "He's a Russian businessman who saw the writing on the wall in Russia and got out with as much of his money as he could manage. He originally set up business here in Paris, but in addition to the club we're going to tonight, he's got one in Amsterdam, another in Prague, and one he recently opened in South Beach."

"Miami?" Jessie sat up a little straighter. "Really?"

"It's his first foray into the US market, and it won't be his last if I know Yuri. But he got his start selling black-market goods on the streets of Moscow, and he's never forgotten his roots. You'll find his clubs cater to a lot of the Russian gangs that control large portions of the illegal drug market, as well as weapons trafficking and prostitution. He doesn't touch anything himself, not directly. But he can and does make deals happen."

"Even if the Guild isn't Russian?"

"Yuri may prefer to socialize with comrades from the home country, but when it comes to business, all he cares about is the color of your money. Although if asked, I'm quite certain he prefers to deal in euros or American dollars."

"And he's just going to let us walk into this club? Into Oz?"

"Yuri's certainly not going to welcome former MI6 operative Darien Troy and current CIA analyst Jesslyn Coltrane into his midst." Darien gave her a brief grin—quick and wicked—that caught Jessie by surprise. "But Ari has established a reputation and earned a level of respect with Yuri's clientele, so he's going to let Ari walk in without a problem. And you happen to be Ari's date for the evening."

"Right—arm candy. How could I forget," Jessie muttered darkly.

Darien's expression said that amused the hell out of her. "The club is a converted warehouse. The main floor is your standard Paris dance club—loud music, expensive drinks, beautiful people. It seldom gets going before midnight and draws a typical mix of night junkies. Mostly people who want to be seen mixing with a dangerous crowd, and tourists with more money than sense looking for adventure."

"Got it."

"Just about anything is available for a price. Drugs, sex—if you want it and can afford it, you can buy it. But we don't care about the main floor. It's the lower level we want."

"If that's the main level, do I even want to know what's on the lower level?"

"Nothing legal, I can guarantee that much." Darien regarded her coolly, a disconcerting expression on her face. "This, Jesslyn, is called a lesson in trust."

Jessie ignored the sudden dryness in her mouth. "You want me to trust you."

"Actually, I don't give a damn whether you trust me or not. I need to know you can follow my lead."

So this was it. What it all came down to. Jessie knew that, in the world of covert operations she skirted and Darien lived in, it wasn't always possible to play by the rules. What was important was that you had your partner's back and vice versa.

"I can do that," she said softly and saw something flicker in Darien's face. Approval or something like it.

"Good." Darien paused as she reached into her jacket pocket and withdrew a hammered silver choker with an intricately carved stone pendant. "I'd like you to wear this."

It looked very old and Jessie wondered if it was some kind of heirloom. "This is beautiful. It's quite old, isn't it?"

"It's not a family treasure, if you're at all worried about it," Darien said with unexpected gentleness. "To be quite honest, I'm not sure of its provenance. I bought it at a souk in Morocco."

"It will certainly go perfectly with the dress I'm wearing. But I get the feeling that's not what you have in mind."

"You're right. I've added a few enhancements since I first bought it. Now it will let you capture the faces of everyone you see or come in contact with. Once we get back to the house, we'll run a biometric analysis on each of the faces you've recorded and compare the results against a database containing photographs and artists' composites of known and suspected terrorists. Maybe we'll get lucky. Worst case, we add to the list of faces that are on file."

"All right." Jessie turned her head and let Darien place the necklace around her neck.

Darien leaned back and studied the results. "It suits you," she said. "There are just a couple of more things you need to remember."

"Like what?"

"Don't drink anything tonight, not even bottled water. No matter how vigilant you are, it's still far too easy for someone to slip something into your drink.

"Drink nothing. Got it. What else?"

"I want you to stay close to my side. Do not wander anywhere by yourself. I mean it, Jesslyn. I need you to understand, if I have to come looking for you, I'll assume you're in danger and come prepared to kill."

Jessie swallowed. "By your side—like glue. I've got your back."

"Good to know."

The amused tone of her voice made Jessie smile as she watched Darien close her eyes. But the silence was more comfortable this time.

❖

When Zoey pulled the Mercedes in front of the club a short time later, the spotlights on the roof allowed Jessie to see a lengthy queue of people wanting to get in. "This could take all night."

"Don't worry about it," Darien assured her and waited for Zoey to open the passenger door. Climbing from the vehicle, she paused and extended her hand, helping Jessie exit.

Ignoring muttered complaints and expletives from the people waiting in line, she kept one hand lightly pressed against the small of Jessie's back as they approached the entrance to the club. A pair of doormen stood there, keeping the line in check and determining who would be allowed to pass through.

The larger of the two, a muscular man with shoulder-length dark hair and a weapon bulge under his jacket, sent a scowl in their general direction before recognition set in. He then broke into a wide grin, flashing a gold-and-diamond-studded grill. "Ari, welcome back to Oz. It's been much too long. When did you get back?"

"Just a couple of days ago," Darien responded, her Russian fluid with the cadence of a native. "How's business been, Nikolai?"

The big bouncer shrugged. "You know how it is," he said. "But I think it will get better now that you're back. At least, it should make the boss happy. And is this lovely lady someone you've brought for your good friend Nikolai?"

Jessie kept her face appropriately expressionless, following the instructions she'd been given earlier and pretending she had no understanding of what was being said. But even if she hadn't understood, she would have known when Nikolai turned his attention toward her, his eyes a little too appreciative. Even before he reached one hand to touch her.

Jessie's eyes widened, but before she had a chance to react, Darien clamped her hand on Nikolai's forearm, stopping him with a barely restrained violence. Nikolai stared at her hand on his arm, then looked up in surprise and attempted a smile. But his smile slipped and faded as Darien arched a brow and held his gaze.

She leaned closer and her eyes narrowed as she spoke in a deliberately quiet tone. "The lady's with me, Nikolai. That means you can look, but don't ever, ever touch. Try to touch what's mine again and you won't like the consequences, my friend."

Jessie tensed when she saw Nikolai studying Darien with neutral eyes. His expression was clearly uncertain as if he was weighing his options, and a heavy silence thickened between them. She wondered how long Darien would allow the standoff to continue when she saw her give a slight shake of her head. It was barely perceptible, but it proved to be enough to have Nikolai stand down.

"Sorry, Ari. No offense, I didn't understand that's the way it is. I didn't know she was yours that way."

For a second or two longer, Darien's hand remained on his arm. Then the moment passed, and when she released him, she made a show of straightening his jacket and smiled as she fixed his tie for him. "Even if she wasn't mine, Nikolai, you should never touch a lady—any lady—unless she invites you."

For all his size, Nikolai nodded and took a step back, reinforcing what Jessie suspected was Ari's reputation as someone not to be taken lightly. By anyone.

"I'd appreciate it if you could tell Yuri I'd like a chance to pay my respects."

"Sure thing, Ari." Nikolai appeared to hesitate. "Yuri will want to know—will you be going downstairs later tonight?"

"I just might," she said, relaxed once again, as if the tense moment was forgotten. "But first, I promised this beautiful lady we would dance."

"Of course. I will have someone clear a table for you." Nikolai pressed a throat mic and spoke to someone on the other end, issuing a rapid series of instructions. When he turned back, he appeared affable once again. "Will you require anything else?"

"If I do, I'll let you know." Darien turned toward Jessie and almost smiled as she extended her hand. "Let's see if our table's ready, shall we?"

CHAPTER NINE

It was only a few minutes past midnight and inside Oz, the party that would last until morning was just getting warmed up.

The club pulsed to a booming techno beat. The air was filled with smoke—both the acrid scent of cigarettes and the more pungent smell of recreational drugs—and was thick enough Darien believed a person could get high just by breathing. Expensive perfumes and sweat were added to the mix as heated bodies gyrated with frenetic energy under flashing strobe and laser lights.

Silent and watchful, she used the shifting movements of the crowd to screen her as it flowed apart and then came together again. She scanned faces, looking past the smiles and laughter, searching for anomalies, for anything out of the ordinary. Nobody seemed out of place, looked back furtively, or tried to avoid her gaze.

She detested crowds. There were always too many variables to consider. Too many possibilities beyond her control. But there was little else she could do if she wanted to see Yuri because if there was one certainty to this evening, it was that Yuri adored crowds. He loved being the center of attention. Loved to keep his gangster friends entertained.

The smoke burned her eyes, but she didn't see anything that warranted concern. It was just another night in Oz. Ignoring the push and pull of bodies, and with her hand holding Jessie's, Darien weaved her way through the crowd, following a waiter who had materialized to lead them to a table.

They were halfway across the floor when someone grasped Darien's shoulder. She reacted instinctively, pushing Jessie behind her while reaching inside her jacket for her SIG as she swiftly turned.

A reed-thin twentysomething man with thin blond hair stumbled back, grinning foolishly. "Hey, Ari, it's been a while. You need anything?" He had to shout to make himself heard above the music.

Darien slid her hand away from her gun and shook her head.

"Things are moving fast tonight. But I still got hash, some blue-sky blond, and maybe a bit of X if you're interested."

Darien shook her head once again. "I'm good."

The young dealer shrugged. "If you need anything later, you know where to find me," he said, then melted back into the crowd.

Jessie cocked a brow, but Darien ignored her unspoken question. What could she say that would begin to explain any of this? This was simply a night at Oz. She reached for Jessie's hand once again, keeping it firmly gripped until they reached a table on the edge of the dance floor. Darien held out a chair for Jessie, then pulled a chair for herself and sat close beside her.

"What happens now?" Jessie asked, her mouth pressed close to Darien's ear so she could be heard.

Darien shrugged, but she remained alert. "Now we wait. We sit for a little while, let people see us and know we're here. We'll dance as if we have no cares. And then, when the time is right, we'll go downstairs."

Over the next hour, surrounded by heat and smoke and gyrating bodies, Darien sat, casually holding Jessie's hand, mindlessly drawing circles with her thumb. She ordered drinks, the ice melting quickly while the drinks remained untouched. She had almost reached the point where she was starting to think nothing was going to happen tonight when she felt the back of her neck tingling in primal warning.

Glancing around nonchalantly, she noted two silhouettes outlined in a far window above the dance floor. Looking down from what she knew to be Yuri's office. Showtime. She got to her feet, tugged on Jessie's hand to get her attention, and indicated the dance floor. *Let's dance,* she mouthed.

The seconds ticked by as Jessie regarded her with a raised eyebrow. But she stood without saying a word and followed her out to the dance floor. Turning toward Darien, Jessie wrapped her arms loosely around her neck as she began to move, the delicate curve of her breasts pressed against Darien's chest.

Darien responded automatically, placing her hands on Jessie's hips, vividly conscious of the subtly provocative sway, and as they moved together, the chaos around them slowly blurred and faded. The crowd, the heat, and the smoke disappeared. All that remained was the inescapable vibration of the heavy bass coming through the floorboards and the softness of a beautiful woman with tousled blond hair and eyes the color of warm honey.

They stayed like that, with Jessie in the protective circle of her arms, as one song ended and another began. Fast or slow, it didn't matter. Wistfully, Darien thought she would have liked to spend the rest of the night like this. With Jessie. Possibly exploring this unanticipated but potent attraction she was feeling toward the woman in her arms.

As she thought about it, she wondered if perhaps it was a simple case of it having been too long since she'd experienced any kind of closeness with a woman. That had to be it. She was also willing to concede this particular attraction might be connected to long-forgotten feelings she'd once had for Grace, although those emotions had been about the love a child would feel for a parent rather than the clearly sexual heat Jessie was generating.

At another time, it was something she would need to explore. But already she could feel reality press against her from all sides. Darien took Jessie's hand and drew her away from the dance floor. Once again, Jessie didn't question her. She merely sent a quick curious glance in her direction, then allowed herself to be guided through the melee toward a doorway leading to the lower level.

The two security guards posted at the top of the stairs merely nodded as she and Jessie approached. Drawing Jessie closer to her side, they passed without comment and continued to the bottom of the dimly lit stairway, where they were met by another Oz employee.

"Yuri has cleared two seats for you," he said and led them the rest of the way into the heart of Oz.

It was a packed house tonight, but unlike the main floor, this level was filled with the heady aroma of money and power. And blood. Beyond the entrance, Darien could see that the row upon row of arena-style seats were already filled with patrons, clearly and loudly focused on the bloodthirsty spectacle taking place in the very center of the room—a raised octagonal ring surrounded by high netting.

"Illegal cage fighting?" Even over the sudden roar coming from the crowd as one of the fighters in the cage was taken down, she could hear the edge in Jessie's voice.

"Yes. It'll run the gamut of techniques and disciplines—boxing, Brazilian jujitsu, wrestling, Muay Thai, karate, judo, and anything else the fighters can think of. But this—what you'll see here—is as far from a mixed martial arts event as you can get. The only rule here is there are no rules. That guarantees Yuri a huge following, and the house gets to keep a large percentage of the take."

No rules. No gloves or padding. No referees.

It was truly no-holds-barred combat, Darien knew only too well, and what it lacked in finesse, it made up in terms of spectacle. Matches were won and lost in an instant with explosive barrages of hard punches and sheer strength. Just pure violence while onlookers orbiting the ring, and those watching on closed circuit televisions in the private rooms around the perimeter, openly wagered and screamed for blood.

Their escort stopped and indicated two seats in the front row, where the scent of blood and sweat and violence was the strongest.

"Up close and personal with blood and mayhem. Great. Any closer and we'd be in the damned cage," Jessie said dryly. "Obviously Nikolai let Yuri know you were here."

"Nikolai only let Yuri know I want to talk to him. By then, Yuri already knew we were here. Security cameras on the roof would have picked us up as soon as we got out of the car out front," Darien replied, wincing as the current match ended with a blow that stopped the recipient cold. He dropped like a felled tree.

Almost immediately, cage attendants descended on the hapless fighter and removed him from the area, while the announcer focused everyone's attention on the winner. Moments later, the only sign anything had taken place was the remaining blood splattered on the canvas floor.

"Well, Jesus," Jessie muttered, her face paler than when they'd arrived. "What do we do now?"

"Now? It's like one of your chess games. We wait for Yuri to make his move."

❖

Yuri's move caught Jessie by surprise. It came through the loudspeaker system as the ringside announcer informed the crowd that they had a special guest in attendance. Ari was in the audience. And before she could do more than raise an eyebrow in the direction of the expressionless face of the woman beside her, Yuri escalated.

"Perhaps we can persuade this fine champion to enter the cage for us tonight. Shall we try?"

As spotlights picked Ari out, the announcer urged the crowd to join him in convincing Ari to fight. It started slowly at first, but he was soon whipping them into a roaring frenzy until the building felt like it was shaking, and all Jessie could hear was a chorus of voices shouting Ari's name in sync with the pounding of their feet on the floor. Jesus.

Through it all, Darien remained in her seat, her face impassive. But Jessie would swear she could feel her pulse accelerating as she watched her. She wasn't sure what was supposed to happen next, but the crowd settled down when the big bouncer, Nikolai, appeared and crouched at Darien's side.

"The boss wants you to know he's amenable to a one-on-one meeting with you. Said to tell you he'll have some time after you finish your match with our current women's champ. He also wants you to know he's going to show his appreciation by doubling your usual take for the fight."

Darien's expression didn't change as she appeared to consider Nikolai's request. "That's what he wants? A quick tussle with his flavor of the moment?"

"She calls herself Rogue and she's undefeated for a reason," Nikolai warned her quietly. "She's big, she's tough, and she fights dirty. She's got a mean left hook and a damn good right cross. She's also been accused of cheating, although no one's been able to prove anything."

How does someone cheat in a contest where there are no rules? Jessie glanced at Darien questioningly, not certain what she planned to do. But she appeared to make her decision quickly, and Jessie wasn't overly surprised by her terse response.

"Let's do it."

Nikolai didn't appear surprised either as he tossed her a roll of tape.

Before Jessie could think to say anything, Darien removed her SIG Sauer from her belt holster and handed it to her. Next up was the Kel-Tec PF-9 she kept in an ankle holster, along with a knife in a leather sheath strapped to her left arm. And then, amidst wolf whistles and catcalls, she stood and began taking off her clothes.

"Jesus, Ari, what're you doing?" Nikolai actually seemed rattled. "We got lockers you can change in. You know that."

"Relax, Nikolai," Darien said, sounding not the least sympathetic. "It's nothing they haven't seen before. Hell, I've been in public beaches wearing less, and they're all going to see me like this when I step into the cage, so why bother pretending to be modest."

Nikolai walked away with a shake of his head. But Jessie could see that in spite of the cool tone of voice, Darien's eyes were bright with anger. In short order, boots, jacket, shirt, and pants were all removed, folded, and placed on her vacated seat.

Trying to appear as if she wasn't staring, Jessie could also see Elle had been correct in her assessment. Black most definitely suited her and Darien always looked fantastic fully dressed. Whether it was in the jeans and leather jacket of their first meeting or the custom-tailored black silk jacket, open-collared shirt, and pants she'd just removed. But under her clothes…*damn*.

Her breasts were small, taut beneath a black sports bra, while black knee-length spandex shorts clung to her narrow hips and thighs, revealing legs and an ass that were off the chart. Everywhere else, sleek muscles flexed beneath the golden cast of her skin.

Jessie's heart skipped a beat and an intense rush of heat swept through her body. She hadn't been this affected by a woman in, well, she couldn't remember when. Maybe never. There was nothing comfortable or even remotely familiar about this attraction. Instead, it was all yin and yang. Push and pull.

Darien Troy was intelligent. Independent. Beautiful. All characteristics that invariably appealed to her. She was unbelievably drawn by the hints of vulnerability she detected in Darien, existing just below the surface. But she was also unquestionably lethal, and Jessie felt confounded by the attraction in spite of the dark aura of violence that surrounded her.

Maybe it was *because* they were polar opposites. Or maybe it was because she'd been feeling restless of late. Feeling as if there was something vital missing from her life, and from herself. Then reality kicked in and she looked warily at Darien. "You knew this was going to happen."

Darien glanced at her as she removed the silver hoop from her eyebrow. "I've known Yuri for a few years," she said matter-of-factly. "There's a cost to doing business with him, so I had a pretty good idea this was what he would want in exchange for agreeing to a one-on-one with me."

"That's why you were wearing that"—Jessie indicated the shorts and sports bra with a wave of one hand—"under your clothes and why everyone here knows you. You fight here regularly."

"I wouldn't call it regularly."

"What would you call it then?"

"I'd call it often enough to build a legend." She handed Jessie the tape Nikolai had given her. "Could I get you to help tape my hands?"

Even with Darien talking her through the process, Jessie had barely enough time to finish when an attendant came to escort Darien into the cage.

Once in the cage, she moved with the unconscious grace of an animal. Her whole body changed, shifting into battle readiness, her muscles flexing as she slowly stretched them out. She balanced easily on the balls of her feet, light steps and motions.

It was then it hit Jessie and she almost laughed out loud. *Some trained observer you are.* She'd been so caught up in admiring Darien's body that she'd failed to notice a marked difference between Darien and Ari.

Ink.

There was a great deal of ink covering Ari's body. There was a powerful cobra coiled around her left arm. A Celtic triple goddess was positioned on her right deltoid. And a large, boldly colored dragon spread its wings across her back.

The artwork was beautiful. The effect…erotic.

But when the hell did she do that?

The announcer introduced Darien's opponent, Rogue, while Darien continued to walk around the cage, her movements slow, measured. In control. Feeling the canvas floor beneath her feet, she knew from experience the one inch of padding would provide almost no protection when she went down.

Best not go down too often, then.

In Yuri's arena, there were no niceties. This was strictly a blood sport, designed to entertain his criminal underworld customers and provide a venue that encouraged them to drink and gamble. There were no trainers in each corner calling out last-minute instructions. No handshakes in the middle of the cage.

The announcer directed the fighters to their corners and blew a whistle to start a fight that would continue until one of the participants dropped and was unable to get up again. No other rules were considered necessary.

Rogue, dark haired, big, and muscular, came at her in a traditional approach. Circling, jabbing. Testing. After watching her for a few seconds, Darien decided she had no interest in prolonging this match. That dictated her best response would be to fall back on her Krav Maga training and finish the fight as quickly as possible.

Rogue swung first, throwing a hard strike. Darien watched her and calmly wiped the blood from her mouth with the back of her hand. She spun out of the way from the next meaty fist, easily dodging what could well have been a teeth-rattling blow. And when Rogue followed with yet another blow, she pivoted and came up under it, hitting her hard. Rogue stumbled back, appeared momentarily confused and disoriented, but gamely fought through it.

The bright lights prevented Darien from seeing the audience, but she heard them howl their approval. She felt it stir her blood, became energized by it. She didn't feel it when Rogue kicked her in the ribs. What she felt was a profound sense of freedom, a liberation she always experienced in the ring. She parried Rogue's next blow and got in a combination of well-placed strikes of her own.

She focused on timing her next move. She seized an opening and responded with a flying roundhouse kick. It was not necessarily the hardest blow she'd landed. But the moment she connected with Rogue's head, she knew it was the only one that mattered.

The kick was perfectly placed. It lifted her opponent off her feet and dropped her hard to the canvas, where she remained. Motionless. The crowd responded with a deafening roar and began chanting, *Ari, Ari*, louder and louder in appreciation.

It took Darien several seconds to realize the match was over. The cage attendants materialized and carried the unconscious Rogue away but closed the gate behind them, leaving her trapped inside.

Uncertain, feeling a flicker of unease mix with temper, she tried to see beyond the lights. Tried to figure out what was happening. Several minutes passed, and as she circled the perimeter of the cage, she heard the gate open and turned to see an angry-looking tattooed giant enter. Heard the gate close behind him.

This can't be good.

Approaching the side of the cage where she'd left Jessie seated, she saw Nikolai standing behind her, leaning casually against her chair, his hands on either side of Jessie's shoulders. "What's going on, Nikolai?"

The big Russian shrugged. "The boss isn't happy you took his champion out so easily. Some important people have lost a lot of money."

"Then they shouldn't have bet against me."

Nikolai nodded. "There's that, but it's not enough. The boss said to tell you he'll double your cut if you take on one more challenger."

Darien's temper rapidly approached flash point. What Yuri wanted—no, what he clearly desperately needed—was one big moneymaker match tonight. For himself and for his special customers. He was counting on it being her. "He's already doubled my cut and I'm not interested in any more challenges. I didn't come intending to fight."

"Maybe not, but right now, it doesn't really matter what you intended. You know how this is played, Ari."

The message was clear, and she had mere seconds in which to make up her mind.

She needed access to Yuri, needed information and contacts potentially only he could provide, and if she wanted to talk to him, he was leaving her no choice but to give in to him on this. Not that it mattered, because she knew she wasn't getting out of the cage until she agreed.

"All right, what challenge are we talking about?"

"Turn around and meet Cyborg. Your challenge."

Not normally one to turn down a challenge, Darien stared at Nikolai. "Tell Yuri this isn't funny."

Nikolai shrugged once again, almost apologetically, as if to indicate he had no choice. He was simply carrying out the instructions his boss had given.

A quick glance over her shoulder confirmed the aptly named Cyborg was still there. Staring at her, measuring her, while bouncing on the balls of his feet. And if the expression on his face was any indication, finding her to be a less than worthy opponent.

Darien's chin lifted and she returned the evaluation.

Cyborg was at least six inches taller than she was and looked to outweigh her by well over a hundred pounds. He showed signs of habitual steroid use, which would potentially make him more aggressive. He was also either angry because he was being forced to fight a woman and was planning to take her apart. Or he was happy to have the opportunity to go up against Ari's skill and reputation and was planning to take her apart.

Neither option left her feeling particularly comfortable with the turn of events.

She knew she had speed, while Cyborg clearly had strength. But if she was going to survive the next few minutes, she would need to throw him off balance because she really hated to lose, and she wasn't going down without giving it her all.

Deliberately turning her back to him, she called out to Jessie, "Jessie, baby, could you do me a favor? Have Nikolai place a small wager for me. Say, twenty thousand on me to win."

Jessie's eyes widened while, behind her, Darien could hear Cyborg growl. "You think you're going to win against me? A skinny little bitch like you? You're one crazy mother, aren't you?"

His accent placed him as British. Of course, the Union Jack tattooed over his heart might have given that away sooner if she'd been paying attention. Not that it mattered.

"That's right," Darien responded with a laugh. "I'm crazy. Jessie, baby, make that fifty thousand. And if you're good, I'll use my winnings to buy you something pretty. Would you like that?"

There was no whistle this time to start the fight. The look of horror on Jessie's face told her all she needed to know.

She turned in time to meet Cyborg's fist as he landed a hard blow to her face. She felt no pain, and the blow staggered her long enough for him to grab her and lift her off her feet. His face inches from her own, he used arms as thick as tree trunks to squeeze her ribs until she was positive she felt them pop. He squeezed until she could no longer breathe, and then he squeezed some more before he sent her flying violently as he body-slammed her to the canvas.

Darien groaned, struggled for a breath, and staggered to her feet, only to take a roundhouse kick to the side of her head. She had wanted to make him angry and off balance with her comments. Had hoped it might give her an opening she could use to her advantage. Obviously that wasn't going to happen. What she got instead was a world of hurt, and there was blood dripping into her right eye.

Time to change tactics.

She knew she'd taken damage, but she'd fought through worse. As Cyborg delivered another powerful strike to her side, she focused on the crowd, felt their frenetic energy, and used it to boost what little adrenaline she had into overdrive. With her breath ragged and the taste of blood in her mouth, she let her mind go blank. And in an animalistic reaction, right down to the snarl in her throat, she became the street fighter she normally kept under tight control. Doing whatever worked. Fighting coldly, relentlessly, her fists and feet merciless.

The shift in her approach momentarily confused her opponent and had him watching her warily. He crouched as he moved forward and began to circle. She responded by bringing her fist up hard and fast, an uppercut to the jaw that snapped his head back, then hit him twice more before he dropped.

He was back up quickly enough, blocked her next strike, and followed through with an elbow of his own that made a solid connection with her head. Twice she was slammed hard enough to make her ears ring as she was sent skidding on the mat.

Having met with some success, Cyborg came back with the same move, clearly working on the premise that if something worked once, keep doing it. But as Darien knew only too well, in a street fight predictability could get you killed. When he picked her up, this time she was ready for him.

Damn. This is going to hurt.

Timing it just right, she caught him flush with a head butt. Shifting her weight, she followed through by driving her knee up into his groin. Hard.

He bellowed and dropped her like a stone, doubled over as he clutched himself. Fighting to stay on her feet long enough, Darien sent a kick to his head. Watched his eyes roll back as he fell before dropping to her knees. But she didn't have to worry because Cyborg wasn't going anywhere. Not anytime soon.

It was over.

CHAPTER TEN

Jessie stood and watched Darien move to the side of the cage and reach for the netting to hold herself steady. That she was hurting wasn't in question. Her eyes were nearly all pupil, dilated with pain. One eye was already swollen, her lip was bleeding, and she was holding a hand to her ribs. Damage was also evident in the way she moved, if you were looking for it. Stiffly. Carefully. Lacking the smooth and fluid motion Jessie already associated with her.

But, obviously, it wasn't enough that she had somehow defied the odds and won. It was also apparent she had no intention of letting anyone see how badly she hurt. *Probably doesn't fit with Ari's persona.*

She wished there was something she could do to help, but she could only watch and wait for an opportunity to get her out of here. When two attendants arrived to carry out the barely conscious Cyborg, Darien followed them out of the cage and dropped into the seat Jessie had vacated.

"You're going to have one hell of a bruise," Jessie said, lightly skimming her fingertips along Darien's cheek.

"I've had them before. I'll live." Speaking seemed to take too much effort and Darien bent over, resting her hands on her knees while trying to catch her breath. "Can you help me get dressed? I don't want to meet with Yuri like this. Impressions are critical to keeping Ari's reputation intact, and Yuri needs to believe I'm capable of delivering."

"Understood."

It took several minutes, but between the two of them, they managed to get Darien back into her clothes. While she was dressing, Nikolai returned with a damp cloth, which Jessie used to clean up Darien's face. She was relieved to find most of the blood wasn't hers. But she could do nothing about the rapidly forming bruises and the other obvious damage the battles in the cage had left behind. She didn't even want to think about the injuries that weren't visible.

Nikolai appeared to share her concern. "Ari, why don't I have the doctor check you out?"

"No, I'm good. It's not as bad as it looks. Let's go see Yuri. If I need to, I'll get checked out after I leave here."

Jessie wanted to argue, thinking that having a doctor check Darien out sooner rather than later made a great deal of sense. But then she realized they'd been speaking in Russian and she wasn't supposed to understand. Swearing silently, she bit her lip and promised herself she'd make sure Darien got medical attention as soon as they got out of Oz. Someone—Zoey or Ben—would surely know a doctor she could call.

She remained silent as she helped Darien regain her feet and slipped an arm around her waist, aware of just how much Darien was leaning on her for support. But she didn't say a word as Nikolai led them back up the stairs and to the second level where Yuri kept his office.

Yuri Berezin proved to be nothing like Jessie expected. In his midfifties, he was pale, tall, and elegantly slim, with a lion's mane of red-gold hair and light blue eyes. He walked over to them as they entered his office, both arms extended.

"Ari." There was obvious pleasure in his voice, but when his lips brushed both of Darien's cheeks, she winced, and he immediately looked dismayed.

"Thank you for seeing me," she said as she drew back.

Yuri gave a dismissive wave of his hand in Nikolai's direction, and after the bouncer left, he tipped Darien's face up with a fingertip. "Please sit. I'm sorry you were hurt tonight. But you cost several of my regular customers a great deal of money when you defeated Rogue so easily, and they were looking for blood. If I hadn't offered them yours, they would have come looking for mine. It was just business—I trust you understand."

Darien shrugged and eased her body into a chair. "I'm fine, Yuri. Nothing for you to worry about. But quid pro quo. I helped you out with your customers tonight. Now I'd like your assistance in return."

Yuri remained silent and looked at Jessie. Darien clearly followed his thinking and released a soft sigh. "Don't worry about my beautiful Jessie. Although she only speaks English, I find I've grown quite fond of her. But then, I don't keep her around for conversation."

"You surprise me, Ari. I wouldn't have thought you to be sentimental."

"Sometimes, I surprise myself," she responded wryly.

"Love can make fools of us all." Yuri laughed while Jessie fought back the urge to throttle them both. "Tell me how I can help."

Darien leaned back, hissed, and drew in a breath. "I need a contact."

"Tell me who you wish to meet and I will make it happen."

"I want to meet the head of a group that calls itself the Guild."

Yuri's expression darkened and his posture changed almost immediately. "The Guild?"

Darien nodded. "The original organization is old, from nearly twenty years ago. A merger of sorts brought about when the heads of three splinter groups came together as one. They set up their base in Prague and were initially bent on funding the destabilization of Russia, but by the time they disappeared, around five years later, they'd expanded their sights to financing groups targeting a number of Western interests."

"I remember them. Why does this long-dead group interest you?"

"Because they're no longer dead. Someone has resuscitated them."

"Are you certain about this?"

"Quite certain. A couple of days ago, someone sent a message to the media on behalf of the Guild claiming responsibility for the missile strikes that brought down the three passenger jets that everyone's talking about. The ones that have been all over the news."

The air rippled with an undercurrent as a muscle in Yuri's cheek began to spasm and his already pale face became bloodless.

"I have seen the papers, but they are filled with rumors. Unfounded allegations."

"Yes, but now there is a new rumor circulating. Someone is trying to buy more missiles and I have no doubt it will prove to be connected to the Guild."

Something in the set of Yuri's body changed again and his expression became guarded. "What is it you're asking, Ari?"

She met his gaze steadily. "I want you to get me an introduction, Yuri. I want a chance to broker the weapons."

"I thought you dealt primarily in small arms. Assault rifles and occasional RPGs."

"I do. But I find I've become more ambitious, and given the opportunity, I believe I can provide anything. I have recently gained access to missiles including American-made Stingers and TOWs, and Russian RPG-7s." Darien fell silent and Jessie could tell she was watching Yuri closely, gauging his reactions. That Yuri knew something was obvious. Jessie could see it in his eyes.

"These are dangerous people," Yuri said after a lengthy silence. "This connection you seek, she is crazy, I think, and not someone you want to be doing business with. Not if you want to live to do business another day. You need to think this through, Ari. If it's more business you want, I can introduce you to others. For a small commission, I can get you all the business you can handle. But this…what you ask—"

"I need this, Yuri, or I wouldn't ask," Darien said. "Introduce me to your contact at the Guild. I will make it more than worth your while."

He made them wait the length of several heartbeats while he mulled over his decision, and until he actually spoke, Jessie was uncertain which way it would go. But finally, with more resignation than enthusiasm, Yuri nodded. "I cannot promise anything, but I will see what I can arrange for you."

"That's all I can ask."

"I will make some calls and get back to you. Will you be available through the usual channels?"

"Yes." Darien rose to her feet. And though she tried not to show it, Jessie could see the night's events had taken their toll on her. She was clearly exhausted and moving slowly, sluggishly as they left Yuri's office.

It wasn't until they were completely out of the building that Jessie felt a measure of relief. She welcomed the kiss of the cool early morning air against her flushed face. But she remembered what Darien had said about external cameras and remained silent, helping Darien remain on her feet while they waited for Zoey to bring the car.

Zoey's anger shimmered visibly as soon as she saw the condition Darien was in. But to the girl's credit, she didn't say a word. She merely helped Jessie get Darien settled in the backseat of the Mercedes, then got back in the driver's seat.

Darien briefly murmured her thanks, leaned her head back, and fell silent as Zoey eased the car away from Oz. She didn't say anything else until a short time later when, clearly hanging on to the last vestige of control, she asked Zoey to pull over. Zoey responded immediately without question, but even then, Darien barely made it out of the car before she stumbled to the side of the road. Falling to her knees, she was violently and wretchedly ill.

Jessie felt helpless but did what she could. She stood close so Darien could lean against her legs, held Darien's hair out of her face, and passed her a bottle of water Zoey produced so she could rinse her mouth.

She then helped her get back into the car and sat beside her in relative silence. She knew one of them would eventually break the ice, and it turned out to be Zoey, after taking a hard look at Darien in the rearview mirror.

"You're concussed again, aren't you?" There was concern evident in her voice, and fear. But there was also a great deal of anger.

Jessie looked at Darien and saw everything only too clearly. The fatigue, the headache, the simmering emotions ruthlessly held in check. But as she watched, she saw Darien gather herself. "It's a possibility."

"But the doctor told you—"

"Zoey." Darien turned her head and looked at Jessie.

"Don't look at me to defend what you did," Jessie said, while keeping her tone neutral. "It's obvious you knew what you were walking into when we went to Oz tonight."

Clearly that was something Zoey didn't need to hear. "You fought in that damned cage even after what the doctor said? Goddamn it, Dare.

She warned you. One well-placed blow, another concussion, could cause permanent brain damage or even kill you. And you promised… you promised me you'd be careful. What were you thinking?"

Darien pressed her fingers to her eyes, muttered something about being surrounded by stubborn women, and sighed wearily. "It was a calculated risk, Zoey. We need Yuri's help and getting in the cage was the only way to get him to agree to meet with me."

Zoey lashed out before Darien could complete her argument. "But why did it have to be you?"

"Because time's not our ally right now, and Ari could make something happen quicker than anyone else. Why do you think Ben pulled me into this mess in the first place?"

"Because he's a selfish bastard and he only cares about the job. About getting the job done."

"Ah, Zoey, no," Darien said softly. "Come on, you know that's not true."

"Maybe not," Zoey conceded after a long moment, "but you're the one who put it on the line and ended up getting hurt."

"I'm fine—"

"You're not fine." Zoey bit the words out. "You've got another concussion, your face is bruised, your eye's swollen, and you're holding your side, so you've probably also busted a couple of ribs. You only say you're fine like all of that's nothing because you've got some kind of damned death wish. Same as always."

Jessie stiffened as Zoey's words whispered through her. Was that what lay behind the glimpses she caught from time to time in Darien's eyes?

"It's not a death wish." Darien paused, her gaze direct. "I need you to trust that I know what I'm doing. This organization we're after—the Guild—they're dangerous. Deadly. Nobody knows that better than me. They're about to make their next move, and I have no idea when or who they intend to target. I only know it's going to be soon, and innocent people are going to die. They need to be stopped before that happens, Zoey, but to do that, we have to find them. Get up close and personal with them. And Yuri is the only way I know to make that happen quickly."

There was a twisted logic to what she was saying, and Jessie knew she was right, but Zoey clearly wasn't ready to let go. "I don't know about any of that. All I know is lately it seems like every time you go near Yuri, you end up getting hurt."

"That's just because I'm getting too old for this shit." Darien made a small frustrated sound. It was not exactly a laugh, and there was no humor in it, but it was enough to have her hold her ribs and groan. "I'm always tired after I come home from a job. It's why I've always refused to take on jobs back to back—because I need time to clear my head. But now it seems my body needs time to recover as well. Damn it, Zoey, when was the last time I took a vacation?"

The change in direction worked, and Jessie saw Zoey glance in the rearview for just a second or two, as if trying to ascertain how serious the question was. "Do you mean like spending weeks in Djibouti or Kigali tracking a target? Or do you mean taking a sailboat and going to a beach somewhere like Fiji, surrounded by palm trees and beautiful women?"

"The beach." Darien sighed and sank deeper into the soft leather seat. "Definitely the beach."

Zoey laughed. "Then the answer would be never."

Darien glanced at Jessie and gave her a wry smile. "That's what I thought. Do you like sailboats and beaches, Jesslyn? Maybe it's time we all go to the beach."

Jessie smiled back. "I like sailboats and beaches just fine. But I'm not a fan of tan lines."

Darien groaned again, only this time Jessie had a feeling it had nothing to do with her bruises.

CHAPTER ELEVEN

Darien opened her eyes to a throbbing head, a rapidly pounding heart, and a fire burning along her ribcage. The room was dimly lit, and when combined with the faint disorientation she was experiencing, it took several minutes before she was able to process where she was and what had happened.

She had a vague recollection of being driven to this particular hotel after leaving Oz. It was part of the legend she'd created, the place where Ari routinely stayed, and until she heard from Yuri, it would be necessary to stay in character. But with her head and body aching, the drive had proven nearly unbearable.

She remembered getting out of her clothes and slipping into one of the plush white robes the hotel provided, shivering as reaction set in while Jessie argued that she needed to go to a hospital. But she'd refused, and the determined set of her jaw must have said it louder than the words she struggled to say because Jessie finally gave in.

But not completely. What Jessie did was call Ben, who arranged for a doctor to make a house call to her hotel room. Darien recognized the doctor who eventually checked her out as a long-established contact of Ben's. A woman with a gentle touch, a sarcastic mouth, and a willingness to treat a friend of a friend in the middle of the night, no questions asked. For some reason, Darien couldn't recall her name.

She'd bit her already painful lip and remained silent through the inevitable poking and prodding that followed. Nodded when the doctor advised her she'd be better off sleeping sitting up so her ribs wouldn't hurt quite so badly. Released a sigh of relief when there were no more scrapes and abrasions that needed tending and Jessie gently pressed an ice pack to the side of her face.

Before she left, the doctor gave her a shot to blur the edges of pain into something more tolerable. Darien hated needles—a childhood aversion she'd never outgrown—but once the drug began to take effect, she grew drowsy and unable to think clearly. Exhaustion took its toll and everything began to fade. And then she couldn't think at all as she lost the battle with sleep and it pulled her under.

She just hadn't expected she would sleep the entire day, not counting the few times she remembered Jessie waking her up to make certain she was able to regain normal consciousness. But if the sky visible through the window and the green glowing numbers on the bedside clock were any indication, it was exactly what she'd done. The day had been and gone and darkness had slipped into place once again, all while she'd been sleeping.

She groaned softly. In spite of the chorus of complaints from her body, she needed to get up. She didn't know where her weapons were—not her primary, not her backup, not even her knife. The absence of weapons left her feeling vulnerable as hell, a feeling she was far from comfortable with, and she couldn't recall the last time something like this had happened.

She also needed to check her voice mail and e-mail and find out if Yuri had made any progress in getting her a contact with whoever had resurrected the Guild. She hadn't exaggerated when she'd explained things to Zoey. The Guild's next move was coming. She could feel it in her bones. And whatever they chose to do next, it would be fast and it would be deadly, which meant there wasn't time to lose.

But first, she desperately needed a shower.

Time to move.

She briefly wondered if her legs were going to be able to support her once she tried to stand. But the thought caused only a moment's hesitation before she pushed off the bed. She even managed to stay on her feet for maybe five seconds before her head threatened to explode and she was hit hard by a twisting sense of vertigo. She dropped back onto the bed, braced her elbows on her knees, and gripped her skull.

"Going somewhere?" Jessie rose from a chair near the window and walked over to the bed, her voice quiet but laced with steel.

The moment stretched and the silence hummed. Darien straightened. She wasn't accustomed to dealing with nerves, at least not her own. She ran a hand over her face and tried to wipe away the last vestiges of drugged sleep. She grimaced when she came in contact with a bruise.

"The bathroom." Her throat was dry and the words came out as barely more than a harsh whisper. She tried again. "I could really use a shower...make that a shower, some coffee, and I'd kill for some aspirin. Um, by any chance, do you know where my gun ended up?"

"Your SIG's in the drawer in the night table, on the right side of the bed. I've borrowed your backup for the time being. And I'll see about finding you some aspirin. You can take them with food after you've showered."

Darien stared at her for a minute. "I don't think food ranks that high on my list of priorities right now." Mostly she wasn't certain she could keep anything down.

As she spoke, she opened the drawer in the night table and found her SIG exactly where Jessie had said it would be. She pulled it out and felt marginally better, just by having the gun in her hand.

She released the magazine and checked to make sure it was loaded. Once she was satisfied, she ensured the gun was cocked and locked with a round in the chamber, then slid the weapon under one of the pillows on the bed.

Jessie watched her deal with the weapon without comment. "I'm not surprised you're not hungry. But you've not eaten in more than twenty-four hours, and whatever you might have eaten before was left on the side of the road early this morning. Food will help you recover faster. Food and rest. You know I'm right, so don't waste your breath arguing with me."

"I wasn't going to." Darien lifted a hand to her chest, rubbed her battered ribs. "I seem to remember Ben's doctor friend checking me out. Did she say anything I should know?"

"She said you're a mess, but I'm guessing you've already figured that out from how you're feeling." Jessie was clearly not holding back. "You've got a concussion, bruised ribs, an assortment of contusions and lacerations, and you're running a low-grade fever. She suspects you've also got a bruised kidney and said to tell you not to be surprised if you find you're passing a bit of blood. She also said it could be a few days before the vertigo subsides."

"All right."

"The good news is you'll live," Jessie continued. "Of course, that's assuming you don't do anything else that could be construed as stupid. Like getting into a cage fight with someone who looks like they belong in Jurassic Park. Because if you do, I might be tempted to take you out myself."

The urge to turn away was strong. Her body ached and her head throbbed with every heartbeat, making an argument just about the last thing Darien wanted. But the fates did not seem to be cooperating. "It's not as if I planned that part of last night's program," she said defensively.

"No, I'll grant you that." Jessie appeared to hesitate and sighed. "The doctor said you'll probably be feeling quite a bit of pain for the next few days, and she left you some pills that should help. She said you won't have full strength or mobility for at least a week and suggested you might want to refrain from anything more strenuous than an occasional walk to the bathroom or over to the sofa for at least a couple of days. Although she also told me not to hold out much hope that you'll listen. I take it she knows you."

"We've encountered each other on a few occasions in the past."

"Other times when you've been injured, I would imagine."

Darien shrugged and mentally debated the relative merits of whatever medication the doctor had left behind. She hated pills. Any pills. But the thought of taking something that could provide some measure of relief for the pounding in her head sounded appealing.

Too appealing.

She took a steadying breath, but the pressure still pounded against her skull, blurring her vision. "All I really want at the moment is a shower."

Some of what she was feeling must have shown in her face, because when Jessie responded, this time her voice was softer. More gentle. "Can you manage on your own or do you need help?"

I've been managing on my own for a very long time. Since I was thirteen, Darien thought and felt the prickle of her isolation. "I can make it on my own."

And she could, she told herself. But maybe later, after her head stopped throbbing and the room quit spinning. She blinked, swallowed, and reached for Jessie. "But maybe I could lean on you a little? Just to get me started. If you don't mind."

She felt Jessie's eyes sweep over her, saw her smile. "I don't mind. And while you're having your shower, I'll order some food from room service. Is there anything in particular that you think might appeal?"

Darien felt her stomach knot at the thought of food. "No. Just make it something that won't require a great deal of chewing," she said and sent Jessie a fleeting grin.

Jessie laughed and stopped to pick up the robe from the floor. "Here. Use this for now," she said, making Darien suddenly aware she was wearing nothing more than bruises and a thong. "Zoey dropped off some clothes for you earlier. I'll leave something out on the bed for when you've finished your shower."

"Thanks."

Intention was fine, but moving proved to be an entirely different thing. The first step had Darien unsuccessfully trying to stifle a groan.

"Darien?"

"It's okay. Just stayed too long in bed without moving. I can do this. We just need to move slowly until I loosen up a bit." Ideally, after she closed her eyes and rested. For maybe a week.

"No problem. We'll take it as slow as you want."

Jessie offered her arm again, and Darien accepted it gratefully, leaning on her and absorbing the comfort of Jessie's strength as they moved across the room. Her body was stiff, but as she began to move it became easier.

"Will the ink wash off in the shower?"

Darien gave a quick head shake. "No. Not right away. It usually takes about a month or so to fade."

"That's too bad, in a way. It's quite beautiful."

"I'll let Zoey know you said so."

"Zoey did all your body art?"

"She's really quite talented. It was actually her idea to have the ink be part of Ari's evolving persona, and there's something to it because, for whatever reason, it seems to help me slip into character."

Jessie remained silent, her eyes on the coiled cobra.

"Maybe she'll do one for you."

"Maybe." She angled her head up, barely meeting her gaze. "Are you sure you can manage the shower on your own?"

Darien's lips tugged at the corners as a rather provocative image suddenly danced across her mind. She felt the room shift around her and caught herself staring at Jessie. Looking past the sun-streaked blond hair spiked by careless combing and badly in need of a cut. Beyond the warm eyes and the familiar features that called Grace to mind, to where she could see a quiet strength that was entirely Jessie's.

The discovery pleased her even as she wondered what it meant.

❖

The change happened so fast Jessie almost missed it. An infinitesimal tensing of Darien's body. And then something charged and edgy in Darien's expression had Jessie's skin tingling as Darien's eyes swept over her face.

Incapable of doing anything else, she remained motionless, while seconds ticked by. As if to test them both, she shifted her gaze, met Darien's eyes and held them. But as she felt everything else start to fall away, she found herself taking a step back.

"I make you nervous," Darien said.

Jessie felt her face grow warm and thought about lying. Denying. But as she'd yet to recover her breath, she chose instead to say nothing.

Darien stared at her a heartbeat longer. Long enough that she had to know she was making her uncomfortable. "Good," she murmured, then turned, stepped into the bathroom and closed the door.

Jessie was left battling a desire to flee. The hotel suite, with its two bedrooms and comfortable sitting area, was quite large. But as she stared at the door, she suddenly felt confined. Caged.

Darien, she realized tiredly, was proving to be both a lure and a threat to her sanity. She was clearly capable of making her mood shift from nervous to annoyed to concerned to sexually aroused and back again in the blink of an eye. Jessie was finding the process exhilarating, exhausting, and nerve-racking all rolled into one.

Closing her eyes, a stark memory ripped through her, and for an instant all Jessie could see was the angry tattooed giant standing in the cage. She could see him reaching for Darien with his mammoth hands. Lifting her off her feet and squeezing the breath from her lungs before throwing her hard to the canvas.

As the horror of the image faded, it took all of Jessie's willpower not to shudder. Darien was so damned lucky she had come away with only a concussion and bruises. The fight with Cyborg could so easily have left her with broken ribs, a shattered cheekbone, a fractured skull. Or something much worse, she thought, as she remembered what Zoey had said. *Another concussion could cause permanent brain damage or even kill you.*

What the hell had Darien been thinking? In spite of her denial, were her actions rooted in some kind of death wish as Zoey had suggested?

She swallowed and pushed the images and thoughts aside. Trying not to think about the endless possibilities and what could have been, she walked back into the other room, picked up the phone, and ordered a light meal and a pot of strong coffee.

The food had been delivered by the time Darien reappeared. She cleaned up well and looked much better. Fresh from her shower, she was barefoot, but she was wearing the loose fitting cotton drawstring pants and T-shirt Jessie had left out for her, thinking her choices wouldn't unnecessarily irritate all the bruises she'd seen.

The scent of sandalwood whispered around Darien as she moved, and with her hair spilling loose and wet around her face and her eyes huge and dark, she looked about seventeen years old. Young and vulnerable in ways Jessie hadn't expected.

"You look like you're feeling better."

"The shower helped." Darien sniffed the air appreciatively, the steaming spinach-and-feta omelet capturing her attention and drawing her closer to the table. "Turns out, I may be hungry after all."

"Good. I hope this is okay. I tried to go for simple and easy to eat," Jessie said. "And if you're good, I got ice cream for dessert."

"I can be good, but it really depends—what kind of ice cream?"

"It's called Death by Chocolate. Is there any other kind?"

"My favorite." Darien closed her eyes and a slow mesmerizing smile curved her lips.

And suddenly she didn't look seventeen anymore.

Jessie tried to ignore the heat the smile generated each time it appeared and concentrated on pouring coffee into the two cups on the table. She hoped Darien didn't notice the slight trembling in her hand as she offered her one of the cups. Watched her bring it to her lips. And thought, *Oh God, what a face.*

Ever the pragmatist, a quiet voice in her head reminded her that a woman who allowed herself to be drawn too closely to a face like Darien's would get exactly what she deserved. But she would probably enjoy every minute of it.

Everything became sharper, more intense, and the sudden urge to touch Darien stunned her. To move closer and lift a hand to her face. To taste her mouth and feel the strength and all that passion that lay just beneath the smooth surface. She felt herself flush, closed her eyes, and swallowed. Faintly chagrined, she realized she needed to get her surprisingly awakened libido back under control.

It wasn't that hookups didn't happen in the field. Christ, based on her experience since being recruited to the agency, if they didn't happen in the field, they'd never happen at all. As she thought about that, she recalled a brief affair she'd had with a reporter she'd met a couple of years earlier.

They'd been introduced by a mutual friend and had gotten acquainted over cheap wine and amusing stories. Recognizing a mutual interest and desire, they had both known what they were getting into was temporary. Friendly more than frenzied. And when the affair had run its course, they'd each gone her own way. No hurt feelings.

But Jessie knew instinctively the same thing could never happen with Darien. Not that the idea of starting something physical didn't have a lot of appeal on so many different levels. The woman created heat just by walking into a room and too often left her wondering—

Jessie quickly shut down that train of thought and rubbed an ache at the back of her neck. No. She didn't need to be reminded how foolhardy it would be to get involved with Darien. For too many reasons, not the least of which was Jessie preferred women who were friendlier. Less intimidating. Less lethal.

And there were other things, she thought, needing to remember that while they both liked to do things their own way, Jessie believed in rules. She needed some semblance of order. Darien, on the other hand, clearly didn't play by anyone's rules but her own.

Maybe that wasn't important in a temporary—and purely physical—relationship. But there was also Ari to consider. Sometime in the past few hours, she'd come to the uncomfortable realization that Darien was able to so easily become Ari—a cage fighter, an arms dealer, and whatever else she needed to be—because she had created the legend as close to her own likeness as possible. Ari was an extension of Darien.

There was also the inescapable fact that Darien was clearly working on an agenda she had no intention of sharing. It implied a lack of trust which, if nothing else, infuriated Jessie. It also made Darien dangerous, both to herself and to anyone else who got too close to her.

But mostly, mostly Jessie knew she wanted more. Deserved more. And she doubted she would ever get more from Darien Troy. Jessie exhaled slowly, but the wanting didn't go away.

"Let's eat."

❖

Darien's chest tightened, but she didn't allow herself to look away when she saw something flicker briefly in Jessie's eyes. A question. Whatever it was, for the moment it remained unasked. Perhaps because Jessie had already learned that some questions should never be asked, while others could never be answered.

Choosing to ignore the undercurrents that hummed like a prelude in her blood, Darien held out a chair for Jessie and they both sat to eat at the small table by the window. But she could feel Jessie watching her closely as she sampled the food. "This is good," she pronounced and murmured her thanks. Refusing to give an inch, she concentrated on the food on her plate with the same single-minded purpose she had used to bring down her opponents in the cage.

At least, she conceded, Jessie let her have a few minutes of undisturbed time to refuel before she pushed her own plate away.

Appetite clearly forgotten, Jessie aimed a long level look in her direction. "Can I ask you a personal question?"

In the act of spearing a ripe, fat strawberry, Darien looked up. Everything suddenly became sharper, more intense. Even the silence intensified.

Not many people questioned her. Fewer still attempted to go toe-to-toe. But the scowl on her face didn't appear to be discouraging Jessie. Neither did the silence that followed. Jessie simply continued to watch her with an expectant look on her face.

Darien frowned and thought she could stop this simply by saying no. *No, you can't ask me any personal questions. No, I will not answer even if you ask.* But then she surprised herself. "I should warn you I'm not a fan of sensitive chats. But I guess you can always try."

"Meaning you won't necessarily answer?"

"Just ask your question, Jesslyn." She kept her words slow, deliberate. "Take a chance and we'll see what happens."

"All right, I'd like to ask you about last night."

"What about it?"

"You expected what happened—that you'd end up fighting in that cage—and you had to know what you were doing was dangerous, at the very least reckless, given what Zoey said about your previous history of concussions. But you didn't let it stop you."

Never one to turn down a challenge, Darien met Jessie's narrowed stare. "That's right. But you knew that last night. What is it you really want to know?"

"There had to be other ways for you to approach Berezin without getting into that cage, without risking getting hurt or worse." Jessie didn't even try to keep the frustration out of her voice. "I guess I'm trying to understand. I want to know why you chose to do what you did."

"Maybe I didn't care—"

"You didn't care," Jessie repeated, abruptly cutting her off. "Why doesn't that surprise me? I mean, Jesus, if someone has something you want badly enough, you simply go after it, is that it? Even if it means getting into a cage and fighting in a contest without rules. And if someone gets hurt in the process—damn it, if you get hurt in the process—you're telling me you don't care."

Darien sighed and ran a hand through her hair in frustration. "You didn't let me finish, Jesslyn, and now you're twisting my words."

"Am I?" For a few seconds, Jessie's expression didn't change. But then her eyes lost their sharp focus and Darien saw her lips tremble. Saw her lick them as she tried to speak. "Then tell me, Darien. Tell me what last night was all about because from where I'm sitting, you could have been seriously hurt—even killed. But you didn't let that stop you."

"No, you're right," she answered softly. "I didn't let fear of being hurt stop me. But you're making it sound black and white, and the problem is the world isn't always as clear-cut as you'd like it to be."

"Damn it, I know it isn't."

"And there are plenty of ways to die. Believe me. I'm intimately acquainted with most if not all of them."

Jessie flinched and closed her eyes. "I don't doubt that."

Watching her, Darien sensed Jessie was flirting with shutting her out, no longer prepared to hear her out. That inexplicably made the need to explain, to have her understand suddenly more acute. "I don't know how it's done in the CIA, but in my world, everything isn't always neat and tidy, and information seldom comes with a ribbon wrapped around it. Maybe it doesn't make sense to you, but over the years, I learned what's important is to figure out how to get what you need and stay alive. Nothing else matters."

"You're saying it's just a matter of technique."

"You have your way and I have mine, so yes. Last night was simply a calculated risk. It wasn't as if getting in that cage was something I'd never done before, which meant the odds were in my favor, and I didn't care to wait. I needed to make something happen as quickly as possible."

"I wish I could believe you," Jessie murmured.

Her words were soft, but they pierced through Darien's defenses and hurt. "Why can't you?"

"Because I'm so afraid Zoey was right."

"Right about what?"

"That you have a death wish."

❖

Jessie watched Darien become unnaturally still, while her secret-clouded eyes suddenly seemed unnaturally dark against a face that had become unnaturally pale.

"Is that what you really think?" she asked.

"Tell me I'm wrong."

Slowly Darien shook her head. "You're wrong," she said. "You don't know what you're talking about."

"Don't I? I think you're taking unnecessary chances and I believe it's because of what happened to your mother fifteen years ago. And if something goes wrong and you get yourself killed, then at least you won't have to feel pain anymore. It won't hurt anymore. But ask yourself one thing—do you think putting yourself at risk is what your mother would want?"

Darien recoiled. A flash of anger flickered across her face and she balled her hands into tight fists. "What the hell do you know about my mother?"

"I know only the bits and pieces Ben shared with me," Jessie answered softly. "I know she was killed, that her death was connected to the Guild, and that you and Ben and my mother somehow came together and went after the people responsible."

"Then you know all you need to know."

"No, I don't think so." She took a deep breath and tried again. "I think there are a lot of pieces still missing from the story I was given. Enough pieces that it makes me wonder how I'm supposed to help if I'm kept in the dark."

Darien responded by pushing away from the table, her meal forgotten as she stumbled to her feet. "Leave it alone, Jesslyn. In fact, leave me alone. Go back to the house in the Latin Quarter and work with Ben and Elle. Or better yet, go home. Back to Langley. You'll be safer there. You'll all be safer if you're not standing too close."

Jessie felt Darien's words sear through her, bringing not warmth but a penetrating chill. She'd gotten too close, she realized. She'd slipped too close to the place Darien kept walled away. Possibly even from herself. But two could play this game. "My life is my own. I decide what's best for me, not you. And certainly not someone at Langley."

"You can choose to live how you want," Darien said, her voice calmer, almost casual. "But letting you get hurt trying to help me isn't part of the program and it won't happen on my watch. If for no other reason than I owe Grace that much."

Jessie's lips compressed into a thin line. "That's another question that needs answering. What does my mother have to do with this? With you?"

She got no answer. Darien held her gaze another moment, then turned and walked gingerly back to the bedroom, closing the door behind her. But as Jessie turned and stared at the closed door, all she could think was there were still too many shadows lurking behind Darien's eyes. Too many secrets and half-truths swirling around her.

Worse, whatever she was holding back was potentially making her act recklessly. Making her too willing to take risks. Making her think nothing of gambling with her own life.

As she fought back yet another wave of frustration, Jessie realized her greatest fear—that whatever Darien was hiding would get Darien killed. And that Jessie's mother was somehow deeply involved.

But by asking her to leave, Darien had also inadvertently allowed her to glimpse an area of even more dangerous vulnerability, entirely at odds with the person she allowed others to see. Darien Troy operated with a strong inner compass that compelled her to protect other people from harm. She was unwilling to jeopardize the few people she allowed to get close even if that meant putting her own life in danger.

CHAPTER TWELVE

In the light cast by a corner floor lamp, Darien stared at the blister pack of pills the doctor had left for her on the night table. The temptation, she admitted, was powerful. The pills shone like a beacon offering deliverance, and she couldn't help but think it would take so little effort. Two tiny pills and she could escape into oblivion. She could already feel the mind- and body-numbing effects.

So what are you waiting for? Just reach out and pop a couple into your mouth.

Too easy, she thought. She rubbed her eyes in an effort to alleviate the throbbing in her head and eased onto the bed, groaning as pain flared in her ribs. Closing her eyes, she walled off the pain. She then settled in as best she could and ignored the little white pills.

At the best of times, she hated pills. And right now, she knew their fleeting appeal had little to do with having reached her threshold of tolerance for physical pain. No, it was all about deluding herself into thinking they might help keep her nightmares at bay.

It was something she had to work at, but during the waking hours of each day, she had learned to push the memories aside. The problem came at night. That was when the memories were able to sneak past her guard.

Although she'd slept for the better part of the day, she still felt drained. She wasn't sure whether it was physical or mental, or if the difference even mattered. She'd taken another hot shower, letting the water take the worst of her aches away. She'd then forced herself to stay awake for the last two hours and had done everything she could to keep from thinking, just to be sure.

She'd hoped she was too tired to dream. But when she finally slipped beneath the covers and closed her eyes, the dream was waiting for her. Just like it always was. It took her back into a world of darkness. And it showed her all too clearly what she tried so hard not to think about.

The past.

As the images flooded her brain and her mind clouded with memory, she found herself at thirteen again. Surrounded by the smell of her own blood. The stench of garbage and urine. The scent of death. Trapped in a cold, dark alley in Prague with her mother's rapidly cooling body only a few feet away. Close enough to see. Too far to touch.

There were rare moments when she could almost forget. More times than not when it all came thundering back. Especially in her sleep. When it felt as if only minutes—or a few hours at most—had passed since that cold November day.

She could feel the fists striking her face, hitting her body. Taste the hand clamped over her mouth to smother her screams. Feel other hands roughly touching her. Hurting her. She was helpless, frightened, and she felt herself being pulled down, pinned against the cold, hard ground.

Just when she thought she couldn't take any more, the dream stopped, only to start all over again. She was thirteen. Surrounded by the smell of her own blood. The stench of garbage and urine. The scent of death. All she could see was her mother's rapidly cooling body only a few feet away. Close enough to see. Too far to touch.

This time, the scream ripped from her throat and would not be stopped. It filled the air as she came awake fast and hard, with fear sucking the air from her lungs. She choked back another scream and sat up in bed. She ignored the protest from her ribs at the sudden movement and tried to steady herself.

For the first time in years, comfort came in the sound of a woman's voice and in the gentle touch of her hands.

"Darien, you're dreaming." Jessie's voice was soft, barely a murmur. "It was just a dream. You're safe now, I promise. Come back. I'm here with you and I won't leave you."

Slowly the images faded and everything inside her stilled. As Jessie's words slipped past her defenses, she shuddered and tried to keep herself from splintering like shards of glass.

"Breathe, Darien. I've got you. But I need you to breathe."

For a moment, it wasn't possible for her to follow the simple instruction. There was no air. She simply couldn't breathe. But finally her lungs started to work again. She inhaled deeply and breathed in the soft, sweet scent of the living, breathing woman holding her close.

For so long, there'd been no one. During all the years that had passed since her mother's death, whenever she wrenched herself awake from a nightmare, she'd always pulled her knees close to her body, sat in the darkness, and hugged herself. Sometimes she'd imagined something like this—having someone else there to hold her. But no one was ever there, and she always felt empty and alone.

Now she could feel Jessie pressing against her, holding her, massaging her neck and shoulders. Murmuring words without meaning except to say she was there.

Darien didn't fight it. On the contrary, she wanted to keep Jessie close. Her presence allowed her to feel sheltered, safe, and protected, and temporarily smothered the loneliness she believed she could never escape.

Blindly, she reached out and wrapped herself in Jessie's embrace, absorbed the warmth of her skin, and held on with all her might.

❖

"It was just a dream. You're safe."

Although Darien had yet to say anything, Jessie didn't stop talking to her. Softly, carefully. A continuous litany of comforting words meant to ease her back and not shatter whatever balance Darien had managed to find in the minutes since she'd woken up screaming.

But Jessie knew the words were also meant to allay the fears that clouded her own mind. She pushed back the momentary panic that had gripped her when she'd heard the first scream. She'd been in her own room, on the phone with Elle getting an update. Terrified that someone had managed to somehow get to Darien when she was in no condition to defend herself, she'd dropped the phone.

She'd grabbed Darien's backup weapon and run toward the other bedroom, not certain what to expect but determined to help. The screams had been bad enough. The silence that followed a hundred times worse. But what she found was Darien sitting up on the bed. Alone.

She was shuddering and pale. Eyes wild and glazed with terror and dark against the pallor of her face, her knees were drawn up against her chest, while her arms were wrapped around her legs. She was rocking and muttering, "Oh God. Oh God," over and over again as she continued to rock, continued to try to force air in and out of her lungs.

For several minutes, Jessie alternated between cursing Darien and herself as she tried to soothe, to calm. She'd never felt anything as cold as Darien's skin. Nor could she remember a time when she had felt as helpless.

She watched Darien struggle for air, saw the sheen of perspiration on her skin. Even now her body was still trembling, and although the tremors had begun to subside, she could still feel the tension coiled in her muscles. Just as she could still see the shadows in Darien's eyes.

It was telling that even if it was because Darien was too weak to argue or too tired to care, she accepted Jessie's presence beside her on the bed. It was also all too clear that, at least for the moment, the edge that helped keep Darien detached from those around her and one step ahead was gone as she allowed Jessie to hold her. Rock her. As she accepted her touch.

For her part, Jessie wasn't certain what she should say to her. She couldn't begin to describe her own feelings, had no clue as to Darien's. So they remained as they were on the bed. Jessie sitting up with her back against the stack of pillows, Darien resting in her arms.

"Are they always this bad?"

The edgy silence continued as she tried to consider whether Darien hadn't heard her or was simply sidestepping the question. But after a moment, she heard a sigh shudder out and listened as the words began to form. "Sometimes it's worse than others. It hasn't been this bad in quite some time."

"I'm guessing that's a good thing because you scared me half to death as it was." She tipped her head so she could see Darien's face. "Do you want to tell me about it?"

She felt the tension in Darien's body increase before she shook her head. "It's just a nightmare."

"All right. Not to suggest you've had any stress in your life lately that could bring on a nightmare, but you said sometimes it's worse than others, so I'm guessing this is a recurring dream. Does anything in particular trigger it?"

"Breathing."

A faint smile pulled at the corners of Jessie's mouth. "Well, at least now that I know, I'll be better prepared."

Darien released a small strangled laugh before falling silent again. Restless with memories she probably didn't realize were still visible on her face and still shadowing her eyes, she shifted out of Jessie's arms, but surprisingly, remained close enough that their bodies were still touching. "I'm sorry I frightened you."

"It's okay."

Darien remained quiet for what felt like a long time. Jessie had hoped she'd keep talking, but as she looked at her, she realized another piece of the puzzle had just slipped into place. "This is why Zoey doesn't live with you, isn't it?"

Seconds dragged by as Darien stared at her. "Just how much did Ben tell you about me?"

Jessie shrugged. "Not all that much, really. But I'm an analyst, remember? That means I'm quite good at looking at disparate puzzle pieces and coming up with reasonable assumptions."

Darien caught her lower lip with her upper teeth and bit. The gesture was totally unconscious and sexy as hell. Then she turned her head, and her hair formed a curtain to hide her profile. "Zoey was having enough problems with flashbacks of her own when I first took her in. And while it didn't happen all the time, having me occasionally wake her up in the middle of the night screaming didn't help."

"What did you do?"

"Believe it or not, I actually tried to work through it with one of the psychiatrists attached to MI6. It helped a bit, but not nearly enough. Then I tried staying up all night, not going to sleep until Zoey left for the school we'd found for her."

Jessie tried not to let her reaction show. "How did that work out for you?"

"About how you'd expect. All I did was get my days and nights confused. I thought I'd eventually get used to it, but instead I was tired all the time, and when it almost got me killed while doing a job in Mogadishu, Zoey and I both knew we couldn't go on like that."

"So you bought the house in the Latin Quarter and gave Zoey your old place."

Darien nodded then shivered and winced, reminding Jessie of why they were here and what had transpired earlier. Reminding her that Darien was still hurting.

"You know what? We can talk about what I know and don't know later. Right now, just tell me what I can do to help. Tell me what you need. Can I get you something? Some coffee or water or something stronger? There's probably something in the minibar or I can call room service, if you'd like."

"Nothing, thanks. I'm good."

But she wasn't. She looked cold and pale, and though her face was impassive, Jessie had only to look in her eyes to see the echoes of pain lingering there. "If I ask, will you answer another personal question?"

Darien met her gaze and said, "Why would you stop now, Jesslyn? You've been on a roll tonight."

"Who hurt you?"

In the span of the heartbeat before she turned away, Darien gave an impatient shake of her head. "No one—it doesn't matter."

But it did matter. Jessie could see it. Feel it. She wanted to push, but wasn't certain how hard. Just as, damn it, she wanted to shake Darien. Shake all the demons crowding her and get to the bottom of whatever had driven her to scream the way she had.

Perhaps Darien saw some of what was on her mind.

Anger wouldn't have stopped Jessie from pushing. Nor would a demand to back off. But the plea that leaped out from Darien's shadowed eyes, along with the weariness etched in her face, did. "You know what? We can talk later. Right now, more than anything, I think you need to sleep."

"Sleep's highly overrated." There was an odd catch in Darien's voice. The faint lines around her eyes and mouth tightened and her hands visibly trembled for an instant before she fisted them. "Besides which, there's really not much point. As soon as I fall asleep, especially in this state, the dream will come."

"You could always try to dream of me," Jessie said lightly. Darien turned to study her, her stare dark and haunted as she struggled to come up with an appropriate or smart comment. When neither was forthcoming, Jessie wondered only for a second or two if she knew what she was doing. Then she stopped thinking.

Reaching out, she put her arms around Darien again and drew her head onto her shoulder. She felt her immediately stiffen, felt her body tense and push against her, and figured she was about to bolt. But something in her expression had gotten to Jessie, threatening to break her heart. Whatever was eating away at Darien was very real and very deep. So she held on.

"Please don't fight me," Jessie murmured. "I just want to help."

"You can't help."

"Actually, I can. But only if you let me."

She found Darien's skin still frighteningly cold to the touch and began rubbing her gently to warm her. She felt like silk, but Jessie could also feel the strength in the muscles that lay just beneath the deceptively soft exterior.

Darien's breathing quickened, and she remained stiff in her arms for the longest time without saying another word. But little by little, Jessie felt her begin to relax, and finally, after a few more minutes had passed, she released a ragged sigh. Tilting her head back, Darien looked at her.

"What is it?" Jessie asked.

"Are you planning to hold me all night?"

The quiet question swirled around Jessie while Darien's breath feathered warmly on her neck. "Yes, if that's what it takes to get you to sleep through until morning. Go to sleep, Dare."

Surprisingly, she didn't argue. All the fight seemed to have gone out of her, and as she closed her eyes, Darien let out another soft sigh. "You'll stay?" Her words a sleepy plea, Darien didn't wait for an answer before she reached out blindly with one hand and held on.

"I'll be right here," Jessie whispered, filling the darkness with her promise. "I'm not going anywhere. Now go to sleep."

Darien held out only long enough to hear her response. In the seconds that followed, Darien's breathing evened out and she slowly slipped into what Jessie hoped was a deep, dreamless sleep.

Once she was convinced Darien was truly asleep, Jessie shifted and settled her more comfortably in her arms. Feeling strangely exhilarated and not tired in the least, she looked at Darien and, in the involuntary honesty of sleep, saw her in a way she'd not seen her before. With her dark hair strewn across her face, she looked young. Soft. Vulnerable.

CHAPTER THIRTEEN

S omehow, she'd forgotten.

Or perhaps she'd never really known how wonderful just being held by a woman could be. How soft and how warm it felt. The sensation should have made her pull back. But instead, it made a shambles of all the defenses she'd spent years building. And as she lost the battle with sleep and gave herself over to Morpheus, god of sleep and dreams, Jessie's arms wrapped around her gave Darien a sense of comfort and security she'd not known in years.

It felt so damn good, so rare. It smothered the loneliness she'd always believed she could never escape, and she wanted to keep the feeling close for as long as possible. It was almost enough to keep her from sleeping, just so she could prolong the moment.

But in the end, it didn't really matter. Maybe it was from the pain or from exhaustion or a combination of the two. Or maybe it was simply because she was breathing the same air as Jessie while being held in her arms. Whatever the reason, her eyes drifted closed, she succumbed to the lure of sleep, and she slept for almost four hours. Deep, sweet sleep without nightmares—only pleasurable images and sensations.

When she finally awoke into the gray light of predawn, she did so as she always did. Surfacing fast, alert and braced.

She ran a quick inventory and was pleased that this time there was no disorientation. Her head was still aching, only less so. But that was to be expected as she dimly recalled the doctor saying postconcussion symptoms could linger a week or more. Her ribs were still tender, but that was also to be expected. More importantly, she knew exactly where she was and whose arms were holding her.

It had been a very long time since she'd awoken next to a woman. Closeness wasn't something she allowed herself. And even the last few occasions had only been about the job. The woman had been an MI6 operative whose life she'd just saved, and after spending the night crawling through the dark to safety, they'd managed to find a hole-in-the-wall hotel before collapsing together on the single bed and sleeping for nearly twenty hours.

She sensed Jessie was only sleeping lightly and knew she would have felt the change in her breathing the moment she woke up. But she was in no hurry to move, in no rush to leave the safe haven she'd been given, so she stayed perfectly still where she was. Wrapped in Jessie's arms with her head pressed against Jessie's chest. Drawing in one deep breath after another. Breathing in the faint scent of lavender soap on her skin and holding on so tight Jessie's heart couldn't beat without Darien feeling it.

"Are you feeling better?" Jessie's breath was soft and warm.

"Surprisingly so." Her voice was rough with sleep. Turning slightly, she pushed her hair away from her face. "Thank you. I would guess I owe you one."

"For what?"

She felt Jessie's eyes skim lightly over her face as she pondered the question. "For making sure I was all right. For holding me until I could breathe again. For staying with me while I slept. All of it."

As she spoke, she felt a sudden hunger—greater than her will to deny it. Her body hummed with heat and life and she remembered her dreams. Remembered Jessie had been featured prominently in them. Caught in the moment, she recognized she felt something for Jessie. Something new, different, and uncomfortably strong.

Before she could think about what she was doing or stop herself, not even sure she wanted to, she turned to face Jessie and, in the gloom that shrouded the room, found her mouth.

Not hard. Just hot, sweet, and soft. Lingering.

❖

God, the woman can kiss.

For an instant, that was all Jessie could think. Only Darien's lips existed as they moved over hers. Seducing, giving, demanding, until she wanted to do nothing more than surrender. She wanted to inhale the heated fragrance of Darien's skin. Wanted to keep tasting her. Simply wanted her. Over and over again.

But only for an instant. Even as her body began to respond, the last vestiges of self-preservation kicked in, and she forced herself to draw back. Forced herself to ignore the way Darien's lips tasted, and the way it felt when those smoky eyes were trained on her with desire.

"What are you doing?"

"I would have thought it was obvious, but since you're asking, I must be doing something wrong." Darien's smile was surprisingly mischievous. "I'm trying to say thank you."

She leaned in closer, lifted her right hand, and skimmed her thumb along Jessie's cheekbone. Leaned in farther and slid her lips along her jaw, the smooth column of her neck, her collarbone. Nuzzled her throat.

Jessie forced herself to remain dead still. "Darien, don't."

Her tone said it all.

In that fractured instant, Darien rolled away. She lay on her back and stared up at the ceiling as the silence lengthened, heavy and oppressive. Irritation and hurt flitted across her face as her smile dissolved into a mask, leaving no hint of expression on her face.

"I'm sorry if I made you uncomfortable. My social skills may not have been the best to begin with, but I don't normally misread signals so badly. All I can think is I've been alone in the field for too long. Clearly I was out of line, but I can assure you it won't happen again."

Jessie felt trapped between conflicting desires. Keeping to herself emotions she wasn't yet ready to face, she tried to make amends. "Darien, no. It's not that...you didn't. Misread anything, that is. It's just that—" The situation had quickly gone off the rails and she wasn't helping matters. She wasn't sure she could explain what she was thinking, even to herself. She reached for the bedside lamp and turned it on. Watched Darien's eyes narrow in defense and lost her train of thought. "Jesus, you're so damned beautiful."

"I'm sorry, is that why you're not interested?" Darien's eyes had become as flat as her voice, and all the warmth that had been there in the minutes before fled.

"Of course not. It isn't—damn it, none of this is as clear-cut for me as it is for you."

"I don't know what that means."

There were no easy answers. Moistening her lips, Jessie laid a hand on Darien's arm and immediately felt it vibrating with tension. "It means I'm not sure how to handle this, and I'm well aware I'm not making any sense."

"Try a little harder, Jesslyn."

"I'm trying. Damn it, you confuse the hell out of me. I'm attracted to you…I want you," Jessie admitted as an inchoate yearning coursed through her. "Enough that it's distracting. Enough that it's starting to hurt."

Darien breathed out a sigh. "Then I fail to see the problem, because from where I'm standing, I see two adults capable of acting on what would seem to be a mutual attraction. I want you. You want me. Sounds pretty simple."

"It does when you put it that way. Except I can't go where you want us to go." As she spoke, Jessie looked at Darien's mouth and felt another flash of desire. She tried to swallow and found her throat dry.

"All right." There was a calm acceptance in Darien's voice. "Not that you need to tell me, but can I ask why not?"

"Of course you can ask. It's just that hasn't it occurred to you that some attraction—our being attracted to each other—is inevitable given all the adrenaline that was flowing last night?"

Darien shook her head and sent her a slight smile which still held a spark of sexuality. "It might have, except we were attracted to each other, or at least I was attracted to you, well before last night's adrenaline rush. And I think you know it, so that particular line of reasoning won't work."

She had a point. "Okay, maybe. But there are a couple of other reasons why this just can't happen."

"Do tell." With her arms crossed, Darien leveled a look at her for longer than she cared to be scrutinized.

Damn her. "Fine. In simple terms, one is that, as a rule, I don't let myself get led by my libido."

Interminable moments passed before Darien responded. "I have a bad habit of disregarding rules, but even I'd have to say that's a pretty good one. Although I think we've already established this attraction between us is more than an overactive libido. You said there were a couple of other reasons. What else, Jesslyn?"

Jessie hesitated, caught in a moment of indecision before she forced herself to push on. "I don't believe sex—and more specifically sex with me—is going to solve whatever's troubling you."

Darien straightened and pushed a strand of hair from her face with unnecessary force before giving her a granite stare. "I don't believe I was looking to solve anything by having sex with you."

"Weren't you?"

For a moment, it looked as if Darien had more to say. Possibilities pushed in from all directions. But then unexpectedly she stilled, and over the next few seconds the only tell was her expression, which became disquieting. Caught somewhere between anger and confusion.

"What is it?" Jessie asked.

Darien looked away as she slowly shook her head and released an odd laugh. She bit her lip before saying anything. "Bloody hell," she whispered.

"Talk to me, Darien. What's going on?"

There was no response. Jessie stared at Darien, uncertain what was going on. But she had pushed her away only minutes before, so why should she be surprised if no answer was forthcoming? "Darien?"

"I hate like hell to say this, but it's possible you may be right."

It was not the answer she'd expected. "What do you mean?"

"Earlier. There's no question I was feeling grateful. For your kindness. For caring enough to stay with me. I also realized I didn't want to be alone. I've spent most of my life alone, and in every part of the world there are shadows. And suddenly you were there." She turned back to face Jessie. "My intent—I'm not so sure anymore. I just know I didn't want to think, at least for tonight. I wanted to forget what year it is, what day, what hour. I just wanted to feel... something. Anything. And I thought—well, it doesn't really matter what I thought. Obviously, I was wrong on all counts."

Jessie felt her throat close. Darien's voice, so sad and haunted, cut through her, and she suddenly wasn't sure whether she should continue with this conversation. Or *if* she could continue.

She looked at Darien and as the silence lengthened and thickened, she could see her withdraw into herself, could almost see the protective barriers Darien had already started bringing down around herself, slamming them home, slipping the locks in place.

Whatever she had seen on Darien's face only a short time before disappeared. And then there was nothing left. None of the hunger. None of the longing. None of the humor. Nothing. Any trace of the woman from earlier, the one who'd offered her mouth and her passion, was gone. All that remained was a bruised woman who stared at her with eyes far too dark in a face far too pale.

She could leave it there. She should leave it there. Jessie knew she had struck a nerve, and an intelligent woman, a rational woman, would know better than to push someone like Darien Troy until her back was against a wall. Jessie pushed anyway.

"Maybe you weren't wrong. Let's leave it at that for the moment because I happen to think there's a bigger issue."

Jessie saw a flash of heat in Darien's face before it went cold. Watched as Darien slowly fisted her hands again as her chin came up and she asked, "Bigger than my wanting to use you for sex so I could stop myself from thinking? What could that possibly be?"

"We have no trust between us."

Darien frowned. "Tell me you're not serious."

"I am. I need honesty. Trust. We're supposed to be working together, but you don't even trust me enough to tell me what's going on and what you're doing. We can't work together effectively without trust. But I'm somehow supposed to put all of that aside and trust you enough to sleep with you? It doesn't work that way, Darien. At least not for me."

❖

Somehow Darien breathed, even as her throat constricted.

It stunned her how badly she had wanted Jessie. But like a breaking wave, the heat of desire had collapsed, replaced by a sense of regret that left her chilled. And on the heels of regret, the loneliness returned.

It wasn't, she realized, that she didn't still want Jessie. She did. So much that she ached. It was more a realization that she was standing at a crossroads. Knowing what happened over the next few minutes, along with the choices she made, would determine how she moved forward—how she and Jessie moved forward—with the job at hand and everything else.

"Just so we're clear, it's not you." Darien winced at how cliché the words sounded. "What I mean is I don't actually trust anyone."

"You can trust me."

Jessie's words scraped at her still-raw wounds. Without thinking, Darien slipped out of the bed, ignoring the pull of bruised muscles as she walked over to the window. Standing twenty-five floors above the street, she watched the lights of Paris glowing softly in the early morning light and stared out at the awakening city. "I don't know what you want from me."

"What I want is for you to talk to me," Jessie said in a calm voice. "I know you think it's none of my business, and you could be right. But then again, maybe not. It doesn't really matter anymore."

"What's that supposed to mean?"

"It means you're not doing this alone anymore. Tell me what's going on, Darien. Tell me what your nightmares are all about. Help me understand this connection you have with the Guild. I'm good at what I do, but I'm no good to you if you put blinders on me. Let me help you. Trust me."

It was as if the walls in the hotel room suddenly closed in. "You ask too much. You ask the impossible."

"I don't think so. I think you might surprise yourself."

As Darien gazed at the reflection in the window, for an instant she thought she saw another woman's face standing behind her. A loving presence long gone from her life and the only person she had ever fully trusted. In that moment, she wanted to be a child again, safe in her mother's embrace.

She shook her head, and the vision wavered, then vanished. And she was suddenly afraid that if she dropped her guard she'd lose the fight. But with her next heartbeat, she realized the fight might have already gone out of her.

She turned back to look at the woman on the bed, and tried to bring everything into perspective. Jesslyn Coltrane might be a government operative, but that was where any similarity between them ended. And she was asking for more. Ironically, she was now the one asking for a demonstration of trust.

Darien shifted uncomfortably, tension thrumming through her body. To explain her history with the Guild, to put it in perspective, wasn't just about trust. She would need to go back to where and when it all began. And she really didn't want to delve into the past. Revisiting old pain was an exercise in futility, especially when nothing would change. Nothing could change. There would always be too many ghosts waiting there. Too much pain. Too much death.

For a long moment, she said nothing. Pushing her hair from her face, she looked across the room at Jessie once again. And in that one instant, as their eyes met, another wave crested.

Darien stood frozen. Said nothing. Did nothing.

Then slowly she forced herself to speak. "You're right." There was a beat of silence as she swallowed against the tightness still in her throat, barely recognizing the rough edge to her own voice.

"I'm right?" Jessie repeated uncertainly.

"Yes. You're right in thinking what's happening with me and the Guild is connected to my mother."

The words were torn from somewhere inside her, the shock of the truthful statement mirrored in her voice. Darien tried to focus on Jessie's face and not on the memories crowding her as an all too familiar ache settled in her chest. Because she knew if she let herself, she could still see and hear and feel other things. Everything.

"They—my mother was killed in an alley in Prague when I was thirteen. And when it happened, it was like something inside me died too, only it was worse."

"Because you were still alive?"

Darien nodded stiffly. "Since that day, I've had this dream. Over and over again. No matter what I do or don't do. It just keeps coming back. I close my eyes and I see it happen. Sometimes it's only flashes, like looking through a kaleidoscope. But then there are other times when it comes back so strong and so real I get so I can barely breathe."

"Like tonight. That's what the nightmare was about? Your mother's death?"

"Yes. Intellectually, I know it's just a dream. I'm well aware it's been years since it all happened. But here"—she tapped her chest above her heart—"sometimes in here it feels like it was only yesterday. And then there are times when I'm right back in that damned alley."

"You were there?" Jessie's eyes filled with comprehension even as her hands tightened on the light blanket covering the bed. She looked like she wanted to reach out, to touch her, and was doing what she could to prevent herself from acting on her impulse.

"We were supposed to be going to Paris. But at the last minute, my mother received word about a terrorist group her team had been tracking. A group believed responsible for the execution of two Mossad agents. She changed our plans and we went to Prague instead."

"You told me before your mother was Israeli. Am I correct in assuming she was an intelligence officer?"

Darien sighed. "If you're asking if she was Mossad, then the answer is yes. But at the time she was killed, she was *kidon*, and had been for more than a year."

Jessie sat up straight, one brow rising. "You're not just talking about your mother being an Israeli intelligence operative," she said in a quiet voice. "You're talking about her being part of Mossad's ultrasecret kidnapping and assassination unit."

"The unit *allegedly* responsible for carrying out kidnappings and assassinations," Darien corrected dryly but without amusement.

"That's semantics and you know it. The point is your mother took you with her to Prague while she was pursuing terrorists. What in God's name was she thinking? You were only a child."

"Actually, no. That's not correct." Darien slowly shook her head and a faint humorless smile touched her lips. "I was never a child— at least, not in the way you mean it. And certainly not in any way you would recognize. Even growing up as Grace Lawson and Reid Coltrane's only child."

CHAPTER FOURTEEN

It all made horrible sense, Jessie realized.

They were both the children of covert operatives. But while she had been protected by her parents, sheltered in academia until she was old enough to decide what she wanted for herself, Darien hadn't been given a choice and had grown up in a world of black ops, surrounded by spies and assassins. She would have learned and absorbed, becoming more dangerous with each day that passed.

She confirmed Jessie's assumption a moment later.

"My mother started training me when I was maybe five years old. And over the years, I received training from some of the best, including Ben and both your parents."

"That's how you know my parents?"

Darien nodded. "By the time I was thirteen, I excelled in several martial arts disciplines. I could strip down, clean, and reassemble any weapon from an M16 to a backup five-shot revolver. I was an excellent sharpshooter. And I'd been working as a courier for nearly two years."

Oh, Jesus. It certainly explained a lot. But there was still the question she had to ask. "What happened in Prague?"

Darien's expression darkened like a cloud occluding the sun, and she turned to look out the window again. Her eyes appeared fixed on some distant point, but Jessie knew she was no longer seeing the familiar vistas. The Louvre, the Seine. The street life. Because she was no longer looking through the eyes of a woman, but rather through the eyes of a thirteen-year-old girl. A girl who'd lost whatever semblance of childhood she'd had in an alley in Prague.

"My mother set up a meeting with a contact near our hotel. She told me to give her an hour to take care of business. After that, we would do some sightseeing and have an early dinner." Her voice grew softer. "I didn't mind. She'd bought me a new camera. I was eager to try it out, and the concierge had suggested I head toward Charles Bridge. But by the time I realized it was a setup, it was too late."

Darien fell silent. She didn't move, didn't blink. Jessie wasn't even sure she breathed, and the pain caused by her grief and regret was tangible. *You weren't just there when your mother was killed.* In spite of what Ben had said, that her mother had been set up, Darien somehow believed she was responsible for what happened.

Jessie's thoughts automatically went to Grace. She couldn't imagine losing her mother, let alone feeling responsible for her death.

In the window's glass, their gazes met. Sensing what was coming, Jessie prodded gently and prepared for the words to spill. Even knowing it would be dangerous for her to see Darien as a still-grieving child instead of a woman who coolly carried out government-sanctioned hits. "What happened, Darien? Tell me."

"They had to have watchers. In retrospect, it's the only thing that's ever made sense. They knew what I looked like, knew when I was approaching, and they were ready for me. I should have been paying attention, but I wasn't. I was focused on the camera, checking the light and deciding on apertures and angles, when I was accosted on the street in broad daylight. There were three of them. Heavily armed, well trained. And in the blink of an eye, they pulled me into an alley. I tried to fight them—" She squeezed her eyes tight and clearly battled control back in place.

Jessie almost stopped what she was doing. Almost reached out and offered comfort. But she knew she was close to uncovering something important, something at the heart of what was driving Darien. *Forgive me,* she thought and pressed on. "What did they do?"

"They had a bit of fun with me, and then at some point, they must have contacted my mother." Pain flickered in her eyes before she closed them and she shifted her weight from foot to foot, as if preparing to flee. "She should never have come alone. But she wasn't thinking clearly. She just reacted and came for me. No backup. No plan. Just her. My mother. They grabbed her when she came charging into the alley, then held me down and made me watch as they beat her half to death. And then they put a bullet in her head."

Goddammit. No wonder she still has nightmares. "Can I ask— do you know—why didn't they kill you too?"

"Didn't they? I'm not so sure." Darien said. She shook her head as if to banish the thought. "After they shot my mother, I waited for my turn. I expected to be next. I'm not sure, but at that point, I think I wanted to be next. But the shot never came, and then they let me know they had other plans for me."

"What kind of plans?"

"There was a brothel. They owned it." She paused, swallowed, then went on. "They had some customers with particular appetites. Customers who liked them young. Liked my type."

Jessie fought past the tightness in her throat as a wash of horror swept over her. "What did you do?"

"I took things one day at a time and did what I had to do to survive until I could get away. And then I went after them."

❖

Jessie blinked and remembered what Ben had said. *By the time we caught up to her, she was operating with one simple premise. She wanted revenge, and if someone got in her way, they bled.* "You're talking about seeking retribution. Vengeance. On three cold-blooded killers. Is that what you're saying?"

"Call it what you want, Jesslyn."

But Jessie could see the hurt on her face, along with the devastation. "I'm not judging what you did, Darien. I'm just trying to understand."

"Then try and understand this. I couldn't walk away. Not then." Her face and her eyes grew dark. "I would get up every morning and look in the mirror. I would see my face staring back at me, but nothing was the same. And I couldn't walk away until I knew who it was that murdered my mother. Who it was that destroyed my life. I couldn't walk away until I made them pay, even if it got me killed. But I was okay with that because I was comfortable with the first rule of revenge."

"There are rules?"

"Yes. It was something I read. Something from Confucius that said before you embark on a journey of revenge, you should dig two graves."

"And knowing that, you still went after them. By yourself?"

"By myself? In the beginning, yes. Growing up as I did, it wasn't like there was anyone I thought I could turn to." She broke off, wrapped her arms around her waist, and turned back to stare out the window. "It took me almost ten months to get all three, and I really didn't expect to survive. Didn't really care and nearly didn't, as it turned out."

"What does that mean?"

"The last of the three was a clever bastard and proved to be more of a challenge than I bargained for. By the time Grace and Ben arrived, I'd been ill for a while. I think there'd been too many nights sleeping in doorways and eating whatever scraps I could beg or steal. Grace and Ben saved my life. And then they helped me finish it."

"And after? After the three men who killed your mother were dead. What was there left to finish?"

"There was still a criminal organization to deal with—a network of human trafficking and prostitution, arms dealers and drug dealers, with the profits feeding terrorist activities. It needed to be shut down. Permanently. It's what my mother was trying to do when they killed her. I think I just wanted to finish what she'd started."

Jessie understood. "That's why you thought it couldn't be the Guild that brought down those planes. Because you believed you and Ben and my mother destroyed the organization nearly fifteen years ago."

Darien squared her shoulders and gave a terse nod. "Once the three leaders were dead, the rest was surprisingly easy. Without them, the networks they'd built fell in total disarray, fighting over leadership, while we systematically destroyed everything they controlled. Warehouses, nightclubs, brothels, meth labs. The whole house of cards came down. Or at least, that's what we thought. Until now."

Jessie felt breathless, as if she'd just stepped off a tilt-and-spin carnival ride. "And just like you did at thirteen, you're also telling me you're willing to do anything to go after them now."

"Yes."

"No matter what?"

"No matter what. The Guild—then and now—is still responsible for my mother's death. Somehow something wasn't completely destroyed. Something survived. That's my failure and I'm going to rectify that now."

"Even if you get hurt?"

"Jesslyn, I've stood on the edge of this particular abyss before, battered and bruised but still standing. I'm not afraid. And I won't go down without a fight." Darien rubbed her face as if to shake off the last few minutes, then met Jessie's gaze. "Now you know it all."

Not entirely. Jessie stared at her. She knew there were questions she still needed to ask…like what Darien had planned and how she could help. But some of those questions, she could see by the look on Darien's face, would have to wait.

That was okay, because she realized Darien had given her exactly what she'd asked for. Her honesty. Her trust. "Ben told me he raised you from the time you were in your early teens. Is this how you ended up with him?"

"Yes. When it was all done, when we thought there was nothing left of the Guild, I had nowhere to go. No family to go to. I was prepared to strike out on my own, but Ben took me back to London with him, and eventually to MI6." She paused, bit her lip. "I had to go through a lot of psych evaluations before I could officially join, but I wasn't worried. I knew I wasn't crazy."

"I know that." Jessie paused. Through the shadows, she had seen something flicker in her expression and she needed to know. "But why Ben?"

"You're asking why Ben and not Grace. That's what you want to know, isn't it?"

Jessie nodded and simply waited. Didn't breathe. She could see the question had hit a little too close, and Darien's expression offered a glimpse of the emotions she kept so tightly under wrap.

"That's one you'll have to ask your mother sometime."

She began breathing again. "All right, I'll do that. Can I ask one last thing?"

Darien looked up and Jessie thought she saw something different. "I can't believe there's anything left to ask." A slow smile curved her lips. "What haven't I told you?"

"I think I just want to know—do you ever get tired of what you do?"

She went so still Jessie was afraid she'd finally overstepped her bounds. But it was too late to take the question back.

"Tired?" Darien blinked. "It must be obvious by now that I started down the path I'm on not for any noble purpose or calling, Jesslyn, but for revenge. Pure and simple. But anger and vengeance can only sustain a person for so long. It's like living without a soul. So, yes, I'm tired. Tired of adrenaline and lies and not really knowing who I am. I have been for quite some time, and I'd like not to do what I do anymore. When I told Ben it was over for me once we finished this, I meant what I said. Instead of living from assignment to assignment, mission after mission, I think I'd like to just be."

"That sounds nice."

"Yes, it does, and I still have hope." She paused and raised her eyes to meet Jessie's. "Did we just bond?"

Jessie laughed. "Now that's a scary thought."

"Isn't it, though?" She grinned. "But the truth is when it all gets to be too much, I remind myself of something your mother once said to me."

"My mother?"

Darien nodded. "She said that things have a habit of working out the way they are meant to be."

Jessie smiled. "My mother's a big believer in looking back not with regret but for what you can learn."

"Unfortunately, I've learned what I do is necessary." Darien bit off a sigh. "And until this particular job is finished, it does no good to think about anything else."

CHAPTER FIFTEEN

As the promise of the new day spread across a blood-washed sky, Darien leaned against the balcony railing and let the breeze whisper around her. She loved this time of day almost as much as twilight. She loved the play of otherworldly shadows and light on the city, and the photographer in her wished she had one of her cameras in her hands.

Around her the soft silence stretched, deepened, allowing her thoughts to run unchecked and uncensored in her head. She just wasn't sure what was more painful—her thoughts or the third degree she'd just experienced.

She couldn't remember a time when she'd divulged as much deeply personal information. Not even to the psychiatrists who had endlessly grilled her prior to clearing her into the ranks of MI6.

Not that she'd ever blamed them. After all, how many thirteen-year-olds were brought to them having survived taking down three powerful organized-crime heads? And how many thirteen-year-olds could boast having one of the agency's most respected covert operatives as her unofficial, self-appointed guardian?

She knew the team of psychiatrists had been charged with checking her fitness for duty. Ensuring she wasn't a sociopath or a psychopath before she was entrusted with additional skills and cut loose to kill on behalf of Queen and adopted country. But she was also aware while the multitude of tests they ran only confirmed she was bright and had an aptitude for languages and technology, they'd been frustrated by the lack of personal information she'd shared with them.

Jesslyn Coltrane could teach those long-forgotten psychiatrists a thing or two about how to get information from an unwilling subject, she thought wryly. For some unanticipated reason, she had been able to tap into Darien's carefully guarded psyche with remarkable ease. The words had felt as if they had no choice but to spill out, and she had handed Jessie pieces of herself she'd never meant to share with *anyone*.

Perhaps her nightmare had left her vulnerable and susceptible to Jessie's questions. All Darien knew was not since her mother's death had she been able to talk like that with anyone, and she'd forgotten what it felt like to share.

But the aftermath of opening herself up lingered. She would have thought she would feel some sense of relief, but she didn't. She felt drained. She feared she'd said too much. And the realization of just how badly she wanted to take some—or all—of it back threatened to bring her down.

At least for now, Jessie appeared to have no more questions left to ask. She'd called room service and ordered breakfast, then muttered something about a shower before she wandered off, correctly sensing Darien's need to be alone.

But the sense of loss surprised her. Darien didn't know what to make of it or what it meant. She only knew she was tired and in no shape to be reading anything into her own thought processes and emotions.

Still, her mind lingered on the moment just before Jessie had walked away. They'd stood so close and Darien had suddenly ached to taste her again. Something had passed between them, and she knew all she had to do was step forward. So she took a step back instead and let the moment pass. It was better that way.

Abandoning all thoughts and questions, she headed for her own shower, a marble and chrome extravagance with a double-headed shower and limitless hot water. When she was done, she dressed in jeans and a loose cotton shirt and tucked her SIG into the holster she clipped to the back of her jeans. That act in itself felt familiar, normal, and she felt better for it. Less a stranger in a strange land.

A quick glance in the mirror as she ran a brush through her hair revealed tired and faintly bloodshot eyes. Her head was still aching, but the swelling on her face had receded and was all but gone, leaving only a bruise across one cheek. She wasn't worried about that.

Of greater concern to her was the much larger bruise covering her ribs. The pain was bearable, but she knew it left her flexibility compromised. She tested her ability to strike with her fist, found it distinctly wanting. But she knew she'd experienced worse, just as she knew it would not be enough to prevent her from doing whatever was necessary should the need arise.

The knock at the hotel-room door jackhammered through her as she walked out of the bedroom. Her instincts immediately went into overdrive just as another knock was followed by a familiar voice calling out, "Room service."

Darien relaxed, slipped her gun back into its holster, and opened the door. "I wondered when you'd get around to showing up."

Ben smiled and pushed a loaded room-service cart into the room as he moved past her. Elle followed close behind, pausing long enough to close the door.

"Elle would have had us here last night when Jessie dropped the phone in the middle of their conversation. But I checked and was able to assure her everything was fine. GPS showed you were here, right where you were supposed to be, and your vital signs were coming through nice and clear, although your heart rate was up a bit." Ben lightly skimmed the bruise on her face with one hand. "Now I see why Jessie asked for a doctor. Are you all right? How's the head?"

Darien ignored the ever-present headache and responded with a dismissive shrug. "Unintended consequences, nothing more."

"She's got a mild concussion. She also needs to eat something, so it's good you've brought the food with you," Jessie said as she walked into the room, her hair still damp from her shower.

She looked good in jeans and a black turtleneck. Damn near edible, even. Darien licked her lips. "She keeps trying to mother me," she muttered.

"Trust me, I don't feel the least bit motherly toward you," Jessie responded with a grin before turning to Ben. "Did I just hear you say you were able to track Darien's vital signs?"

Darien's breathing unraveled and she was left to stare at Jessie while Ben explained the tiny GPS-enhanced tracking device implanted in Darien's hip. For her part, Jessie ignored her, focusing instead on removing the covers from heaping platters of food and placing them on the table.

Fearing her thoughts were visible on her face, Darien turned her attention to the food and forced herself to relax. Tried to ease the tension from her shoulders and neck, which was making her headache worse. She hadn't been hungry until that moment, but the delightful aroma emanating from the table made her mouth water and her stomach sit up and beg as she approached for a closer look.

Automatically, she reached for the closest carafe and filled four cups, then quickly discovered the coffee was hot and strong and wonderful. It helped clear her head if not her headache, and for the next few minutes she allowed the conversation to flow around her while she concentrated on enjoying the abundance of fresh fruit and french toast smothered in maple syrup Jessie had ordered. Relishing the normalcy.

When she finally leaned back in her chair and released a satisfied sigh, she found Ben looking like he was trying not to laugh. "It's good to see your appetite's finally back. But are you sure you've had enough?"

Darien noticed the flicker of amusement in Jessie's eyes as well. Shrugging, she grinned in response. "I didn't realize I was so hungry. And to answer your question, yes, thanks. I've had more than enough."

"Good. Jessie relayed the gist of what happened when she called looking for a doctor, but now would be a good time for you to bring Elle and me completely up to date. Where things stand with Yuri, and what comes next."

Darien was aware of the moment his eyes focused on her bruised face. Looked deeper, seeing, she was sure, much more than she wanted to reveal.

"I know you need more time to recover," Ben continued. "And I truly wish I could give it to you. But my every instinct is telling me the Guild's not going to give us that time."

She kept her gaze steady as she met his eyes. "I agree." She began by relaying the conversation she'd had with Yuri at Oz, concluded with his agreement to facilitate a meeting with the Guild, and deliberately left out everything in between. Ben stared at her with eyes that saw entirely too much, but he didn't mention the oversight.

Darien knew Ben was unhappy that she'd gotten back into the cage so soon after the last time. Nor did she believe she was hiding anything from him. The doctor would have already given him an update on her condition, and knowing they'd gone to Oz, he would have deduced how she got in that condition. She knew she'd hear about it sooner or later. She'd just as soon wait for later.

But Ben was a professional, and he would understand what she did even if he didn't like the tactics she'd chosen. What was important was the result, and her bruises would heal and fade.

"Do you think Yuri will come through?" Ben asked.

Darien thought about that for a moment, then gave a dry smile. "Yuri doesn't trust his own reflection in the mirror, but he has no real reason not to come through. It's my guess, though, that he's not particularly happy about it."

"Why's that?"

"It's not that he doesn't want to help, especially because he thinks there's money to be made and he wants to be part of the action. It's more that he thinks this woman leading the Guild is—"

Elle released a strangled sound. "Wait a minute. Are you saying it's a woman we're after?"

Darien turned too quickly and tried not to wince. "Yes, and Yuri thinks she's crazy, although considering his usual associates, I'm not sure what that means. But it doesn't really matter. He's a businessman, so he'll arrange an introduction and do whatever is needed to ensure he gets a cut on any deal."

"Damn," Elle said. "It's great that we're finally getting somewhere, but I hate it that it's a woman. I mean, I know it happens. I've been around enough to know women are often involved in carrying communications and money between terrorist cells. But this—for some reason I'm having a hard time accepting it."

"What's hard to accept?" Darien asked. "The concept of women as terrorist leaders isn't new, Elle. Women have long been involved in terrorist movements and have been counted among the leaders in a number of organizations, including the Japanese Red Army, Italy's Red Guild, Peru's Shining Path, and Germany's Red Army Faction."

Jessie nodded in agreement. "Women have also been responsible for carrying out numerous bombings and deadly attacks. Take a look at Russia and the Black Widows suicide bombers. In fact, it's believed more than half the suicide bombers in the world since 2002 have been women." She passed Darien two tablets. "It's just aspirin, but it'll help with both the inflammation and your headache."

"Thanks." Aware of Ben's eyes watching her every move, Darien quickly popped the tablets in her mouth and chased them down with the last of her coffee. When his cell phone buzzed softly, she was grateful for the distraction. A moment later, both Jessie and Elle reached for their own phones as they began to vibrate.

❖

Jessie pressed the phone tightly against her ear and swore she could feel the tension coming through the satellite connection to Langley before she heard the deputy director's taut, low voice on the other end. But once she did, try as she might, she found it difficult to swallow.

Oh God, oh God, oh God. Her vision blurred and her throat tightened as guilt cloaked her.

She had known from the start they were working to a tight timeline. The Guild had confirmed it in their original media communiqué, indicating they were just getting started and warning that their next move was imminent. And every threat analyst Jessie knew had arrived at the same conclusion. Escalation would come swiftly. They would need to work fast if there was any hope of stopping the Guild before that happened.

But her call had just made it perfectly clear. They were too late. The next move had already been made.

She felt a knot of coldness deep within her. Maintaining a tight grip on the edge of the table, she ignored the pounding of her heart and struggled to put any personal feelings on hold while she listened. Just beyond the table, she could see Elle's face had turned ghostly pale as she nodded and listened to someone—probably Adam—undoubtedly giving her the same news.

A quick glance farther into the room showed that Ben was no longer in her line of sight, but Darien seemed to be acting on some kind of prescient instinct. She had turned on the television and was quickly working her way through the available channels. And even though she'd left the television on mute, Jessie could see all the networks were carrying the same story.

The only problem with the live feed was that the images left nothing to the imagination. Still listening to her mother's voice, Jessie watched smoke streaming from what had once been an upscale shopping mall. The aftermath of the explosion had left a gaping maw filled with rubble, smashed glass, and dangling wires. The feed managed to convey the silent screams of sirens as emergency vehicles converged on the scene, while the dazed and the injured were assisted from the wreckage of the building.

The information she was receiving from Grace indicated synchronized attacks had been carried out in three different countries. A shopping mall in Moscow. A courthouse in Ottawa. A school in Berlin. Simultaneous bomb blasts in three cities resulting in chaos, death, and destruction.

Jessie knew she had encountered worse in her career and would again as long as she stayed with the agency. But it would always be the loss of innocent lives, the children, that would tear her up. As she watched the images continue to unfold, all she could think was they never had a chance.

After she ended her call, she stared at the television no longer seeing the images, turning her head only when she felt Darien's hand squeeze her shoulder and heard her murmur, "Are you all right?"

"Not really, no." She blinked, feeling helpless and almost consumed by anger and grief. Her body was trembling and she was uncertain she could say more without emotion bleeding through in her voice. She was faintly surprised when she felt Darien reach for her hand and found herself holding on tightly, almost painfully. Darien didn't object. There was a real strength in her, and she was clearly willing to let Jessie share some of it.

"How do you do it?" she heard herself asking. "How do you deal with all the blood and death?"

"You try not to think about it," Darien said with surprising gentleness. "You fight through the emotions until you manage to find some kind of internal distance. And then you go back to fighting the good fight."

Easier said than done. "I really hate it when kids get hurt." She stared at the flat screen a bit longer. "I want this all to be a really bad dream. Have they indicated how many casualties?"

"No, but if it's any consolation, I'd say this time it's not going to be about a high body count."

"What do you mean?"

"It's Saturday," Darien said. "The greatest number of casualties will come from the shopping mall. The good news is it was hit early, just after it opened but before it got busy. As for the other targets—the school and the courthouse—one would expect them to be mostly empty during the weekend. If the goal was a high body count, the bombings would have been carried out later, on a weekday, when the school and the courthouse would have been fully occupied."

"But they weren't."

"Exactly. That would suggest the targets were selected because they were symbolic more than anything else. Like the school."

"To what end?" Elle asked as she put down her phone.

"Why does any person or group resort to acts of terrorism? Most often, it's to intimidate. To instill fear. To disrupt lives. And to send a message. The Guild just did what they set out to do. They demonstrated their capacity. They showed everyone they can carry out actions that clearly took months to plan. More importantly, they've shown they can reach people where they live—right in the middle of their normal, everyday lives where they least expect to be touched."

The minutes stretched as Jessie listened to Darien and Elle talk while continuing to stare at the television images. Russia. Canada. Germany. "They're not just random targets," she said out loud, even as she continued to process the limited information she had.

"I wouldn't think so," Elle responded.

But Darien was watching her intently. "Where are you going with this?"

"She's now hit six of the G8 countries," Jessie said. Her mind raced three moves ahead. "The next G8 summit—it's just a few weeks away. It fits. The US, Russian, and French presidents will be there. So will the chancellor of Germany, and the prime ministers of the United Kingdom, Canada, Italy, and Japan."

"All those world leaders in one location would be a powerful draw," Darien said softly.

Jessie nodded. "The Guild's original goal was to destabilize Russia. That could be accomplished much more easily if they were to weaken all of her allies."

"And nothing would do that faster that taking out each country's leader. Short-term, all of those countries would be reduced to chaos."

"Jesus, it makes horrible sense."

"And it's crazy enough it just might work. Where's the next summit being held?"

"In the US. On Cabot Island."

"Where's that?"

Jessie smiled faintly. "Not surprising if you don't know, since it's one of more than three thousand islands off the coast of Maine."

Darien raised her eyebrows in silent question.

"It's called the Maine archipelago," Jessie explained, "and it includes everything from small granite ledges to Mount Desert Island, the largest of the islands at just over one hundred square miles."

"You're not kidding, are you? That's really where they've chosen to hold the next summit?"

"I'm afraid so. Most of the islands are uninhabited, and federal and state agencies and conservation groups own about fifteen hundred. But the rest are private property. About a third of the islands are ten acres or more. Some have thriving villages serviced by daily ferry service from the mainland, and I believe fourteen are inhabited year round. Mostly in Casco Bay, Penobscot Bay, and south of Mount Desert."

"It sounds like you know the area quite well."

Jessie smiled faintly. "I should. My family maintains a summer home there that's been in the family for generations, and I spent every summer vacation there when I was younger. I can remember spending endless days on the water, sailing and exploring as many islands as I could. My goal was to touch them all before I finished high school."

"And did you?"

"Lord, no," Jessie laughed. "But not for lack of trying."

Darien went very still, her expression suddenly difficult to read. "It sounds like an idyllic place."

"It was—it is."

"But you're also describing a security nightmare for the summit."

"You don't know the half of it," Jessie said. "The boating season in Maine typically lasts from the first of July through Labor Day. Between local boaters, tourists, sports fishermen, and commercial fishing boats, the waterways are filled with craft of all sizes and shapes, from kayaks to yachts. I understand the logistics have been driving Homeland Security and the FBI crazy since the location was chosen for the summit."

"Then why the hell was it picked?"

"I'd like to tell you it's because the authorities thought the island would make it easier to prevent the clashes between police and protestors that have become synonymous with high-level meetings. And in part, that's true."

"What other reason is there?"

Jessie grinned wryly and shrugged. "Because the current US president has a summer home there."

"Wonderful," Darien murmured. "Leaving us with a terrorist threat, a logistical nightmare, and a rapidly shrinking timeline."

❖

"Your level of patience is nothing short of amazing," Jessie said. It was clear that, as far as she was concerned, they'd been waiting far too long for Yuri to make contact with Ari, and her voice was lined with frustration.

Glancing up from the computer, Darien saw the sheen of impatience showing in Jessie's eyes and ignored her sarcasm. "Patience is my stock in trade, Jesslyn." She smiled, knowing it was also a fundamental rule of revenge. "Waiting is the first thing a sniper learns to do."

"So we just wait?"

"Everything happens when the time is right. In the meantime, we wait. Keep busy."

"Doing what?"

"A little of this, a little of that. For example, come and tell me what you see." She pointed to the computer she'd been using to familiarize herself with the area surrounding Cabot Island. The screen was currently displaying satellite images of the Maine archipelago.

But unlike Jessie, who would look at the images with a view to protecting the island and everyone on it, Darien had been viewing it through the eyes of a hunter. Looking for weaknesses that could be exploited. Searching out points of vulnerability.

The distraction worked. She watched Jessie's shoulders relax as she focused on the laptop, staring at the screen. "I see too many places to hide. Too many places from which to launch an attack. Even if Homeland Security clears an island, what's to stop someone from going in behind them and storing missiles or weapons or whatever they need? "

"You're right." She glanced at Jessie and sensed she'd been waiting for a moment like this. "What is it you want to know, Jesslyn?"

Jessie blinked, appeared to hesitate for a second. "I guess I want to know how you would do it. What would you do if you were hired to take someone out during the summit?"

Picking up a pen and some paper, Darien studied the blank page in silent consideration before she began jotting down notes under Jessie's watchful eyes. She knew the island itself would be well fortified. DHS personnel would set up a security buffer zone around the island, restricting both airspace and access by water. Soldiers and police officers would form a ring around the island while coast guard gunships with anti-aircraft batteries would circle the waters. Military jets and marine helicopters would perform routine flyovers.

The causeway from the mainland to the island would be closed to all but authorized vehicles for the duration of the summit. Even then, there would be multiple checkpoints to clear, including bomb-sniffing dogs, numerous credential checks, walk-through metal detectors, and X-ray bag screening.

But if she was seriously hunting any or all the heads of the G8 countries while they were on the island…how would she do it?

Clearly there would be opportunities to launch a short-range tactical missile strike from one of the countless islands that made up the archipelago. Or from a pleasure yacht, one of hundreds out on the water beyond the buffer zone.

Both scenarios—the second more so than the first—warranted serious consideration given the Guild's success to date with missiles and bombs. Adding a distraction would help, possibly a suicide bomber trying to get across the causeway. It would cause chaos and prevent DHS from using the causeway as an escape route.

When she was finished, she laid the pen down and examined her notes. It could work. But as she stared a little longer and let her mind run free, she suddenly found herself contemplating an entirely different possibility.

Before Jessie could say anything, she reached for the pen once again and began writing quickly. Drawing the basics of a plan that called for simultaneous attacks using GPS and computer-controlled airplanes. Miniature jets capable of flying up to four miles at more than three hundred miles per hour. Each replete with electronic jammers and armed with 40 millimeter thermobaric grenades.

Watching over her shoulder, Jessie swore softly. "Baby drones?" When she nodded, Jessie bit back another oath. "All I can say is thank God you're on our side."

The comment elicited a brief smile, but that was all. The problem with the exercise Darien had just completed—the problem with considering how she might handle such a job—was she would never take on a job of this nature in the first place. Because no matter how it was handled, there would be no getting away from collateral damage.

Innocent people would die. The fact that many of them would be military and law-enforcement personnel wouldn't make them any less innocent or any less dead.

Any response she might have considered making would have to wait as her cell phone began to vibrate. She immediately felt a wave of adrenaline flow through her body, but her hand remained steady as she reached for the phone. Conscious of the three people watching her, as soon as she heard Yuri's voice on the other end of the connection, she got up and moved to stand by the window, creating the illusion of space and distance, if nothing else.

CHAPTER SIXTEEN

Jessie's gaze followed Darien as she moved to the window and stood in the exact center of a nimbus of light. She heard her greet Yuri softly in Russian. Over the next few minutes she watched as Darien fell silent, the phone pressed against her ear, and sensed her withdrawal even though Darien never moved away from the window.

Darien appeared oblivious to everything around her, her concentration fixed exclusively on whatever information Yuri was relaying. She listened with a calm detachment, occasionally acknowledging her understanding while her expression remained solemn.

But as the seconds ticked by and the conversation continued, something changed. Yuri must have said something unexpected, something that caused Darien to stiffen. Tension spread visibly like darkness and appeared to settle somewhere between her shoulder blades. The frown that formed on her face wasn't encouraging. Neither was the prolonged silence that followed when she finally disconnected her call.

For the longest time, Darien remained by the window as if held there by the dying sunlight. With her eyes closed and her hands locked together, it was patently obvious she was fighting combustible emotions, making an effort to regroup. The tight silence stretched before she opened her eyes again and turned back to the room.

She unclenched her hands and let them fall to her sides. Squared her shoulders. But as Jessie waited and watched intently, she could see there were new shadows in Darien's eyes, and a bone-deep weariness that hadn't been there earlier.

Whatever was troubling Darien went deep, and it made Jessie want to reach out to her. But it wouldn't help. This was neither the time nor the place, and she was not the only one observing Darien. Ben and Elle were staring just as intently, both clearly impatient to know what the next move was going to be in the complicated chess game they were all playing.

Jessie wanted to know but let her silence tell Darien she would wait until she had her thoughts in order. Ben was not inclined to give her time. "What did Yuri say?" he asked. "Are we on?"

As if coming out of a fugue state, Darien nodded stiffly. "The Guild has agreed to meet with Ari," she said. "They'll provide a list of the weapons they want, but Yuri indicated thermobaric weapons will be at the top of their shopping list. He says they're on a short clock, but they're prepared to pay top dollar to get what they want as quickly as possible."

Elle leaned forward. "I'm not familiar with—what did you call the weapons they want?"

"Thermobaric weapons. They're fuel-rich high explosives," Ben explained. "When dropped from an aircraft or fired from a rocket launcher, the initial explosion injects a fine flammable mist into the air to form a cloud. When it's detonated, it generates an intense high-temperature explosion that literally sets fire to the air above its target."

"The fireball creates a vacuum and everything in the vicinity collapses," Darien added. "It also sends out a shock wave in all directions that lasts longer than more conventional explosives."

"So whatever doesn't get obliterated in the blast gets flattened by the shock waves or suffocated by the vacuum," Elle concluded.

Darien nodded. "That's what makes them ideal weapons when dealing with tunnels or caves, which is why American Special Forces used them in Afghanistan. But because they deliver massive firepower in a relatively compact size, they're also considered highly portable and ideal for remote targets…like Cabot Island."

As she spoke, something caused Jessie's spider-sense to tingle and left her feeling uneasy. It wasn't *what* Darien was saying, which was bad enough. There was something else at play. She could hear it in the tension in her voice.

Thrusting her hands deep into her pockets, she studied Darien's face carefully, looking for a source of concern. What she saw as her eyes traced over the lines that shaped Darien's face was the same thing she'd been seeing since their first meeting. Slanting cheeks and a sensuous mouth. Dark unreadable eyes.

But something was off. Something just beneath the surface. She watched Darien turn back to stare out the window, her arms folded over her middle in a stance that was becoming familiar, and sensed she was struggling to contain a surge of unwelcome emotion.

The only problem was Jessie had no idea what was causing it. She just knew it hadn't been there before Yuri's call, and she needed to find out what it was before they went too far afield. She weighed the pros and cons, then made her choice and began to probe.

"I don't know why, but something isn't sitting right. Maybe it's happening easier than I thought, I'm not sure," she said. "But since this meeting is what we've been waiting for, I suppose I shouldn't question our luck."

Ghost-gray eyes turned in Jessie's direction. But if Darien was surprised or irritated by her reaction, it didn't show. "There's nothing to question. It's not luck. It's simply a case that the Guild's original broker, Ivan Sakharov, hasn't been returning calls. Rumor has it he's disappeared."

"Really?" Jessie drawled the word out into two syllables.

"Yes, really." Darien tipped her head in acknowledgment. "It obviously brings to an end the search you've been conducting for the broker. But it does prove you were right about the Russians, and according to Yuri, Sakharov's lack of response has rattled Nadia. It's caused her to become impatient, and therefore open to using an arms dealer she hasn't met or dealt with before. Namely, Ari."

"Who's Nadia?"

There was a subtle hesitation before she answered. "Nadia Petrov," Darien said in a curiously flat tone, "is the current head of the Guild."

The words were measured and gave away nothing but the facts. But Jessie could hear something in her voice. "Do you know her?"

"Not exactly, no." There was a tense pause during which Darien continued to look vaguely unsettled. "But unless I miss my mark, she's going to turn out to be related to Dmitri Petrov."

"And he is…?"

"He *was* one of the original three leaders whose gangs came together to form the Guild…and the last one to fall."

The chill in Darien's words rippled along Jessie's spine as the picture suddenly became clear. "Oh, Jesus," she murmured. "Damn, are you all right?"

❖

For the span of several seconds, the skin on Darien's neck prickled as if Dmitri's hand still held her there. She brought her hand up and rubbed the spot, trying to stay focused on the moment until she heard only the thunder of her own heart, beating in a frantic rhythm. "I'm fine."

Part of her actually meant it, but she knew she didn't quite manage to hide the faint edge in her voice. Or the fury that no doubt burned in her eyes. When Jessie continued to stare at her, she finally conceded. "Okay, maybe I'm not entirely fine. But I've learned the hard way to take it the way it comes, one day at a time. And I won't let this get in the way of what needs to be done."

Ben looked at her and Darien realized she had become the sole focus of his attention. "Are you certain? Dare, I need to know if you can handle this. There's no shame in admitting it if you can't. We'll just find another way."

Darien smiled faintly. "There is no other way." She spoke in a quiet, tempered voice that held only a calm acceptance. "You know it as well as I do, which is why you brought me into this mess in the first place. You needed Ari to connect with the Guild. Well, Ari now has an invitation to come to the table, so there's no turning back. What I need is for you to help keep me alive while I'm doing it. End of discussion. Let's just get it done and worry about picking up the pieces later."

Jessie looked from Darien to Ben, and back again. It was clear she wasn't particularly comfortable with the direction the conversation had taken. Nor, it seemed, was she fooled by the civilized tone.

Probably, Darien thought wryly, because what Jessie saw in her expression wasn't the least bit civilized.

Ben wasn't happy either. But after pausing long enough to look at Darien again, he chose to put the personal aside and focused instead on the business at hand. "When and where do they want to meet with you?"

Darien closed her eyes a moment and drew in a breath. "They want to meet three days from now, at five thirty in the morning."

"All right. Where are they proposing to meet?"

"That's where things get really curious," Darien said. "They want to meet on the Black Forest High Road, twenty kilometers out of Baden-Baden. According to Yuri, I'm to travel by motorcycle and wait alone by the side of the road. Once they've confirmed to their satisfaction that I'm alone and that I haven't been followed, they'll initiate contact."

"No, that's crazy," Jessie said. "You're still recovering from a concussion. You're in no condition to travel any distance, let alone go to Germany by motorcycle. As for going alone, that's beyond crazy. Please, tell me you're not considering doing what they're asking."

Darien turned her head and their gazes met. "Worried about me?"

"Yes." The word barely came out.

Darien inhaled sharply and felt a fleeting instant of surprise. "Don't be. I'll be fine."

Before Darien could say anything more, Ben intervened. "Worry not. She won't have to ride the bike to Germany. We'll use one of the surveillance vans to transport both Darien and her bike. She won't have to actually get on the bike until we're close to Baden-Baden."

He was, Darien realized, once again acting as her sense of caution. Particularly since at times it was clear he didn't believe she possessed any. She watched him move to the laptop, his fingers quickly flying across the keys as he scrolled through a series of maps until he found the one he wanted.

"We can set up surveillance along the highway, roughly here and here." He tapped the screen a couple of times before he turned back to look at her. "We should be able to track you and record everything that happens, while being close enough to provide some support in the event you need it."

"Close but not too close. They sound paranoid and the whole point of surveillance is not to be caught watching."

Ben held Darien's gaze a heartbeat longer. "Unfortunately, it means even if we respond immediately, it will still leave you alone in their crosshairs for longer than I'd like."

"I'm aware of that, but it'll have to be enough because this may be the only chance we get," Darien said. "As for being in their crosshairs, all I need is a chance to convince Petrov to let me provide the weapons she needs. I've done it before. And if it starts to get hot, I'll have to make do until the cavalry gets there."

Jessie stiffened and looked for a moment as if she wanted to disagree. But then she shrugged. "I don't like it," she said, "but since I have little to offer as an alternative, I guess we're going to Germany."

The tension that had been squeezing Darien's shoulders slowly began to dissolve. "Think of it as an adventure. In the meantime, we need to know the players before we can anticipate their moves. We have three days to see what our collective databases can tell us about Nadia Petrov."

"What do you hope to find?"

Answers, she thought, but only shrugged.

❖

As darkness waned and the new day began to spill through the window, Darien released a tired but satisfied breath and saved the file she'd just compiled. Removing the flash drive from the computer, she clutched it in her fist and pushed away from the desk, knowing she was holding everything she'd been able to learn about Nadia Petrov. Hoping it was enough to give her an edge in understanding her opponent.

Dmitri's daughter.

She would have been sixteen when Dmitri died, three years older than her father's killer. An only child, her mother had been a prostitute already several years removed from her life, leaving Nadia to grow up alone on the fringes of a criminal underworld ruled by her father with a harsh hand.

She'd gotten her education on the streets of Grozny in the Chechen Republic before she'd moved on to Moscow. There were records documenting some early arrests for what were mostly petty crimes—theft and black marketeering. But she had also spent time in a corrective labor colony in Mordovia, southeast of Moscow, allegedly for the murder of a former lover.

The most recent photograph Darien had been able to find was at least three years old. It had been taken by chance, by a low-level intelligence officer charged with capturing and forwarding for identification the faces of everyone attending the funeral of a noted arms dealer. Luck. But sometimes that was all it took. And it provided a clear image of the woman Dmitri's daughter had become.

Tall, blond, and dark eyed. Athletic. Attractive, although it was obvious she'd not had an easy time of it, and she looked older than her thirty-one years. But it was more than that, Darien knew, as she walked to the window and gazed out at the waking city. She wrapped her arms around her body as a flicker of recognition coursed through her.

They had followed different paths to where they were today. But as she contemplated what she'd learned about Petrov and the pieces came together, she was disturbed by the similarities she saw in their lives.

Neither had a real family growing up or anything resembling an ordinary upbringing. Both were loners. Both of their lives had been shaped by violence and death at an early age. Both had been on their own for a long time and had problems with authority. Both were survivors.

But even as she recognized there were things in Petrov's life she could relate to, Darien knew they were about to face off in a contest where there could be only one winner. She stared at the flash drive as if it held some kind of answer. All the while feeling as if, in some way, she was looking into a mirror.

"Don't go there," Jessie whispered softly. "You're nothing like her."

Darien hadn't heard Jessie approach. Feeling slightly chagrined, she turned around and gazed into her concerned eyes. "Are you trying to read my mind again, Jesslyn?"

Arching a tapered brow, Jessie's gaze searched her face. "It doesn't take a mind reader to figure out you're looking at Petrov and seeing shades of yourself. And along with kinship, possibly feeling some guilt for your part in shaping who she's become."

"You don't really know me well enough to say that. Not with any degree of certainty. But even so, you can't deny the similarities."

Jessie shook her head. "Trust me, I know enough. I know for a fact Nadia Petrov kills ordinary people trying to lead ordinary, everyday lives. Men, women, children, it doesn't seem to matter to her. And she does it seemingly without giving it a second thought. Without remorse. You, on the other hand, don't do that. You hunt the worst, criminals without a conscience. And I know everything you do is designed to help make the world a safer place for ordinary people."

Darien's laugh was soft. "You know all that, do you?"

"Yes. You're nothing like her."

CHAPTER SEVENTEEN

Baden-Württemberg, Germany

Just after five in the morning three days later, Darien found herself standing on the side of an all but deserted two-lane blacktop cutting through the Black Forest region in southwestern Germany. She flipped up the visor on her helmet and inhaled air so sweet and clean it almost burned her lungs.

Releasing a soft sigh, she couldn't help but think that driving fast was one of life's simple pleasures. But going fast on a motorcycle was even better. She loved taking the Ducati on the twisting roads. It was powerful. Responsive. She loved leaning her body into the curves and racing the wind. It was one of her favorite distractions, a way to relax and leave behind some of the chaos she tightrope-walked over most days.

But on this day, the ride had nothing to do with relaxation and proved much too short when she stopped, as instructed, on the side of a near empty highway. The Black Forest High Road was shrouded in darkness and still damp from the previous night's rain, while a soft southerly breeze whispered hypnotically. It was just cool enough to fan her face as it faintly stirred the trees that stretched for mile upon mile.

Removing her helmet, she got off the bike and stretched muscles still bruised from Yuri's cage, while her senses remained alert to every sound and movement in the shadows that crowded the road. She felt a tingle of anticipation dance across her skin. But for now, only the breeze, the low murmur of nearby running water, and the faint rustling of leaves disturbed the stillness.

Of course, she wasn't really alone. Far from it. She knew that somewhere along the quiet stretch of road, there were two surveillance vehicles. Hidden under the cover provided by the trees, they were maintaining a watchful eye on her.

Jessie and Elle were riding with Ben in one of the vans, several kilometers to the south. A second van was positioned several kilometers to the north of her location. The second team was led by a British intelligence agent named Nicola Spencer, a woman she'd met years before and had worked with closely on a number of occasions. Often enough to have developed a level of comfort and trust with Nicola watching her back, and she knew that was why Ben had arranged for Nicola to be here.

The knowledge stopped her from feeling isolated, and as the silence stretched, she found herself hoping they were doing the right thing. Because doing the wrong thing was guaranteed to be a fast way to die.

"Tango one, your heart rate's up. Is everything okay?" Ben's voice came though her earpiece clearly, almost as if he'd been reading her mind.

"Everything's quiet," she replied softly. "Hey, Tango two. Did you know that according to local lore, this region of the Black Forest is where sorcerers, werewolves, and even the devil himself is said to walk?"

"That's the kind of knowledge that'll keep you up at night and give you nightmares, Tango one." Jessie's dry response didn't quite muffle the laugh she tried to stifle. She was also wrong. Rather than disturb or frighten her, the thought of encountering sorcerers or werewolves actually delighted Darien. They were simply creatures of the darkness and the night, much like her. Kindred spirits.

She caught a glimpse of two hawks gliding in slow circles, using the subdued light as cover as they searched for prey. She followed them with her eyes until they disappeared, then turned in a slow circle. Taking it all in.

The air carried with it the distinctive scent left behind by the rain, underscored by the smell of fallen pine needles, wet flowers, and damp earth. She let the scent merge with the silence, then felt both fill her, blissfully enjoying the moment and reveling in the temporary peace she found there, even as she waited for a contact whose intent was as far from peaceful as you could get.

As she had so many times over the past few days, she felt her thoughts return to Jesslyn. Somehow, she'd slipped under her skin when she wasn't looking, and there was something about her, something that continued to draw her in. It wasn't just her looks, although it certainly could be her kiss, which continued to stir her blood, long after the memory of it should have faded.

The truth was Jessie seemed to be able to reach her, to touch her in places she didn't want anyone—any woman—to reach. It made her think too much of possibilities, of connections, of not feeling isolated. It made her think of things that had no place in her life and left her feeling vulnerable.

She paused in midthought as something stirred in the nearby woods. She instinctively looked around, all of her senses going on alert as she checked and rechecked her surroundings. But there was still no one in sight, and she realized it was only the breeze disturbing the leaves. She shook her head and laughed at herself.

You've gotten paranoid, she chided.

But even knowing she should be totally focused on the mission, she still found herself fighting half-articulated feelings stirring in the rhythm of her blood. Along with the prickling sensation that someone other than her team was watching her every move.

The surveillance vehicle was a covert operative's dream—a warm and dry mobile observation post filled with state-of-the-art equipment. Settled comfortably in the rear of the van, Jessie leaned forward, elbows resting on her knees as she regarded a bank of dark computer screens, each attached to a digital data recorder.

She was hooked to the console via a headset Ben had given her earlier, after explaining the unit was voice activated. She just needed to talk.

She was also equipped with a PRR—a small personal role radio—meant to facilitate communication between team members. She knew the PRR had a low probability of detection or interception, but it was only designed to be used over short distances. That meant their PRRs wouldn't allow for communication with the second surveillance team located several kilometers away.

Listening vigilantly in case Darien needed anything, Jessie watched while Ben guided Elle through a final series of tests on the satellite connections and signal strength. Once they were finished, one by one, the monitors in front of her sprang to life, washing the van's interior and its occupants with a soft green light.

From her position, one monitor would allow Jessie to continuously monitor Darien's GPS-tracking signal as well as her vital signs. Other monitors used a satellite link to send real-time signals and provided views in a grid covering the surrounding area, automatically toggling back and forth every five seconds. With cloud cover minimal, there would be no interference, so the images on the monitors came through clearly.

"Cool toys," Elle said appreciatively. "And all the comforts of home compared to what we had in Islamabad."

Jessie smiled. "It does have a certain wow factor, doesn't it?"

More importantly, no one should be able to approach Darien from either direction without alerting them. Her lips pulled in a tight line as she thought of Darien alone on the side of the highway, then pushed the thought aside.

But as the minutes ticked by, nothing moved. The only sign of life on the screen was from indigenous wildlife. Mostly small creatures. Rabbits and hedgehogs. The occasional truck rumbled by, but no one else appeared to be coming and they were rapidly running out of time.

"Something's not right," she murmured when she could no longer keep silent.

"They're cutting it fine," Ben responded, "but perhaps it couldn't be helped."

"What are you thinking?" Jessie raised a sardonic brow and tried to suppress her impatience. "That they ran into unexpected traffic?"

Ben shrugged. "Actually, I have no idea what's going on." He sounded calm, but his expression said otherwise. Reaching overhead, he opened a small metal cabinet, pulled out a large thermos, and began filling cups with coffee before passing them along to her and Elle.

Holding a cup, Jessie closed her eyes and inhaled. The steam rising into the air was rich and strong. It smelled like heaven and the scent alone had her energy picking up as her mouth watered. *God, it's like Pavlovian conditioning.*

"Thanks." Settling back into her seat for the duration, Jessie brought the drink to her mouth and couldn't control the sigh that escaped her.

"Problem?"

"Lord, no. This is sinfully wonderful."

"You'll have to thank Darien. She programmed the coffeemaker when we stopped outside Baden-Baden, while we were offloading the bike." Ben flashed a grin and laughed softly. "Only Darien would design a state-of-the-art surveillance van with a built-in coffeemaker, and then load it to go at just the right time with Jamaican Blue Mountain."

Jessie didn't care how ridiculous that sounded. She took another sip and felt grateful.

Silence stretched, and as they continued to wait, the coffee shot both warmth and fragrance into the air until it filled the van. But Jessie couldn't control the shivers that coursed through her body. Adrenaline, caffeine, and nerves were a bad combination.

Ignoring her body's response, she rubbed her neck and continued to watch the surveillance screens, reassuring herself that Darien's tracking signal was where it should be and there was no one else in sight. She picked up her coffee and drained it but no longer felt the heat.

Elle regarded her with an amused expression. "Stop worrying about her. If there's anyone capable of looking after herself out there, it's Darien."

"I know that's true, but I can't help it," Jessie murmured with a calm she didn't feel. "This doesn't feel right."

"I agree." In the dim light, Ben's posture remained unchanged, but his voice held a weary note. He glanced needlessly at his watch and his features tightened. "If Petrov was coming, she should have been here by now. I think we need to call this off and reel Darien back in. There's an MI6 safe house not far from here we can use to regroup. Plan our next steps."

But before Jessie could respond, Nicola Spencer's voice came through the overhead speakers. "Heads up, people. I believe we have company."

Jessie glanced at the GPS tracker on the dash screen, then looked at the satellite feed displayed on the other monitors. Between one heartbeat and the next she saw it. "Is that—?"

A helicopter.

And Darien was alone, exposed by the light of dawn. Chills ripped through her.

"Tango one," she said urgently over the com-link. "You need to get out of there. Now. Head south. Do you read me, Tango one?"

Darien didn't question the instructions. The urgency in Jessie's voice alone was enough to make her move swiftly. As she swung her leg over the motorcycle, she twisted her hair, slipped the helmet back into place, and dropped the visor. With one touch, the powerful bike roared to life before settling down to a soft rumble. Heeding Jessie's warning, she gunned the engine and urged the machine back onto the road. Heading south.

A twist of the throttle and the world quickly became an amalgam of darkness and light—the shadows of the hills and trees, the ethereal blue of the air, the gray sky, and the black undulating ribbon of highway that stretched out into the horizon. She accelerated through a series of curves and listened to the throaty growl of the motorcycle echoing in the stillness of the early morning.

Darien had always credited her instincts for keeping her alive this long, certainly not something to disregard or ignore. Those instincts had told her not to question Jessie's instructions, but she still had no idea what the danger was or what direction it was coming from. All she knew was her instincts were screaming, and as she leaned into a sharp curve in the road, she found herself paying closer attention to her surroundings, looking for the trap she sensed was near.

Just as she rounded the bend, Jessie's voice answered her unasked questions, issuing another warning over her com-link. "SAT showing possible hostiles. Your eleven o'clock."

Eleven o'clock? Darien immediately scanned the sky. At first it was only a shadow, barely discernible against the pewter of the early morning sky. An instant later, she spotted it more clearly. A sleek helicopter, skimming the treetops as it gained altitude.

The windows were tinted dark and there were no numbers visible. No markings at all. Just like that, the day went downhill in a hurry and she knew she was in serious trouble.

Her eyes darted from the road to the helicopter. She needed to reach Jessie and Ben, but as her mind furiously calculated time and distance, she knew she wasn't going to make it. It was only a matter of time—*seconds*—before she was in the helicopter's line of sight, if it hadn't already happened. Certainly not enough time to disappear into the shadows of the towering pines. She was left scrambling for an alternative plan to survive, and surviving the next few minutes had just become highly questionable.

Seconds later, the probability of survival diminished even further as the beat of the helicopter grew louder. It turned, circling to the south over the road, then hovered just over the trees. As if in slow motion, the side door opened and Darien saw a muzzle flash. Gunfire erupted, strafing across the road, chewing up the asphalt around her.

Fly, damn it. She found herself begging, impatient for more speed, as a deep-seated anger settled in her. She had no desire to die, and after everything she'd done and everything she'd been through, this was not the way she'd choose to go. She urged the machine faster. Racing at spine-numbing speed on the slick road, coaxing every last ounce of power the bike could give her.

But then she felt the shock of white-hot searing pain as a bullet struck the Kevlar vest she was wearing, all but knocking her off the bike, while another furrowed through the flesh in her forearm. The exploding burn spread like a wildfire across her torso and down to her fingers. Unable to breathe or maintain any kind of her grip on the throttle, she began to lose precious speed.

The rapid deceleration probably also saved her life. As another barrage of bullets rained down around her, a tire blew. The motorcycle reacted violently, and in the next instant, she was catapulted into the air.

❖

Jessie flinched as she heard the distinctive stutter of automatic weapons fire echoing in the distance. The sound was familiar enough for her to readily identify it, but she knew they were still too far away to be of any immediate help, and she was afraid Darien didn't have that much time. She felt a chill slide over her skin as a bolt of fear laced through her, and she hissed out a breath.

Reaching for the console, she tried to hail Darien.

No response.

She waited through several heartbeats before trying again. "Tango one? Do you read me? Give me your status. Can you lose them?" She swallowed. "Darien? Can you hear me?"

But there was still no contact. Not then and not on her subsequent try.

"Elle?" Jessie inhaled sharply and tried to ignore the dread washing over her. "I need you to help me out. Can you boost the signal?"

Elle quickly tapped some keys, frowned, and intensified her focus as she tapped a few more times before making a disappointed sound. "It's no good," she said. "All I'm picking up is static and dead air. I'm not sure how, but I think we're getting jammed."

From the driver's seat, Ben swore softly as the van sped along the highway, trying to close the gap between them and Darien. More surprisingly, Jessie heard the unexpected sound of nerves in Ben's voice. It took a moment, but she recognized the cause. Fear. For Darien.

An instant later, the sound of renewed gunfire could be heard over the van's engine. A short burst followed by a longer one. With her heart pounding, Jessie turned and stared at the monitor and for a moment, her world narrowed to one goal. Keeping a close watch on Darien's tracker beacon as it moved on the screen, inching toward them. She willed it to hurry as it drew tantalizingly close.

In the next instant, she watched helplessly as it suddenly disappeared.

Her gaze snapped to Ben and her composure wavered. "Oh, Jesus, Ben. Her signal—Darien's signal just disappeared. It's gone."

Oh God, Darien. Please be alive.

Ben's features tightened. "Hang on." As he spoke, he pressed harder on the accelerator, causing the tires to screech as he took the van through the next curve, taking it high and tight and much too fast.

Jessie grabbed the console for balance but was still slammed back into her seat. As she recovered and glanced in his direction, she could see emotion in Ben's face. The beginnings of grief blending with the tension already there. Knowing Darien had been a part of his life for so many years, she couldn't imagine what he was feeling, and her heart ached for him. Her own eyes were burning. Her throat tightened and she had to swallow before she could speak.

"She's strong. We'll find her."

"Um, Jessie," Elle said as she watched the readout on a palm-sized electronic device. "It's not just her tracker that's gone silent. We're not getting any communication whatsoever from her. Just dead air."

Time seemed to slow down and the tension inside the surveillance van grew thicker as they raced to Darien's last known location. Jessie felt numb. She refused to believe they'd lost Darien. That wicked grin of hers was starting to mean something to her and she refused to accept she wouldn't see it again. Pushing negative thoughts aside, she tapped into all of her training and struggled to stay focused.

"We'll get her back."

Ben glanced in the mirror and sent her a weak smile. "Are you trying to convince me or yourself?"

"Does it really matter?"

CHAPTER EIGHTEEN

In the fleeting moments after the motorcycle fell away from beneath her, there was no time for fear, much less anger. Darien landed hard. The impact stole what little remained of her breath and left her momentarily paralyzed as she slid across the asphalt. Unable to stop or begin to slow herself down, even as she felt pain tear through her.

She flew over the edge of the highway and down the embankment, the moss proving to be much less cushioning than it appeared at first glance. She tumbled helplessly over thick undergrowth, gnarled roots, and rocks until her momentum finally exhausted itself, and she came to an abrupt stop by a copse of trees near the bottom of the ravine.

For seconds—or possibly longer—she remained perfectly still, nearly overwhelmed by a bleak sense of disbelief that she'd been taken down so easily. Wanting to deny she was potentially minutes away from capture. From death.

She heard herself moan, low and deep, and the metallic scent and taste of blood filled her senses. She needed to open her eyes. But even before she did anything, in some part of her concussed and swollen brain, she knew instinctively any movement at all would hurt. Really badly. Even something as simple as opening her eyes. At least for now, she was alive. And that seemed to trump everything else.

But then time and her thoughts slowed. Darkness embraced her and everything faded to black.

When awareness returned, the pain in her body also returned, with a vengeance. Everything hurt. She wasn't sure how long she'd been out, but it couldn't have been long. She waited several seconds for the worst of it to pass while she concentrated on trying to breathe.

She tried to think, but her mind was foggy, filled with fractured thoughts and images. She knew she was lying on hard, cold, damp ground. Her leathers were torn and wet, and she was shivering uncontrollably. And then it hit her, all at once. Nadia Petrov. The helicopter. Gunfire. Flying off her bike.

Her eyes flew open. Just blinking took effort, and she lay still for a few seconds longer, knowing she needed to move but unsure about the extent of her injuries. Forced to wait until the world around her stopped spinning while pain manifested itself in countless ways.

Swallowing against the waves of nausea that were threatening to take her under again, she forced herself to push through the discomfort as she tried to move. Slowly at first. Testing her extremities, starting with fingers and toes, grateful to discover everything was still functional—more or less.

But even the slightest movement hurt, and she began to think her head was worse than she'd originally believed. It was throbbing fiercely, and she knew she was dangerously close to sinking back into oblivion where nothing mattered. Clearly, that was not an option.

As the will to survive reasserted itself, she fought against the beckoning darkness and forced herself to concentrate. To breathe. One breath at a time. Even then, it took all the effort she could muster to remove her helmet and assess the damage.

Her heartbeat was erratic, and beneath the Kevlar her chest throbbed where at least one bullet had struck her. It made breathing difficult, but it wasn't too bad if she didn't breathe deeply. Bruises were already making themselves felt all over her body, and her arm screamed in protest, bleeding where another bullet had done some damage. Pain was radiating up to her shoulder, and she could feel blood snaking down her forearm and seeping through the tear in the sleeve of her jacket, its scent a sharp bite in the damp air.

She would need stitches, she thought, absurdly irritated by the realization.

But the good news was she didn't think anything was broken. The Kevlar-and-titanium vest under her jacket had unquestionably saved her life, and the ruined leathers had done their job. They had saved her from leaving multiple layers of tender skin on the road. Or worse. The definitive diagnosis was she was alive. Painfully but undeniably alive. And if she wanted to stay that way, she needed to start moving, get out of the area as quickly as possible.

As if to support her decision, the distinctive sound of a helicopter penetrated her thoughts. It confirmed what she had suspected—that her pursuers hadn't gone away. They would be scanning the crash site, looking for any sign of movement, of life. But, at least for the moment, they were still in the air. In spite of a brief lapse in consciousness, she didn't believe there had been enough time for them to land and commence a ground search.

She tried hailing Ben and Jessie, but met with no success. Not even static. Tried for Nicola, but got the same result. Nothing. After three fruitless attempts she gave up.

She pulled the tiny communications earpiece out and stared at it numbly in the shadowed light. It had probably become disabled during the crash, not that it mattered. Without adequate light and the proper tools, there was little she could do to fix it. Assuming she got out of this mess, she promised herself she'd see what she could do to make it more resilient. In the meantime, it meant she was on her own.

With her control hanging by a thread, she forced herself to sit up.

She hissed as pain flared and pulsed through her with every heartbeat, threatening to take her back under. But she persisted, reaching down and slipping her Kel-Tec PF-9 from her ankle holster. She balanced the weapon carefully in her left hand while she waited for the dizziness to subside.

Considering it was the lightest and flattest 9 mm ever mass-produced, the weapon felt unusually heavy. But she was nearly as good a shot with her left hand as she was with her right, and under the present circumstances, nearly as good would have to do. She just didn't fancy the odds of taking on an as yet undetermined number of well-armed assailants.

She needed to move.

Sore and bleeding, it took a bit longer before she tried to stand up. On the third attempt, she managed it, clenching her teeth as she staggered to her feet, only to be thrown off balance by her inability to use her right arm. She struggled not to fall, then almost immediately was forced back down to her knees, lowering her head as the light-headedness threatened to overwhelm her.

Keeping her forehead down on her knees, she ignored the pain slicing through her head like a knife. She could feel her skin go cold and moist—shock?

It didn't matter. Instinctively, she knew any further delay was out of the question. The cool light of dawn was already spreading and would make it easier for whoever was out there to find her. That made pain secondary to the need to escape. To survive.

Looking up, she saw the trees towering above her, their branches lifted to an unseen sky. Only minimal light managed to filter through the dense canopy. That was a good thing. The trees would make it difficult for whoever was after her to track her from above and would force them down to the ground.

That would buy her some time. And she was strong, she reminded herself. Resilient. She took two quick, deep breaths, feeling them burn in her bruised chest, buried the pain deep enough, and got back to her feet.

Her abused muscles immediately made their objections known. She sympathized but overruled them. Biting down hard on her already bloodied lip, ignoring the pain that jolted through her every time her feet struck the ground, Darien began to move as fast as she could, running parallel to a stream flowing twenty feet below.

Adrenaline fueled her muscles and served as a temporary painkiller. She knew it wouldn't last, but for now, it allowed her to swiftly cover ground, barely aware of her surroundings. It wasn't easy. The terrain was dense, wet, and irregular, littered with fallen trees and moss-covered stumps. She knew one wrong step could bring it all crashing to an end. Just as she knew there was really very little choice.

She was running for her life.

Jessie opened the door and jumped out the back of the surveillance vehicle before Ben had brought the van to a complete stop. She stumbled and nearly fell but managed to stay on her feet. Once she was clear of the van, she quickly glanced up into the hazy sky, looking for the helicopter she could still hear somewhere in the vicinity. But the sound of the beating blades was growing more distant, and she knew it was moving away.

"Bloody hell," Ben shouted at her. "Are you trying to get yourself killed? I thought you were smarter than that."

Jessie ignored him, not really giving a damn what Ben thought. She needed to find Darien, and her only objective was to follow the skid marks she'd seen scored into the asphalt. Slowing only when she reached the edge of the road, she looked down and felt her heart stutter painfully as she tried to make sense out of what she was seeing.

For a long drawn-out moment, she simply stared down. Wanting to deny the evidence, willing to trade everything for a chance to change reality. "Oh God." The words escaped her as she stared, unblinking.

Thirty feet below her was what remained of Darien's motorcycle. The once gleaming Ducati was now a barely recognizable tangle of twisted and crushed metal resting haphazardly against a tree, one wheel bent and pointing toward the sky. Jessie felt her heart freeze in her chest and struggled to accept that the scene below was real as she scanned the nearby area. But try as she might, she could see no sign of Darien.

Please let her be okay.

She swallowed painfully and tried not to think of Darien lying somewhere nearby. Hurt...or dying...or...no, she refused to go there. But as she looked for Darien, she found herself simultaneously calculating the odds of Darien's survival and bracing herself for what she believed was inevitable.

Daylight barely penetrated the forest canopy, but as her eyes became accustomed to the interplay of shadows and gloom, she began picking up minute details. Bent branches and other signs where Darien's body had disturbed the ground as she'd hurtled from the road toward the bottom of the ravine.

Conscious of Ben and Elle following close behind, Jessie began her own descent, scrambling precariously, her boots sinking and slipping on the soft wet earth that made up the steep incline. Mindful of the rough terrain, she followed the broken trail Darien's impromptu slide had left behind, coming to a stop near the bottom when she saw where Darien's fall had ended.

The imprint of her body was still visible in the mud and flattened vegetation, and for an instant Jessie swore she could smell sandalwood, Darien's distinctive scent. It was her imagination, of course, but it propelled her into action.

She quickly searched the surrounding area, expecting to find her battered and broken. But in the gray muted light, the only thing her eyes picked up was Darien's badly dented helmet, with traces of blood visible on the shattered visor.

"At least she's still mobile," Ben said, echoing the thoughts running through Jessie's mind as he stepped up beside her.

"But she's hurt," Elle added quietly, staring at the blood on the helmet. She glanced at Jessie with a measure of sympathy on her face.

Jessie nodded. *Damn it, Darien. Where are you?*

She pushed back unwelcome images and knelt where Darien's body had most recently been. Trying to see what she might have seen. Trying to concentrate on picking up any signs she'd left behind.

"Whoa. Hold on," Elle said suddenly. "I've got something."

"What?"

"We're no longer being jammed. The terrain's causing a bit of interference, but I'm picking up Darien's signal." Elle studied the electronic device she was holding in one hand before pointing with the other. "She's moving, somewhere in that direction."

Jessie jumped to her feet, looking in the direction Elle had indicated. Her vision narrowed and almost immediately she picked up the trail Darien had created through the uneven terrain. Not stopping to think, she set off at a rapid pace, leaving Ben and Elle to follow in her wake.

❖

Ignoring the branches that slapped at her as she ran past, Darien scampered over gnarled roots and rocks, going down hard on a couple of occasions, adding bruises and losing precious time. Shaking, she got up and kept moving, ducking under low branches. Expecting any second would be her last.

A few minutes later, she was forced to stop. After the last fall, she'd gotten turned around and she was no longer certain what direction she was going in. Was she still moving away from her pursuers or toward them? Her shoulders sagged, and she tried to remain still but could do nothing about the rapid rise and fall of her chest.

She tried to listen for any sounds that would indicate she was being followed. But the woods had settled into an eerie silence, and the only sound she could hear was her own heartbeat—faster and harder than she would have liked. She swore softly and tried to make as little noise as possible.

She was becoming increasingly light-headed. Loss of blood, she thought dispassionately, aware that the damage to her arm was bleeding steadily. Another concussion coming on the heels of the last one was also a possibility, as another wave of dizziness threatened to bring her down.

But every fiber in her body told her she'd be killed if she stayed where she was. Inhaling as deeply as she dared, she pushed off and started moving once again. Zigzagging and using trees and shadows as cover.

She was just starting to think she might actually make it when someone reached out and grabbed her, dropping her hard to the ground. She could feel stones digging into her back as she fought to breathe past the bare hand covering her mouth.

Whoever had her was in for a surprise. She wasn't going to be taken out without a fight. If she was going to die today, she wasn't doing it lying on the ground. And she had no intention of dying today.

She struggled violently to dislodge the body on top of her and kicked out hard. She heard a grunt followed by a muttered curse and then, "Stop. Damn it, Darien, stop fighting. It's me."

Darien froze. Her vision cleared and she saw Jessie Coltrane's beautiful features inches from her own. With her gaze absorbing her face, she blinked, as if Jessie might not be real. But she was still there when Darien opened her eyes once again.

Reassurance flooded through her. Her adrenaline rush calmed and she stopped struggling, sending Jessie a faint smile as she released a soft breath. She waited, felt Jessie shift as she settled next to her on the ground. And in that moment, she knew she would live to see another day.

"Don't move," Jessie mouthed.

"Not moving," Darien mumbled in response and kept still. Not that she had a lot of choice. Dizziness swept over her and she braced against the surge of nausea she knew would follow in its wake.

Settling back, she closed her eyes.

❖

"Darien?"

There was no answer. Deathly pale, damp hair clinging to her face, Darien lay completely still on the ground, and in the darkest part of her very existence, Jessie suddenly feared she was dead.

Ah, hell. Don't do this. She'd been alive and ready to kick her ass only seconds before. She couldn't just—

But as adrenaline flooded her senses and her vision narrowed, Jessie stared at the blood matting Darien's hair and the streak staining her face. She reached for Darien's hand. Found it cold as ice, lifeless, and she couldn't feel a pulse when she placed her fingers on her inner wrist. Couldn't feel anything.

God, no. Darien was so still Jessie couldn't tell if she was breathing, and as she moved her hand slowly toward her neck, she realized she was afraid to touch her. Afraid that when she pressed her fingers against her pale, smooth throat, she would find no pulse. There would simply be nothing and Darien would be gone.

Praying she was wrong, she quashed the rising sense of panic and forced herself to focus on the task at hand. Forced herself to act as she slipped one arm around Darien's shoulders. She felt her head fall listlessly over her arm while her fingers hovered. Swallowing, she reached for her throat and searched for a pulse.

An instant later she breathed a sigh of profound relief. She could feel Darien's pulse, beating strong and steady beneath her shaking fingers.

With her eyes not straying from Darien's face, she spoke quickly into her PRR. "This is Tango two. I've got her."

Almost immediately, she heard Ben's voice. "Is she okay?"

"I—I don't know. She's not responding." She couldn't find any more words. But that was okay. What she'd said was enough and she could hear the others drawing near.

Shifting and settling Darien's limp body against her own, she gently called to her. "Darien? Come on, Dare, open your eyes and look at me. Quit scaring me."

Nothing.

As she waited for some kind of response, Jessie leaned closer, her eyes fixed on Darien's face. Looking for a sign. Anything. She knew it was the excess adrenaline coursing through her own body that was making her shake and her voice sound rough—it sounded almost like a stranger's—but she kept talking to Darien. Holding her. Encouraging her. Willing her to come back. Never looking away from her face

It probably took less than a minute. She wasn't sure. Slowly Darien roused and Jessie felt a wave of relief. Darien's breathing was still shallow and her gaze was unfocused, her eyes clouded and hazy beneath a layer of long, thick black lashes. But when recognition followed, Jessie knew she had never seen anything more beautiful in her life.

"Welcome back," she said and released the remnants of panic. "You're going to be all right. But, Jesus, don't ever scare me like that again."

Darien looked up, blinked, and licked her lips. "Sorry. Bad time to take a nap, but it's been that kind of day. Who knew motorcycling was a full-contact sport." Her voice caught but the corners of her mouth twitched weakly before she released a soft groan and closed her eyes.

Jessie couldn't help but smile as she watched her. Bone, muscle, skin. Alive.

"Jesslyn?"

"Yes?"

"I think Petrov tried to kill me."

Her voice was slurred. Jessie frowned and stared once again at the blood trickling down her forehead. Her concern deepened as she remembered the dented motorcycle helmet and worried about another head injury.

"And it looks like she came pretty close to succeeding." She gently wiped the blood on Darien's face with her shirt sleeve. "We were about to call you in when the helicopter showed up. I tried to warn you, but we weren't sure whether you heard anything before they jammed us. After that we couldn't raise you."

"I heard you…at least I remember hearing something. I'm pretty sure I heard you telling me to head south."

"I did." Jessie offered a smile. "And I'll be eternally grateful to whoever trained you to respond without question."

Darien laughed, the sound reassuring Jessie more than anything else had up to that moment. "Then you can thank Ben. Any idea what happened with Petrov? I seem to have lost track of where she went… or what direction I was going in."

"I understand falling off a motorcycle will do that. For now, all I can tell you is her helicopter has left the area, and they didn't get a chance to put anyone on the ground. We've got team two picking up what's left of your motorcycle, and then they'll sanitize the area. In the meantime, we need to get you out of here and get you checked out."

"That sounds good to me. But please, Jesslyn, promise me—no hospital. I hate hospitals."

Jessie smiled as she heard the faintly pleading note. She reached for her hand and was about to respond when she caught herself staring at the blood seeping through a tear in Darien's jacket sleeve. "Your arm looks like it's bleeding pretty badly."

Darien nodded and winced, hissing in obvious pain. "I got tagged a couple of times just before I went down. It's not bad, I don't think, although it stings like the devil." She swallowed and her hand tightened briefly around Jessie's fingers. "Honestly, I'm all right. Do you think we can get out of here now?"

But Jessie wasn't about to be put off. "You got shot? What do you mean a couple of times? Where else, Darien?" she asked. "Where else did you get hit? Where else do you hurt?"

"My chest. At least they missed my head…but they caught me almost dead center. It knocked the breath out of me, that's all. If it wasn't for the titanium in the vest…" She closed her eyes, took a hitching breath and tried to straighten up.

"If you hadn't been wearing the vest, you'd be dead." Jessie felt her chest vibrate with rage.

"I know—oh, damn."

"What's wrong?"

"It's nothing. It just hurts. Everything hurts. I'd really like to get out of here. Please, can we just do that?"

The soft pain-filled voice nearly broke her, but it was also what got through. "Shit. I'm sorry. Ben says there's a safe house somewhere near here, but that means you're going to need to move so we can get you out of here, and it's probably going to hurt like hell."

A quick nod of her head was almost all Darien seemed capable of managing. "I already hurt like hell, so I don't think it'll make much difference. Trust me, if it gets me out of here, I can do it."

"Are you certain?"

When she nodded again, Jessie reached out and grasped her chilled, unsteady hand tighter. "All right. Focus on me, take a breath, then let it out really slow," she said and eased Darien up as she exhaled. She was aware Ben and Elle were standing nearby and had been following the conversation, but her eyes never left Darien's face.

Darien was clearly determined to tough it out and her expression never changed. But by the time she was on her feet she looked decidedly paler.

Ben seemed unusually quiet as he watched their progress before expressing his concern. "Are you going to be okay to walk," he asked, "or should I have someone go get a litter?"

The comment earned him a scowl. "Ben Takahashi, the day I need to be carried out—" Darien never finished. Her knees gave way and she started to go down, with only enough time to whisper, "Oh, shit."

Jessie and Ben caught her and held on before she hit the ground.

CHAPTER NINETEEN

Outside the eighteenth-century timber-framed farmhouse, the air remained cool even as the sun struggled to break through a cloud-filled sky. The weak sunlight was bright enough to fill the second-floor bedroom, filtered only by the sheer white curtains. It was also warm enough for Jessie to feel its heat as she stood by the window, gazing at a panoramic view of verdant meadows and valleys surrounded by forest.

The safe house was set back from the main road and was all but invisible behind a thick wall of spruce, fir, and pine trees that stood guard on either side of an unremarkable wooden gate. The gate itself looked as if it hadn't been used in years, but it had opened smoothly upon their arrival and was connected electronically to the extensive security system protecting the property.

Beyond the trees, the house was surrounded by a gently rolling field. Not all that different from the neighboring farms, except for the small circular asphalt landing pad located behind the house. It was currently occupied by the sleek Agusta helicopter that had brought the doctor Ben had called—a retired British intelligence officer with a shock of white hair and sharp blue eyes.

Moving restlessly away from the window, Jessie sank onto the wing chair Ben had positioned near the side of the bed and leaned back. It provided her with an unobstructed view of Darien, sitting on top of the bed wearing only a snug-fitting tank top and silk boxers. Ordinarily, that might be an enjoyable sight. But at the moment, all she saw was a woman who looked much too pale. Pushed beyond fatigue and into exhaustion. Vulnerable. And all too human.

Darien needed food and probably wanted a bath, or at least a shower. She had pushed her hair back behind her ears, and it framed a face that was marred with scratches and still held traces of dried mud and blood. There was a nasty bruise and a scrape on her forehead still seeping blood. She was holding her right arm gingerly against her chest, and Jessie could see the temporary bandage they'd wrapped around her forearm was soaked through with blood.

But the line of her jaw was rigid and the hard set of her mouth dared anyone to challenge her. She was clearly not happy, a point emphasized by the single word she hissed as she narrowed her eyes against the light being shined into them by the doctor. The word had been uttered in a language Jessie didn't know, but she didn't have to understand it to recognize its meaning.

The doctor gave no indication he'd either heard or understood, and Jessie caught herself staring when he lifted Darien's T-shirt. She'd never considered herself squeamish, but the bruises covering Darien's chest had her throat tightening, and she momentarily looked away.

Denial came hot and hard and fast, pounding in Jessie's blood. It had been close. Too damn close. If the shot had been just a little higher, it would have caught her vulnerable throat where no Kevlar provided protection. That's what had made the difference between having Darien here, glassy eyed but gamely glaring at the doctor and—

Her stomach roiled at the thought and she sat still for a long moment, trying to banish the unwelcome images from her mind. And when that didn't work, she found herself wondering if this was what Dorothy had felt like just before she was pulled into the tornado.

While the doctor frowned, poked, and prodded, muttering things only his patient could hear and respond to, the wait felt interminable and the tension in the room vibrated. But after checking Darien out thoroughly, he looked up and stated he could see nothing to cause undue alarm. Nothing life threatening.

"I can guarantee she'll be sore for a few days," he said. "But I didn't feel any cracked ribs and I can't see anything to prevent a full recovery, as long as she doesn't do anything else to put herself in harm's way."

Darien looked up at that moment, and for an instant Jessie thought she read uncertainty mixed with the pain evident in her eyes.

But before she could be sure, the doctor stepped into her line of sight, and by the time he moved, Darien's expression was carefully blank once again, her eyes clearly trying to focus on the doctor.

❖

"Can you tell me your name?"

"Darien Arianna Troy."

"Well, Ms. Troy, my name is Aaron Price. I'm a doctor and your friend Ben here has asked me to take a look at you, to see what damage you've managed to do to yourself."

"Darien." Her voice was barely above a whisper and she paused to clear her throat. "Please call me Darien."

"All right. Darien, do you know where you are?"

"Not exactly, no. I'm guessing it's a safe house and that I'm still somewhere in Germany." Although unhappy that her voice sounded raspy and weak, Darien took a small measure of satisfaction that she could manage a coherent response.

"Do you remember how you got here?"

She paused and realized she had no immediate answer for that one. She felt bone tired. *All that running for your life will do it.* But as she tried to remember more, she found herself slamming into a thick wall, her thoughts foggy and colliding. Flickering like an old movie.

She could remember standing on the side of the road, teasing Jessie over the communications link about local folklore while waiting for Nadia Petrov to arrive. She remembered the helicopter arriving, sending a deadly hail of bullets raining down on her, and the blinding flash of pain when she was hit. She could remember flying off her bike and tumbling down the slope toward the sound of running water, before running for her life.

But then—nothing. At least nothing tangible. No matter how hard she tried.

Giving up, she shook her head, licked her lips, and watched with mild interest while the doctor—Price—held her wrist and checked her pulse. She could have told him he would find it to be a little faster than normal, but he didn't ask, and she saw no reason to volunteer the information. He didn't seem to mind as he continued checking her vital signs.

"Your temperature's up a bit and your pressure's a little low. But it's nothing we can't handle," he said. "Now I want you to follow my finger."

Her lips twitched. "Why? Is it going somewhere?"

"You must be feeling all right if you're up to giving me sass, young lady." But he sounded pleased and he was smiling as he held his finger up and waited for her eyes to follow while he moved it. Behind him, she thought she heard both Jessie and Ben laugh.

As she finished doing what the doctor asked, she told him of her recent concussion. She watched his smile fade, but he refrained from making any comment. A moment later, he cocked his head and looked at her. "This next bit's going to be more difficult for you, Darien."

"Oh? How so?"

"I need to remove the bandages on your arm so I can assess the damage, and it's most likely going to hurt. So if it's okay with you, I'd like to give you a shot of something. I can't give you too much with that head injury, but I can at least try to take the edge off before I proceed. Any known allergies?"

Darien exhaled and shook her head. "No allergies, but let's keep it to a local."

Price looked at her with questions and skepticism in his eyes, and she felt forced to explain. "I'm not a fan of pain, Dr. Price. But I've had some experience with narcotics and I hate how they make me feel even more."

There was a tense, silent moment before he shrugged. "All right." He pulled on a pair of latex gloves and began the task of removing bandages and methodically cleaning and stitching, trying to put her back together.

Just like Humpty bloody Dumpty.

Beyond clenching her left fist and an initial painful intake of breath, Darien didn't make another sound as Price cut through the bloodied field dressings covering the bullet wound. She gritted her teeth and gathered her resolve around her like a cloak, ignoring the pain radiating up her arm and the persistent pounding in her head.

Once she had successfully distanced herself from the pain, she looked down and watched Price make progress on her arm. With the bandage removed, she could see now where the bullet had entered her right arm at a shallow angle just above her wrist and continued for several inches. *No wonder it hurts.*

She watched him inject something that stung ridiculously but then numbed the area, providing an incredible measure of relief while he cleaned debris out of the wound. He then began making a neat row of tiny stitches. "This will probably scar, which is too bad because it's a nice arm. But it should fade given time. Or you can see a plastic surgeon once you get home."

Darien bowed her head tiredly. "I'm not worried," she said. "It's certainly not the first scar I've gotten and I somehow doubt it will be the last."

Price nodded and continued working on her arm. Once he was finished, she obliged him by lying down and raising her chin a notch. But she couldn't prevent a wince and closed her eyes when he probed the contusion on her forehead before adding several more stitches to a cut just below her hairline.

When she opened her eyes again, she watched warily while he put a brace over the fresh bandages on her forearm and slipped a cotton sling around her neck. She met his gaze and expelled a long breath but didn't say anything.

"It's meant to stop you from doing any further damage to yourself," Price said in response to her unasked question. "Not that I hold much hope in that regard."

Darien knew he was right. If stopping Petrov meant she needed to act, she would block out the pain, disregard any personal risk, and do whatever had to be done. But for now she was beyond thinking, beyond caring. The past twenty-four hours had yielded little sleep and an excess of adrenaline. And she knew the adrenaline that had been insulating her was no longer working, just as the combination of pain and lack of sleep had her eyes gritty and burning.

She bit her lip and struggled to remain alert. Noted that her hands had begun to shake. She took an extra moment, inhaled a slow measured breath, and tried to sit upright, but only managed to prop herself up on her elbows before she was forced to abandon her effort. The failure left her feeling even more bruised, and agonizingly vulnerable.

She was aware that Price was maintaining a watchful eye on her and had remained where he stood by the bed. He reached for her wrist and checked her pulse one more time, then started calmly responding to Ben, who had somehow held his questions in check until that moment.

Darien tried to concentrate and listened to Price explain his primary concern—the combination of a mild head injury on top of a recent concussion.

"Two recent concussions," Ben corrected.

"Two?" Price all but glared at her, but she refused to look away. She could feel his displeasure and could hear the mild reprimand in his voice. Their gazes held a moment longer, but any scathing lecture he might have delivered was forestalled when Jessie placed a gently restraining hand on his arm.

Distracted, he glanced at Jessie before turning back to her. By then, Darien knew the moment had passed. Nodding to himself, Price cleared his throat and explained the head injury would likely result in some blurred vision, headaches, and possibly some dizziness. But none of it was exactly news to her—she'd been experiencing all the symptoms he was describing since regaining consciousness after crashing her bike.

"Maybe we can blame her not telling you about the second concussion on the fact her brain's a little scrambled," Ben said with a smile. "What about her other injuries? How long before she's able to be back on the job?"

"Darien's lost a fair bit of blood, but I'm guessing no matter what I suggest, she'll be back on the job sooner than she should be," Price responded dryly.

Darien choked back a laugh then clutched her side and groaned.

Jessie immediately leaned closer, reaching for her hand. "What's wrong, Darien?"

Aware of the comforting heat of Jessie's touch, Darien allowed herself to be distracted by the circular motions of Jessie's thumb on the back of her hand. She closed her eyes, tried to clear her throat, and finally managed to say, "Nothing."

"Don't give me that. Tell me. What is it?"

"Don't let him make me laugh. It hurts too much."

It was Price's turn to laugh. "That's because of the bruises on her chest. Just maybe they're what will keep her still for a while."

The scowling words all but visible on the tip of Jessie's tongue were preempted by Ben. "Head injury. Bruises. What else?"

Aaron Price scratched his chin thoughtfully. "The bullet that struck her arm didn't break any bones, but I'd recommend she go for some physical therapy. The rest of her injuries are mostly cuts and bruises, and no more than one should expect after flying off a motorcycle."

"So she'll be okay?" Jessie asked.

"I'll give you a qualified yes," he said. "Her blood pressure's a little low, but she's strong and she'll be fine as long as she doesn't overdo it. Perhaps you'll have more luck convincing Darien that means allowing herself time to heal, keeping the stitches dry, getting enough rest, and letting her body get to a point where all the bruises are actually gone before she adds new ones."

"Good luck with that," Ben responded dryly. "You'll find she's damn near impossible to manage."

No one paid much attention to Darien's aggrieved sigh. But that was all right. At least the worst was over. Then again, maybe not. Before leaving, she watched the doctor draw a syringe. "What is that and is it really necessary?"

Price met her gaze. "Your biggest risks right now are shock and infection, so yes, it's necessary."

He didn't wait for her to agree as he lifted her T-shirt, slid her shorts down until he found bare skin, and injected Darien's hip over her muttered protest. He then pulled a thin blanket up to her shoulders, wrote down an emergency number where he could be reached, and handed it to Jessie.

"I'll leave some tablets for the pain, but because of the head injury, I'd rather she not take anything for a few hours, if she can handle it."

"Please don't bother. I've no interest in taking any painkillers," Darien murmured, but she wasn't certain anyone was paying attention. Wearily closing her eyes, she listened to the rise and fall of voices before they grew distant and faded. And as the shot began to take effect, she felt the throbbing in her arm and head slowly ebb.

CHAPTER TWENTY

The sun that had been struggling to break through the clouds had disappeared again as Jessie looked down from the window and watched Ben escort the doctor back to the waiting helicopter. All too aware that her nerves were starting to fray, she walked back toward the bed and regarded Darien. Her eyes remained closed, but there was tension visible in the stillness of her body, and as she searched her face, she knew Darien was still awake.

"Now that everyone else is gone, do you want to tell me how you're really feeling?"

A blink—just one blink—was the only immediate response she got as Darien opened her eyes. But if carefully controlled and cool detachment was what Darien was aiming for, the effect was spoiled by the pain evident in the lines of strain on her face and the stubborn lock of sweat-dampened hair falling across her forehead and into her eyes.

As the silence stretched between them, the temptation to brush the hair back from her forehead was so strong that Jessie actually lifted her hand to do so. Thankfully, she caught herself at the last instant, crossed her arms, and hugged her elbows tight. "I'll interpret your silence to mean you're hurting like hell."

Darien blinked again, but this time she met Jessie's gaze. "How is it you know me so well after such a short time," she mused, her words sounding soft and almost as bruised as her body.

"Lucky, I guess." Jessie smiled a little. "But just so we're clear, I have no intention of listening to the standard answer I believe you give for everything from a paper cut to multiple gunshot wounds."

Darien bit her lip and groaned. "Please don't make me laugh, Jesslyn. I'm begging you."

She considered Darien's words before opting for mercy. "All right. But you have to be honest and tell me how you're really feeling."

"You *really* won't let me tell you I'm fine, will you?"

Darien looked at her and sighed when she shook her head. "No. I want the truth, Darien, because what happened today was much too close. I need to believe you're okay."

"I *am* okay."

"You could have died."

"But I didn't die. I'm right here." As Jessie waited for her to say more, Darien blew out what sounded like an exasperated breath. "All right, how about if I admit I've been better? Would it help if I told you I feel like I've been run over? Not that I ever have, but I have a feeling this might be what it would feel like."

Jessie tried hard not to laugh. "That good?"

Darien gave a wry shrug and as she looked up a ghost of a smile touched her lips. "All things considered, I'm well aware I was lucky this morning. That it could have been worse. As it stands, it's only bruises and a few stitches, all of which will heal, and I'm not only alive, I'm pretty certain I'll survive to fight the good fight another day."

Darien's gaze on her face suddenly felt different—almost like a caress—and as Jessie listened to the soft cadence of Darien's voice, something in her mind focused, sharpened. She became keenly aware of the liquid heat that inexplicably ran through her veins every time Darien looked at her.

Except this wasn't all that inexplicable, was it? She suspected she knew exactly what it was. She could even pinpoint the moment things had changed. It had happened when she'd heard the sound of gunfire. When she'd feared for Darien's life.

She closed her eyes then opened them instantly. She didn't like the bleak vision that appeared, showing her just what could have happened. Shuddering, she raked a hand through her hair and pushed the image back into a dark corner of her mind. But pretending what happened hadn't changed anything was next to impossible, and she had to come to grips with an attraction she wished she wasn't feeling.

You are so screwed. She wasn't ready for this. Wrong place, wrong time. Certainly not when there was still a job to be done and a terrorist organization that not only needed to be located, it needed to be stopped. Fight the good fight indeed.

But denying or ignoring whatever was simmering between her and Darien simply wasn't working any longer. She leaned closer and took a deep breath.

She quickly discovered that was a mistake because she ended up inhaling the faint scent of sandalwood that had been teasing her senses. She also realized if Darien tilted her head up, she could easily kiss her mouth, and Jessie surprised herself by actually considering it. It took a long moment to rein in the impulse.

As the seconds ticked by, Jessie realized Darien had been silent for much too long. She needed to say something. Something amusing. Something blasé. But as she inched closer, still wanting to but not allowing herself to touch, a modicum of truth slipped from her lips before she could stop it. "It seems I need you to do more than survive, Darien."

Darien flashed a half smile that failed when the lines of strain bracketing her mouth grew more pronounced. Her expression became grave and watchful, and although it was obvious she was in pain, it was equally apparent she was determined to tough it out. At least her eyes were brighter than they'd been since she'd awakened in the safe house, the sharp intelligence clearly visible once again. "I'm sorry," Darien said. "It's not been one of my finer days. I didn't mean for that to sound quite so flippant."

"I know you didn't. But I'm serious. For at least the next week or so, I not only need you to survive, I also need you to not fly off motorcycles. Or cage fight. Or do anything else that will add to the damage you've already inflicted on yourself.

"I hear you." A grin—lightning quick and just as lethal—made a brief appearance. "But I'm afraid that's a promise I can't make."

"Why not?"

"Because it's not me you need to tell. You need to talk to Nadia Petrov."

Jessie stiffened. "What do you mean? Why Petrov?"

"Because unless I'm seriously mistaken, she set me up and tried to kill me earlier this morning."

"Well, I know that—"

"No, I mean she tried to kill *me,* Jesslyn. Not Ari." Her smoky gaze narrowed before her eyes slid closed. The silence stretched until she continued in a quiet voice. "If Petrov truly believed Ari was an arms dealer, this morning's meeting would have taken place. But it didn't. Instead, she tried to kill me, and with a little bit more luck or slightly better aim, we wouldn't be having this conversation."

❖

Darien licked her lips and tried to remember when the thought had first occurred to her, but everything was hurting too much and the answer wouldn't come. The only thing she knew for certain was that her words had rocked Jessie, and as they stared at each other, Darien was certain she could all but read her thoughts.

Was it possible? Did Petrov know who Ari really was? Did she know Darien was the woman who had killed her father and helped destroy his organization fifteen years earlier? And, if that was the case, how the hell had it happened?

She knew a lot of time and effort had gone into crafting her cover story. Creating Ari. If the legend had remained intact as it should have, Nadia Petrov would have gone ahead with the meeting that morning. Everything should have gone according to plan. She would have negotiated the purchase of the weapons, and they would have followed the weapons back to Petrov's lair, effectively terminating the threat, capturing everyone involved, and putting an end to the Guild once and for all.

That was how it was supposed to work. That was how it should have worked.

But instead of following a carefully scripted plan, the day had swiftly and decisively gone to hell. Her legend appeared to have been compromised from the start, their communications had been expertly jammed, and but for a bit of luck, she would have been killed. Now, the only thing that mattered was figuring out how to stay alive long enough to see things through.

She closed her eyes, aware for a moment only of how fiercely her head was pounding and how badly the stitches in her arm burned. But even as her thoughts began to spiral into free fall, she had to admit she appreciated the irony the situation presented.

The children of Arianna Troy and Dmitri Petrov going head to head all these years later.

The events from fifteen years earlier had bound them, and it was clear neither had managed to break completely free. Nor would they—not while there were loose ends. And there was no question. As tangled as it was, the skein that was their lives was continuing to unravel. There were loose ends everywhere.

"Your bike," Jessie said suddenly. "Yuri said Petrov wanted you to come alone on your motorcycle. That would seem to imply she had a certain level of knowledge. Personal knowledge. Is there any way she could she have traced you through the Ducati? Could it have helped her somehow find out who you really are?"

Darien shook her head. Wincing, she bit her lip and tried to sit up without much success. "The Ducati was set up for Ari as part of the legend from the time of purchase. Complete with all registration documents and its license plate."

"All right. What about Yuri?"

"Again, I'd have to say no. It's not that I haven't considered the possibility, but Yuri's only ever known me as Ari. And the first time we met goes back a long time. Almost ten years. I was working a covert operation, and the team arranged for me to get into a small fight club where Yuri was part owner."

"Ten years ago? Jesus, Dare, even I can do the math. Are you telling me you started cage fighting at eighteen?"

"Actually, I'd been fighting for more than a year by then, but I never fought anywhere Yuri would have either seen me or heard of me."

"How can you be certain?"

Darien would have laughed if she had the energy. "Because my earliest fights took place in Thailand. In some hardscrabble villages no one ever heard of, where I was gathering information on a British gun runner selling arms to the FARC. And trust me when I tell you, my own mother could have had front-row seats to any of those fights and wouldn't have recognized me."

As her determination to continue wavered, she felt the walls closing around her, pushing closer. She needed time to think. Maybe after her head stopped throbbing, and after the world stopped spinning, she'd be able to think.

She was grateful that Jessie's presence kept even darker thoughts at bay because the meeting with Petrov on the side of the Black Forest High Road had morphed from a simple covert operation into something much more sinister. It became a trap.

It became an execution.

❖

Darien's voice faltered and Jessie could see she was rapidly fading. It occurred to her that in what was really a short time since she'd met her, Darien managed to end up looking pale, bruised, and battered far too often for a kick-ass former MI6 operative. Possibly someone needed to remind her she wasn't indestructible, and Jessie had a feeling that responsibility had somehow fallen to her.

She sighed and felt a wave of anger wash over her, mixed with a surge of protectiveness that jolted her. How the hell had it happened? How had it all come apart?

Without thinking, she pushed Darien's hair out of her eyes allowing the shadows in the room to play across her face, highlighting all the intriguing planes and hollows. A dark angel, she thought. Just looking at her could literally stop her breath and make her want. It left her questioning how and when Darien had become so deeply embedded under her skin.

Leaning closer to the bed, she hesitated, then gave in to temptation and lowered her mouth until she was just a breath away.

Darien stared at her. "I don't think—"

"Good. Don't think."

The instant their lips met, Jessie almost pulled back. But as the spark inside her ignited her blood, she wondered how she could have forgotten what one kiss could do to her. She kept her hands on the bed, not touching Darien other than with her mouth. Softly. Gently. And then she ended it before it really got started, not giving Darien a chance to respond.

Licking her lips, she looked at her, watched Darien's eyes slowly open. She saw them darken and for the first time noticed the tiny black flecks in the sea of gray.

The silence vibrated as the seconds ticked by. "Why did you do that?" Darien asked.

"Because I wanted to. I'm sorry. Not for kissing you. I'm not sorry about that. I'm sorry because I know I'm probably confusing the hell out of you. Still, I think it's only fair, because I'm confusing the hell out of myself."

"As long as you're being fair," Darien murmured wryly.

Jessie's smile widened. "You know, I'm really starting to like you."

"That's good, isn't it?"

"Maybe—probably. Only problem is I also think you're seriously crazy."

Darien became silent and for a moment she clenched her jaw while her eyes seemed to grow smokier. Bad choice of words, a faux pas, Jessie decided. She watched shadows chase each other through Darien's eyes and correctly concluded she'd gone too far.

But before Jessie could try to take back the words, Darien responded with a softly spoken, "You're probably right."

"No, I'm sorry—I really didn't mean anything by my comment. I was only teasing."

"It's not a problem. I know you were teasing. You just happen to be right."

"So long as you know I don't think it's a bad thing."

"So you're saying it's good that I'm crazy?"

"No—yes."

Slowly, unexpectedly, Darien smiled. "Which is it?"

Trapped by the smile, Jessie stumbled. "Oh, hell, Darien. I don't know. Both, I guess." She stopped and looked closer. "And from the look of you, I'd say you're also done in. I should let you get some sleep for a while. We can talk after you've rested. Maybe we can even come up with a plan for how we're going to stop Petrov and the Guild from attacking the G8. Something that doesn't involve leaving you dangling like bait."

"Jesslyn, don't, okay?" Her smile was already gone. Now her hand tightened as her voice slowly faded as well. "I'm fine—or I will be, in short order. I'll have you know I have remarkable recuperative powers."

"I don't doubt that. It's probably the only reason you've survived this long."

"I've survived this long because I'm good at what I do."

"But you can't deny you were put in a totally vulnerable position today." Jessie sighed unhappily. "You were left alone on the side of the road with your support teams too far away to be of any real use other than to pick up the pieces after Petrov's attack. I've no idea what I was thinking when I agreed—I should have seen the inherent weaknesses in the plan."

"Let it go, Jesslyn." The expression in Darien's eyes matched the intensity in her voice. She gave her a tight smile and extended her hand, waiting until Jessie reached out with her own to grasp it. "I wasn't put in a vulnerable position—Ari was. And there was no other way to do it if this was going to work."

"Except that it didn't work, did it?"

"No, but it should have. It was a solid plan, it made sense, and I was the right choice. It's exactly for situations like this that Ari was created. It should have worked."

"It should have worked," Jessie agreed. "Now we need to figure out why it didn't and why you were nearly killed. You, Darien, not Ari." She looked away for a moment, chewed the inside of her cheek before turning back to meet Darien's eyes. "We have to figure out how the plan went off the rails so badly and what we're going to do next. Because the more I think about it, the more I think your earlier assessment is correct."

"What assessment is that?"

"I think you were compromised. I think Nadia Petrov knew exactly who was standing on the side of the road. I think she knew exactly who she was trying to kill. And I think as soon as she realizes she failed in her attempt, she's going to try again."

❖

A short while later, a noise at the bedroom door had Jessie automatically reaching for Darien's SIG Sauer on the night table. She aimed it steadily as the door opened. Ben and Nicola Spencer stood in the doorway, frozen, the silence deafening until she lowered the weapon and laid it back on the table.

"Your mother and I have been friends for a very long time," Ben said. "You might be her favorite daughter, but I doubt she'd be too forgiving if you shoot me."

"I'm her only daughter," Jessie responded dryly. "But you're probably right. Sorry."

Crossing the room, Ben approached the bed, his expression softening as he looked down. "No problem. We just wanted to check on our girl and see if she was finally sleeping."

"She is, and I'm hoping she actually stays that way for a couple of hours." Jessie glanced at Darien, saw her stir restlessly, but for the moment she didn't open her eyes. "Are you sure—"

"We have the doctor's assurance that she'll be fine." Normally taciturn, Ben squeezed her arm, surprising Jessie with the gesture. "She just needs time to rest and to recuperate. As soon as the helicopter returns, I've arranged to have it bring us back to Paris. Darien will recover more easily at home."

"And then?"

Ben shrugged. "And then everyone—including Darien—continues to do whatever needs to be done to neutralize Petrov and the Guild. We have just over a month before the start of the summit. That doesn't leave a lot of time."

Ben paused, and as he turned to face her, Jessie thought she detected something else in his normally stoic face. Concern? She studied him a moment longer, trying to read whatever was troubling him before giving up. "What is it, Ben? Has something else happened?"

"Not exactly. But Nicola and I have been discussing how things turned out this morning. Too many things don't quite fit, and it started us thinking that Darien might just be an integral part of Petrov's plans. In fact, we believe—"

"You believe Nadia Petrov knew who was standing on the side of the Black Forest High Road this morning." Jessie sighed. "I guess that makes it unanimous, then, because Darien and I talked about that very possibility earlier. She believes Petrov knew exactly what she was doing and who she was going after, and I'm finding it harder and harder to disagree."

"That's why everyone here will be heading to Paris instead of London."

Uncertain what she was hearing, Jessie turned her head and quietly studied the redheaded British agent. "Oh? Why is that?"

"To cover Darien's back," Nicola responded with a shrug, but her lips twitched with a smile. "I can't speak for the others, but I got to know Dare when she was still with British intelligence. She saved my life once in Kuwait, another time in Jakarta. I returned the favor in Benghazi, so in my books I still owe her one. Not that she's counting."

"I'm guessing she wouldn't," Jessie said.

"It's one of the things I appreciate about Darien—her seemingly innate ability to be in the right place at the right time. That, along with her marksmanship, her right cross, and her to-die-for skills in the kitchen."

Jessie laughed. "It sounds as though you like her."

"I do. But more than that, I respect her. Admire her. Worry about her. Maybe you should know I was there when Ben first brought Darien back to London when she was a kid. And I've a pretty good idea what she went through." Nicola stopped herself as if maybe she'd said more than she wanted to. "I just want to make sure Petrov doesn't hurt her...or worse."

"Then it seems we want the same thing."

There was a moment's pause—a few seconds, no more—during which Nicola looked at Jessie. "You remind me a lot of your mother."

Jessie tried not to roll her eyes. "I'm starting to think my mother has worked with everyone."

Nicola chuckled. "The Grace I know likes rules, order. I'm guessing you do too. Darien, on the other hand, has never met a rule she didn't eventually break. It's probably why MI6 didn't work out for her."

"Your point?"

"My point? There are always operatives such as myself willing to help Darien when she needs intel, an extra pair of eyes or, on rare occasions, someone to watch her back. But she doesn't let anyone get too close." Silence ran for several beats and Jessie's frown deepened, but Nicola didn't flinch, simply met her gaze as she continued softly. "It appears she's let you in further than she's ever let anyone."

Jessie kept her face carefully expressionless. "Is that what you think?"

"Yes." Nicola smiled thinly. "But it won't make a difference because Darien isn't about to let anything stop her from doing whatever she thinks needs to be done. And she won't like thinking Petrov outsmarted her."

Ben shrugged, clearly agreeing with Nicola's assessment. "It's part of what makes her good."

"What are you trying to tell me?" Jessie asked.

"Expect crazy."

CHAPTER TWENTY-ONE

The trip back to Paris was uneventful, and for the next two weeks, life fell into a routine for Jessie. Her days were filled combing through satellite images and CIA and NSA intercepts. Searching through feeds, filtering and translating information, while others pounded the streets working assets and following up on every available piece of intel.

Different approaches but centered on one goal. Finding Nadia Petrov.

Jessie sighed tiredly, only too aware that with each passing day, the clock ticked inexorably toward the third week of July. Everyone knew where Petrov would be at that time. But in spite of their collective efforts, they were no closer to determining how she planned to get there or where she might be now. She was a ghost.

Their one potential lead—the helicopter used to carry out the attack on Darien—led nowhere. They had been able to track the chopper, only to discover it had been stolen from a heliport in Frankfurt then scuttled immediately after the attack.

After the discovery of the burned-out helicopter shell, Darien stopped making appearances during the daily team progress reports. But each morning, there was always evidence she'd been working late in the night.

It was there in the notes left on the neatly stacked building schematics, architectural drawings, satellite images, and photographs of Cabot Island and the Maine coastline that Darien continued to study. Providing an assassin's perspective.

Funny, that didn't bother Jessie as much as it once had.

But the hours Darien was dedicating at night made Jessie wonder when she possibly found time to sleep. During the day, she knew Darien routinely spent time working out at a nearby gym, focused on recovering from her injuries. She also ran endlessly, determined to rebuild her already indefatigable stamina. On some occasions, when she ran in the early morning, Jessie would run with her. But, more often than not, she ran after dark and it was Zoey or Nicola who kept her company.

Which was just as well.

She still didn't know what the hell had possessed her to kiss Darien like she had that morning in the safe house. But that simple kiss now haunted her, disturbed her sleep, and pulled her attention away from the data she was supposed to be concentrating on.

Darien, on the other hand, seemed singularly unperturbed.

Not that she was totally indifferent. On several occasions, Jessie had been aware of Darien's watchful eyes and her dark, assessing gaze. But Darien had made no attempt to engage her as she had previously in the hotel, or reprise their first kiss in the kitchen. And so the kiss in the safe house remained a ghost. An apparition that was seemingly haunting only her.

Releasing a soft sigh, she pushed away from the computer console, her eyes burning from reading screen after screen of intercepted transmissions.

"Taking a break?"

She turned to find Elle watching her from the doorway. "I'm not getting anywhere, so it seems as good a time as any. Why? Do you need help with something?"

"No, I just think you're looking too damn pale."

Jessie chuckled. "These monitors may give off light, but I doubt I'll be picking up a tan anytime soon."

Elle shook her head as she took the seat Jessie had just vacated and pulled the keyboard closer. "Not the kind of fix I was thinking of for you. I was thinking you should wander down to the gym and find Darien. I've a feeling that woman could put some color back in your face in no time."

"I thought she scared you."

"Just because I'm afraid of the woman doesn't mean I can't fantasize."

Jessie laughed again. She didn't say anything more for fear she'd reveal too much. But as she headed downstairs, the thought of visiting the gym suddenly sounded appealing. She could work out some of her frustration—sexual or otherwise. After that, maybe she could sit in the steam room for a while. Relax, then come back and grab a quick bite to eat before settling down in front of the computer for a little bit longer.

Making a U-turn on the stairs, she went in search of some workout clothes, a frisson of anticipation trickling through her. Thirty minutes later, she walked into the gym Darien frequented and looked around.

The main room was massive and filled with plenty of well-maintained equipment—free weights, cycles, cardio, Pilates, and strength-training machines—while a running track circled the perimeter of the room. And though the gym was clearly popular and she was dressed to blend in, Darien was easy to spot.

With her face serious, her hands taped, and her hair pulled up into a ponytail, she was quietly working a speed bag. Left, right, left, right, maintaining a smooth rhythm. She was clearly inwardly focused, intent on rebuilding her strength and speed in light of the injury to her right arm, and appeared oblivious to a group of young men working out nearby, gamely pretending not to notice her.

Except that they were preening rather than paying attention to form, trying to keep an eye on her, and seemingly having difficulty accepting the fact she was ignoring them. They couldn't possibly be regulars, Jessie thought, and tried hard not to laugh. Otherwise they would know Darien was there to work out, not to hook up with a stud for a one-night stand…even if that had been where her interests lay.

Not that Jessie blamed them. She took a minute to admire Darien's long, lean frame. What the woman did to a pair of black running shorts and a muscle shirt was sinful. Kick-ass gorgeous. Her T-shirt was cropped, exposing a few inches of well-defined abs and a flat stomach that made Jessie want to drop to her knees and press her lips across that smooth expanse.

Her heart pounding, Jessie forced herself to look away, certain Darien knew she was there even though there'd been no eye contact. She tried to concentrate on what she was doing and began working through a set of stretches before heading for the running track to begin her own workout. She quickly slipped into the zone.

She was just starting her second kilometer when she felt someone approach her from behind then fall in line alongside. She glanced over, but she really didn't have to. She knew it was Darien, having already picked up the faint scent of the sandalwood soap she favored. Having already felt her heat.

When Darien acknowledged her with a brief nod, Jessie couldn't help but tease, "I see you managed to lose your entourage. Did you wear them out?"

Darien's response was succinct. And while it wasn't in English, at least this time it was in a language Jessie had no trouble understanding—both the words and the sentiment. She laughed and opted to make up for the teasing comment by allowing Darien to set the pace.

Thankfully, Darien settled on an easy, comfortable stride, something that wasn't especially fast, but would nonetheless eat up any distance. Even so, by the time Darien finally reduced their pace to a slow jog, sweat had beaded along Jessie's hairline, and she was feeling the stretch and pull in her muscles.

They finished their cool-down lap near a bench by the first turn on the track, where Jessie had left her gym bag. Picking up the bag, Darien indicated with a nod of her head. "Interested in the steam room?"

The image of unwinding in a dark steamy room with Darien beside her wrapped in only a towel flashed in Jessie's mind. Swallowing past the heat the image generated, she folded her arms across her chest. She felt herself go damp, but she suppressed the urges threatening to overwhelm her and forced herself to smile with determined brightness.

"Um—sure." She'd lost her mind. There was no other explanation.

As it turned out, they spent only fifteen minutes in the steam room, but it felt much longer and she was grateful when they finally headed for the showers. But even the cool water temperature didn't help her regain her equilibrium or control over emotions that had suddenly roared to life within her. She had foolishly thought she had managed to keep them at bay, but now they threatened to erupt like a volcano.

Turning her head, she watched Darien finish dressing. Saw her strap her ankle holster on and slip into her leather jacket. Why did she find that sexy as hell?

She had no answer. Nor did she have an answer for why, a moment later, she locked the door to the locker room while simultaneously reaching for Darien. Her previously dormant inner bad girl wanted to come out and play.

There was no prelude. No coaxing. No soft whispered words. Instead she placed one hand on Darien's chest, backed her up against the now-locked door, and slipped one hand around her neck to draw her closer.

And then she kissed her hungrily.

❖

For a moment, Darien was too stunned to react.

But her body had no such problems. Her pulse rate accelerated and her blood pressure spiked as Jessie's mouth began to skim over hers. It sent a wave shimmering over her skin that almost instantly transformed from warmth to burning heat, pervasive and persuasive. And as the heat seeped into her blood, it called to something deep inside her.

Slowly she began to respond, tracing Jessie's mouth with the tip of her tongue in sensual intimacy before she pulled Jessie's bottom lip between her teeth. She heard the sharp catch and release of Jessie's breath, drank in her sigh, and felt her shudder as Darien traced the sides of Jessie's neck and grazed along her jaw before sliding her fingers through soft blond hair, still damp from her shower.

She drew her closer, deepening the contact as they continued to kiss. Long enough to get lost in the wonder of it and for a breathless moment, she gave herself to the heat. The need. The desire.

Tongues touched. Probed. Savored. Jessie tasted of passion and hunger. The contact left Darien dizzy and made her want more.

Steeped in the feel and taste and scent of Jessie, she didn't know how long it was before the low murmur of voices outside the locker room finally broke them apart. They stared at each other for another endless moment before Darien lowered her head until their foreheads touched.

Inhaling the light scent of Jessie's shampoo and soap and the subtle essence of woman, she tried to catch her breath, to slow her heart rate, to form a coherent thought. She should have been better prepared for this, she mused, feeling the exquisite pressure that built inside as she watched Jessie's eyes flutter open, faintly dazed.

She'd known from the start that Jessie elicited strange and conflicting emotions from her—part urge to devour and part wish to go gently and slowly, to savor. And she'd known Jessie had begun looking at her differently since Germany, with what she could only interpret as increasing interest…and possibly longing.

She just wasn't certain what it all meant. Where it might lead. The only certainty was that Jessie somehow touched all the dark, lonely places inside her.

"What are we doing, Jesslyn?" she asked softly. "I thought you didn't want this."

"I did say that, didn't I," Jessie whispered back.

"Yes, you did." Without giving it a second thought, she slid her hand down Jessie's arm. Grasping her hand, she brought it to her mouth and kissed her knuckles, then turned her hand over and kissed her inner wrist.

"Stop that," Jessie said, but there was no heat in her words. "I can't think when you do that and I'm trying to be serious."

Darien smiled. "All right. What are you trying to tell me?"

"I think I'm trying to tell you I'm sorry. I know I've been sending you mixed messages, and if you let me, I want to fix that."

Darien raised an eyebrow. "Really? How do you propose to do that?"

"I plan on being completely straightforward." Jessie's smile slowly faded and the expression on her face became a match for the intensity in her voice. "I don't want there to be any misunderstandings. Nor do I want you to have any doubts about what it is I want."

"All right. And what is it you want?"

"I want—I've wanted to do that…to kiss you…again…for some time now. Definitely since the safe house in Germany. And I want a chance to do more than just kiss you because in spite of all the missteps we've taken so far, I think I've wanted you since the first time I saw you. And nothing that's happened since then has changed my mind."

As she listened to the telling silence, Darien breathed a deep sigh of understanding and acceptance. "All right. So long as you're sure this is what you want."

Jessie nodded. "I am," she said and leaned in for another kiss.

Darien closed her eyes and licked her lips. "There's a small hotel…it's about two blocks from here—"

"Why a hotel? Why not your house?"

"If we go there, all the people working at the house—Ben and Nicola, Elle and the others—it won't take long for them to intuit what's going on."

"Does that bother you?"

Darien shook her head. "It's been a long time since I've cared what others think of me. But I thought you might—"

Jessie stopped her by pressing three fingers against her lips. Shivered when Darien took the opportunity to draw them into her mouth.

"I've been out since I was fifteen, if that's what's worrying you," Jessie said, her voice slightly breathless. "Elle certainly knows, and since Ben's such a good friend of my mother's, the odds are he knows as well—probably has for years. But that's beside the point because the truth is I don't give a damn what anyone else thinks either. If anything, I believe they'll admire my taste in women."

Darien nipped one of the fingers that had been pressed to her mouth. "I don't know about your good taste, but you certainly taste good."

"That's really bad." Jessie choked back a laugh. "Look, I want you, I'm pretty damned certain you want me, and I want us in your bed. So unless you're hiding a husband, a wife, or a dozen lovers nearby, there's nothing else to discuss."

Darien grinned. "No husbands. No wives. No legions of lovers."

Even if she had been so inclined, further conversation proved impossible when the voices outside the locker room grew more insistent and someone banged on the door. Releasing a soft groan, Darien lowered her head and kissed Jessie one more time, giving her a taste of what she was feeling. "Come on. Let's get out of here."

Stepping aside, she unlocked the door. But as she swung it open, she was almost immediately confronted by two angry looking women. Unconcerned, she stepped into the space between them and

Jessie, sent a wordless warning in their direction, then watched them back away before she reached for Jessie's hand and drew her along.

"You're going to have to teach me how to do that," Jessie said, squeezing her fingers and giving her an amused look as they reached the sidewalk in front of the gym.

"Do what?"

"Make people back down just by raising an eyebrow."

They slowly made their way past the people who crowded the narrow pedestrian streets—tourists out enjoying the city and locals trying to make their way home. They hadn't gone far before the light rain that had been falling off and on all day began to fall in earnest.

It didn't really matter to Darien. She was feeling remarkably lighthearted and Paris was a walking city. Even in the rain, there were always plenty of cafés, restaurants, churches, and museums you could duck into if you didn't want to get wet.

Of course, just because she enjoyed walking in the rain didn't mean Jessie did as well. All too soon, Jessie's hair and jacket glistened wetly, while the cool, damp air had put color in her cheeks, highlighting her delicate bone structure. Looking around, Darien pointed to the closest café. "Do you want to stop and wait out the rain before we continue on to the house? I can get you a glass of wine or maybe a cappuccino, if you'd like."

"Thanks, but if it's all right with you, there's no need to stay. I actually don't mind the rain, although I'd love it if you could get me a mocha to go."

Darien thought about that for half a beat. "You sure you want to keep walking?"

Jessie nodded, and for a brief instant, Darien could see intense emotions swirling just under the surface of her eyes. Unapologetic longing. Desire. And a touch of nerves.

"The rain's not that bad," Jessie said. "It's really just a drizzle—okay, a heavy drizzle—and it's cut down on the sidewalk traffic, don't you think? Unless you've changed your mind?"

"Don't be crazy. Why would I want to change my mind?" She gave Jessie's hand a gentle squeeze, then pulled a black watch cap from her pocket and slipped it on Jessie's head. "This should keep your head a bit warmer until we get back to the house."

Adjusting the cap, Jessie smiled. "Thanks. But what about you?"

"I'm good."

"Okay then—that's good. We're good." Jessie's face lit up and her relief was evident. "We'll keep going as soon as you get me a mocha—a large one with a ton of whipped cream, if that's okay. It's the perfect walk-in-the-rain treat."

"A ton of whipped cream. Right. Well, never let it be said I'd stand between a woman and her idea of a perfect treat." With a laugh, Darien went into the café, returning a few minutes later with the requested large mocha which indeed was topped by a mountain of whipped cream.

Ignoring her warning that it might be too hot, Jessie immediately lifted the reinforced paper cup, inhaled the rich scent of chocolate, cinnamon, and coffee, and brought the drink to her lips. The low moan of satisfaction that followed sounded unbelievably sexy, but when the tip of her tongue darted out to lick the cream residue on her upper lip, Darien felt as if she'd been hit by a bolt of lightning. A clear reminder, if she needed one, that it had been much too long since she'd been enticed by a woman.

And she was certainly enticed. Enthralled. Captivated. With her heart pounding wildly in her chest, she experienced a fleeting moment of jealousy aimed at the mocha Jessie was holding with such reverence, and she spent the remainder of the walk home in a sensual haze.

Thankfully they encountered no one as they slipped into the house. The only indication anyone was even around was the muffled sound of voices coming from the direction of the computer room when they passed the fourth floor on their way to the fifth.

Darien released Jessie's hand when they entered her bedroom, leaving her momentarily standing near the foot of the bed. Long enough to close the door and take both their jackets and the watch cap Jessie had been wearing, hanging them up to dry on an antique coatrack in one corner. She then took an extra minute to light candles and put on some music. Something soft and bluesy. Perfect for a rainy night.

Satisfied, she turned back to Jessie, whose face was lit by the flickering glow of the candles while the music washed over her. She looked so beautiful. Alive. With a light shining in her eyes that came from within and owed nothing to the flames that seemed to dance in time with the music.

Reaching for Jessie's hand once again, Darien searched her face through half-closed eyes and felt her throat tighten. And then she drew her into her arms, brushing her lips lightly against Jessie's mouth.

"What was that look?" Jessie asked.

"You—you take my breath away." She could feel need cresting inside her, and without thinking she slid her hands into Jessie's hair, drawing her closer for a longer kiss. Chocolate blended with lust and long-simmering desire, and Darien flicked her tongue along Jessie's lower lip for an extra taste.

Jessie moaned softly and deepened the kiss, simultaneously moving her hands to undo her shirt. Darien stopped her and saw surprise and concern flicker across Jessie's face when she pulled back.

"Is something wrong?"

"Not a thing. Tell me what you want, Jesslyn."

"That's easy." She laughed softly. "You. Better yet, you and me. In your bed, in every imaginable way."

"That's pretty direct."

"I wouldn't have thought you'd have a problem with direct."

"I don't. But as long as we're laying it all on the table, I think you should know I'd like us to take our time."

Jessie groaned. "Take our time?"

"Mm-hmm."

The first rumble of thunder echoed outside and it made Darien smile. She'd always done her best work in the rain, she mused, as she traced a fingertip along Jessie's cheek and down her collarbone, stopping only when she encountered the top button. She followed the trail of her finger with her lips, lingering on her throat while she undid the first button and felt a wave of heat course through her.

She paused before moving on to the second button, her mouth gently tracing the newly exposed skin. As much as she wanted to touch Jessie, she knew a quick tumble would not be enough. Never be enough. Not with Jessie. And as each subsequent button was convinced to release its hold, it stirred her hunger for more.

Pushing the shirt aside and pressing her mouth against a newly bared shoulder, she felt Jessie arch her back, giving herself over to long slender fingers and a gently questing mouth. And when the last button was undone, she scraped her teeth across her skin and sent Jessie's shirt tumbling to the floor.

Pure appreciation edged out all of Darien's thoughts as she paused and let her gaze roam over the barely there scraps of material that covered Jessie's breasts. Seconds later, she used her teeth to coax the material into joining the shirt on the floor. Cupping one small pale breast, she ran her thumb across a pebbled tip and watched Jessie's eyes close before adding hot breath, sharp teeth, and a soothing tongue over sensitized skin.

As she continued, Darien chuckled softly when her mouth found a particularly sensitive spot, one that sent a shudder rolling through Jessie. Not giving her a chance to recover, she trailed a finger down her bare chest to the button on her jeans. And then she dropped slowly to her knees, worshipping every inch she uncovered with her lips as she sent Jessie's jeans sliding to the floor, leaving her with only black French-cut briefs.

Jessie's skin was like silk, warm and smooth as Darien ran her hands over it. The line of her spine, her buttocks, her thighs. Exploring every curve and hollow. Memorizing textures and tastes. Touching. Licking. Biting. Standing up, she paused long enough to kick off her shoes and socks and pull her own T-shirt over her head, tossing it to the growing pile on the floor as she shimmied out of her jeans.

When she'd finished, the skin-to-skin contact drew a trembling whimper from Jessie, and Darien paused. "Are you okay, Jesslyn?"

Jessie opened her eyes and stared into Darien's. She drew in a shuddering breath and sighed, "Oh God, yes."

Jessie hadn't known how wet she was until Darien parted her, dipped a finger, and trailed wet heat up to her mouth. For a moment, she forgot how to breathe.

"You taste so sweet. Somehow, I knew you would."

The low voice sent heat sparking through all her nerves until it settled between her thighs. And then there was no more time to think as Darien kissed her. Her mouth was hot, demanding her full attention. She responded by wrapping her arms around Darien's neck, her tongue answering Darien's initial fleeting touch. Teasing. Twisting. Wanting.

Pleasure bloomed. Lost in the moist heat of Darien's mouth, she was only vaguely aware of being gently nudged onto the bed, a task made easier by her weakened knees. She felt Darien's hands keeping her steady when the mattress dipped, shivered when she felt warm, slightly roughened fingertips slide along her arms and to her cheeks, gently tucking her hair behind her ears.

The bed shifted again a moment later as Darien's long lean body stretched out until she loomed over her, arms rigid as she braced herself. Bending her head, Darien placed another kiss on her mouth. At once gentle and possessive. And then a ghost of a smile flitted across her lips as she flicked her tongue along her lower lip.

"So hot," Darien murmured, dipping lower to nip her throat before she began working her way slowly down her chest and across her abdomen, only to pause at her belly button.

Jessie's breasts felt unbelievably heavy and tight with need. She grabbed Darien's shoulders, digging her nails in and arching her hips in unmistakable demand. She felt the vibration more than heard Darien's faint chuckle, then almost cried in relief when she felt her shift and resume moving inexorably downward.

Going up on her elbows, Jessie watched Darien's slow progress. Watched her smoke-gray eyes darken as she used her beautiful mouth to coax the thong along, and then used her teeth against the sensitive skin she found there. The combination—sight and sensation—had her dropping her head back onto the bed while her pulse pounded and desire sent heat radiating through her body.

When Darien paused, Jessie groaned. "Oh God, please don't stop—"

"Trust me. I have no intention of stopping. By the time I'm finished, you won't be able to think of anything for the rest of the day except the feeling of me loving you." A moment later, she trailed her lips across Jessie's hip bone, settled her open mouth over her, and gently exhaled. The moist heat was almost too much for Jessie and sent her stimulated nerve endings dancing wildly. God, she was so close. *So close.*

As if she could hear her silent supplication, Darien opened her, parting soft folds and gently stroking the wet heat she found there before delving into her with her tongue. Slow and sweet and tender.

When the tip of Darien's tongue slowly circled her clitoris, a shudder rolled through Jessie. Emotions and sensations melded, coursed through her body, and flooded every cell when Darien slipped inside her. Everything was so much more powerful with her inside. Suddenly breathing required thought. Her heart rate increased, started racing, and she shuddered ever closer to a peak.

Greedy for more, Jessie moaned and writhed. Lost in sensation, she drifted near the edge of an abyss. Almost afraid that Darien would try to keep things slow, she grabbed handfuls of her thick, dark hair and pressed against her talented mouth in wordless demand. *Please.*

Darien didn't disappoint.

Let go, Darien's spirit whispered as she edged the tension higher and higher and helped Jessie take what she needed. *I'll catch you*, her heart promised as she increased the pressure with her mouth and sent Jessie catapulting into a breathless, screaming orgasm and all Jessie could say was Darien's name.

Awareness returned when she felt Darien begin to lift herself off her body. Uncertain whether she meant to leave the bed, Jessie reached out and wrapped one arm around Darien's waist, stilling her movement. "Where do you think you're going?"

Darien released a soft laugh. "I thought you might need to breathe and I figured it would be easier if I wasn't crushing you."

"Breathing's nice. Having you on top of me is nicer." Jessie watched the banked fire in Darien's eyes grow infinitesimally hotter before her eyes skimmed down to look at her mouth. Full. Unsmiling but soft. Perfect. Emboldened, she gripped the back of Darien's head and brought it back down until her mouth was within reach, her body taut with the anticipation of kissing her. "And I don't know what you're thinking, because I'm nowhere near finished with you."

In Darien she discovered an enthusiastic, wickedly talented lover. She also noticed that each time they came together, Darien loosened up a little more, laughed a little more. Opened up to her a little bit more.

But not completely.

It made her wonder if Darien was afraid of what was happening between them. Afraid of exposing too much of herself. Not the former MI6 operative. Not the contract assassin. But the real woman. The living, breathing, feeling woman.

She would need to move carefully. But that was for later. For now—she claimed her mouth. Hot, possessive, demanding her full attention while she continued to hold her. Jessie had no doubt Darien could have easily removed her restraining arm and was indescribably pleased when instead she felt surrender shudder through her.

"Jesslyn, you're going to have to help me."

"What do you mean?"

"I don't have a frame of reference for this." She closed her eyes briefly. "You probably need—want—more, and I don't know what I have to give. I don't even know how I feel except that I'm glad you're here with me."

"I'll take that—for now."

"Good because I just know I want more of you." A low groan came from Darien's throat as she pressed her mouth to the hollow in Jessie's neck. "I want all of you."

"Then I don't see a problem because it seems we both want the same thing."

For an instant, Darien went still. She lifted her head and looked as if there was something she wanted to say. But as she opened her mouth, Jessie put a hand over her lips preventing her from saying anything else. And then her hands were in Darien's hair and she was covering Darien's lips with her mouth, kissing her once more. Kissing her with increasing hunger. Kissing her like Darien was there for her alone.

Jessie shifted, pressing against Darien with her thigh, touching nerve endings tight with unfulfilled stimulation. She felt the low groan reverberating in Darien's chest and smiled. "We'll figure it out, Darien. Later."

CHAPTER TWENTY-TWO

When Darien awoke, she was immediately conscious of two things. Dawn was just breaking, the light coming through the window, thin and gray. And Jessie was lying awake beside her on the bed, a potent reminder of what they had shared.

Gently shifting, she inched up and tried but couldn't remember a time she had awoken beside someone. *Ever*. It had also been a long time since she'd allowed any woman to get this close. To her, not Ari. Touching her where it mattered. Making her lose control.

Slightly dazed, she looked down at Jessie. But as she absorbed both the warmth emanating from her and the heated fragrance of her skin, she realized how different this felt from anything she'd previously experienced. There was a connection, gossamer threads, binding them together. And then a new thought occurred.

This didn't just feel different. It felt bloody marvelous. Which begged the question: Why did being with Jessie like this affect her as nothing had before?

Stretching sleepily like a satisfied cat, Jessie lifted her gaze and smiled at her, and Darien immediately felt her throat tighten and her heart rate increase. She almost laughed, knowing Jessie shouldn't have this effect on her. But with those warm eyes and softly tousled hair, Jesslyn Coltrane was proving to be a force to be reckoned with.

"Good morning." Reaching over, Jessie brushed Darien's hair back from her face and gently rubbed her thumb under one eye. "You don't sleep nearly enough. I'm sorry if I woke you up."

"Don't worry, you didn't. I haven't slept for more than two to three hours at a time in longer than I can remember." Darien laughed quietly. "But I have to admit, the sleep I did manage last night was some of the best sleep I've had in years."

"Good to know."

She felt Jessie's eyes on her and her skin tingled under the intensity of her gaze. "Um, Jesslyn—"

"Uh-oh. I'm not sure I like the sound of that." Her smile seemed to dim a little. "Does that mean we won't be doing this again?"

"No...not at all." Unable or possibly unwilling to stop herself, she leaned down and touched her lips to Jessie's mouth, letting the kiss deepen slowly while ignoring the more primitive urges coursing through her, the ones that wanted to ravish and devour. "Before you ask, I've no regrets about last night, and have no doubt—we will take this up again, tonight at the latest. That's a promise."

Jessie nodded and licked her lips. "I'm good with that. What happens now?"

Darien stared at her for a moment then slowly smiled. "For now, I'm thinking a shower first then breakfast. Then we save the world. Does that work for you?"

Jessie nodded and continued to watch her without saying anything.

Acting on impulse, Darien eased from the bed before turning and offering her outstretched hand. When Jessie accepted her hand, she knew she'd made the right decision. She threaded their fingers together and brought them to her lips. Saw Jessie's eyes flash with sudden heat and felt a quickening in her blood.

"Jesslyn?" Her voice was a pleading whisper. "I don't think I can wait for tonight. Shower?"

She left herself open, allowing Jessie to read the unmistakable invitation, and was rewarded when Jessie let her pull her from the bed.

❖

By early evening, Darien had lost all sense of bonhomie.

Under normal circumstances, she would have said nothing was impossible. But finding a woman who didn't want to be found was proving to be a definite challenge. Nadia Petrov had covered her tracks like a pro, and as potential leads continued to evaporate, she remained an elusive ghost. In spite of their collective talents, assets, and efforts, they were no closer to finding her. And while rumors continued to abound, it was starting to look like no one had actually seen Petrov in more than three months. Not and lived to tell about it.

Fifteen days. They were fast running out of time, and while the search continued, Darien knew the unspoken fear was that unless luck started to turn their way, Petrov would remain in the wind until it was too late to stop her. Her mood grew darker thinking of that prospect.

She knew no one could stay hidden forever and reminded herself that Petrov's father had proved to be equally difficult to track. That she had found him in the end was of little comfort because it had taken her months. And while she was now a much better tracker than she had been then, time was something they simply didn't have.

Watching another day wind down, Darien tried to cope with the ever-increasing intensity of her headache while frustration settled once again in a knot between her shoulder blades. She heard the bedroom door open at the same time she realized she was rubbing her temples and quickly dropped her hands to her side.

"You look pale. When was the last time you ate?"

Jessie's question coming out of the blue penetrated the haze Darien was in. She knew she should have eaten long before now. She didn't have to be told. But the only thing she could recall putting into her system all day was coffee. "I'm not sure."

"That's what I thought. What am I supposed to do with you," Jessie said half to herself as she moved closer and placed her hands on Darien's shoulders. And then she kissed her. The touch of her mouth was electric and sent a charge racing through Darien. It also left her unable to do anything but respond—with pleasure.

"Wow," Jessie murmured, licking her lips as she drew back. "Don't know why I waited, because I really wanted to do that."

"And do you always do what you want?"

Jessie appeared to consider the question before sending a quick half grin in her direction. "It's not something I've normally done in the past, but it would seem I've picked up some new habits since I've come to Paris."

Darien smiled for the first time in hours, leaned closer, and kissed her back, letting some of the intensity she was feeling show. "We could always skip dinner."

Jessie laughed. "Not unless you prefer your women comatose because I'm famished, and if I don't get something to eat, I'll pass out. Not surprising because I doubt anyone's eaten since breakfast, and don't think I didn't notice that you didn't eat this morning."

"I had other things on my mind this morning..." She grinned faintly as she recalled exactly why she had been so distracted that morning. "Not to worry. I'm sure I can quickly put something together so you don't faint."

"I'm sure you can, but why bother? I think we should just go out for dinner. That way, for once, you won't need to worry about cooking."

"Are you asking me out, Agent Coltrane?"

Jessie hesitated ever so slightly. "I'd love to, but not right this minute. Go grab your jacket and I'll tell Elle and Ben and Nicola we're all going out for dinner. I don't care where. You can pick."

Darien stared at her a moment longer. "Bossy little thing."

"You don't know the half of it," Jessie said with a laugh.

❖

As the shadows lengthened and evening settled over the city, Darien chose a small nearby restaurant that appeared constantly busy and seemed to cater primarily to a mix of students and neighborhood locals—youthful, boisterous, and confidant. A young woman near the entrance greeted Darien with a wave and pointed to a booth at the back.

As they squeezed past the crowd waiting for takeout by the counter, Jessie saw the menu scribbled on a chalkboard and laughed with delight.

"Hamburger and *pommes frites* okay?" Darien asked.

"Oh God, yes. That sounds perfect."

After conferring with the others, Darien went to place their orders while they made their way to their booth. A few minutes later,

Darien joined them. Once she had her back to the wall so she could face the door, Jessie could see her slowly begin to relax—or at least relax as much as Darien ever did in a public venue.

She never fully dropped her guard and continued to maintain a predatory focus on everyone who came and went in the restaurant. But as she stretched her legs, she seemed to be following the animated conversation at the table and occasionally joined in while they waited for their meals to arrive.

The food proved to be worth the wait. When a large platter was put in front of her, Jessie realized the meal might be viewed as traditional American fare, but in a city devoted to fine dining and elite restaurants, it would never qualify as fast food. Especially not when it was accompanied by a glass of the house red.

Set before her was a serious burger. The char-grilled patty was hand pressed, thick and juicy, stacked with lettuce and tomatoes. The sesame seed bun was homemade, the fries crisp and fresh cut, accompanied by an assortment of dipping sauces. And the scent was incredible. Greedy for a taste, she took a first bite, closed her eyes, and sighed contentedly as the flavors melted in her mouth.

"Hungry?"

Jessie grinned, finding the food too good to mind the teasing note in Darien's voice. "Yes, as a matter of fact, and this is perfect. I just can't believe the woman who insists on feeding us healthy food brought us to an American-style diner."

Darien made no attempt to hide her amusement. "I'll have you know, even though I don't eat it, beef in France is typically grass fed and extremely lean. So that hamburger you're doing your best to inhale still qualifies as a healthy choice."

"I don't care. This is really good," Jessie responded good-naturedly, concentrating on her food until the sharp edge of her hunger had abated. "Are you planning on finishing your fries?"

❖

"I think I'm going to have to double the distance I run tomorrow if I've any hope of working that dinner off." Jessie released a rueful laugh and linked her arm with Darien's as they left the restaurant and started back to the house at a leisurely pace.

"That's probably not necessary." What was meant to be a quick glance was extended and Darien allowed her gaze to roam with both directness and appreciation. "In fact, I wouldn't change a thing if I were you."

Jessie's eyes widened and a flush swept across her face. "That's sweet," she said carefully, then added a quick grin. "But then you're probably just saying that because you'd like to maintain a competitive advantage."

Darien rolled her eyes and grinned. "I didn't make you eat most of my fries. So you're going to be hard-pressed to lay the blame at my feet." She tilted her head to one side. "As for being sweet, I doubt you'd be able to get a single person who knows me to agree with you."

"That may be, but I would take that to mean none of them know you very well."

Darien took the comment seriously and wondered how it was Jessie seemed to know her so well, especially so quickly. "That may be," she repeated before a reluctance to continue down a personal road had her steering the conversation in another direction. "By any chance, are you suggesting you'd like me to slow down or hold back when we run?"

"No, not really. I was teasing—mostly."

"Good, because I was thinking you might like to go running with me at Bois de Vincennes tomorrow morning."

A small crease appeared between Jessie's brows. "Oh? Why's that?"

"No reason other than it's an amazing place to run," Darien responded and slowly watched Jessie's frown disappear. "I think you'll like it."

"Then I guess it's a date."

Darien was smiling as they rounded the corner near the house. But before she could conjure an appropriate response, she stopped abruptly.

A stranger stood at the top of the front steps, holding what appeared to be a small white bakery box. Male, Caucasian, mid to late forties, edging over six feet and in decent shape, with shoulder-length blond hair and high Slavic cheekbones. He was dressed in the uniform of a delivery service and there was a small van parked by the curb, the logo of a local patisserie featured prominently on its door panels.

All very normal in appearance. Except for one thing. Deliveries were never made to this address. Never.

Darien didn't make any conscious decisions. She simply acted. She held out one arm to stop Jessie's forward momentum, simultaneously reached inside her jacket for her weapon. And as everything shifted into slow motion, she slipped her fingers around the SIG's grip and pulled it loose from her holster.

Stay back. She wanted to scream the words to Jessie, but years of training ensured her plea remained locked inside her head. She felt Jessie bump into her arm. Heard her start to say, "What—"

The rest of Jessie's comment was lost as Darien's gaze sharpened and her focus zeroed in on the stranger standing at the door. Just as behind her, she momentarily heard Nicola and Elle laughing at something Ben had just said, and then their voices also faded into the evening air.

Vigilance had been a part of her daily life since earliest childhood. She had grown up in the business, and it had been constantly drilled into her until situational awareness became as natural as breathing. She could recall failing to remain vigilant only once, in Prague, and the consequences of that failure still haunted her. That made the possibility of failing again too painful to even consider.

She pushed Jessie behind her as her eyes met those of the courier. Saw a flash of surprise followed by swift recognition on his face. Watched him reach swiftly for his weapon. He was too late.

His age marked him as a seasoned professional. She was faster. No doubts, no second-guessing. Before his gun cleared his jacket, she had already fired several rounds in rapid succession.

The muted sound of the shots echoed faintly, the suppressor silencing the man's death, still audible as he tumbled down the steps and fell to the sidewalk. A moment later, quiet descended on the street once again.

Darien had known the outcome even before she'd taken the first shot, but she still kicked the weapon away from a limp hand just to be sure. She dropped to her knees beside the unknown killer and studied the face of an ordinary looking man with blond hair and blue eyes staring sightlessly at the dark sky. She felt his blood seeping into her jeans as she confirmed there was no pulse, aware the sound of footsteps behind her meant the others were fast approaching.

She wasn't concerned about Nicola and Ben. Both had been in the field too long to be distressed by what had just happened. But Jessie and Elle weren't field agents. They were analysts, and regardless of training scenarios and family bloodlines, the fallout from what they had just witnessed would need to be dealt with in the not-too-distant future.

For now, it was enough to know they were safe.

Darien holstered her weapon and turned her attention to the small white bakery box the would-be killer had been holding. At this point, it was an unknown, therefore the only thing that mattered.

The box had hit the steps when it had been dropped and lay partially open, but not enough for her to see inside. Taking a slow, deep breath, she reached for it with steady hands and gently eased it open. Not completely. Just enough to be able to see what it held without disturbing its contents.

She blinked and froze.

She was staring down at a timer, and as she watched, the green numbers slowly counted off the passing seconds.

"Oh God," Jessie murmured, staring at the tableau in front of her. The blond man lay where he'd fallen at the bottom of the steps, an expanding pool of blood around his head and torso. There was no doubt he was dead. No doubt Darien had just killed him.

But if that wasn't enough, there was the bakery box Darien had just opened. A bomb, she thought numbly, licking her lips and trying to pretend her heart hadn't just skipped a beat. She watched Darien cradle the box with extreme care, saw her sleek dark eyebrows draw together in concentration as she scanned the device. *A bomb that's set to explode in less than four minutes, if that timer is accurate.*

"Jessie," Darien called to her softly. "Listen to me. I need you and Elle to go with Ben and get as far away from here as possible. Do you hear me?"

"And what the hell do you think you're going to do?" Jessie asked in disbelief, her voice barely a whisper.

"I'm going to disarm this. Trust me. I know what I'm doing. I've done it before. But I need to be clearheaded and able to concentrate on what I'm doing, and that means I need you out of here."

Jessie understood all too well. She was no expert, but she'd had just enough explosive ordinance disposal training to know what was involved.

She knew if Darien miscalculated in any way, if she moved too quickly, if she cut the wrong wire, or if there was a hidden motion switch, there would be no second chance. The bomb would go off as intended and it would take anyone unfortunate enough to be nearby with it. Clearly Darien didn't want her or Elle at risk of getting hurt— or worse.

Jesus. She didn't want anyone to get hurt either. But what Darien was asking her to do was impossible. There was no way she was leaving her alone with the timer on the bomb rapidly ticking away the seconds. Darien just didn't need to know that.

"All right."

It took every ounce of willpower she had to do the only thing she could do. Conscious of nothing but her pounding heart, she stepped back into the muted shadows of the street. Out of the way and beyond Darien's peripheral vision so as not to pose any kind of distraction.

She knew Darien would believe she had done as she'd asked. Just as she knew Darien would be unhappy when she discovered Jessie had been less than honest with her. But there would be plenty of time to deal with the fallout of not having listened later. After the bomb was disarmed.

She saw Nicola frown, looking at her with unspoken questions. But not for long. Darien, still studying the bomb she was holding, quietly called out to her. "Nicola?"

"I'm right here, Dare. Tell me what you need."

"Something I can use to cut these bloody wires. You're usually a walking tool kit. You wouldn't happen to have—"

"Wire cutters?" Nicola laughed softly and reached into her bag for a small leather pouch from which she pulled out wire cutters and handed them to Darien. "I've been carrying them since Jakarta. This will make the first time they've actually had to be used."

"Hopefully they're still sharp then," Darien said dryly. "Now make yourself useful. Get out of here. Go with Ben and make sure all of you are at a safe distance in case this thing does what it's supposed to do."

Nicola rolled her eyes, turned her head, and cast a faintly amused glance at Jessie. "Darien?"

"What?"

"Be a dear. Shut up and cut those wires so we can deal with the body in front of your house. Preferably before one of your neighbors comes along and calls the police."

Darien remained silent for a moment. "All right, but if I mess this up and kill us both, you and I are going to have words."

Jessie choked back a nervous laugh, heard Elle mutter something between an expletive and a prayer, and watched over Nicola's shoulder. She knew enough to be aware Darien would have to cut the wires in the correct sequence in order to prevent detonation. First the wire that led to the primer, then the reactor wire, and finally the wire that fed the ignition timer.

She held her breath. As she watched the numbers continue to count down, she felt an icy calm wash over her. It would be any moment now. An endless heartbeat later, Darien cut the timer wire and the numbers stopped.

Ben came around beside her where he could see what she was seeing—the timer, a set of snipped wires, and several thin cylinders of C-4 nestled in the box. "Nice job, Dare."

Darien nodded.

Only then did Jessie place a hand over her racing heart, beating fast and hard beneath her palm. But as she swallowed dryly and closed her eyes, she tried not to think about how Darien's face had become a blank slate. She tried hard not to think of what it might mean.

To no one's surprise, the dead man carried no ID. No markings or tags on his clothes. No cell phone. Even his weapon—a Makarov PM—was a standard Russian military and police issue sidearm. There was nothing that would help identify him. Still, Jessie had no doubt Darien would find him in one of her databases.

Before her heart rate returned to normal, Ben had already arranged for a crew to photograph and fingerprint the body, and then sanitize the area, removing any trace of what had happened. Through it all, Jessie noticed Darien was unusually quiet. She could sense her withdrawal and knew instinctively that no matter how hard she tried to hold on, Darien had already retreated into the persona she had presented when they'd first met.

She remained off to one side, her body still, a wholly unreadable expression on her face, responding only occasionally to something Nicola said to her. So Jessie wasn't surprised to see her disappear into the house once everything was done, heading straight to the computer room where she locked everyone else out.

Entering the house, Elle raised her eyebrows, her lips compressed into a thin line. Jessie couldn't miss the unspoken questions and sighed. It was clear from Elle's expression that her original nervousness and distrust of Darien was back and stronger than ever, only now it was coupled with the horror of having witnessed her first killing.

In that regard Jessie could relate. She had somehow managed to relegate her own shock at seeing Darien kill someone to a far corner in her mind. But she knew she would never completely erase the image and had no idea how to help ease Elle's mind.

Silence lengthened before Jessie gave in to her uncertainty and shrugged. "At a guess, it's probably better that we don't know what she's doing. But if you really insist on knowing, I suppose we could always see if we can beat her security system."

"I doubt you'll get very far," Nicola said with a laugh. "Personally, I think the best thing we can all do is let her be."

She gave Nicola time to say more, but when she didn't, Jessie pursued it. "You're suggesting we just wait?"

"You can take my advice or not, it's up to you. But I've worked with Darien often enough to know she'll come down when she's got something, and she's always come through. In the meantime, I don't know about anyone else, but I think I could use a drink."

"I think I like the sound of that," Elle said weakly.

Moving to a built-in bar, Nicola took a look. "I know there's still some of the single-malt scotch Ben likes so much, but that's because no one else will touch it. No ice, as I recall," she added, pouring a healthy splash into a tulip-shaped glass.

"Perfect," Ben said.

"Thankfully, there's wine for the rest of us. We've got a cab, a merlot or two, and a couple of pinot noir. Elle?"

"I'll take whatever's going, thanks."

"What about you, Jessie? Any preference?"

Preference? Jessie looked over, grateful to have something to think about other than whatever Darien might be doing. "The pinot sounds good."

Nicola nodded, selected a bottle and stared at it briefly. "Interesting, don't you think? Even though she lives in what is widely considered the world's top wine-producing country, our Dare seems to favor American wines from California. I wonder what Freud would say about that?"

Jessie laughed. It was impossible not to and she felt infinitely better for it. "I don't know about Freud, but I think a taste of home sounds good right about now." Pushing her hair behind her ears, she reached for one of the wineglasses Nicola had just filled, then sat down to quietly nurse her drink and wait.

There wasn't a lot of conversation, but it wasn't really needed. Jessie was certain all of them were thinking about known and unknown assassins, ticking bombs real and metaphorical, and whatever information Darien was unearthing upstairs.

They didn't find out what Darien had been doing until almost two in the morning. That was when Jessie got up to fetch another bottle of wine and saw a silent figure moving out of the dark hallway, just before Darien stepped into the light.

Her hair was wet from a recent shower and she had changed into a white T-shirt tucked into a pair of well-worn jeans that hugged her narrow hips and traced the length of her long legs. Jessie couldn't help notice how tired she looked and wondered what was keeping her upright. Possibly a connection to the laptop under her arm?

She indicated the bottle in her right hand. "Hey, stranger, can I entice you with a glass of wine or would you rather something stronger?"

"Wine sounds good."

Darien appeared reluctant to move and remained still for a few seconds longer before she made her way into the room. Once she did, Jessie was better able to see the shadowed remnants of the evening's activities in her bloodshot eyes and the lines of strain on her face. Curiously, it lent her an air of vulnerability that seemed completely at odds with the don't-touch-me vibe she was giving off.

She waited until Darien was perched on a stool with a glass of wine in front of her before asking, "So what did you find?"

Darien took a deliberately casual sip before answering. "In a hurry for show-and-tell?" Meeting Jessie's gaze, she smiled wanly and shrugged, then set up the laptop. "Why don't I start with what I've managed to put together on our visitor from earlier this evening? After that, the dots become fairly easy to connect."

While the others gathered around the laptop, her fingers tapped a few commands and conjured up an image. The blond hair was shorter in the photograph. But there was no mistaking the blue of his eyes or the face of their would-be killer.

"His name was Sergei Korolev," Darien said. "Russian born and educated, and until five years ago, he had made a steady if unspectacular climb in the military, including serving for a time in Russian special ops."

"What happened five years ago?" Ben asked.

"Rumor has it Korolev was passed over for promotion and took it out on his commanding officer. Rather violently. He disappeared shortly thereafter. When he resurfaced, he was working as an enforcer for some heavy hitters in the Russian mob. After that, he branched out, doing work for anyone who needed and could afford his services, including some of the Colombian cartels."

Jessie leaned closer and stared at the computer. "You're saying he became a hired gun?"

"Yes. He wasn't known to support any particular causes, had no ties or loyalties. He simply went where the money was, and going by the healthy bank account he had, he stayed rather busy. I was able to locate roughly twelve million before I took a break, and there's likely to be more. I just need a bit more time to find it. But here's the critical link." Darien tapped more keys and the image on the screen morphed.

The picture that now filled the screen was clearly taken from a distance. But there was no mistaking the two people in the photograph. Standing near a massive ship berthed at a shipyard were the recently deceased Sergei Korolev and Nadia Petrov.

"How the hell did you get this?" Ben asked. "No, never mind. I don't need to know. Do you have any idea when it was taken?"

Darien nodded and drained the rest of her wine in one tense swallow. "Two days before the Guild brought down the three jets."

"Boy howdy," Elle said quietly. "Ben may not want to know, but I'd sure like to know how you got this information so quickly when we've been searching for Petrov around-the-clock for weeks and haven't been able to find anything."

"Believe it or not, we caught a break—through him." Darien indicated Korolev's image with a finger. "I got a hit when I ran his face through the database, and that led me to a contact I've used on a number of occasions. At the time the photo was taken, he was tracking Korolev, not Petrov. He knew Korolev was arranging to move weapons to support some mercenary action in the Ivory Coast and was only interested in following the weapons that came off that ship. He didn't know or care who the woman was."

The room grew quiet while each of them stared at the image and processed the information they'd just been given.

"I still don't get it," Elle said. "What's the connection? Why would Nadia Petrov choose to meet with Korolev just before launching a major offensive? He's a mercenary, a hired gun, as you said. Not someone you'd need when you're attacking passenger jets and—" She fell silent when Jessie put her hand on her shoulder. "What is it? What am I missing?"

"Petrov wasn't hiring Korolev to be part of her large-scale plans, was she?" Jessie said softly, her eyes seeking and finding Darien's. "This was personal. She knows you—knows exactly who you are. She knew bringing down those planes would draw you into the investigation, and she hired Korolev to take you out, which he tried to do in Germany, and then again earlier this evening. She's got big plans. She's finishing what her father started and is settling old scores along the way. But you've already figured that out, haven't you?"

Darien nodded. "It's the only thing that makes sense. It's also what we're going to use to bring her down."

Jessie chewed her bottom lip, suddenly fearful she knew where this conversation was going. But in spite of the nerves, she pressed on, keeping her voice light as she asked the question. "What are you saying, Darien?"

"She's targeting me. So I'm going to offer Petrov the one thing she seems to want badly enough that she'll be willing to come out into the open to get it. I'm going to offer her the chance to get me."

CHAPTER TWENTY-THREE

Darien shivered, pulling her arms closer and wrapping them protectively around herself. But as always, the gesture proved useless and she remained caught in a struggle she had no hope of winning. The nightmare was on her again and there was no way she could fight her way out of it. She forgot who she was, where she was, forgot everything except the memories of childhood as they crowded around her.

She was thirteen.

Surrounded by the smell of blood. The stench of garbage and urine. The scent of death. Trapped in a cold, dark alley in Prague with her mother's rapidly cooling body only a few feet away. Close enough to see. Too far to touch.

It was all too familiar and she wept. She could feel the wetness of tears mixing with the blood on her face, but she couldn't move. She wanted to scream. No, please. Not again. *And perhaps a sound managed to escape her constricted throat. Because in that moment, from the battered ruins of her beautiful face, her mother's eyes suddenly opened. Her mouth opened and she started to make a sound.*

Darien jolted out of the dream, throat straining around the scream she wouldn't voice, swallowing it before it could escape. With her heart pounding wildly and mind in disarray, she fought for self-control and tried not to trip over the last vestiges of memory and nightmare. But it still took her a minute to push through the fog to register where she was. Not in an alley in Prague, curled in a fetal ball of pain and misery, but on an Air France Airbus, flying through the darkness over the Atlantic bound for New York.

"Bad dreams again?" Jessie murmured beside her, lightly stroking her arm.

Her eyes were open but it made no difference. She still saw her mother lying on her back, her ruined face turned toward her. The image was as real as her own heartbeat. For the space of several breaths, she found herself unable to speak and felt Jessie's hand close around hers, holding it tight.

"Just relax. I've got you. Take deep breaths, nice and long and slow."

One breath. The words made her feel tenderly stroked, and for a moment, she allowed herself to savor the scent and feel of having Jessie near her. Close. Warm. Real. A second breath. She breathed her in and wasn't surprised to discover Jessie's presence and whispered reassurances began to soothe and calm combustible emotions. She could almost take a full breath again.

She tried to swallow, but her mouth was bone-dry and she reached for the bottle of water she'd left in the cup holder by her seat. The water had become lukewarm and she grimaced, but she drained it anyway. By the time she finished and was cradling the empty bottle in her hand, she had worked the knot out of her throat and had shaken off the chill of memories.

"Do you want to talk about it—about your nightmare?"

A sound somewhere between a laugh and a groan escaped her. "Why bother? It's always the same—the same nightmare, the same pain. An hour spent talking about it is an hour of my life I'll never get back."

"I can't help you if you close me out, so I guess I'll owe you an hour." Jessie's slow smile pulled Darien closer. "Was the dream about the alley in Prague? Where your mother was killed?"

Darien let out a sigh. Leaning her head back, she closed her eyes. She could still feel the residual tension and tried to sort through the images lingering along the dark edges of her mind, only to find herself fumbling when the usual pieces didn't fit. But the feel of Jessie's hand holding hers kept her anchored.

"Darien?"

"Sorry—yes. The dream was about Prague. It always is. I'm really tired of dreaming about it, but I can't seem to make it stop. And each time I have the dream, I feel like I'm left hanging on by my fingertips."

"What would happen if you just let go?"

"I don't think I want to find out." She could feel Jessie's gaze on her face, waiting for her to continue. But as more pieces of the puzzle slipped into place, her voice died.

"What's wrong?"

"I'm not sure. It's always been the same. Except—"

"Except what, Dare?"

Opening her eyes, she turned her head and frowned when she caught her reflection in the window. The image was shadowed, distorted, and stared back at her like the image from her dream. She tried to put her thoughts into words. "Except this time, for the first time ever, there was a difference."

"How was it different?"

"She—my mother—she opened her eyes. I mean, she was still dead. I knew she was still dead. But she opened her eyes and stared at me. She opened her mouth and it felt as if she was trying to tell me something. But of course she couldn't, could she? She was dead." She paused for a moment. "I wonder what Freud would say about that?"

"Freud believed dreams represent an ongoing wish, that they are the way the id communicates its deepest, darkest desires."

"So Freud would say I wanted my mother to open her eyes, to still be alive?" Darien considered it for a long moment but found herself too tired to feel anything beyond resignation. "Now there's a surprise."

There was no possible response and they sat quietly for a long time, the silence filled only with the drone of the jet's engines and the distant whispered conversations of other passengers.

"Can I ask you something?"

Startled by Jessie's softly worded question, several seconds ticked off the clock before Darien formed a response. "Of course. You should know you can ask me anything."

"Why is that?"

"I don't know. It's just the way it is. Ask your question, Jesslyn."

"All right. I'd really like to know—what did you do with it?"

Darien's frown deepened. "What did I do with what?"

The small smile that had been dancing around Jessie's mouth widened. "What did you do with Korolev's millions?" she asked softly. "You said he had a healthy bank account and I don't know why, but I got the impression his account's not that healthy anymore. I'd like to know what you did with the money."

Uncertain how it came to be that Jessie could read her so well, and wondering what she would do once Jessie learned all her secrets, Darien released a wry laugh. "I donated it."

"You donated it. To whom?"

"I'm not sure. Several different groups. There was Doctors Without Borders, a wildlife reserve in Kenya, a farm program in Tanzania. A couple of others, I think. I've got the list on my laptop if it's important. How did you know?"

Jessie gave a faint shrug. "There was something in your voice when you spoke about the money. Were you at all tempted?"

"To take the money for myself? Why would I do that? It's not as if I need it."

Jessie choked back a laugh. "You've no need for twelve million dollars?"

Darien shook her head. "I've done all right for myself, Jesslyn. Trust me when I tell you I don't have any need for Korolev's money." She hesitated before continuing. "I realize to most people, maybe even to you, Korolev was in the same business as I am."

"I don't think that."

"Maybe. Maybe not. I just know I'd like to believe I'm actually making a difference. It could be I'm deluding myself so I can live with what I do. I don't know. As for the money, rather than just let it sit there until someone else—maybe some terrorist group—accessed it to fund who knows what, I gave it to organizations that can do some good with it. It's not as if I haven't done that before."

"Of course you have." This time, Jessie didn't hold back her laugh while Darien continued to frown at her. "I mean, good God, you're a modern-day Robin Hood, aren't you?" But she squeezed Darien's hand, taking away any possible sting her words might have had.

❖

As the jet continued to fly inexorably closer to New York, Jessie slid to her left. The new position enabled her to shamelessly watch Darien as she stretched her long legs and wandered toward the front of the cabin in search of more water.

She saw her encounter a member of the cabin crew, saw the flight attendant's hesitation before succumbing to Darien's dazzling smile and considerable charm. A lethal combination and very few people seemed to be immune, she thought.

And why not? Darien was strong, tough when she had to be, intelligent, and it showed. But it always came back to that smile. It was her smile that had first caught Jessie's attention. It drew her in and continued to hold her.

Feeling the heat pooling deep within her, she watched Darien's face grow more animated as she elicited a laugh from the flight attendant. Lost in the moment, Jessie almost missed Ben's approach. She looked up, then moved back to accommodate him as he quietly slipped into the seat Darien had vacated.

"She should be sleeping," he said with a nod in Darien's direction.

"She managed to get a bit earlier, but then she had another nightmare," Jessie responded. "They're coming more frequently and it's not going to get any easier, the closer she gets to confronting Petrov. I hate to admit it, but I'm worried about her."

Ben's face remained impassive. "You two seem to have gotten close."

The words were said casually, but Jessie was fairly certain she detected a warning note in Ben's tone. "Is there a question you'd like to ask?" she said lightly.

"No. I'm simply making a statement. I don't want to see her hurt."

Jessie knew he was only speaking out of concern for Darien— out of love, when it came down to it. But knowing didn't alter her reaction. She felt a flare of anger. Sharp and quick. "You believe I'm going to hurt Darien?"

"Not intentionally, no." A muscled flexed in Ben's jaw. "But she's about to walk into the line of fire."

"Do you think I don't know that? Or hate the fact that if something goes wrong, no one's going to be there to help...*I'm* not going to be there to help?"

"What I think is that Darien needs to be focused on surviving whatever Nadia Petrov has planned while buying the rest of us enough time to stop Petrov from attacking the G8. Not thinking about anything else."

"You think I'm going to be a distraction for her?"

Ben's dark eyes fixed on her. "You're a complication where Darien's concerned. I've been watching her with you, and she's different. You've changed her. It doesn't help that Grace will be meeting with the two of you once you're in Maine. Things between Grace and Darien...I think Darien is finding the prospect of a reunion difficult."

"What are you saying?" Warily, Jessie tried to focus, but her throat grew tight and her voice no longer sounded like her own. "If there's a problem between Darien and my mother, why am I only finding out about it now?"

"There's no problem. Not exactly. I am concerned about how this might play out if Darien has to explain things to Grace."

"Explain what exactly? That she's sleeping with me?"

"Yes."

"That's enough, Ben." Startled, they both turned at the sound of Darien's voice. She was standing close, two bottles of water held in fisted hands. Her voice was neutral, but there was no mistaking the anger radiating from her in waves.

Ben stood and faced Darien, mere inches separating them. The tension between them was palpable and Jessie bit her lip as she saw their eyes lock in some kind of silent combat. Neither said anything and when the silence grew strained, Ben finally spoke.

"I don't want to see you get hurt," he said. "I know you're still angry with me because I withheld information, and that's on me. But you're not thinking. I shouldn't have to remind you that emotions will get in the way of the job. They'll get you killed. And starting when we land, you need to have your head completely in the game or you're not going to survive."

"Other than this damned-near-constant headache, my head is just fine. What I need is for you to back off and let me be the judge of what's best for me," Darien said quietly.

She began to brush past him, but Ben stopped her, her name a question on his lips.

She hesitated after turning back to face him and had to see the regret visibly etched on his face. "Forget it, Ben. I've moved on."

"No you haven't. Not completely. And I was out of line."

"Yes, you were." Darien appeared on the verge of saying something else. But whatever it was, it died as she pressed her lips tightly together then released a soft sigh. "It's been a long day, Ben, and we could all use some sleep."

Ben studied Darien's face, clearly looking for something. Whether or not he was satisfied with what he saw, Jessie didn't know. But he gave a curt nod before he turned and walked away. Darien waited a moment longer, then slipped back into her seat. Without saying a word, she handed Jessie one of the bottles she'd been holding.

"Thanks," Jessie said. She uncapped the bottle and took a long drink while watching Darien closely. The shadows under her eyes told of too little sleep and too much adrenaline. She looked tight, almost brittle. Or at least she did until she somehow schooled her face and all expression faded.

Seconds ticked by. When the silence had gone on long enough, Jessie reached with one hand and caught a loose strand of hair, holding it aside so she could see Darien's eyes, her expression. She was clearly not happy. Fair enough. Neither was she. "We've still got a long night ahead of us. Do you want to tell me what the hell that was all about?"

She was surprised when Darien turned and briefly kissed the hand that had just touched her cheek. The anger ebbed from her expression as other emotions swam in her eyes. "I'm sorry, Jesslyn. But as long as tonight is, tomorrow will be an even longer day. Would you mind if we left any serious conversation for another time?"

Yes, I mind. The words echoed in Jessie's head, but they remained trapped there. She knew it would do no good to confront Darien when she clearly didn't want to talk. And especially not when they were about to initiate a carefully choreographed dance meant to draw out a cunning enemy. She swallowed her disappointment.

"No problem. We'll have plenty of time to talk about things once we get to Maine and are out on the water." She hesitated, but only for an instant. "You know Ben only said what he did because he cares."

"I know," Darien said then surprised her by releasing a wry laugh. "But be careful around him, or before you know it, he'll be giving you a copy of *The Care and Feeding of a Contract Assassin.*"

Jessie stared at her for a moment. "Does it come with pictures?"

CHAPTER TWENTY-FOUR

They landed at JFK just after sunrise, the eastern horizon a palette of deep lavender, orange, and gold as the jet made its descent into New York. Jessie and Darien walked through the Jetway, caught up in a tide of tired passengers eager to deplane, before they managed to separate themselves.

They also left the rest of the team behind without looking back. No words, not even glances were exchanged. Everyone knew their roles and what was at stake.

And no one does paranoid like agency operatives. Darien laughed softly to herself, knowing she was no different as she gazed at her fellow travelers. The habit had been ingrained since childhood, enhanced by years of training, and was now as much a part of her as dark hair and golden skin.

She didn't pay much attention to anyone and wouldn't, unless they showed more than a passing interest in either her or Jessie. Then she would memorize everything about them. But nobody stood out.

They had one more flight—a relatively short hop to Bangor on a private Beechcraft Bonanza—then a drive to Bar Harbor, on the edge of the sea, where they would pick up the boat they would call home for the foreseeable future.

The car Jessie rented turned out to be a dark gray BMW roadster. "It's not quite a Ducati, but I thought you might enjoy driving it," she said with a smile. "But I can drive if you're too tired."

"No, I'm good."

Slipping into the driver's seat, Darien started the engine—a comfortable throaty rumble—and grinned as she found herself staring at a cockpit with enough dials to rival the jet they had flown in from France. There was too much traffic, however, and with stops for groceries and to-go coffee, no opportunity to see what the car could really do. But she still checked mirrors as often as the road ahead.

By midafternoon she was barefoot in shorts and a tank top, standing on the deck of the *Tao*, a sleek white forty-five footer not unlike most of the other boats currently docked at the marina. She took a long, deep breath, conscious of the warmth of the sun, the cooling breeze, the scent of the sea, and the unmistakable feeling she was being watched. Her instincts were twitching.

Showtime, she thought and wasn't surprised. She had already completed an electronic scan for bugs of any kind, and for now the boat was clean. But she knew it was unlikely to stay that way.

She looked around casually as she rolled her shoulders and tried to stretch back muscles still cramped from too many hours on planes. She checked the nearby boats, then looked toward the parking lot, searching places where someone might hide if they wanted to see without easily being seen. There were only empty cars and she didn't see anyone who looked out of place. But she knew they were there.

Hearing soft footsteps approach from below deck, Darien smiled slightly, knowing the sound meant Jessie had finished checking out their accommodations. Then she felt Jessie's hands settle on her shoulders and begin to work on the knots, and she closed her eyes.

"Hey," Jessie said. "Everything okay?"

"Define okay," she murmured, before adding, "You've got magic hands."

Jessie laughed. "You don't know the half of it."

No, she probably didn't. There was still time and she hoped to find out. She closed her eyes and enjoyed the moment. But as her awareness intensified, she also felt the tension being transmitted through Jessie's fingers. "You feel it too, don't you?"

"There's a spot on the back of my neck that's been burning since we got here," Jessie responded softly. "I'm not sure why because I didn't anticipate they'd make a move of any kind so quickly."

"At a guess, they've been on us since we left Paris."

"Why would they do that? I wouldn't have thought this would escalate so quickly."

"I don't think this is about making any sudden moves. It's too soon and Petrov can't afford to have her desire to take me out ruin her plans for the summit leaders. That means she'll need to coordinate the two events as closely together as possible. So I think she's just keeping an eye on me, trying to anticipate what I might do."

"And what is it you're going to do?"

"Watch and wait. Anticipate. Distract."

She turned and got her first glimpse of Jessie, looking far too edible in shorts and a bikini top. For what seemed like a long time, although it might have only been measured in seconds, she simply looked. Her pulse throbbed at the base of her throat as her gaze traveled, pausing in places that caused the beat of her heart to increase. Like the slope of Jessie's breasts and her pale, gently curving mouth.

She leaned closer and brushed her mouth lightly over Jessie's, soft and gentle, then licked and kissed her way down to her collarbone. She wanted nothing more than to linger. But what she was feeling was different. Real. More so than anything she'd ever experienced. She was also all too conscious of the unknown eyes watching them.

She forced herself to draw back before she lost what passed for control around Jessie. "Why don't we take the boat out for a bit, get used to how she handles. By the time we get back we'll need fuel, and we can get an early dinner at the marina restaurant."

Jessie flashed a look out of eyes hazy and filled with something that made Darien wish they were alone. In bed.

"Is that your best offer?"

Darien gave her one last look. "It is, for now. Can you untie us?"

Jessie nodded and went to work, efficiently handling the dock lines while Darien got the engines started. They were purring smoothly by the time Jessie hopped back on board.

Jessie sat in a swivel chair on the flybridge and kept an eye on wind and current as Darien maneuvered the big boat away from the dock and moved slowly out of the marina. The boat came with both old-fashioned throttle levers and joystick controls and she could see Darien testing both, getting familiar and comfortable with how the boat handled as she lined up a channel marker.

She made a turn once she cleared the marker and brought up more speed with a nudge of the throttle as they moved into open water. The boat's response was immediate and Darien's mouth lifted at the corners, but her eyes were covered by dark aviator sunglasses, so Jessie couldn't tell what she was thinking.

As if you could, she told herself. Ignoring the debate in her head, she asked, "Do you know where we're going?"

"No idea whatsoever. I just want to see how the *Tao* handles. Make sure there are no surprises. Since this is your home turf, why don't you decide?" She indicated the navigation system in front of her with the wave of one hand, while keeping the other on the wheel to control the boat. "See anything you like?"

Jessie stared at Darien's hand and felt adrenaline spike. "Yes."

Darien laughed and the mood shifted like quicksilver to sensual delight. "How about picking a direction first?" she said, extending her free hand.

Jessie took it, weaving their fingers together. Felt the warm, solid strength of Darien's hand and swallowed. "Why don't we head toward the Cranberry Isles? It won't be as busy as anywhere around Mount Desert."

Darien altered the boat's course and a moment later had them heading southeast. "Cranberries. Sounds tasty."

Jessie shook her head and fought against a smile, then realized something. "You've never been here and I swear you didn't even look at the GPS or the navigation system. How the hell did you know to do that?"

"I studied the maps while we were in Paris. Remember?"

"And that's all it takes?"

When Darien shrugged, Jessie realized her study of the maps was indeed all it took. A photographic memory of some kind. And though Jessie had grown up exploring the coastal Maine waterways, Darien already appeared to know them as well as, if not better than, she did. She kept all of those maps in her head. Amazing.

"Here," Darien said after a few minutes. "Why don't you take the controls for a while?"

"Really?"

Darien slid out of the pilot's seat. "You know the area, but you don't know the boat. I'd like you to feel comfortable enough that if I'm ever out of commission, unable to help, you'll be able to do whatever needs to be done."

Jessie had been eager to get her hands on the big boat, but she didn't like the sound of the possibility Darien had just described. Reality, she realized, had just raised its ugly head.

To anyone out on the water, or even at the marina, she and Darien looked like an ordinary couple, enjoying a vacation on the beautiful waters of coastal Maine. Except that they weren't a couple and this wasn't a vacation. She had made a mistake—a rookie mistake that could prove lethal in the field—by allowing the line between appearances and reality to blur. But as Darien's words had just clearly reminded her, they were rapidly approaching the apex of a dangerous operation and lives were at stake, not the least of which was Darien's.

She clenched her teeth but managed somehow to smile. "I hear you."

She started to move toward the wheel, but Darien stopped her. "I'm sorry, Jesslyn. I'm just trying to stay one step ahead and make sure we have contingency plans in place. That's all. I don't want you to worry. Come and take the wheel."

Darien gently tugged on Jessie's hand, pulling her closer and touching their entwined fingers to her lips. The look on her face left Jessie slightly breathless, filled with a heady anticipation, and it suddenly felt like she was being offered something other than control of the *Tao*.

But she also acknowledged that steering tons of yacht on a crowded waterway was probably a safer bet to dealing with the look in Darien's eyes. At least for the moment. She swallowed, realized Darien was saying something, and forced herself to try and concentrate. Something about—

"Video games?" Darien repeated. "Have you ever played video games?"

"Of course." She'd played more than her share over the years. "Want to play later?"

Darien laughed but didn't respond to the double entendre beyond a raised eyebrow. "The joystick's no different. Just like a video game. But don't just play with the joystick. Before we head back today, I'd like you to be comfortable with both sets of controls."

Jessie nodded and took the controls, happy to be concentrating on something other than the heated blood coursing through her veins. "Sweet," she murmured as the boat responded to her touch.

Darien remained close but let her learn firsthand how the boat handled and how to correct for things like wind and currents and tides. Once it was clear she was comfortable, Darien showed her how to enter waypoints and set the autopilot using the touch-screen navigation system.

"How is it you know how to use all this equipment?"

"I've probably used something similar at one time or another. And it's technology, right?"

Jessie watched her a moment longer. "So you read the manual?"

"Yes." She gave a slight grin. "I'm sure I did, at some point."

She was clearly trying not to laugh, Jessie realized. She was also trying to keep a close eye on the radar continuously sweeping the navigational chart on the computer screen. "What are you looking for?"

"Anyone following our course a little too closely."

"And?"

With a quick shake of her head, Darien reassured her there was nothing close enough to worry about. Slowly relaxing, Jessie watched the rock wall of the shore recede and felt the memories of long-ago summers stir inside her. The scent, the taste, the very feel of the experience was familiar, and she was fifteen again, determined to explore every island.

As she shook off the past and slipped back into the day, she began appreciating the stunning natural beauty of the Maine coastline she hadn't enjoyed in much too long. The warm July sunshine and the refreshing sea breezes, the scenic bays, craggy peninsulas, the sparkling water. Even the whales were enjoying a perfect summer day, and she grinned as Darien pointed to first one, then two more humpbacks breaching not far from their starboard bow.

❖

Darien noted both she and Jessie were more relaxed as she brought the boat back to the marina.

It had been an uneventful day, which in her experience made it a good day. The water had been calm and the boat had handled exceptionally well, better than she could have hoped. She felt reassured that Jessie could deal with the big boat alone if she needed to. And if she was being honest with herself, the day on the water had helped her more than if she'd been able to spend the day catching up on lost sleep.

The presence of military speedboats patrolling the water and a trio of helicopters buzzing occasionally in the air overhead proved surprisingly reassuring while serving as a constant reminder. There was a job at hand and an as yet unseen enemy. It helped her stay focused. Calm. Grounded. Ready to face whatever waited just around the next bend.

More importantly, she had taken the first step in becoming very visible, letting anyone who wanted to or needed to know that she had arrived. She was here in Maine. And while it went against years of indoctrination and training, she had to remember this time, she wasn't the hunter. She was the prey.

The trap was now set, and all she needed was for Petrov to take the bait. And she would. Her need for vengeance was too strong, something Darien could readily identify with and understand. Except, at a guess, she had more experience with revenge than Petrov.

Did Petrov know enough to dig two graves?

She shook her head in a futile attempt to dispel her thoughts, then watched Jessie jump onto the dock and found herself pleasantly distracted. Even if it was just for a second or two, she paused to admire Jessie's very shapely derriere as she bent to tie a line to one of the cleats. A moment later, she choked back a groan and pulled her bottom lip between her teeth when Jessie turned and caught her looking.

Behave, Jessie mouthed, then crossed her eyes.

Darien laughed out loud and shrugged semi-apologetically before heading below. She paused long enough to grab a change of clothes—shorts, a silk tank, and a white cotton shirt—then left the master stateroom head for Jessie while she made her way to the forward head. A quick shower should do the trick. Preferably cold.

When she returned, she found Jessie sitting on the edge of the bed wearing a thin red silk robe, towel drying her hair. Jessie looked up and smiled, her face pink from sun and wind. "I just realized, unless we're talking casual, I have nothing to wear that might be considered appropriate for dinner."

"Good," Darien said as she slowly approached the bed. Closer until all she could smell was the delicate scent of shampoo mingling with a scent that was pure Jessie. "Don't wear anything."

Jessie laughed. "I can't go out to dinner dressed in—" Her words faded and her eyes grew wide when Darien stopped only inches from her face.

She bent toward Jessie, to where she could feel Jessie's breath against the damp strands of hair that clung to her face.

"Darien?"

The soft kiss Darien brushed against her cheek made Jessie shiver. "I think you should stay right here, wearing exactly what you have on—and nothing else—while I get dinner from the restaurant and bring it back."

"You want me to stay here wearing only this robe?"

"Yes...no." Darien shook her head and reached for the sash holding the robe closed. It came undone with a single tug, and then she lifted her hands to the lapels and gently pulled them apart. "You're so very beautiful. You take my breath away, and I want nothing more than to make love with you. I want to feel you wrapped around me. I want to hear my name on your lips and feel you come apart in my arms. Give yourself to me, Jesslyn. I promise I won't hurt you."

"Don't make promises you can't keep."

"I guess you'll have to trust me," she said, her lips a breath away from Jessie's. "I never make promises unless I intend to keep them."

She closed the final distance and brushed a kiss on Jessie's lips, warm and soft, fully intending to leave, to pick up dinner. But Jessie clearly had ideas of her own and changed the tenor of the kiss as she pulled Darien down onto the bed with an irresistible pressure. She went willingly, felt as the kiss deepened, became demanding. It filled her with hunger and a sudden rush of heat that seeped into her body and flowed in her blood.

And Darien responded, losing herself in the moment, giving in to the onslaught of sensations and emotions that flooded her. Without reservation. No hesitation. No holding back.

CHAPTER TWENTY-FIVE

In the hazy predawn light, Darien opened her eyes feeling disoriented. She didn't know how long she'd slept or what time it was. Nor could she say what had awoken her. But for the first time in a very long time, she had woken up without the images of Prague filling her mind.

As she slowly reflected on that surprising knowledge, awareness of her surroundings amplified and she found herself listening to the sound of water slapping softly against the hull. She breathed deeply and smiled, drawing pleasure from the gentle rocking motion of the boat and the warmth emanating from the woman lying beside her.

Jessie looked so right there, sprawled on her stomach with the covers pooled around her hips and long spiky lashes shadowing her cheeks. She was as achingly beautiful asleep as she was awake. And sexy as hell.

Darien squeezed her eyes shut for a moment. She knew she could easily get lost just watching her sleep and swore she could feel every breath she drew. Hear every beat of her heart.

She was no longer surprised to discover Jessie could make her blood run fever hot with a single look. Or make her ache without even trying. But she was amazed at how quickly a very real bond had formed and how Jessie made her want things Darien had never previously considered possible.

Funny how just a few weeks can change everything. She could so easily get used to this, she thought, and wanted to keep the feelings close.

Coffee. She needed coffee.

She slipped quietly from the bed, taking care not to disturb Jessie. The air was cool and damp, and she shivered as it brushed against her bare skin. But it was simpler to bend down and retrieve the shorts and T-shirt she had tossed aside the evening before than try to find her jeans. Not if she didn't want to wake Jessie up. Without giving it another thought, she scooped up the clothes from the floor and went to the head.

Just as she returned to the stateroom minutes later, her instincts started to quiver and hum. Darien had learned long ago never to question them, and she moved to the night table and retrieved the SIG Sauer she'd left there. She checked it out of habit, even though she knew she would find it the way she always left it. Fully loaded with one in the chamber. But she felt better having checked, and she tucked the gun at the small of her back before making her way to the galley.

Still uncertain what had caused her instincts to twitch, she left the lights off. She moved quietly through the shadows, flipped the switch on the coffeemaker, then stood motionless in the darkness. Breathing slowly, shallowly, making no sound, she let the sounds of her surroundings wash over her as she listened.

At first, all she heard was the distant wail of a foghorn. The whisper of a breeze laced with salt. Water slapping against the dock pilings. Her blood pulsing through her. But then a faint noise alerted her. The unmistakable sound of someone approaching on the nearby dock.

Darien waited, listened, and a moment later, she heard the sound of footsteps on the wooden planks, closer now. Soft. Cautious. As her training kicked in, she slipped out of her deck shoes and reached for her SIG, holding its familiar weight comfortably in her hand. And with her bare feet making no sound, she advanced toward the stairs.

Sometime overnight, a thick fog had rolled in and enveloped the coast in a shroud of gray. It was nearly impenetrable, visibility limited to only a few feet. But she could feel someone's presence in the movement of the air, and as she cleared the stairs and slipped onto the deck, she realized there might be barely enough light to see—but just enough light to kill.

She waited in the misty shadows, keeping perfectly still until she saw the intruder materialize through the shifting veils of fog.

Whoever it was would be getting a surprise, she thought. Weapon locked and loaded, she waited until they got a little closer. "You may as well come the rest of the way," she said. "But you're going to want to come in nice and soft because I have a SIG in my hand and I can guarantee one thing. I don't miss—not at any distance."

A heartbeat later, she watched the intruder morph.

"Hello, Darien. It's been a long time," Grace Lawson said before she stepped closer. But she kept her hands visible and empty, coming in soft as requested.

Everything inside Darien went painfully still. She slowly lowered the gun to her side, but kept it in her hand. Grace was Jessie's mother and someone she once knew. A friend of Ben's. A friend of her own mother. But right now the only one who had her complete trust was Jessie. Anyone else would have to earn it.

"You're lucky," she said. "My normal response is to shoot without asking any questions. In this case, that also means tossing people over the side when they try to come aboard without permission."

Grace was smart enough not to argue. "Point taken," she said and smiled, suddenly looking years younger and even more familiar.

Time fragmented and Darien felt the keen slash of memories, reminding her of another life, another time, and a woman she had once loved nearly as much as she had loved her own mother. "Why are you here, Grace? Is there a problem that couldn't be communicated through channels over the satellite phone? Ben warned me it was likely you'd want a face-to-face meeting, but I can't imagine why."

"Can't you? There was a time you would have been happy to see me." Grace fell silent, studied Darien, and then sighed. "I was recently reminded it's been a long time since I've seen you or talked to you. And with things rapidly coming to a head, I thought it was time to change that."

"Time? You thought it was time?" Tension shimmered in her voice as a whisper of anger seeped into Darien's blood. "Well, isn't that bloody marvelous."

There was no visible change in Grace's expression, but Darien heard the slight hitch in her breathing. She watched Grace swallow and saw her gather her rather formidable reserves around herself before she finally spoke.

"It's been nearly fifteen years, Darien. Even you would have to admit it's been a long time. Plus we are both aware you have my daughter with you."

"Yes, how about that," Darien said dryly and forced herself to smile. "Imagine my surprise when one of the operatives you sent to Paris turned out to be your daughter. Especially after you went to such lengths to make certain our paths never crossed, all those years ago."

It still hurt, she realized. Damn. Fifteen years later and it still hurt that Grace had chosen to walk away from the child she had been, leaving Ben to deal with the inevitable fallout. Darien willed the hurt into a dark corner of her mind. But it took more effort than she'd anticipated, and she had to struggle to keep her expression neutral, her voice steady.

"You had to know Ben would bring me in," she continued. "So it stands to reason you knew Jesslyn would end up meeting me— working with me—when you sent her to work with Ben."

"I thought that might be the case. But I couldn't allow it to influence my decision to send Jesslyn. She's good at what she does, which made her the right choice. And I stand by what I believe was the right decision."

When Darien didn't respond, Grace paused, stared at her for a long few seconds, then adjusted her stance. "As for the decision I made fifteen years ago—to leave you with Ben—I don't expect you to understand, Darien, but I believed I needed to protect my family. My daughter. And I did what I thought was best for all concerned."

In spite of her best effort, Darien felt her pulse accelerate and struggled to present a calm she didn't feel. "You honestly thought I would hurt Jesslyn?"

"Not intentionally, no. But try to put yourself in my position, Darien. Even before we finished destroying what we all hoped was the last of the Guild, you were out of control. Dear Lord, you were almost feral." She paused as if expecting an argument. When none came, she continued. "You were only thirteen, but you'd lived your whole life in the shadows and had just spent the better part of a year hunting and killing people with single-minded purpose. If you can remember that, how could you expect me to risk…?"

How could I expect her to risk Jesslyn, Darien silently finished for her and briefly closed her eyes. "You know what, Grace? It's ancient history. It can't be changed. None of it can and we're both better off forgetting about it. But there is one thing you should know. Jesslyn is more than good. She's the best."

She realized her mistake almost as soon as she said it, even before Grace's head snapped up. She'd clearly revealed something of her feelings. In her voice or through her words. Grace confirmed her suspicion an instant later.

"What have you done, Darien?"

Darien remained silent under the intensity and weight of Grace's scrutiny before she moved out of the shadows. "It would be a mistake to think you still know me," she said, leaving Grace's question unanswered while calmly tucking her gun back at the small of her back and indicating the stairs. "Jesslyn's still asleep, but the coffee should be ready by now. You're welcome to have a cup while you're waiting for her to get up. Maybe she'll be more inclined to answer your questions. Do you still take it black with one sugar?"

"I'm surprised you remember."

"I remember everything, Grace."

Darien willed away thoughts that intruded, willed away old hurts, leaving only an aching emptiness. She started to turn and saw Jessie standing near the top of the stairs. Wearing one of Darien's white cotton shirts, with only a couple of buttons done up. Her eyes were wide, but her mouth was flattened into a hard line, while the bleak expression on her face said she had heard too much.

Jessie's head was spinning and for a moment all she could do was breathe. Too late she remembered Ben's caution about things not having ended well between Darien and her mother. At the time she had wondered what he meant. Now it seemed she had finally found out, but she still wasn't certain she was putting it all together correctly. Was she?

She looked at Darien, noted sadly that her beautiful face was singularly without expression, then turned to stare at her mother. "Did I just hear you correctly? You abandoned her because of me?"

Her mother flinched and looked as if she wanted no part of the conversation, but Jessie wasn't about to allow that. "Damn it, mother,

I just heard you tell Darien you left her behind to protect me. Is that what happened? Is that what you did?"

Before Grace could respond, Darien stepped in front of Jessie. Blocking her view of her mother, she waited until Jessie's eyes connected with hers. "I'm going to get changed and go for a run." She lifted her hand and briefly touched Jessie's face. "It'll give you and your mother some privacy so you can talk. It'll also give me a much-needed chance to clear my head."

"I don't think that's a good idea." Jessie realized Darien wasn't listening and felt a chill that had nothing to do with the cool air whispering over her skin. "Damn it, Darien, no. You're just giving Petrov an easy chance to grab you. Which means the last thing you should be doing is going anywhere alone."

Darien showed no reaction beyond a low, mirthless laugh. "I'm the last person you need to be worried about when it comes to being able to look after myself. If you haven't figured it out yet, I'm certain Grace will be only too happy to fill in any blanks you may have. And the whole point of our being here is to give Petrov just that chance."

Jessie looked at her and frowned. Clearly she and her mother needed to talk. But the distance Darien was throwing between them was a much bigger problem. Tension swirled between them. It felt tangible, had weight and substance, and worse, she couldn't think of any way to change things, to stop what was happening. Her inability to think left her frozen, a part of the fog-bound tableau on the deck, as she watched Darien disappear down the stairs.

She was still standing there under her mother's watchful eyes, too numb to move or say anything, when Darien returned a short couple of minutes later. She had changed into black spandex shorts and a black long-sleeved T-shirt and had pulled her hair back in a loose ponytail. She looked as dark and dangerous as she ever had, exuded strength, and walked with the same easy confidence she always did. But Jessie could also sense her growing isolation and felt compelled to try again.

"Dare, please listen. I'm really not sure this is a good idea." For an instant Jessie thought she'd gotten through. Thought she had seen the barriers Darien had erected around herself begin to fracture.

"This hurts," Darien murmured. "Why did I think it wouldn't?"

"What hurts, Darien?"

But even as she asked the question, a mask closed over Darien's face, reminding Jessie just how good she really was at that, at shutting out the world and everyone in it.

"I have to go. Sooner rather than later, Petrov needs a chance to grab me. And we all know it'll be better for everyone concerned if I'm alone when she comes for me."

Unsaid was that if anyone—if Jessie—was around her when Petrov finally made her move, she could become collateral damage. It didn't need to be said. But damn it, surely if they used their collective intelligence, they could come up with a better plan than this. "Darien, wait. We need to think this through."

Not surprising, Darien didn't listen. Instead, Jessie watched her turn away, moving like a wraith with unnerving silence as she disappeared from sight without looking back. Jessie continued to stare into the fog long after Darien's shadow had faded before finally turning to face her mother, who was watching intently. "I need some coffee."

She didn't bother to wait for a response as she led the way down to the galley, flipping the light switch on as she passed to chase away the suddenly oppressive darkness. She reached into a cupboard, brought down two mugs, and filled them with coffee, adding a single sugar cube to one before passing it to her mother.

"Talk to me," she said, clasping her own coffee mug tightly in both hands, trying to absorb its warmth. "Explain how the woman I thought I knew all my life could have left a thirteen-year-old child behind to fend for herself. Especially a child who was still trying to deal with her mother's murder."

Jessie saw her words hit home and the bright galley lights emphasized Grace's sudden pallor. There was a long silence, and then she heard Grace's soft voice ask, "How much do you know about what happened in Prague fifteen years ago? How much did Darien share?"

"I would say she told me most of it. About the men that grabbed her, and witnessing what was done to her mother. About escaping the brothel and going after the killers. And about you and Ben finding her and helping her finish the job."

Grace drew in a soundless breath. "I'm surprised she revealed so much. The Darien I once knew would never have been so forthcoming."

"She's changed. Even in the short time I've known her, I can see that she's changed." Jessie slumped onto the couch, her forearms resting on her knees, hands still seeking the warmth of the coffee mug, while she stared up at her mother's eyes. So like her own, but nothing she saw gave her a clue. "It's my job to sift through and interpret intel, but the one thing I could never understand and Darien never willingly shared was how she ended up with Ben in London. Straight into the waiting arms of MI6. It was like she never had a chance to do or be anything other than what she is."

"A killer?"

"A very talented and very deadly operative," Jessie countered without heat. "So imagine my dismay when I hear you say you chose to leave her with Ben to protect me. How in hell could you have done that to her?"

"Actually, darling, I was thinking of you."

Jessie flinched. "How can you say that?"

"Because it's the truth, Jesslyn. I knew you but I also knew Darien. And even though you were only fifteen, I knew instinctively you would take one look at her—at that wild and beautiful woman-child—and that would be it for you. At the time, the thought terrified me."

Somewhere a foghorn called mournfully. As the sound thinned and faded, it left only the faint slapping of water against the hull to disturb the silence.

"Well, it may have taken fifteen years," Jessie said softly, "but it turns out you were right all along."

CHAPTER TWENTY-SIX

The morning sun had burned away the remnants of fog by the time Darien stopped for coffee at a small café close to the waterfront. The breakfast crowd of tourists and locals had thinned. But as she chatted with the young waitress—maybe nineteen, and saving so she could go away to college—she learned business would remain fairly steady before surging again at lunchtime.

"I don't mind, I like to keep busy," the girl said. She gave Darien an appraising look and sent her a cheeky grin before adding, "And the tips are really good, especially from the boating crowd."

Taking her coffee to a small outside table near the front door, Darien took a sip then rested her head against the wall behind her. She watched as people parked nearby, got out of their cars, and picked up coffee to go before piling back into their vehicles and driving off. Others jogged by or walked dogs. They smiled and nodded to her. She raised her coffee in salute and smiled back.

Just another runner cooling down, enjoying the view. Reflecting on the morning.

The ever-present scent of the sea and the looming evergreens had done their job, serving to calm and soothe her. And as she had hoped, the run had helped to clear her head. It always did. But it had also yielded an unexpected side benefit. It had helped ease the headache that seemed to have become her constant companion since her last fight at Oz.

It was only fair, she thought wryly, since she had picked up other companions in the exchange. She'd been keenly aware of them, the unseen eyes that had her senses tingling from the moment she'd left the boat.

She knew, of course, that some of her watchers would be part of the joint MI6-CIA team Ben and Grace had put on the ground. Assigned to monitor, but not interfere. Waiting for Petrov to make her move so they could track her back to wherever she was hiding.

But there were others. When she'd stopped to fiddle with a lace on her running shoe and had glanced back, all she'd caught were shadow figures. Nothing else really popped, which told her they were good. And that made sense. At this late stage in the game, she expected Petrov would have pulled out all the stops and was going with her best resources.

Darien shrugged. There was still nothing she couldn't handle.

For some reason, possibly lingering restlessness, at the end of her run she'd continued into the heart of the village instead of turning into the marina. It was only afterward, when she found herself aimlessly looking in shop windows, that she realized she was avoiding a return to the boat. The thought annoyed her.

Under normal circumstances, she would not consider herself a coward.

But then these aren't normal circumstances, are they?

No, far from it. She considered the nature of her restlessness and acknowledged she ought to be in constant motion, hunting for Petrov. Not sitting here, highly visible, waiting for Petrov to act. She hadn't anticipated how heavily the passive stance would weigh on her. But she should have known. She needed to act, to get things started. Get things done. Then move on.

Seeing Grace again hadn't helped. Her unexpected appearance had stirred the dust and detritus Darien believed was keeping the past securely covered. She had exposed all the wreckage, the grief, and the regret Darien had tried for years to hold in check. And she had reminded Darien of how long she'd hidden herself away, believing it was easier than interacting with people. Easier than explaining what had happened and what she'd done. What she'd become.

And now? Avoiding Grace and whatever tales she would have told by now would not solve anything. Not that she believed there was anything Grace could tell Jesslyn that she herself hadn't already told her. And even if Grace provided details Darien had left out, she truly didn't think any new revelations would have the power to cut the threads binding her to Jesslyn. Or at least she needed to believe that.

She gave herself a mental shake. The past was the past and couldn't be changed. There was a job to do. An operation that dictated Petrov would come for her. And no one needed to tell her she needed her head in the game if she intended to survive.

Ordering another coffee to go, she paid her bill and overtipped her waitress, hopefully contributing to the girl's college fund. She then slowly made her way back to the marina.

❖

If still waters ran deep, Darien Troy ran endless fathoms. It was the only thing Jessie could think of as she watched her coalesce from thought into a living, breathing woman.

She had been gone longer than Jessie had anticipated, but she was finally returning from her run, the sun slanting across her as she walked slowly down the dock toward the boat. The run appeared to have done her good. Her face was glowing, her golden skin flushed and damp with a faint sheen of perspiration. And her body, in the black T-shirt and running shorts, could make a grown woman weep.

Watching her made Jessie's nerves awaken. She felt her pulse kick up and her throat go dry, while her body was ignited by a thousand different emotions. Memory sliced into her awareness, taking her back to the night she had met Darien. Inexplicably, she hadn't been able to take her eyes off her that night. And now, now that she'd gotten to know her better, now that she had been with her and had become intimately acquainted with both the heat and tenderness of her touch, the flood of sensations left her breathless and wanting with an elemental hunger.

A killer, her mother had said.

Yes, she was. Unquestionably lethal. But she was so much more. In the time they had been together, she had seen other sides. Darien had let her in physically, holding nothing back. They had also grown closer emotionally. Laughing, talking, or simply sharing quiet moments.

Darien would never be an easy person to live with. Or to love. Jessie already knew that. But more importantly, she could provide the strength Jessie wanted in her life, needed in a partner. She would challenge her. Hell, they would challenge each other. Endless possibilities opened up before her.

She knew she was getting ahead of herself. They hadn't talked about anything beyond the present moment. She didn't really know what Darien wanted, or what she dreamed beyond the nightmares of Prague. But her mother was right. Darien was it for her. She knew that as clearly as she knew she needed to take her next breath.

Of course, she also knew there were things that would need to be dealt with between here and then. Critical things. First she would need to ensure Darien survived whatever Nadia Petrov had planned for her. And they needed to ensure the Guild was prevented from carrying out its larger agenda of terror and destruction.

But after that? After that, she would take her time and convince Darien she both wanted and needed her in her life. That they could make it work. A walk in the park, after saving the world.

"Something smells good," Darien said as she stepped onto the satin teak deck.

"I thought you might be hungry after your run. So I made French toast—I have it in the warmer. I also picked up some of Maine's much vaunted blueberries to go with it. They were frozen and came from last year's crop, but I confess I've been nibbling on them and they're really quite wonderful." Heat rushed into her cheeks. She was rambling and she knew it. The problem was so did Darien, who was looking at her with an expression somewhere between suspicious and cautious.

"Are you okay?"

No. "Yes."

"Did Grace leave, or will she be joining us for breakfast?"

"She left."

Jessie extended her hand. She waited until Darien grasped it and laced their fingers together before she drew her close and led her down to the galley.

She nudged Darien down at the table, then quickly moved away. It was either that or she was going to grab her and pull her into the stateroom and onto the big bed. Because all she wanted to do at this moment was abandon herself to the heat pulsing through her, to the sweet ache of wanting Darien. But what she really needed to do was get her head back in the game.

It was really good advice she was giving herself, and she was trying hard to follow it. But it was made more difficult when Darien was sitting within arm's reach, looking like temptation personified.

She brought the French toast out of the warming oven, slid some on two plates, then put one in front of Darien, the other beside her on the table. She remembered to get the berries and butter and maple syrup, some ice water for Darien, and juice for herself. Finally, with nothing left to do or get, she took a seat at the narrow table and began to eat.

"So how was the run? See anything interesting?"

Darien sent her a sideways look. "It was good. Absolutely beautiful, actually. Mountains and ocean and trees, along with a few gut-wrenching hills to keep me honest. And lots of company."

Jessie went still and looked at her. "Company?"

"Some combination of the home team and Petrov's crew, I would imagine. I have to admit it wasn't the most comfortable I've ever felt while running. It felt too much like I had crosshairs on my back." Darien looked at her and shrugged. "But we both know it's going to happen sooner rather than later, and more importantly, it's going to net us what we need. Petrov. Tell me why it bothers you so much."

Because it risks you too much, she wanted to say. "Because the longer I think about it, the less I like this plan. There has to be another way—a way of getting Petrov without putting you in jeopardy."

"There probably is, but nothing any of us have been able to come up with until now, let alone in the time we have left." Darien sighed. "Jesslyn, the one thing we know to be true is that Petrov wants me. I can't say for certain, but I would hazard a guess she wants me as badly as I once wanted her father when I went after Dmitri all those years ago. I know what that feels like."

Jessie remained silent, choosing to wait for Darien to continue at her own pace.

"What I can tell you from personal experience dealing with revenge is she's not going to give up. And since she's going to come after me anyway, this way we get to follow my tracking signal back to wherever she's hiding. We not only get her and her weapons, we neutralize her plans and save the day."

"I know all of that," Jessie said quietly, "but those of us who are going to be tracking your signal aren't the ones walking into the line of fire. That'll be all you. What if she just kills you right away? Have you even thought of that?"

"It's always a possibility, which is why this is a calculated risk," Darien admitted. "But the probability that Petrov will choose to kill me quickly is quite low. There's no satisfaction in that. She wants to hurt me. She wants to make me suffer before she kills me."

"How can you be so sure?"

"Because it's how I felt about Dmitri. I wanted to look him in the eye. I wanted him to know who it was ending his life…and why. I wanted him to be left with no doubt."

"Darien." The tight edge in Darien's voice made Jessie ache and it was all she could say. Just that. Just her name. She swallowed hard and almost looked away. "I think that's what scares me."

"What scares you? Me?"

"Jesus, no. Never you. What scares me is that she wants to hurt you. And if something happens while she has you, if something goes wrong, I'm afraid I'm not going to be there—none of us are going to be there in time to help. Damn it, Darien, do you have any idea, any idea at all, what that would do to me? If you get hurt or if—"

Raising her hand, Darien pressed her fingers against Jessie's lips as she whispered, "That's not going to happen."

Jessie swallowed hard against the tightness in her throat. "You do know you're not Superman, don't you?"

"I guess that explains why I couldn't find a cape to fit." Darien laughed and leaned in closer. "I need you to trust me, Jesslyn. Trust me that it'll be all right. That we'll get through this."

"How can you say that with such certainty?"

"Because I have to." Darien leaned forward, eyelids at half-mast, then briefly brought their lips together. "It's what I need to believe in order to do what I have to do. Just like what I need right now is to make love with you. I need to be who I am when you and I are together."

A slow smile spread over Jessie's face as she shot Darien a look and saw she meant it. "I knew there was a reason I liked you. You're a woman who knows what she needs."

"Right. I'm what every mother wants for her daughter."

"Wrong. You're what the daughter wants for herself."

CHAPTER TWENTY-SEVEN

The afternoon sun was sitting low, close to the horizon as Jessie took another turn in the pilot's seat behind the wheel. She had a headset on and was talking to Ben and Grace and someone from Homeland Security. Hourly check-ins had now become the order of the day.

Darien stood next to her, uncertain suddenly why they were even out here. She should be out running, giving Petrov a chance to grab her. Instead, she was listening to the steady throbbing power of the big diesel engines and the soft cadence of Jessie's voice. Alternating between watching the radar screen and using binoculars to take a closer look at any boats in their vicinity.

She stayed within arm's reach of Jessie, not because she needed to worry about how she was handling the boat, but because she enjoyed feeling her heat. Her lips quirked as she thought about that. She liked that almost as much as she liked the fact they were both relaxed—with the silence and with each other—in spite of the circumstances surrounding them.

So incredible and unexpected. Jessie was the only woman she'd ever been with who knew who and what she was, what she did. No lies. No pretending to be something or someone she wasn't. She was finding that powerful. Heady.

She wondered if she would live long enough to enjoy it.

Anything new? she mouthed silently when Jessie made eye contact.

Jessie shook her head, frustration evident as she continued listening to whoever was now talking on the other end of the line. Darien well understood how she was feeling. Waiting was the hardest part of the game, and the clock was counting down. Time was running short and they all knew it.

As with previous days, they'd spent the better part of the afternoon circling just beyond the buffer zone Homeland Security had established around Cabot Island, before slowly expanding their route, moving farther and farther out. The multitude of pleasure boats that had been out on the water earlier had lessened, and Darien was interested in anyone who had chosen to stay too long in the area.

Nadia Petrov was out here. She could feel her. In a few minutes, they would turn back toward the marina. Darien would go for another run, giving Petrov yet another opportunity to grab her. If it didn't happen then, she and Jessie would have dinner. Try to relax. And wait until morning when Petrov would be given her next opportunity.

"Does it look to you like that boat is in trouble?"

Even as Jessie spoke, Darien was already watching a fishing boat take shape through the binoculars. A gleaming white Boston Whaler, powered by a pair of 225 hp Mercury engines, appeared to be dead in the water. "Can you bring us closer?"

Jessie turned her head slowly, the slight breeze teasing her hair around a face already grown pale before their eyes made contact. Even if she hadn't known that everything they'd been doing until now had been leading them to this moment, she would know they were the only boat within sight of what appeared to be a disabled vessel. And even if it hadn't been marine law, simple decency dictated they stop and offer what assistance they could.

"Just put us on an intercept course," Darien said softly. This was not how it should go down, not with Jessie so close to the line of fire. But sometimes you had to deal with the opportunities that presented themselves. She could feel the adrenaline of battle begin to flow through her, leaving her body humming. "Bring us in nice and slow. And call Ben." She turned away for an instant and stared through the binoculars. "Have him check the registration on that boat. Number M-E-3-7-4-7-Z-W."

"Darien?" Jessie's voice was reed thin.

Darien nodded. "Keep it nice and slow, Jesslyn. Wrong place, wrong time, but this is what everyone's been waiting for, so let it happen naturally. As soon as I'm clear of the boat, I need you to go. Don't look back. Don't give Petrov any reason to do more than what she came for."

She started to turn away, intent only on getting through the next few minutes. One minute at a time. Jessie's voice stopped her.

"Darien, wait."

She turned back to face her.

"I—I love you madly." Jessie licked her lips. "I thought you should know, just for the record."

Darien inhaled sharply. "Can you actually fall in love with someone—with someone like me—in such a short time?"

"Yes, I can," she replied softly. "I think I've been waiting for you my whole life."

Darien's eyes burned and her throat tightened. "Then just maybe we have a future waiting for us. I think I'd like to find out." She wanted to go to her, wanted to hold her. She did neither.

"I'd like that. So don't you dare get yourself hurt."

"It's not part of my plan. I'll be back, Jesslyn. I promise you."

She saw Jessie square her shoulders, adjust her headset, and punch in her call. Heard her speak softly to someone and waited until she was finished. Darien then moved to starboard, watching as the distance separating the two boats gradually decreased while Jessie carefully maneuvered closer.

Time and space converged. Everything slowed. Nearly stopped.

She could make out three people in the other boat, not counting whoever was piloting it. Two men, both quite large with expressionless faces, stood like bookends and casually kept what looked like assault rifles barely hidden beneath their jackets. A third man, heavyset with dark closely cropped hair and a scarred face, made no such attempt at pretense. He raised the weapon in his hands, aimed it at her chest, and smiled.

Not wanting to risk Petrov's crew getting any closer to Jessie, Darien waited only until the space between the two boats narrowed enough to allow her to vault over. She landed lightly in front of the three men, stared down the barrel of a gun, and slowly raised her hands to indicate her willing surrender.

The men seemed nervous, agitated, and almost immediately, the big one to her left stepped forward. His hands moved roughly over her, searching for weapons while the scarred man, the obvious leader, watched. No one moved any closer until she felt the cool metal of handcuffs as they slipped over her wrists.

"No fight?"

"There are at least three of you, you're armed, and I'm cuffed. Even you should be able to do the math and calculate the odds."

He cursed, then backhanded her across the face. She went with it, didn't fight it, but the pain was still immediate and made her eyes water. Darien pushed it back, working her tongue over her lip, tasting blood. She could feel the sheer size of him as he stepped closer, and she found herself looking into a wide Slavic face with dead pale eyes. "Do you have a name?"

"Dzhokhar Alaudin. But it will do you no good. You will not live long enough to use the knowledge." He leaned close, his breath hot against her face. "I knew Dmitri when I was a boy. If Nadia allows, it will be a pleasure to kill you when the time comes."

Are you sure you don't want to try recalculating those odds, Dzhokhar Alaudin, she thought and smiled thinly.

But before she could respond, a blinding pain exploded in the back of her head. Sharp and exquisite. Almost immediately, a wave of blackness swallowed her and she sank to the deck without a sound.

❖

For an instant, Jessie froze, She stared at the empty space that only moments before had been occupied by Darien. Remembered how dark and solemn Darien's eyes had been, how penetrating her gaze in the seconds just before she'd turned away. Before she'd willingly stepped into danger knowing she was doing so without backup. Slowly she willed the disparate pieces back into place. It might not have gone down while she was running, the way they had all anticipated, but it had gone frighteningly according to plan. Petrov's people—the men in the other boat—had come for her and Darien had surrendered to them quietly, without a fight. So there had been no reason for them to hurt her.

Watching Darien drop like a stone after one of the men struck from behind had sent a surge of adrenaline coursing through Jessie. Adrenaline based in fear as she remembered her own words. *What scares me is that she wants to hurt you.*

She shoved the thought away. It wouldn't help, but it could bring her to her knees.

Caught between frustration and despair, Jessie took a deep breath and tried to find her emotional bearings. There was still a job to do. They needed to find Petrov and stop her. They needed to get Darien back. Jessie knew she wouldn't rest until she had her back, safe, and in her mind she began going over immediate possibilities.

She reached for the satellite phone and punched one on the speed dial while continuing to stare out at the horizon. The boat was heading into open water, disappearing in the encroaching darkness. They needed to quickly track Darien's signal. In the meantime, the clock continued to run hard.

"What's happened?" Ben's voice demanded.

"Petrov has her. Please tell me you've picked up her signal and are tracking her."

She could hear Ben talk to someone. Somewhere near Ben, she could hear other voices. Faint. Indistinct. And Jessie could almost feel the intensity of the silence coming from the phone while she waited for an answer.

"Ben?"

"Bloody hell, they're trying to jam the signal."

"Yes, we knew they would. And you said we would be able to counter anything they used. Are you able to track her?" she asked breathlessly and experienced a sudden chill as she waited. "Ben? For God's sake, do you have her?"

When he still didn't answer, Jessie wrapped her arms around her abdomen and began to pace, struggling to contain her impatience. Her mind crowded with images of Darien. Laughing. Serious. Impossibly tender. Lethal. So many facets, and while she knew she had barely scratched the surface of what Darien might be capable of, she was in the hands of a woman who had killed people indiscriminately.

Finally, she heard Ben's voice. "The signal's cutting in and out, but it's not completely blocked. We've got her, which means we've got Petrov."

Jessie felt relief sweep through her. "Thank God."

"Jessie?" Her mother's voice suddenly came through her headset. "You need to be aware—DHS has been given a clear directive. If they don't think we can reach Petrov in time to stop her from launching her attack on the island, they will level her boat and anything in the surrounding area."

Even if we haven't rescued Darien. She hadn't said the words. But then she really didn't have to. Jessie knew their choices were limited, just as Darien would have known the risk. "That means every minute…every second counts."

"Jessie," Ben added softly, "Darien has her wits and years of training. In this business, she's as good as it gets."

"I know. Just tell me what you want me to do."

"Stand by. Just stay where you are. Ben and I will pick you up. We have a crew we'll leave behind to bring your boat back to the marina."

❖

Pain was the first thing Darien knew as consciousness returned to her world. Her head was pounding and her body ached. She also knew she needed to open her eyes, but experience had taught her that would make things worse, at least temporarily. Still, there was no time like the present.

She sucked in a breath and gritted her teeth as she cautiously opened her eyes. Almost immediately, her vision doubled and swam. But in that brief moment, one thing became all too apparent.

She had no idea where she was. She had lost all sense of place and time and couldn't make sense of her surroundings. Had she gotten hurt again? Suffered another concussion? She hated the uncertainty, hated not knowing.

As awareness of her surroundings amplified, she saw she was in a small, windowless room. But she could still hear the familiar cry of the seagulls and the air was laced with the scent of salt, confirming what the sensation of motion beneath her feet had already told her. She was on a boat.

And then she remembered. A white Boston Whaler. A man named Dzhokhar Alaudin. She remembered being struck in the back of the head and knew that didn't bode well. But as she slowly assessed her situation, she knew the possibility of another concussion was the least of her problems.

Her hands were tied. The handcuffs she vaguely remembered had been replaced by a coarse rope around her wrists, and she had been strung from a hook embedded in an overhead beam, leaving her arms extended, stretched taut. The position was uncomfortable, but she was confident she could get out of it. She would just need to swing her legs up around the beam, then unhook herself.

But before she could contemplate making such a move, she would first need to find a way to clear her head. She closed her eyes and tried to hold on while another wave of dizziness crashed over her.

Think about something else. Like getting home.

She thought of Jessie and imagined her every touch, every whisper, every sigh and murmur. And in that moment—a moment of perfect clarity—she knew whatever happened, Jessie would be with her. Part of the soul she thought she'd lost in the aftermath of Prague.

"Good. You're awake." The voice was female, faintly accented. "Are the ropes too tight? Are they hurting your wrists? Not that it matters, of course."

Nadia Petrov. As her footsteps brought her closer, Darien turned her head to get a better look. The small movement left her head reeling and sent pain shooting down her arms. But it allowed her to finally see her adversary face-to-face.

Petrov didn't immediately say anything else as she paced in front of her, looking agitated as she tapped the gleaming weapon she held in her right hand against her left palm. She then walked around Darien, studying her. "For a long time, I heard so many stories. I heard how smart you are. Yet you allowed me to capture you. I must tell you, that was not very smart. You think maybe your being here will help your people find me. But I think all you have done is make it easier for me to kill you."

"That remains to be seen."

Petrov's mouth twisted. She drew back her arm and slapped Darien with enough heat to snap her head to one side. "This is not up for negotiation. You killed my father. I will kill you. It is the way it must be. Nothing can save you from your fate."

Darien worked her jaw, absorbed the pain, then licked her lip gingerly with the tip of her tongue. "Nadia—can I call you Nadia?"

She watched Petrov remain motionless for a moment, clearly debating her choices before she nodded her head.

"Then listen to me, Nadia. As someone who's had a great deal of experience with revenge, I can tell you it provides only temporary satisfaction. Once you've finished what you set out to do, you'll discover you're empty. There's nothing left."

"That's because you see nothing beyond your own insignificant existence. Do you believe you are my only reason for being here? If so, I am afraid I must disappoint you. I have plans for things other than your death. Important plans that will take me far."

"By attacking the summit? By killing eight world leaders and countless others?"

Petrov let out a breath, but it didn't seem to calm her rage. "Yes. I would have thought you, of all people, would understand. Perhaps I have overestimated you."

Darien turned over the immediate possibilities, then mentally shrugged. "Try me."

"I know who you are, Darien Troy. I have known who you are for many years—almost from the beginning. Does that surprise you?"

Surprise didn't begin to describe what she was feeling.

The heat of Petrov's gaze raked over her as she stepped closer, staring at Darien through dark, soulless eyes. "You have nothing to say?"

Darien remained silent.

"Answer me, damn it." Petrov slapped her again.

Her cheek stung and her eyes watered as Darien forced herself to face Petrov, to meet her gaze. The silence lengthened before Petrov spoke again.

"Information is not that hard to get if you know who to ask and are willing to pay. My father taught me that. And there were all those rumors. The men"—she released a sharp, humorless laugh—"the men found it difficult to believe a young girl could do so much damage and kill such powerful men. Men like my father. But I believed what I heard because I knew what was in my own heart. I understood what you had done. More importantly, I knew why."

Darien closed her eyes, sensing what was coming.

"So I watched and studied you and learned. You became my role model."

The deep guilt Darien had harbored over her part in shaping who Petrov had become rose to the surface. "Your role model?"

"Yes. It is as I said. I watched you and I learned. I also made two promises. I swore on my father's grave I would finish what he started by helping Chechnya gain independence from Russia. And I promised myself when the time was right, I would deal with you. But then I realized I could do both." Petrov paused as if savoring the moment. "Bringing down those jets was what you would call a stroke of genius, don't you agree? It guaranteed someone—either your old friends at MI6 or someone from the CIA—would want to involve you. Bring you into the game. And I was right."

Darien struggled to keep the sudden surge of emotions from showing. "You killed all those people to draw me into a game with you?"

"You should see your face." Petrov laughed. "After everything you have done, I did not anticipate the thought could upset you. But as much as it would please me to have you think you are responsible for all those deaths, the truth is you were only partial motivation. The other should be obvious. I needed to demonstrate my capacity. My power."

"You succeeded. You had my involvement within a couple of days of bringing down those planes. And you showed the world what you were capable of. So why continue large-scale attacks—the mall, the school, the courthouse? Why not wait until the time was right and simply go after the summit?"

"Because"—she ran the muzzle of her gun along Darien's cheek—"before I brought down those jets, the men in my world—the ones who control the drugs and prostitutes, the ones who launder money and finance wars, *all* of them—viewed me as inferior. Incapable of assuming the mantle of leadership once held by my father. Not just a woman. The daughter of a whore."

"But you showed them they were wrong," Darien said softly.

Petrov stared at her. "Perhaps you do understand. Yes, I showed them how wrong they were. And as I escalated, it worked even better than I could have dreamed."

"How?"

"In every way that counts. Over the years, I built a small network, but until recently, I was still operating on the outside. Finding my own sources of funds, negotiating my own deals. But showing everyone what I'm capable of changed that. It opened doors and has given me real power. For the first time in my life, I command respect."

Darien remained silent, mostly because she hated the idea of agreeing with Petrov.

An instant later, all emotion faded from Petrov's face. "Killing you will cut the last connection to my past. And after tomorrow, Russia will be brought to her knees while her allies will be too busy trying to deal with their own internal power struggles to offer any assistance. Chechnya will rise and reclaim her independence, and the people will sing my name long after I am gone."

Petrov wasn't exactly mad, but neither was she completely sane. Darien considered how best to respond and decided there was little risk in the truth. "I think you've overlooked a critical point. The CIA, MI6, DHS? They'll call for a tactical strike if they believe they can't stop you from launching your attack on the summit."

"They won't attack as long as I have you. As long as they think you're still alive."

Darien shook her head. "That's where you're wrong. They'll launch a strike whether I'm still here or not. I'm quite expendable."

Petrov stared at her, barely suppressed rage filling her eyes. "You're marked, aren't you? A laser tag of some kind to track you. They will use it to lock on to you." She lashed out in anger. She'd still been holding a gun, and the solid metal connected hard with Darien's ribs, stealing her breath. "I can kill you now and have your body thrown overboard."

"It's too late." Struggling to breathe, she had to force the words. "They'll already have your coordinates. You won't make it out of this alive."

"You are wrong. I plan on living a very long life," Petrov said coldly. "But I'm afraid the same cannot be said for you. You will live only long enough to see me destroy the world leaders attending the summit. Long enough to know you have failed. And then—well, then you will die."

Darien didn't see the next blow coming. Or the one after that.

Pain didn't have time to register as the hook she was attached to broke free. Unable to break her fall, she landed hard, forcing the air from her lungs as her head rocked back on the wood-plank floor. She saw a blinding flash of light.

And then there was nothing.

CHAPTER TWENTY-EIGHT

Inside a building set up as a temporary command post, oblivious to the chaos around her, Jessie stared at the images on a large flat screen. Since shortly after midnight, they had been receiving a continuous satellite video feed of Nadia Petrov's location, making it clear they were no longer searching for a needle in a haystack.

Thanks to Darien's GPS tracking signal, they knew exactly where Petrov was—onboard a gleaming blue-hulled custom yacht currently anchored on the leeward side of an uninhabited island about ten miles offshore. It was not lost on Jessie that Petrov had named the yacht *Reprisal*.

Watching the activity on the monitor was proving to be easier than listening to the discussion taking place at command, between the various agencies involved in the operation. There was no consensus on a course of action, and the discussion had become heated as Grace went nose-to-nose with a pair of suits from DHS and a three-star general. Arguing logistics and what would constitute the best approach. Deciding whether to launch an armed incursion or to call for an airstrike and obliterate the yacht and any weapons onboard before they could be used.

Both scenarios significantly threatened Darien's life. At least for now, the green tracking dot from her tag continued to blink steadily, reassuring Jessie she was still alive, somewhere onboard the yacht.

Wandering away from the never-ending argument, she found Ben silently staring out the door into the remnant of the moonless night, as if somehow it offered him hope. She recognized his stillness now and knew it was his way of containing his emotions. His way of dealing with the fear they shared for Darien.

"I'd trade places with her in a heartbeat," he said without looking up.

"I know," she responded. "Darien knows that too. Hopefully, she knows how we all feel about her and will use that knowledge to give herself strength to hold on. At least long enough for us to bring her back."

"Maybe, but it doesn't sound as if those boys from DHS are going to leave anything to chance. Darien doesn't figure into their plans. Nor do I think they're going to give her the time she needs to get away."

"I know. I listened in on part of the discussion." Jessie paused and licked her lips. "I'm not in my element here, Ben, but I want to go after her."

"Believe me, I know how you feel. But you can't do that any more than I can. There's too much on the line, too many lives at stake. And Darien would never forgive us."

"I know that. But we both also know it's not straightforward revenge Petrov's after. She doesn't just want to kill Darien. She wants her to suffer first, and that scares me." Jessie knew the longer Darien was with Petrov, the more the scales tipped against her. "I tell myself not to think about it—about what's happening to her, what she's going through. I know if I think about it, I'll fall apart and that won't help her. It won't help anyone. But it's all I can think about. I'm crazy about her, Ben. And I can't help her."

She thought she saw a look of understanding in Ben's eyes.

"Don't tell Grace," he said, and the corner of his mouth tipped up, "but you're exactly what I hoped for Darien all these years. Someone who could help her learn to love herself as much as she was capable of loving someone else. Enough to make her want to live past the age of thirty."

Ben fell silent, and as they stood together in the cool gray mist watching a thin ground fog swirl, Jessie lost all sense of time. She didn't notice the approaching dawn until she heard the sound of footsteps and turned to see her mother and the general approach.

Grace didn't have to say anything—the status of the operation was evident by the expression on her face. Jessie knew the window for Darien to get away from Petrov had all but closed.

"General Bartlett's arranged to get you onto a coast guard search-and-rescue helicopter," Grace said.

"When?"

"In a matter of minutes. Our hope is it will get you close enough to Petrov's yacht without raising too many questions. Close enough for you to be able to communicate with Darien."

Jessie felt her body start to hum, felt faintly breathless, and recognized what she was feeling as the resurgence of hope.

"You need to contact Troy and tell her to get the hell out of there," Bartlett said. "The order's been given to launch the birds at first light. Once they're launched, there'll be no turning back. The orders are to level the yacht and everyone on her."

❖

Darien opened her eyes, fighting to get past the initial disorientation. She was lying on the floor. Her head was pounding, her eyes burned, and she had to struggle to breathe deeply as she tried to fight both nausea and chills. It was then she heard the sweetest sound.

"Dare, can you hear me?"

Her tiny earpiece was somehow, miraculously, still intact. Still working. It was her only connection to the rest of the world—and Jesslyn. Hearing Jessie's voice, even faintly, told her help was close at hand. The knowledge flooded her with a rush of emotion. "Where are you?"

"Oh, Jesus. Tell me you're okay." The relief in Jessie's voice was clear. So was the tension.

"I'm all right."

"Dare, listen to me. You need to get out of there, now. Your window's just about gone. I'm on an SAR chopper…damn, we'll be going out of range in just a few seconds, but we'll be close by. Darien? Do you hear me? We'll pick you up, that's a promise."

"I'm counting on that," Darien murmured hoarsely, her throat tight. "But Jesslyn, if you don't find me…if we don't see each other—"

"No. Don't say it. We'll find you. I'll find you." There was nothing else as the helicopter Jessie was in flew out of range.

For the next several heartbeats, Darien remained frozen. Numb. She knew the odds, had known them all along, and for the first time in her life, she was afraid she might lose. She'd never doubted herself before and it left her momentarily shaken.

But not for long. Instinct and training and a strong dose of self-preservation kicked in. She wasn't prepared to lose. Not now. Especially not to Dmitri Petrov's daughter. Jessie had said her window was about to close. That could only mean someone was about to launch an attack, intent on wiping out Petrov and her deadly arsenal. And that meant she needed to get off the *Reprisal*. Now.

She stumbled awkwardly to her feet, biting back a groan as a sharp, nearly blinding pain slashed through her when she tried to use her bound hands. She realized her left hand wasn't working and that every breath brought a new stab of pain. Dizzy, she staggered toward the stairs, using her teeth as she moved to work at the rope binding her hands.

She was trembling from a combination of pain and exertion by the time she reached the top of the stairs. But she managed to get one hand free, leaving the rope dangling from her injured left wrist. She stopped, grateful to discover a thick fog shrouding the boat and everything on it, and stood for what seemed like forever. Calculating the distance to the side of the yacht.

It was now or never. She moved from the stairway but was still ten feet away, seconds from making her escape, when a loud voice behind her yelled out for her to stop.

There could be no complying. She took off, and three successive shots followed, their sound deafening. The exploding burn came a second later. Her hip and her side screamed in protest. She staggered but didn't slow down. Running hard, she hurtled over the edge of the boat, a free fall into the dark water below that drove all thought from her mind.

In the seconds that followed, the water enveloped her. It wrapped cold arms around her, and for an instant, dark oblivion beckoned. She felt more than heard the next shots fired in her direction. But she was free, gasping for air and treading water before using a steady stroke to put distance between her and the boat.

She began calculating, knowing the human body cooled much faster in water than in cold air, and with the water temperature somewhere below sixty degrees, her chances of survival depended on being able to hold out until rescue came. She was losing blood, and as the minutes passed, she knew it wouldn't be long before the stiffness of hypothermia set in.

She paused when she thought she heard something. Thought she saw something streaking overhead. And realized there was no more time. She gulped in air and dived. A moment later, the world around her lit up and shockwaves buffeted her as Petrov's yacht exploded.

Jessie sat in the cargo hold of the SAR helicopter. From her position, she could just make out the screen in front of the copilot and felt reassured by the constant presence of the green GPS dot that showed her where Darien was.

She was still watching when she heard the words come over her PRR. "The Predators are in the air."

A chill swept over her. "How long do we have?" Jessie asked.

No one answered. But it really didn't matter. Less than a minute later, the explosion lit up the sky where the *Reprisal* had been. It blinded her for an instant as orange-red fire erupted, almost close enough for her to feel the heat.

The percussion rumbled and deafened as the rockets impacted, sending a shower of wood and fiberglass and metal soaring into the air. Jessie stared in disbelief as the water appeared to boil, and smoke rose toward the sky.

She hadn't thought it would be any harder being this close, but she could feel her emotions crowd her as the helicopter flew over the site in the first red streak of dawn. Searching blindly, since Darien's tracking signal had gone silent in the minutes before the Predators had unleashed a rain of fire.

God, Darien. After all she'd done and been through, she didn't deserve this. Jessie stared sightlessly at the empty space between her boots.

"Jessie…" She felt a hand squeeze her shoulder and looked up into Ben's face. He looked stricken, pain etched in his features. But she also saw sympathy in his eyes as he reached for her hand and laced his fingers with hers. "Come sit by me, we can look together."

Moving numbly to the open side of the chopper, with the wind pulling at her hair, Jessie fixed her eyes on the dark water below as they moved in a coordinated search pattern. Scanning. Searching the widening debris field, but finding nothing. No sign of life. Only the churn of water, as the remains of Petrov's yacht slowly disappeared into the ocean, and the bodies were pulled into the Zodiacs searching below.

Each time a body was found, Jessie's stomach sank and her heart stuttered. Each time, after an endless wait, the same report came through clearly over her PRR. It wasn't Darien.

But each time she felt hope fade a little more.

It might have been seconds but could just as easily have been hours later, when one of the crew members leaning out of the chopper called out. "There!"

Grabbing binoculars, Jessie sighted, tried to see where he was pointing. And then her blood ran cold. She could see a body lying partially across a large square piece of debris. Facedown, dark hair floating in the water, T-shirt torn to the skin in numerous places. Jessie's stomach rolled and her mind went blank.

Oh God, no. Don't do this to me. Don't let me lose her.

The helicopter banked and moved closer. Jessie saw two rescue swimmers jump into the water, their powerful strokes bringing them swiftly to Darien. They turned her over gently, one checking for a pulse before looking up toward the chopper and shaking his head.

Jessie's heart fractured. But as she watched Darien's head loll listlessly, one of the two swimmers suddenly began puffing air into Darien's lungs while the other attached her to the harness that would lift her out of the water.

"Bleeding and unresponsive…no pulse…hypothermia…"

The message came through the PRR garbled and broken. But it didn't matter. All that mattered to Jessie was Darien needed help and it was taking too long for them to get her into the helicopter.

When they finally laid her on the deck, she appeared lifeless. Cold and pale, her lips were faintly blue, as blood and seawater ran off her face. More blood flowed freely from her hip and from her side, and there was a large contusion visible near her temple. Ben immediately slipped into position and started the rhythmic chest compressions, while Grace placed the mask over Darien's mouth. Sinking to her knees, mindless of the cold water and the blood pooling around Darien's lifeless body, she steadily worked the bulb.

Simultaneously, a medic began to cut Darien's wet clothes. He quickly dealt with the bleeding, applying field dressings to her wounds, then covered her with a thermal blanket.

Jessie tried not to think about how much time had passed since they'd first pulled Darien from the water. Or how long it had been since she last took a breath of air on her own. But even as she watched Ben and her mother desperately working to coax life back into Darien, she felt herself dying inside.

Come on, Darien. You're too strong to let anyone take you out like this. Fight, damn it. You promised.

A moment later, she watched with fear and uncertainty as all activity ceased and the medic felt Darien's throat. Jessie waited through the longest heartbeat of her life and closed her eyes to the words she feared would follow. But then she heard, "I've got a pulse. It's slow, but it's there."

Her eyes flew open, but it still took several seconds for the words to hit home. "She's not—?"

Before anyone could say anything, Darien made a sound. A painful, choking, strangled sound as water spilled from her mouth. Ben and the medic turned her onto her side, and Jessie heard her harsh intake of air. One breath. Then another. Still coughing up water, she struggled to pull air into her lungs before finally drawing a ragged breath.

Watching the rise and fall of Darien's chest with each new breath, Jessie slumped against her mother, grateful for the support. She wasn't certain what the medic was doing as he continued to work on Darien.

But she knew he was finished when he wrapped the thermal blanket tightly around Darien and sat back on his heels.

"I'm not certain whether it's the hypothermia or that head wound keeping her unconscious," he said. "Why don't you try talking to her?"

Jessie didn't need to be told twice.

"Darien? Dare, open your eyes and look at me. Please." She heard the fracture in her own voice, but she didn't care. She continued speaking, asking Darien to come back to her. Pleading with her not to leave. "Damn it, Dare, you promised."

Just when she thought it was never going to happen, Darien's eyelids finally began to flutter, and then her eyes opened. Dazed and unfocused. But Jessie knew she had never seen a more beautiful sight in her life.

❖

Darien stirred and immediately knew three things. Pain was slicing through her head with every beat of her heart. Breathing required a herculean effort. And she felt trapped, held down and nearly smothered by something covering her.

She was also sure she'd heard a voice. Whispering to her. Calling out her name again and again.

Am I dreaming?

No, she was fairly certain her eyes were open. She could make out shapes, colors. She was also certain the sound she could hear was a helicopter rotor beating the air. *I'm dreaming that I'm awake and lying in the back of a helicopter.*

Her stomach rolled in a queasy swell as she tried to gather her disjointed thoughts. Images shifted and changed. She teased Ben about his father wanting grandchildren while Jessie beat him at chess yet again. Her mother threw her head back in laughter before reaching out to ruffle her hair. Darien wanted to ask her to stay, but before she could say anything, her mother began to fade and then dissolved completely.

But she could still hear voices. She tried to hold on, tried to focus on what they were saying. But she was so cold and the light around her was growing dim again as darkness seeped in from all sides.

"Darien."

She heard it again, and even though it still seemed to be coming from a great distance, it was clearer this time. She could feel the touch of a gentle hand. As she tried to focus, her field of vision cleared and she saw a face. A familiar face. A beautiful face.

"Welcome back," Jessie said.

She swallowed and tried to speak. "Told you I'd be back." Her voice was a hoarse whisper. "And see, nothing that a stitch or two won't fix."

Jessie groaned. "I think this might qualify as more than a stitch or two, but thank you for coming back."

"I promised." Darien saw tears fill Jessie's eyes. She wanted to reach out and touch her but found herself unable to move, bound by a blanked wrapped tightly around her. "Jesslyn."

"Hold still," Jessie murmured. "What is it?"

"I always keep my promises."

❖

With a trembling hand, Jessie pushed Darien's hair aside and traced the contours of her face. Swallowed back a nameless rage as she smoothed her fingertips over the livid bruises on Darien's temple, her checkbone, her lips, then brushed the lines of blood from countless tiny cuts on her face and neck.

The pain in Darien's eyes was so clear it stole her breath, and for a moment, Jessie wanted to come up with some creative way to make Nadia Petrov pay. But then she remembered the yacht exploding and realized the woman was likely already dead. In the next instant, Petrov no longer existed for her as Jessie bent down and pressed her forehead to Darien's.

Darien released a shuddering groan. "I knew you'd come. I knew you'd find me."

"How could I not?" There was so much she wanted to say, so much she needed to say. But Jessie remembered where they were—in a search and rescue helicopter surrounded by crew members. Not to mention her mother and Ben, who were quietly observing her from only inches away.

Ben drew closer and gently squeezed Darien's shoulder. "Well done, Dare."

"Ben's right," Grace added. "We wouldn't have succeeded but for your courage. You saved a lot of lives today. People who will never know what you did and what you risked, but who will owe you their lives nonetheless."

"Does that mean it's over?"

Grace shrugged. "Maybe not completely, but we're well on our way to finishing things. Petrov's body was pulled from the water a short time ago. The threat to the G8 has been neutralized. And we have teams on the ground dismantling what remains of the Guild. This time there will be nothing left for anyone to rebuild. You have my word."

Darien remained silent for a long moment before looking up at Jessie once again. Her face was still much too pale, her eyes were shadowed, and there was an unreadable expression on her face.

"What is it, Dare?" Jessie asked.

"No more," she whispered. "I don't want to do this anymore, Jesslyn."

"Then we won't, love."

"Good. I just want to go home. I just want to be. Remember? Can we do that?"

Jessie considered the question and wondered what she meant by home. Did she mean Paris? She wasn't sure, and quite frankly, as far as she was concerned, it could be anywhere. All she knew for certain was that when Petrov's yacht had been destroyed, with it went the last connection to Darien's past.

As for the future, it stretched out before them like a blank slate. All that mattered was they were being given a chance to create it together.

EPILOGUE

The afternoon sun was just beginning its descent in a brilliant blue sky, its light shimmering on the water, as Jessie walked past a forest of white masts swaying gently at their moorings. Stepping onto the wooden dock, she maintained a precarious hold on the bags containing her purchases, grateful for the near-constant trade wind which kept temperatures more than comfortable.

Less than a minute later, she arrived home—new as of three weeks earlier. The *Arianna*. She was a sleek forty-five foot sailboat with gleaming oak decks and an ocean-going keel. By the time Darien was finished having her retrofitted, she also had a 200-gallon freshwater capacity and boasted a state-of-the-art communication and navigation system.

As she drew near, she heard her name called out. "Jessie, hey, you're back earlier than I thought." And then Zoey appeared, leaning over the railing, grinning widely. "I'm guessing you got everything you went looking for, because from the look of those bags you're carrying, I'd say you bought out all the local grocery stores. I'm also guessing Dare is in for a feast when she gets back later today."

"And then some," Jessie responded with a laugh, knowing each of them, for their own reasons, was looking forward to Darien's return from Paris. For Zoey, Darien would always be her lifeline. Her mentor. Her friend. As for Jessie herself, Darien was simply her everything.

She watched Zoey easily traverse the gap between the boat and the pier and gladly let her take a couple of the bags she was holding.

She then took a moment to simply enjoy seeing the evolution of Zoey, brought about by nearly a month in a tropical paradise.

Her short blond hair was now bleached nearly white through a combination of sun and saltwater, and her skin, instead of goth pale, had a sun-kissed glow. But the biggest change was the ever-present smile on her face.

They went down to the galley together and quickly unloaded the fresh produce she'd bought, along with several pounds of fresh prawns, bottles of wine, and the best bottle of champagne she'd been able to find. Zoey whistled as she took in the spread, stayed and helped clean the prawns, then waved and headed topside.

Jessie found a large pot, filled it with water, and set it to boil. She knew she was a long way from being the kind of cook Darien was, but she was equally determined to surprise her with a special meal for her first night back.

Damn, but she'd missed Darien.

She'd stayed in Nevis only long enough to finalize purchasing and outfitting the boat, then had flown to Washington to meet with Grace and Ben. Something to do with bringing closure to the Guild. Three days into her trip, however, she'd called to say she needed to fly to Paris to deal with some unfinished business.

The term had worried Jessie, partly because Darien was still physically recovering from what had happened to her a month earlier. But mostly because, other than some sporadic e-mails, she'd been strangely silent.

She had to trust that Darien would reach out to her if she needed assistance of any kind. So Jessie forced herself not to contact Ben and ask him to check up on her.

That had been the status quo until yesterday. That was when Darien sent an e-mail saying she had wrapped things up and would be coming back today. She could arrive at any time now, and Jessie could barely contain her anticipation.

Absorbed with her thoughts and dinner preparations, she was caught off guard when she suddenly felt the heat of a body press against her. An instant later, Darien wrapped her arms around Jessie's waist and whispered, "So, did you miss me?"

Jessie laughed, spun in Darien's arms, and briefly found her mouth. "Why would I miss you? Were you gone somewhere?"

"So that's the way it is?" Darien smiled. "No problem, I think I missed you enough for both of us."

Jessie managed one breathless laugh before Darien's mouth was back for more, sending her thoughts scattering in a thousand different directions and igniting a sexual heat.

On some level, she was aware Darien turned off the stove and guided her toward the master stateroom. And it took very little effort to have her stretched out naked on the bed. But then Darien simply stood there. Simply looking.

"Dare? Is something wrong?"

"No." She flashed a grin. "Just trying to decide where to start."

Jessie's laugh was one of relief as she watched Darien quickly undress and join her on the bed. And then they were kissing. Laughing. Touching. Tasting. Creating a sensual world where only their two entwined bodies existed. Thrilling in the rush of the climb and shattering as they fell into blissful satisfaction.

Much later, Darien put the shrimp to boil while Jessie opened a bottle of wine and poured some for both of them. She was aware Jessie was watching her every move but didn't say anything. Simply waited her out.

"You look tired," Jessie finally said. "I promised myself I wouldn't ask, but will you at least tell me—is everything all right?"

"Everything's perfect. Much as I tried to explain, Ben and Grace needed my help to follow the Guild's money trail. I'm sorry it took a little longer than I planned, but as of yesterday all of their accounts are permanently closed."

"And as of today, some well-deserving organizations are the recipients of the Guild's bounty?"

Darien nodded. "Yes, something like that."

Instead of laughing, Jessie put the wine bottle down. And then she was in Darien's arms. For several minutes, she shivered, as if releasing emotions that had been stifled for much too long. Darien understood. Gradually, Jessie's shaking subsided, until finally, she looked up at Darien and smiled wanly. "Thanks. I'm okay now," she murmured. "Is it all truly finished?"

"Completely and totally. Shutting down the money connections was my last official act. As of this morning, I am officially retired. Can you handle that?"

"Does that mean you won't be doing this again?"

"Doing what?"

"Getting shot again. Or getting hurt again. Or scaring me like that again."

"I've no intention of doing anything you don't agree with."

"Good answer." Jessie pressed her lips against Darien's and whispered, "You know I love you, don't you. So damn much."

Darien closed her eyes and felt a profound sense of coming home. "I love you too. And thank you for saving my life."

"You've already thanked me." Jessie frowned. "Don't you remember? At the hospital?"

"Yes, but that's not what I'm talking about. I'm talking about you saving me when you came into my life and loved me, even though you knew exactly who and what I was. And you know what they say, don't you? When you save a life, that life belongs to you."

"Jesus, Darien. When you say things like that…" She shuddered and brought her lips to Darien's once again.

"I just have one question," Darien murmured a minute or two later.

"What's that?"

"What took you so long?"

A flush spread across Jessie's face. "If my mother hadn't left you with Ben, I would have fallen for you fifteen years ago." She paused, then started to laugh. "You know, she actually believed she was protecting me."

"She was wrong."

Jessie nodded. "Yes, she was, but it no longer matters, does it? Because I'm here now. We're both here now—together."

Darien smiled. "That's all that really matters."

About the Author

A transplant from Cuba to Toronto, AJ Quinn successfully juggles the demands of a busy consulting practice with those of her first true love—storytelling—finding time to write mostly late at night or in the wee hours of the morning. She's the author of two previously released romantic thrillers: *Hostage Moon*, a Lambda Literary Award finalist, and *Show of Force*. An avid cyclist, scuba diver, and photographer, AJ finds travel is the best medicine for recharging body, spirit, and imagination. She can be reached at aj@ajquinn.com.

Books Available from Bold Strokes Books

Venus in Love by Tina Michele. Morgan Blake can't afford any distractions and Ainsley Dencourt can't afford to lose control—but the beauty of life and art usually lies in the unpredictable strokes of the artist's brush. (978-1-62639-220-5)

Rules of Revenge by AJ Quinn. When a lethal operative on a collision course with her past agrees to help a CIA analyst on a critical assignment, the encounter proves explosive in ways neither woman anticipated. (978-1-62639-221-2)

The Romance Vote by Ali Vali. Chili Alexander is a sought-after campaign consultant who isn't prepared when her boss's daughter, Samantha Pellegrin, comes to work at the firm and shakes up Chili's life from the first day. (978-1-62639-222-9)

Advance: Exodus Book One by Gun Brooke. Admiral Dael Caydoc's mission to find a new homeworld for the Oconodian people is hazardous, but working with the infuriating Commander Aniwyn "Spinner" Seclan endangers her heart and soul. (978-1-62639-224-3)

UnCatholic Conduct by Stevie Mikayne. Jil Kidd goes undercover to investigate fraud at St. Marguerite's Catholic School, but life gets complicated when her student is killed—and she begins to fall for her prime target. (978-1-62639-304-2)

Season's Meetings by Amy Dunne. Catherine Birch reluctantly ventures on the festive road trip from hell with beautiful stranger Holly Daniels only to discover the road to true love has its own obstacles to maneuver. (978-1-62639-227-4)

Myth and Magic: Queer Fairy Tales edited by Radclyffe and Stacia Seaman. Myth, magic, and monsters—the stuff of childhood dreams (or nightmares) and adult fantasies. (978-1-62639-225-0)

Nine Nights on the Windy Tree by Martha Miller. Recovering drug addict, Bertha Brannon, is an attorney who is trying to stay clean when a murder sends her back to the bad end of town. (978-1-62639-179-6)

Driving Lessons by Annameekee Hesik. Dive into Abbey Brooks's sophomore year as she attempts to figure out the amazing, but sometimes complicated, life of a you-know-who girl at Gila High School. (978-1-62639-228-1)

Asher's Shot by Elizabeth Wheeler. Asher Price's candid photographs capture the truth, but when his success requires exposing an enemy, Asher discovers his only shot at happiness involves revealing secrets of his own. (978-1-62639-229-8)

Courtship by Carsen Taite. Love and justice—a lethal mix or a perfect match? (978-1-62639-210-6)

Against Doctor's Orders by Radclyffe. Corporate financier Presley Worth wants to shut down Argyle Community Hospital, but Dr. Harper Rivers will fight her every step of the way, if she can also fight their growing attraction. (978-1-62639-211-3)

A Spark of Heavenly Fire by Kathleen Knowles. Kerry and Beth are building their life together, but unexpected circumstances could destroy their happiness. (978-1-62639-212-0)

Never Too Late by Julie Blair. When Dr. Jamie Hammond is forced to hire a new office manager, she's shocked to come face to face with Carla Grant and memories from her past. (978-1-62639-213-7)

Widow by Martha Miller. Judge Bertha Brannon must solve the murder of her lover, a policewoman she thought she'd grow old with. As more bodies pile up, the murderer starts coming for her. (978-1-62639-214-4)

Twisted Echoes by Sheri Lewis Wohl. What's a woman to do when she realizes the voices in her head are real? (978-1-62639-215-1)

Criminal Gold by Ann Aptaker. Through a dangerous night in New York in 1949, Cantor Gold, dapper dyke-about-town, smuggler of fine art, is forced by a crime lord to be his instrument of vengeance. (978-1-62639-216-8)

The Melody of Light by M.L. Rice. After surviving abuse and loss, will Riley Gordon be able to navigate her first year of college and accept true love and family? (978-1-62639-219-9)

Because of You by Julie Cannon. What would you do for the woman you were forced to leave behind? (978-1-62639-199-4)

The Job by Jove Belle. Sera always dreamed that she would one day reunite with Tor. She just didn't think it would involve terrorists, firearms, and hostages. (978-1-62639-200-7)

Making Time by C.J. Harte. Two women going in different directions meet after fifteen years and struggle to reconnect in spite of the past that separated them. (978-1-62639-201-4)

Once The Clouds Have Gone by KE Payne. Overwhelmed by the dark clouds of her past, Tag Grainger is lost until the intriguing and spirited Freddie Metcalfe unexpectedly forces her to reevaluate her life. (978-1-62639-202-1)

The Acquittal by Anne Laughlin. Chicago private investigator Josie Harper searches for the real killer of a woman whose lover has been acquitted of the crime. (978-1-62639-203-8)

An American Queer: The Amazon Trail by Lee Lynch. Lee Lynch's heartening and heart-rending history of gay life from the turbulence of the late 1900s to the triumphs of the early 2000s are recorded in this selection of her columns. (978-1-62639-204-5)

Stick McLaughlin: The Prohibition Years by CF Frizzell. Corruption in 1918 cost Stick her lover, her freedom, and her identity, but a very special flapper and the family bond of her own gang could help win them back—even if it means outwitting the Boston Mob. (978-1-62639-205-2)

Edge of Awareness by C.A. Popovich. When Maria, a woman in the middle of her third divorce, meets Dana, an out lesbian, awareness of her feelings brings up reservations about the teachings of her church. (978-1-62639-188-8)

Taken by Storm by Kim Baldwin. Lives depend on two women when a train derails high in the remote Alps, but an unforgiving mountain, avalanches, crevasses, and other perils stand between them and safety. (978-1-62639-189-5)

The Common Thread by Jaime Maddox. Dr. Nicole Coussart's life is falling apart, but fortunately, DEA Attorney Rae Rhodes is there to pick up the pieces and help Nic put them back together. (978-1-62639-190-1)

Jolt by Kris Bryant. Mystery writer Bethany Lange wasn't prepared for the twisting emotions that left her breathless the moment she laid eyes on folk singer sensation Ali Hart. (978-1-62639-191-8)

Searching For Forever by Emily Smith. Dr. Natalie Jenner's life has always been about saving others, until young paramedic Charlie Thompson comes along and shows her maybe she's the one who needs saving. (978-1-62639-186-4)

A Queer Sort of Justice: Prison Tales Across Time by Rebecca S. Buck. When liberty is only a memory, and all seems lost, what freedoms and hopes can be found within us? (978-1-62639-195-6E)

Blue Water Dreams by Dena Hankins. Lania Marchiol keeps her wary sailor's gaze trained on the horizon until Oly Rassmussen, a wickedly handsome trans man, sends her trusty compass spinning off course. (978-1-62639-192-5)

Rest Home Runaways by Clifford Henderson. Baby boomer Morgan Ronzio's troubled marriage is the least of her worries when she gets the call that her addled, eighty-six-year-old, half-blind dad has escaped the rest home. (978-1-62639-169-7)

Charm City by Mason Dixon. Raq Overstreet's loyalty to her drug kingpin boss is put to the test when she begins to fall for Bathsheba Morris, the undercover cop assigned to bring him down. (978-1-62639-198-7)

Let the Lover Be by Sheree Greer. Kiana Lewis, a functional alcoholic on the verge of destruction, finally faces the demons of her past while finding love and earning redemption in New Orleans. (978-1-62639-077-5)

Blindsided by Karis Walsh. Blindsided by love, guide dog trainer Lenae McIntyre and media personality Cara Bradley learn to trust what they see with their hearts. (978-1-62639-078-2)

About Face by VK Powell. Forensic artist Macy Sheridan and Detective Leigh Monroe work on a case that has troubled them both for years, but they're hampered by the past and their unlikely yet undeniable attraction. (978-1-62639-079-9)

Blackstone by Shea Godfrey. For Darry and Jessa, their chance at a life of freedom is stolen by the arrival of war and an ancient prophecy that just might destroy their love. (978-1-62639-080-5)

Out of This World by Maggie Morton. Iris decided to cross an ocean to get over her ex. But instead, she ends up traveling much farther, all the way to another world. Once there, only a mysterious, sexy, and magical woman can help her return home. (978-1-62639-083-6)

Kiss The Girl by Melissa Brayden. Sleeping with the enemy has never been so complicated. Brooklyn Campbell and Jessica Lennox face off in love and advertising in fast-paced New York City. (978-1-62639-071-3)

Taking Fire: A First Responders Novel by Radclyffe. Hunted by extremists and under siege by nature's most virulent weapons, Navy medic Max de Milles and Red Cross worker Rachel Winslow join forces to survive and discover something far more lasting. (978-1-62639-072-0)

First Tango in Paris by Shelley Thrasher. When French law student Eva Laroche meets American call girl Brigitte Green in 1970s Paris, they have no idea how their pasts and futures will intersect. (978-1-62639-073-7)

The War Within by Yolanda Wallace. Army nurse Meredith Moser went to Vietnam in 1967 looking to help those in need; she didn't expect to meet the love of her life along the way. (978-1-62639-074-4)

Escapades by MJ Williamz. Two women, afraid to love again, must overcome their fears to find the happiness that awaits them. (978-1-62639-182-6)

Desire at Dawn by Fiona Zedde. For Kylie, love had always come armed with sharp teeth and claws. But with the human, Olivia, she bares her vampire heart for the very first time, sharing passion, lust, and a tenderness she'd never dared dream of before. (978-1-62639-064-5)